THE REVISE

Richard Crasta grew up in Man ... New York where he is a colum ... runs a small publishing concern called The Invisible Man Press.

The Revised

KAMA SUTRA

A NOVEL OF COLONIALISM AND DESIRE WITH ARBITRARY FOOTNOTES AND A WHIMSICAL GLOSSARY

RICHARD CRASTA

FOURTH ESTATE · *London*

First published in Great Britain in 1994 by
Fourth Estate Limited
289 Westbourne Grove
London W11 2QA

This paperback edition first published 1995
10 9 8 7 6 5 4 3 2 1

A catalogue record for this book is available from the British Library.

ISBN 1–85702–314–5

Author's disclaimer and warning:
Question: Did the 'Pam' episodes really happen?
Answer: No, no, no! They are pure fantasy, pure illusion of maya, like Vijay Prabhu himself, like the entire book itself, like possibly existence itself, life the very idea that Ronald Reagan or Idi Amin could ever have been presidents of their respective countries. This is a book of fiction, with the narrative and imaginative licence that the term implies. I have a very low opinion of my ability to tell the truth, whatever the definition of it is, and if it were at all possible. It is forbidden to read this novel without an abundant sense of humour, and without your acknowledgement that you have been warned that your brain might get twisted out of shape.

The author and publishers would like to gratefully acknowledge the following: *Sunday Mail* for the quote from Pooja Bedi's interview which was published in 1991; *The Dictionary of Famous Quotations* compiled by Robin Hyman for the quote from Winston Churchill's speech.

Typeset in Palatino by Digital Technologies and Printing Solutions, New Delhi
Printed and bound in Great Britain by Cox & Wyman Ltd, Reading, Berks.

To my father,
a great survivor

Contents

Acknowledgements

The author wishes to acknowledge and specially thank the following: the late Seymour Krim, a too-brief mentor and gutsy author, whose encouragement gave me the audacity to begin a literary project that might have my entire ancestral tree spinning in their graves; the poet, friend, and Brahmin Catholic guru Ralph Nazareth, who treated me like a writer when most others were scornful of my dream; the generous Barry Fruchter, who willingly read and re-read my novel; the enormously intelligent and spirited Fred Naiden; poet-novelist Suzanne Ironbiter, Bert Reid, Sunny Tharappen, Franky Dias; Clive Priddle; others who slipped into my life and have since slipped out of it and must therefore be unmentioned; the ducks and geese in the river by my house, who sometimes interrupted my loneliness, and must be honoured on behalf of Mother Nature; my genes, for so prodding on my unnatural course; my bright and beautiful son and *Sesame Street* star James Ashok, who can do nifty things on the computer; my sons Dev and Rohit, who made me laugh; other friends and well-wishers too numerous to mention, whose advice, friendship, faith, and often impatient desire to see the book in print kept me going in the long, often-dark period of the writing of it. And—oops, yes—my wife, who has permitted me to thank all of the above. Thank you, all.

Man, the period of whose life is one hundred years, should practice Dharma, Artha, and Kama at different times and in such a manner that they may harmonize, and not clash in any way. He should acquire learning in his childhood; in his youth and middle age he should attend to Artha and Kama; and in his old age he should perform Dharma, and thus seek to gain Moksha, that is, release from further transmigration. *Or, because of the uncertainty of life, he may practice them at times when they are enjoined to be practiced.*

—*The Kama Sutra* of Vatsyayana

I
DHARMA

The Beginning of Wisdom

The Churchill Factor

I have not become the King's First Minister in order to
preside over the liquidation of the British Empire.
   –Winston Churchill, opposing Indian
    independence (10 November 1942)

MANY YEARS LATER, when the dogs of reality bit me on the behind,
and I wondered at the reason for the extraordinary course my life
had taken, I remembered that distant morning when a dog I was
trying to pet bit me and impressed upon me the fragility of the life
that now powers this tale. At that time Mangalore, a sleepy town
on the west coast of southern India, was just waking up from the
nineteenth century; though the Russians had by now hoisted a dog
into space, life in this corner of the universe was slow as a line of
loaded bullock carts on a hot summer day. In this coconut-tree
shaded town of a hundred thousand people, fewer than a hundred
owned cars, and fewer than a thousand had travelled farther than
fifty miles. Except for a smattering of Studebakers, Prefects,
Vauxhalls, and Landmasters, the town was essentially the same as
it had been a hundred years ago—a town whose easy coexistence
of Portuguese-style churches and small south Indian temples, of
cobra-worshippers and devotees of Saint Anthony, of girls in loose
skirts and women in figure-hugging saris, of tiger dancers and
piano players made it unique, a piece of India and yet not quite of
it.

    At that time I, a rickety, sun-baked, short-cropped and

wide-eyed four-year-old, had just arrived from Bombay with my mother on a vacation, visiting my uncles. The story of how the dog bit me begins, curiously, with a pig, and the pig-eating habits of the locality.

It had so happened that the day before, my uncles' landlady had cut Dukor the Pig, a small, coal-black squealer who had reached his prime. It was a ceremonial occasion, the cutting of the pig, in this Konkani-speaking, pork-fancying, Catholic neighbourhood. You let your neighbours and friends know, and they would reserve their favourite portions at a pre-bargained price. Those who hadn't been warned would be awakened by an unremitting squeal—Vox Piguli—at about five in the morning, continuing till almost six, because the dull, *desi* knife could only put up a poor fight against the thrashing porker, held down by ten family members, usually with a little, pigtailed servant girl grasping the tail. Then, at about seven, the entire neighbourhood would arrive to fetch their meat and their pig blood while it was still hot, wanting to make sure their reserved, choice, and anatomically precise portion was not snatched up by earlier-arriving higher-bidders.

It was the morning after Dukor's brief candle had been extinguished. The family dog, a brown-and-white mongrel with a semi-amputated tail, had been quite frisky, which was to be expected when there had just been a murder in the house and the Great Chain of Being had been temporarily cut at its porcine link.

My mother was languorously engaged in her bi-weekly 'head bath', which meant the smoke-blackened bathroom would be off-limits for the next forty-five minutes while she soaped her waist-length, jet-black hair and poured over herself chembufuls of water from a great black cauldron—a cauldron heated over firewood that gave more light than heat and more smoke than both.

Unnoticed by my adult caretakers, I drifted past the just-watered earth around the banana trees, past the deep well from which water was drawn in round, narrow-necked kolsos (whose coppery smell I loved to inhale with my nose to the cool metal), past puddles of yesterday's rain, to the veranda by the neighbour's kitchen, where Doggie was chained to a pillar.

'Doggie, Doggie,' said I in my friendliest voice, and tentatively reached for the dog in the spirit of idealistic camaraderie that would be such a hallmark of my later years. But the dog, teaching me in an instant the danger that lay in bared but unsmiling teeth and giving me a sudden lesson in the elasticity of dog chains, lunged and sank his teeth in two places: first in my thigh, and then as I fell forward, in my behind.

Was it my shock at this first revelation of the evil buried in benign Nature? Whatever the answer, I was unconscious when my mother found me. Tears flooding her brown eyes, she screamed, '*Arré* baba, what happened to you, my poor baby!' Was it to end like this—that her boy, to whom she had hoped that the mantle of Churchill's greatness might pass, be felled by a dog bite? Wasted, though not yet tasted by more discriminating customers, by History?

For this, her second and favourite child, was the first son she had begotten in the house on 8 Cambridge Road, Bangalore (yes, *Bangalore*, then a loose and lively imperialist army cantonment with skirted women galore, two hundred miles east of coastal, sari-wrapped Mangalore). It was the very house in which the pre-porcine Winston Churchill, as a young lieutenant in the British Army around the turn of the century, had hung up his long johns to dry and indulged in the vices that were to result in his later baldness (and hence his overcompensating pomposity). And surely, I fantasized later, Churchill, being young and single and probably lonely for suitably imperial female company, had splurted his seed onto those very walls (which for the future Preserver of the Empire was a politically incorrect act, but wildly pleasurable nevertheless). And so had I grown up to a chorus of millions of cigar-smoking, bald Churchillian spermatozoa, yelling 'Right on, Vijay!', 'Go for it, Vijay!'; and never in the history of the Free World did one baby owe so much to so many.

'Hees going to be furrpecttly pine, Amma,' Dr Seshadri Doomappa told my mother, fourteen injections later, speaking his heavily-accented English that at other times would have made my mother laugh. Having said this, his lips opened wide for their usual fifteen-second imitation of a soundless, breathless smile. He had taken a risk with my life, injecting me with anti-rabies shots before waiting to verify if the dog had been rabid; and this at a time when the shots themselves had a ten per cent chance of being deadly.

Now, at his white-smocked assurance of a perfect cure, my mother sighed with relief: her sun had not yet set.

But looking back at it many years later, I challenge Dr Doomappa's flamboyantly optimistic assessment. I suggest instead that at the moment of the dog bite, a curse fell upon my life. For did this 'doctor', this smug puncturer of native bottoms, this transmitter of foreign agents into Indian blood, sitting there in the faded imperialist outpost that was the Lady Winelock Hospital, breathing, exuding, and stinking of phenyl like the nurses and the hospital itself, know everything there was to know?

Such as: if a mad dog can transmit madness by biting, can a neurotic dog transmit neurosis? Can a disaffected dog breed disaffection? A maladjusted dog maladjustment? A sexy dog sexual obsession? If you prick us, the dogbitten, will we not bark? If you tickle us, the undertickled needy, will we not laugh immodestly? And if you wrong us, the twice-bitten, will we not write dyspeptic tomes?

The Beginnings of Sorrow

THE SEX LIFE of the average human male begins with his Mummy. This relationship, more intense in some cultures than in others, is energized and inflamed in our culture by unlimited breast-feeding, oil massages, intimate caresses such as may never recur in his often-poor, often-blighted life. And some would argue that that original love affair never ends, that every significant woman in his life merely takes the place of his dear, dear, Mummyji. So momentous is our obsession with this relationship that we idealize it in concepts such as Divine Mother, Mataji, Goddess, the Eternal Female Principle, and so on, and one out of every three Hindi movies reaches its point of emotional crisis with a scene like this:

> SON [ditching his current skirt-chasing interest and rushing to dying mother's bedside]: Maaaan!
> MOTHER: Don't call me 'Maaaan'! I'm not your mother!
> SON [in tears]: Don't say that, Maanji! What all you are talking! If you are not my motherji, who are you—my uncleji?
> MOTHER [sobbing]: I lied to you, *beta*! I'm not your real mother.
> SON: Not my mother? Haré Ram! Then who *is* my real mother? Indira Gandhi?

MOTHER: Your real mother is . . . your real mother is . . . [she croaks].
SON: Maan! Maan! Oh, poor, poor, motherless me!

He bursts into a heartrendingly melancholy song, as the rest of the plot now lurches into the son's tearfully hysterical search for his real mother.

All this while, the audience washes the theatre floor with its tears, and the box office packs in the loot.

This mystical and sometimes exhausting maternal relationship is the prologue to my own tale, which had begun in Bangalore, where I was born on the morn of April 22, 1953, moving from the hospital to the same house that Winston Churchill spilt his seed in, presiding over the seminal staining of a tiny fraction of the Empire's walls. Those early years, before the blight and assorted dogs began to corrupt my paradise, had been so much simpler, so much more benign: as benign as a mother and child walking in a garden—a timeless scene in a timeless dream-movie.

Look at me, then, in my third year of paradise, in my first, full-fledged, technicolour memory: I, a little monkey and recent mud-eater, tugging at the blue-flowered sari of a beautiful lady, my mother, as we amble about the luxuriant grounds of the tree-studded garden compound of Churchill's sometime sub-imperial residence. Mummy's face is powdered, fair, and young, her red blouse is low-cut, and her dark hair falls straight to mid-back, except for two braids pinned together and adorned with a string of jasmine blossoms. Brilliant white sunshine lights the garden's jacaranda and gulmohur trees, its begonias and marigolds and chrysanthemums.

We walk out on to the road, empty except for a jutka trotting by, the horse's silver anklets tinkling; I am lifted up into a soft cocoon of arms, bosom, and perfume; and soon, we are inside a grey, steepled church, Mummy kneeling, I saying, 'Pitty flowers! Pitty eerings!' as I fiddle with her ears and hair.

'Sshh! Sshh!' people say.

And I remember, as I bury my face in her sari and brush my nose against the fair and soft skin of her neck, her rapturous scent—a mixture of soap-of-the-day, Himalaya Bouquet talcum powder, and fresh underarm sweat—a benevolent scent in a benevolent world. Bangalore was then a paradise blessed with cool breezes, pure air, milk-white sunlight, and a forest of trees. And life, for me, was as colourful and rich as a hawker's basket of plastic bangles.

What, then, caused the end of my paradise? The causes, dear reader, all have their roots in my beginnings, in the beginnings of my parents and their getting together and the genes they inherited, in the beginnings of my race, in the poisons planted in me by the dogbite, indeed perhaps in Adam himself (yes, Adam, who was compelled to be a one-hander before Eve came, and who represents the original male condition of loneliness and impossible longings, of free-floating masculine anxiety).

Consider that the primary reason I was born was that my father had a talent for escaping death; just as the reason I am writing this is that I have a talent for escaping life. And to both—his escapism, resulting in my birth, and my escapism, resulting in my strange survival—I attribute my present state.

Indeed, by the time he was twenty-six, Dad, Pater, Paterfamilias, Pop—also known to the world as Melvin Prabhu—a stolid caramel-skinned young man of medium height with thick black eyebrows and a pencil moustache, had escaped or survived numerous falling coconuts, two cobra bites, one earthquake, one charging bullock, two mad dogs, and one plate of lizard-poisoned chutney. Then he made one chhota miscalculation. Just months before the Second World War broke out, he chose to enlist in the army of the Sun-Never-Sets Empire, and was shipped out after his training to swinging Singapore—only to be captured, two years later, by the future inventors of Walkmans.

Not only did Dad survive his four-year imprisonment and the extreme culinary deprivations that destroyed half his prison camp on the east Indian island his captors took him to, but more impressively, he escaped the bomb-happy Americans who, in their eagerness to get at the scarce Japanese (who were about to surrender anyway), had mainly been bombing their own side. Thus it was that one day, Dad narrowly escaped an American bomb by jumping, for some inexplicable reason, into the trench on his right, instead of into the trench on his left as was his usual habit; the bomb killed all the occupants of the trench on the left. Later, as he was wasting away on the starving and bomb-strafed island, the American atom bombs brought about the Japanese surrender and a nick-of-time Allied rescue. Thus do I—though it embarrasses the life out of my bleeding-heart, pacifist soul—owe my existence to three American bombs.

Dad returned, a proud survivor posted to a cushy army job in Bangalore, and soon took a bus down the steep, winding road through the tiger-haunted Western Ghats to Mangalore to go about the much-delayed business of hunting for a wife, through the traditional process in which matchmakers arranged formal social visits for the 'viewing' of the bride.

'My British commanding officer, he wrote in my report, "He is handsome for an Indian,"' Dad told us once proudly, pointing to a photograph of himself, rugged, broadfaced, sunbaked, unnaturally stiff and erect, in an olive-green, beribboned military uniform—the way he looked to me as a child. 'Some *big* families tried to pawn off their daughters on me!'

'But when I saw your mother . . . .'

The encounter took place on a sunny late afternoon in May 1946, on the veranda of a Roman-villa-like residence with peeling yellow paint, evidence of my maternal grandfather's recent decline from big landlord to frayed-jacketed debtor. The veranda looked out onto a two-acre garden dense with coconut, mango, tamarind, jackfruit, and papaya trees, populated by one dog, one cow-and-calf, and one perpetually bleating goat. Here it was that Mummy had entered Dad's life, walking out onto the veranda demurely, her light-brown, long-lashed, almond-shaped eyes downcast, bearing a cup of coffee for the honoured guest. Deftly moving her strikingly long hair out of the way, she had perched herself in a corner chair shyly and soundlessly. At the time, my father was thirty-four, my mother eighteen. And at the vision of her full redbrown lips and her delicate soft skin—a light cream colour and a sign of impeccable lineage—he jumped into marriage with the same alacrity with which he had once jumped into a trench to save his life.

'She was shy, simple, and would not talk to me, but I wasted no time waiting to ask *my* parents to tell *her* parents. I simply told her parents, "I want *her*!"'

'Mehnnnnn!' the goat had bleated in assent, provoking general laughter and good humour amongst the assembled.

But after having escaped death with the skill and comic indestructibility of Brer Rabbit, after having found himself a local beauty for a wife and having married her at a grand wedding during which a band played "Rosalie Mujha Mogachen" and "Oh my darling, Clementine", and after having been merry enough for three years after the war's end as to buy himself a violin and learn to play "Santa Lucia", Dad stumbled through the rest of his life like a wounded, sense-impaired brontosaurus. Perhaps childhood poverty, a narrow escape from starvation and extinction by bombing during four years in a Japanese prison camp, and the slow realization that he was stuck forever as a junior commissioned officer had caused the decline of his felicity and his obsession with only the basics of survival, and therefore his disdain for such superficialities as bourgeois physical appearances: every Christmas of his adult life he wore the same stone-washed three-piece suit, and he never could knot a tie without looking like the victim of an unsuccessful hanging.

I see how hopelessly and genetically interconnected our fates are, for I fear he may also have bequeathed to me his hardheaded unpragmatism and his naïve and disastrous misunderstanding of life. It was only natural then that I would try to enlarge my limited natural inheritance by unconsciously looking for new and improved fathers: at various times, God the Father, Saint John 'Don' Bosco, John F. Kennedy, Father Joseph Maximus, S.J.

Why these Western (or Westernized) stiffs?

Because it is the fate of every educated Indian, whether or not he admits it, never to be completely Eastern, but to be something of a psychological and intellectual masala with some Western ingredients mixed in. In fact, we are all of us irrevocably mixed-up, as mixed-up as a shrouded Hindu corpse in Benares being driven to the Ganga—to its immortal moksha or dissolution in the holy river—on top of a scooter rickshaw: moksha powered by an internal combustion engine, no less!

Indeed, cruel Dame History herself has been a gigantic mixer of our race, starting with the original blending of Aryans and Dravidians, and throughout its later history when the gold and jewel-rich country was the destination of choice for conquerors—Greek, Arabic, Mongolian, Persian, Portuguese, English—not all of whom onanistically spilt their seed here, but some of whom let it sprout in India's fertile soil, taking their pleasures any way they could get them.

When I was born, many years later, there was the problem of naming me, a Christian descendant of Brahmins—and earlier, of colonizing Aryans from south-eastern Europe.*

My mother was like many Mangaloreans whose extreme anxiety not to displease the One True Christian God (which Mom assuaged by making quick prayers and appeals to Jesus, Mary, and Joseph about once every fifteen minutes of her waking life, and also every time she got up at night to pee) had made them conceal their Hindu ancestry from their children. These Brahmin ancestors had supposedly migrated from north India to Goa in the early part of the first millennium after Christ. But it is only in the sixteenth century, when the Portuguese landed in India with the Divine Mission of spreading Christianity and syphilis amongst the Brown Races—winning pepper and souls for the mother country—that most official histories of Mangaloreans begin. What a telling state of affairs: that your consciousness as a race begins from the moment that sword-wielding Jesus freaks from five thousand miles away invade your country.

More than three centuries later, in a now free India, my father and mother were undecided over which heritage of mine, the Western or the Eastern, would prevail in the name they gave me.

Dad was sitting one evening about then in his striped easy chair with his bottle of army ration Hercules XXX Rum beside him, and the day's *Deccan Herald* before him. On that same eventful day, British High Commissioner Sir Alexander Clutterbuck had arrived in Bangalore and the wicked USSR had exploded three atom bombs; advertisements for BOAC, Parle Glucose biscuits, and Lux Beauty Soap floated before my father's bleary eyes.

'Gave the slip to the Japs, ha ha,' he said to himself—a habit of his at the time after his third drink. He hiccupped, whereupon the suppressed ironist and historical determinist in him jumped momentarily to the surface. He would name me Harry Krishna

---

* Read the Glossary at your leisure for more riches on this and on other matters.

Gandhi Netaji Nusserwanjee Tajmahal Prabhu, he announced, compressing in this name India's assorted legacies to the world, the names of two freedom fighters and one industrialist (Jamshedji Nusserwanjee Tata) and the first name of President Truman, whose Fat Man and Little Boy had jointly saved his life and therefore enabled my existence. Buried in this fanciful name lay the excess of a father passing on the mantle of his frustrated ambitions, his unrecognized true worth, to his progeny.

'Harry Krishna? What are you talking, Melvin, we don't have a Harry Krishna Gandhi in our family and, and, he doesn't look like Gandhi, ha ha, what, OK?' Mummy explained to him softly, during a break in his sudden eloquence. She had enough experience by now to know that 'You're drunk' would be the wrong thing to say: Dad maintained, with some justification, that he was a man of self-control, discipline, and moderation.

'Lion I don't fear. But you I fear, Madam,' Pop said, defensively slipping into a joking variation of a popular Konkani proverb: Lion he doesn't fear, Tiger he doesn't fear, but Mouse he fears. And then, retreating from his spirited advance, he said, 'Mother Hen is the queen of her chicks. Your choice, Madam.'

'No, no, *you* say,' Mummy said, trying to placate my father.

'OK, then, we'll name him after a king. Vijay the Great.'

Mummy suspected that no such king had ever lived, but Vijay sounded like a pretty nice name anyway. At that time, the local Catholic Church still badgered most of its members into choosing European names or the names of saints—the same thing, because all of them, at the time, were white. The Church also mildly approved the practice of quasi-European rhyming names such as Lena and Dina and Reena, and Cletus and Titus and Vitus and Litus (if a fifth son had arrived, he would have been named Clitorus, a local joke went). But a few Mangalorean Catholics had begun, slyly, to reclaim their long-suppressed Hindu heritage, choosing religiously neutral Sanskrit-based names like Suresh and Santosh and Prakash, meaning sun and happiness and light respectively. My elder brother had already been named Arun—meaning 'sun'. Trying to offset her impiety by slipping in the sainted Anthony as the middle name, she acquiesced to my Dad's second choice: Vijay.

It must have been a special bottle of rum that Dad was drinking that evening, for that was the last that anybody ever heard from him regarding his ambitions for me. After that, my mother was the sole bearer of that ambition, though her enthusiasm soon declined. But she did her best, with the resources at hand: she had me massaged with coconut oil by a special ayah.

My subsequent demotion came rather rudely. In keeping with the Indian tradition of prolonged breast-feeding, I had fed on the mother's milk of human kindness for three years; but when my younger brother Anand was born, I had to defer (when suitably threatened) to another Christian whose need was greater than mine. It was a loss I would never quite recover from. Milk, liquid cow, condensed milk, cheese, doodh peda, milk and cookies, buttermilk, creamy Polson's butter, milk sweets: long after I shed my milk teeth, these would be some of my passionately favourite things to eat and drink.

The final step in my descent from my milk-fed Eden to middleclass purgatory came six months later. It was an army transfer order, which ejected us from the mountain-pure air of our garden paradise to the urban congestion of India's commercial and cinema capital, Bombay, on which had settled the sad dust and grime of India's industrial revolution.

The Aunt Who Loved
Water Sports

WHEN THE NEXT partner in my erotic education and my adventures in polymorphous perversity, Aunt Meera, entered my life, in Bombay, it was at a time that I desperately needed such a buxom, skirted saviour, when life seemed drab and mean and scary and enclosed by a barbed wire fence, and the food seemed never enough, and the rain seemed always to bring with it a flood, and my mother, full lips ready to kiss, hair parted in the middle and bunned behind like a demure housewife, seemed lost to my younger brother. Bombay could then be divided into two parts: the cosmopolitan part—Colaba, Bandra, Malabar Hills being the best of this—and the part that was a slummy, congested, lower-middle-class village where people lived, ate, and copulated like *chuhas* in holes in the ground, even if these holes sometimes rose up five or six storeys above the surrounding landscape.

From Churchill's ex-residence to this, a three-room shed with an outhouse for a toilet? My father's memory of childhood poverty, catalysed by these conditions, by this fall from economic grace as it were, cast a shadow of poverty on us, a mental poverty that became *ipso facto* truth (truth being a mental state), even though, compared to those who lived in huts and cooked rice on the pavement, we should have considered ourselves privileged.

It was at this time that Aunt Meera, forced by her own

spinsterhood and a temporary lack of living space to board briefly
with us, burst into my life and came to my rescue with soft, dark
chocolates and an unabashed love, a love so uncommon in these
parts that it must have been imported too, like her wondrous
chocolates with their gold and silver wrappings, like her pink and
brown Cadbury's chocolate 'eggs' with almonds at their centres.
Meera, actually my mother's aunt, but hardly thirty-five, was the
most adventurous of her family of seven sisters—Dotty, Maisie,
Kitty, Letty, Winnie, and Dillie being the others, two of them nuns,
three of them the bearers of large families, and one of them in filarial
spinsterhood. It was Aunt Meera who gave me my first definition
of an exotic woman: wavy bob-cut hair, bright red lipstick on
Cupid's-bow lips, fashionable green dot on a broad forehead, large
brown mascaraed eyes actively engaged in seduction, a rustle of
nylon sari, and a dreamy whiff of perfume. Sweeping in one day
from Hong Kong, where she had been typing her backside off for
two years for a small British firm, she had brought along with her
a gramophone, a magic black box bursting with songs by Tony
Brent and Pat Boone. In our granite-floored, bare-walled house,
with dirt collecting in between the unpolished edges of the granite
slabs, the gramophone was an object of holy awe.

Along with her gramophone, Aunt Meera brought a suitcase
full of brightly-coloured trinkets. Later, I learned of a quantity of
watches she'd smuggled in, concealed within her suitcase's false
bottom; but all I noticed then were those wondrous thingumajigs,
so phantasmagoric and foreign to my world: things-in-themselves,
things without a pedestrian, grimly utilitarian use. An aunt who
had extra money, cash to *spare*, and didn't use it all to stuff her belly
was astonishing; but everything about her was astonishing,
including her speech.

'What, Vijay, you little rascal, you *pokri* fellow,' she would say,
in the first few weeks, kissing and hugging me, or fondling my
cheeks between her palms. 'Why you are looking at me with those
big eyes of yours? You want a kiss from your aunty? Already want
to run after girls, is it?'

Given hugs and chocolates like that, it's not surprising that a
child will sense some merit in rascality, as I secretly must have.

And she, falling for my unruly page-boy haircut, my bright

black eyes so new to life, my innocent smile, my way of singing 'Ta-ra-ra-boom-de-ay', was fonder of me than of my sickly baby brother, Anand, or my elder brother, Arun, who had already developed an adult seriousness and was a fanatic about combing his hair neatly and having not one lock out of place: an unwise course, because it discourages adults from indulging in their favourite pastime of ruffling kids' hair. Running her fingers lightly through my rough, uncombable hair, stroking my caramel custard skin, enfolding my spindly arms and legs, she quickly became the magical second goddess of my childhood imagination: a combination of Diana and Eros, extraordinarily beautiful, self-confident and cheerful. And above all, a teacher of life's secrets: it was spinster-she, rather than my prudish parents, who taught me to pee without wetting my feet, holding my little pecker in her own hand during the first, exciting, lessons—which I, dimly sensing her expertise, prolonged by pretending to be a slow learner.

She also launched, simultaneously, my musical education and my erotic vocabulary, teaching me "Dark Moon", "Daylight Come and I Wanna Go Home", "Cindy oh Cindy", "Mama Look a Booboo", "Jamaica Farewell", "How Much is that Doggie in the Window? Bow Wow!" and the nearly-erotic and wicked "Game of Love", which I crooned endlessly in my untrained voice, sincere and calf-like, to entice her and Mom's love: 'A five and a six, and a Kiss Me Quick, Kiss Me Quick, Kiss Me Quick!' She, disregarding the fact that my five-year-old brain was starved in that austere and bookless (except for two free communist-propaganda storybooks my Dad received from the Chinese Information Service) environment, was astonished by my instant memory for the tunes and words of these songs.

'What do you want to be when you grow up?' she said—the first person I remember to have bothered to ask me the question.

'I want so much to be famous, Aunty. I *have* to be famous,' I replied, passionately.

So impressed was she by my answer that she half-humorously reinvented the nickname 'Vijay the Great' which my father had long forgotten, and which, I must confess, delighted me.

As did many of Aunt Meera's picturesque habits: for example, the cigarette she *had* to smoke whenever she went to our hole-in-the-ground outdoor toilet—to counter the overpowering stench, I surmised. And unlike my mother, who was eternally bound in a sari except on the rare occasions when she was changing and briefly exposed her ghagra or petticoat, Aunt Meera often walked about the house in a loose but thin and revealing dress with nothing underneath; or a stylish dressing-gown that made it seem as if her body had been elegantly wrapped—for quick unwrapping. Outside, she often wore sleeveless blouses, exposing her luxuriant black underarm hair. This practice would elicit sarcastic comments from female relatives who noticed their husbands behaving like excited puppies in her presence. 'Poor woman, she couldn't afford enough cloth for her sleeves!' they'd say—comments that Aunt Meera would simply laugh off.

There was something decidedly sensual about Aunt Meera: her flesh was so ample and generous compared with my girlishly slim Mummy, and her hugs warmer and more ecstatic, echoing a secret, passionate love in Hong Kong. But the chocolates tipped the scale, decisively; if she had kept at it, she would have replaced Mummy as my eternal love.

Then, I ran into her 'dark' side. Ah, Aunt Meera: so beautiful, yet so cruel. Why did you have to epitomize that great truth of my life: that women (some beautiful, some not) would often be cruel to me? With a kiss on your surprised lips, I present to you, Aunt Meera, a charge-sheet that my lawyer, if I had one, would present to you.

To begin with: exercising unlawful and felonious control over my orifices.

Because Aunt Meera, in addition to her gramophone and chocolates, had also brought along a king-sized British implement for the administration of enema inscribed, 'By Appointment to Her Majesty the Queen.'

So when Mummy said one day, 'He is constipated, Vijay,' Aunt Meera laughed in reply, her brown eyes lighting up. 'Got just the remedy for it, Lena.'

Fine, Aunt Meera, you *believed* in enemas; in your lexicon, they were like eating your morning oatmeal, *the right thing to do*. So I don't grudge your administering them to yourself a little over-frequently, morning and evening, your face flushed with pleasure. But why *me*?

The effect of these painful enemas, apart from the too-obvious one, was to make me view adults as tyrants whose joy lay in internally hosing down kids . . . so I thought, as they suppressed me and—ouch!—compressed me over a bed: two huge, brutish, stinking adults pinning down a puny child's limbs, while my aunt, her eyes glowing, inserted the thin plastic tube.

'Now stay quiet now. It will feel very good in a little while, so good you'll ask for it everyday now, you *pokri* boy,' she said enigmatically, laughing, as I wailed, 'Please, no no!'

A few weeks later, having been denied an extra helping of vorn (a thick, light brown, soupy kheer made with lentils and jaggery), I flung away the family thermometer (an incident my mother would recount to gleeful visitors for the next two decades, as an example of my wickedness).

I paid for that five-rupee thermometer with a priceless whipping: Dad, Mummy, then Auntie, each politely awaiting their turn according to the official order of precedence, then returning for seconds.

'Tup Tup you will get on your *bum* next time, you see!' said Aunt Meera, eyes flashing three parts fake anger and one part lust, landing a whack on the anatomical portion in question.

She and many Mangaloreans *loved* the word bum, because it was the only permissible quasi-sexual word in the God-fearing social discourse of the time—and only with reference to the bums of minors, particularly minors below the age of reason or protest.

'All bad habits he has,' added Pop, who having performed for the third time, was now trying to restore the circulation to his overworked palm. He had come in from the hot sun a little earlier, and his shirt was still drenched with sweat. Outside, a dog yelped pitifully in chorus to my cries.

After a year with us Aunt Meera, buoyed by the profits from her smuggled watches, moved out of my life and into a large apartment in the upscale Bandra neighbourhood, home of Bombay's film stars. Requiring an electric train ride and a bus change, the visits to her grew rarer and rarer.

And then, in gloomy June, when the Bombay sky opens up to let forth a deluge that will relent only in September, and when a minor deluge actually flooded the neighbouring houses and we were one step away from evacuation, the news came like a sentence of execution. With Dad's transfer to a village near Calcutta, Arun and I were to be sent to a convent boarding-house in Mangalore, a continent away from my parents.

'But it's a dirty village, full of deadly king cobras!' Dad said, trying to persuade us of our good fortune. 'No good schools! You want to become cowherds and catch flies with your mouths?'

I would learn later, much too late, that Dad had begged his haughty north Indian superior for a change of transfer to a town where he could get a school for his tiny children, then had requested his brothers in Mangalore to keep us with them, before settling with hurt pride on the boarding-house; that Mom had had fits of weeping at the thought of being separated from her children, the children she had obsessively taught and fed and stitched clothes for, even as she kept her husband pleased with huge quantities of fish curry, cooked at night when she was already quite tired. But at the time, I understood nothing.

I saw all my worldly belongings disappear into the steel trunk Mummy was packing for us: clothes, nine WIMCO matchboxes, and six empty Gold Flake cigarette packets with which I built houses and which comprised my first and last toy collection. Was I being sent away forever?

Kooooooooo! The metre-gauge train that whisked us southwards over green hills and muddy rivers without undue rest was reddish brown and canary yellow. Southwards and further southwards, tatatatatatat it went, this crudely-welded machine of steel, wood, and bolts, leaving behind entire subcultures and geographical zones, reddish brown, black, and fertile green, until Bombay and Mummy and the box-like Bombay house became dreamy memories.

At Kadur, we were transferred to a vermilion Dodge Fargo bus that sputtered and groaned through a bumpy and dusty eight-hour ride over cloud-shrouded hills into the coastal depression that was South Kandra and on to Mangalore. The day after that, our care and feeding, the welfare of our bodies and souls, became the responsibility of the nuns and their house of bondage called Saint Juliana's Convent.

I did not find the matchboxes and cigarette packs in my trunk when I reached my destination. And I understood. My always practical father had thrown them out on the way.

What I didn't understand then was that my childhood had ended.

Underwear

I NOW SEE that real life and true sex, which I define as debauchery with a female who has played no role whatsoever in your coming into this world or in changing your nappies shortly there-after—began for me in the convent. Not that the nuns came out of it with sticky fingers; the role of nuns in the future sex lives of their charges has yet to be fully documented. Still, there is little doubt in my mind that a black habit that hides twenty times as much as it reveals must provoke dark thoughts in the darkest recesses of the human mind, which, like a cat, is always provoked into curiosity by the hidden dimension (such as: what does a nun's shaved head really look like?). No doubt too that the nuns, my first teachers of dharma (i.e. the religious life, without which sin loses most of its delicious pleasure, as you can notice these days in the West), provided the necessary background for my introduction to real sex.

The convent school, a three-acre complex that consisted of old bungalows with unsightly, box-like additions to accommodate its ever-increasing population, was surrounded by a high redbrick wall strategically decorated with shards of broken glass. Once you were in, you were in! Because the only exit was a massive iron gate manned by a Gurkha: yes the Gurkhas, formerly the pride of the imperialist British Army, were now among the chief protectors of the virtue of India's convent residents. And Virtue was big business at Saint Juliana's Convent, Mangalore.

Mother Ottila, Nun-in-Chief, who cracked the whip over the bevy of nuns who assisted her at this Virtue factory, seemed to have done a good job at keeping them innocent. Once, the nearby priest's seminary had sent the convent its torn clothes, including a few items of male underwear; the nuns, happy to practice their needlework had, out of their ignorance of male anatomy, stitched up the slits in the underpants.

The convent was a little city-state ruled by dolorous nuns: prayers carved in flesh. And it was in this kingdom that I was placed two months past my sixth birthday. Besides me, the place had: fifteen nuns in itchy-brown habits topped with a little whipped cream around the face, fourteen housemaids in the regulation blue-checkered calf-length cotton skirts, twenty boys aged six to ten, and sixty-six girls aged six to seventeen. Kingdom, city-state, nundom: because the outside world—the city of Mangalore and the India that contained it—was, at least until I experienced it during the holidays, merely a concept kicked about in geography class and asserted by the day students. Within these convent walls, my entire world for nine months a year, I knew only a gynocracy: strangely dark-costumed females in absolute power. And in this republic of women, conceived in piety, and dedicated to the proposition that all men are created evil and must therefore be walled out of existence, the only adult male granted a permanent visa was one Father Fernandes, who arrived on his scooter at 6:45 every morning to say Mass and left at 8:15 after a royal 'English' breakfast of fried eggs, bread and butter, bananas, apples, and consciousness-piercing, aromatic Western Ghats coffee.

'*Kyrie Eleison!*' exclaimed Father Fernandes bowing before the chapel's altar, an embroidered gold cross gleaming from the back of his vestment, incense from the incense burner rising up in the air behind him.

It was a little past sunrise, and the muddled light of this September day streamed into the small convent chapel and, mixing with the absurdly yellow electric light, fell on the vermilion-and-blue saints painted on the walls, fell on the faces of the nun-speckled congregation murmuring through the morning Mass, fell on the scapulared sinners nervously regarding the mumbo-jumbo in progress.

Shifting my bruised knees from time to time on the hard wooden kneeler, my gaze was lost in the awesome gold-painted tabernacle, the ever-lit red and gold lamp pointing to that awesome Presence, the Body of Christ, magically condensed into a host the size of a large peppermint.

Now I became aware of a chocolate brown row of nuns occupying the entire back row, praying—lips moving silently, forming 'Hail Mary, full of grace . . .'—and frenziedly counting beads. Or repeating in emotional whispers, 'Jesus! Mary! Joseph!' 'St. Jude, Pray for us!' and so on (it is a truth universally acknowledged that nuns ejaculate frequently).

But the nuns' placement also had a strategic purpose: we, the boarders of Saint Juliana's, were outnumbered by the soldiers of the Good. There were eyes at the back, eyes in front. And behind everyone, in the last row, knelt Mother Ottila, her chubby, arrested face's stern expression tempered by an inner smile as she regarded her virtuous flock at prayer.

And I trembled to think of the sins I had just committed, and not just of the whipping I would get if discovered, but also of the poor impression it would make on Judgement Day.

At the age of six, I had already begun to look out for the end of the world. It had been at most a hot rumour circulating through the Catholic world of late 1959 and early 1960 that the world would end. But the nuns passed it on to us with apocalyptic certainty.

'World is ending, world is ending, pray, children, pray! On your knees, beg God to *save* us!' Sister Maria Antoinetta, standing on the podium in catechism class and tapping the desk with her footruler for emphasis, had implored us in her honeyed voice. Apparently, the news had arrived officially, in a letter to the Pope, from Mary, Mother of God, delivered through the agency of three Portuguese shepherd-children.

'How *wonderful* it would be to die as a little innocent child, pure of heart, and go straight to heaven! Wouldn't it? And now: take down the syllabus for next year,' Sister Maria Antoinetta had continued. But I was not ready to die yet. I wanted to go home and see my mother first.

'*Dominus Vobiscum!*' said Father Fernandes in the sonorous, mock-singing voice of someone in training to be a bishop.

'*Padrin marli puskum!*' echoed in the minds of twenty little boys kneeling in church, mine included—the words meaning, in Konkani: thus farted the priest.

The joke intruded like a compulsive thought, it being one of the few jokes anyone knew, and the secret laughter briefly shushed my fears about the End of the World. Whose signs, Mother Ottila said, anyone could see: Sputnik, Khrushchev, atheists—and, most dramatically, the coming to power in the neighbouring state of Kerala of wicked people called Communists. Communists meant guns, bloodshed, dogs shot into Space, the very doorstep of Heaven, to insult God the Almighty, and oh, horror! Godlessness! All we could do was pray, and children's prayers went straight to God, bypassing screening committees of saints. So said Mother Ottila: Ottila the Nun.

But my fear of the end of the world was balanced by pleasure at my life's first brush with the feminine element—with girls! Girls with brightly coloured ribbons and jasmine and dahlias in their hair, too much talcum powder, mascara, artificial beauty spots to avoid the evil eye, white petticoats to camouflage their delicate forms, thick white underwear . . . .

Girls seemed to drop tears for scores of reasons: the 'Shame, Shame song'*, wetting their chaddies, being beaten with one or more broomsticks or a twig, the untimely death of a beloved domestic cow or goat, the memory of an absent parent or a grandmother, being called harsh or teasing names, being told they were stupid or bad or would be sent to hell, getting their answers wrong in front of the whole class, losing at games, being told the Communists were coming.

Then I thought of my mother, on the platform of Bombay's Victoria Terminus Station, shedding quiet tears and wiping her eyes with her sari's pallav as she waved goodbye.

My reverie rudely cut short by a pinch from Blanche (who like all senior girls had carte blanche to pinch me whenever my

---

* It went:
  Shame, shame!
  Poppy shame
  All the boys and girls know your name!
No one ever knew what 'Poppy shame' meant.

too-genuine devotion seemed to falter and drift off), my thoughts soon drifted to an older un-girl: Sister Domina Mary. What did she want to see me about? I didn't remember her ever looking so angry. My mind ran through my possible trespasses . . . God, is it *that*?

Or could Sister Domina Mary have sent for me about last night? It had happened in my sleep, while I was dreaming of pissing on a tree, or of flying in space flapping my hands like wings. Then I woke up. It was dark, except for a solitary nightlight. I felt a wetness between my legs, under my buttocks. An acrid smell. Oh God! Trouble!

Tiptoeing out, I had squeezed out the shorts onto the wooden floorboard underneath a neighbouring boy's cot to hide the evidence, then hung them up to dry against the bed's headstand—hoping my bedsheet and shorts would dry by morning and my crime wouldn't be nosed out. Then I had tried to keep awake all night so when daylight threatened, I could quickly slip my shorts back on.

All this happened though I prayed incessantly, like the Jews during the Egyptian captivity, pleading every night, 'Not tonight, dear God, please!' I had tried to stay up, focusing my consciousness on the sounds of St. Mary's Convent by night: the pit pit pit trr trr trr whoo whoo whoo of the thickening rain; a late Number 14 or Number 11 bus braking to a stop, then re-starting; an ageing, overloaded lorry groaning down the road. Yet I had finally dozed off, and when Christine Bai, the potato-faced ayah had come to check on my bed and shorts—I can picture her now inspecting a debutante's knickers for semen stains—she had found them soggy with my guilt.

'Made *sussu* in your bed, hah? Dirty fellow! Mutro!' plump Christine Bai had said at the moment of discovery, as always. She called me Mutro: The Pisser. (This was before Morarji Desai made *mutr*, or urine, respectable—and the Indian Prime Ministership less respectable—by admitting he quaffed his own pee, as a form of holistic preventive medicine.) I supposed she had reported her finding-of-the-morning to Sister Domina Mary, as usual.

Sister Domina Mary, wrinkled, fair, sternfaced and tall, wielder of the fastest cane in the East. Her wrath had by now mapped itself on my anatomy: cane marks like juicy red and blue rivers. Sister Domina Mary's sinister, wrinkled face hit you like the lash of her whip, her black veil complementing her dark looks and her sharp, crocodile teeth, her steel cross so large as to seem like a weapon. She had a right eye that continually twitched, as if to confuse the houseflies trying to settle on her nose.

What Sister Domina Mary most relished of her role as boarding mistress was the infliction of 'punishments'. At the end of which, turning away, I would mock her, mouthing a soundless and possibly inaccurate 'You have a big bum!' (Sometimes, I wrote these words out —'BIG BUM! BIG BUM!'— in my exercise book, then crossed them out till only a large blue stain remained.) Miserable tears would follow.

When I grow up, I will come back and beat her, I thought bitterly, walking towards the refectory for breakfast. Or maybe my Daddy will: as an army man, he has a double-barrelled gun, which can kill two people at the same time.

But I stopped myself, thinking: That's a bad thought, the kind of sin for which Jesus has decided to end the world. Jesus, save me, I thought. And please, please, let me have a letter from my mother soon, before the world ends.

There was one advantage to be gained from the end of the world or the threatened coming of the Communists, I thought then. It might save me from Sister Domina Mary.

But that was not to be. 'Sister Domina Mary wants to see you in the dormitory right now,' said Blanche. I followed her like a beaten dog. As I approached the dormitory, girls tittered.

'Filthy fellow!' shouted Sister Domina Mary. 'A thoti's son you are!' Lash lash lash!

And then she dragged me, pleading tearfully against the cane in her hand, to the servants' area in the back with the banana and bimbli trees and the open gutters. 'Please, please,' I cried. Lash lash lash. Stations of the cross, I thought, as I was finally dragged to the granite washing stone to wash my urine-soaked pajamas and bedsheet myself—my shameful secret, of a rebellious penis with a will of its own, publicly exposed.

What really kept me going, I think now, was my hope that somewhere there existed a just world and fair-thinking people. Some day, when all came out into the open, justice would be done—*and children would never be abused ever again!*

But there was also My Sin.

It was a sin so wicked, and so monstrous in my mind that the ten years thereafter, weighed down by guilt, may be described as my post-Leela years. I shuddered often in those years, afraid of dying in my sleep and going straight to hell — even though the cause of the sin, I sometimes thought, was Sister Domina Mary, who by describing me as 'wicked' about ten different times when I was not in the least so had made the appeal of wickedness irresistible to me. It was only at seventeen, when the entire edifice of Sin As Anatomical Knowledge came tumbling down for me, that I was able to dwell coolly on it and write about it—with a pen whose flow had been eased by rational philosophy, writing ambitions, the retrospective vision of mid-pubertal heat, and the discovery that there was no wonder in the world like the wonder between maidens' legs. The Sin and my foolish guilt had now, through a literary metamorphosis, become:

AN IMMODEST PROPOSAL
THE CONFESSIONS OF AN ANATOMICAL DETECTIVE
[OR LEELA, THE ENLIGHTENMENT OF MY EARLY LIFE]

It all happened suddenly, without preparation—the subject hadn't even come up between us—as if some dark, hibernating forces in our natures had suddenly awakened and made us into its puppets. One Sunday evening, as we found ourselves standing in front of Bathroom Row, not a soul in sight, opportunity proved the catalyst.

Leela, like me—though with ribboned pigtails, butterscotch complexion, full, chocolate lips, brooding mystery, and frightened, large rabbit eyes—was a natural victim: the lowest in the girls' pecking order, as I was among the boys. Neither of our parents visited. She wore faded, 'poor' clothes, always with a smudge on her white blouse to match a smudge on her cheek; and she had nude ears—pierced, but bereft of the customary golden earrings. And it was whispered about, because we rarely had sweets with us, that our parents were poor. So we had gravitated toward each other, as if by a primal attraction. We became playmates, playing all the nameless games that are listed in no book and require only the bare, natural equipment: stones, twigs, leaves, flowers, pebbles, legs.

There was also something else: I did not until that cloudy and dark evening know the *real* difference between boys and girls, though circumstantial evidence made me suspect there was some difference. It is God's truth: I had never had sisters, not even girl cousins, and I had been protected from other revelations by careful zoning. Subliminally, I realized that Leela, seven years old like myself, and perhaps three inches shorter than my four feet six inches, had the opposite problem; or the same problem on the opposite side.

That was how, on the spur of the moment, I pulled Leela by the hand, and she understood without words that universal call: *Show me yours*. Together, our faces somber, we charged into a dank and dark bathroom and bolted the door behind us. No time was wasted in trade negotiations. There was none to waste because the nuns would often patrol the area looking for trouble. Down came her white, frilled, coarse-cotton undershorts to reveal her—and here, I use this word so as not to offend the sensitive ears of those who have been raised on tender romantic novels—girlhood. Just a beginner's introduction to the swollen first inch or so, of the cleft: slipping her drawers down an inch or so for a few seconds before she quickly pulled them up again.

Yoo hoo! But to my eternal guilt and shame, I gave uneven exchange. Her prize was a quick look at my diminished *bitto*, for it was just the tip, one leg of my shorts slightly lifted like the opening of a tent, to give her a quick glance at the nib—or what some foolish souls consider to be the high point if not the end-all and be-all of a woman's existence: five, possibly six inches of exaggerated human flesh in its least versatile form. But regardless, oh, thou pre-Lolitan Lolita! Sensuous seed, or seed of coming sensuality! Thou didst oblige!

But I wasn't satisfied. My scientific mind resisted coming to conclusions with one experiment—or so I fooled myself. I needed repeated confirmations of my first sighting of the Promised Land. My life now seemed to have acquired a purpose. Leela and I had grown bolder and the initial guilt had given way to generosity and a ravenous hunger, the hunger of the oppressed for the forbidden.

And during one session recklessly enacted in the Play Room, an older girl named Nina happened to burst in on one of our educational sessions. Nina, whose lips were the reddest I had ever seen, who had a mole on her chinny-chin-chin and slight swellings under her blouse, surprised the bashful two of us by asking for a piece of the action. So I showed her a piece of my little piece, big-hearted Leela showed her the whole of her whatever, and Nina—treachery!—showed us merely the outline of her in-line, camouflaged beneath a thick-and-tight chaddi. A little ungenerous, yet enough of a secret thrill: to see a tight chaddi straining against her swollen, thirteen-year-old pubis.

Seven years old and a *ménage à trois*! Oh, the power of Leela over my soul-lingam; even now, merely to think of a courageous and giving woman who has overstepped the boundaries—Marilyn Monroe going about town and her film sets without panties, for example—gives me a hard-on. Thus did Leela and the good Sisters of the Apostolic Carmel become the architects of my future, overcomplicated sex life.

The Water of Life

UNDER A SALMON-COLOURED October evening sky at the convent, Uncle Gaulbert's scarlet Fiat purred up to the steps of the tiled visitors' parlour, which he climbed with quick chappalled steps to ring an ancient bronze bell.

'What, Vijay? What, Arun? Heh heh, you little twerp, you little *pilkato*, how are you?' he said in his laughing, masculine voice, smiling his good-looking, I'm-doing-wonderfully-ha-ha-ha smile, when he saw us running up to him.

Uncle Gaulbert was a thin, intense man with the sallow complexion of vorn, intensely focused eyes, suave laughter that brought warmth wherever it went, and a thunderous temper that made the roaches want to go back to where they came from. His small face had the ruddy handsomeness of success, proved by his ownership of the tiny red Fiat—yes, he was one of the Hundred (locals who had cars); and also one of the Two (locals who had tiny red Fiats).

He had come to pick us up from the convent boarding-house to take us home for the Dussehra holidays.

Our reply was merely a smile of quiet, shy joy.

Then Mother Ottila said, 'They are all right, Mr Prabhu. But Vijay, you know, he wets his bed. Almost every night. What trouble!'

A moment's shame pulsed through me, and I hated her at that instant, hated Mother Ottila with a vehement hate I had never known before.

Because Uncle Gaulbert, by then, had become the first in a long line of men who were to become my substitute fathers or almost-fathers.

The thing that fascinated me about Uncle Gaulbert was that he stood on his head. Every morning, before breakfast. He said the habit was good for your brain in general, besides being an anti-baldness strategy, but all I could see was that it made him look redfaced and silly. But what awed me was his skill in temporarily suspending the laws of physics, for how else did he prevent his lungi from falling down and revealing his nakedness?

What if Uncle Gaulbert had been not merely my local guardian but my Dad? I wondered, as I slurped green saccharin-laced pistachio ice cream at our first stop, Rayan's Ice Cream Parlour. He would have made a better Dad, since he had more crisp hundred-rupee notes in his purse, and more rollicking, soothing laughter. There would have been almond and pistachio ice creams and Fiat rides, and the nuns would have treated me with the delicacy and awe they reserved for the children of the rich and the 'holy'. The thought was sacrilege.

'Quick, quick,' said Uncle Gaulbert, hurrying out of the parlour into the street. He had long nimble legs from dodging spitters in the cow-dunged streets. Arun and I, clad in our navy blue shorts and soiled white shirts missing an odd button or two, cantered a few steps to catch up with him. Darting up old wooden stairs, ta-dak ta-dak ta-dak, we entered the office of pince-nezzed Dr Bob Colaco, a homoeopathic doctor, the first in a line of many such quacks, dispensing the medical equal of duck soup. I followed Uncle Gaulbert in meek embarrassment, and received 'powders' wrapped in little scraps of paper. The powders, to be gulped down with water, were designed to cure my bedwetting, but tasted suspiciously like the glucose powder which other local quacks gave children for 'strength' or for 'cold' or for boo-boo healing.

Uncle Gaulbert made two more stops. He bought heavy brown shoes for Arun and perfumed, coloured Tata's hair oil for my 'pariah boy' hair.

Now his little red Fiat hummed down the hilly, winding road, past old tiled houses, to the yellow and mossy tiled house by the paddy field—the house that the uncles shared and that had once housed the serpent-toothed Doggie. It nestled in a valley surrounded by trees and old peasant houses and overrun by pigs and pye-dogs and occasional snakes, and ragamuffins who played cricket with bald tennis balls on the road, stopping their game to gape at the occasional passing car or lorry.

'See you tonight, OK?' said Gaulbert, as his car headed back shopwards, two stray pye-dogs trying to nip at his tyres for intruding on their mid-road nap. The uncles would return late in the evening after shuttering up their shops, sometimes picking up a packet of masala wafers or sugared or masala cashew nuts for the children.

The uncles: the masculine, money-churning powerhouses of my boyhood. Their voices loud, their movements sharp. Villagers who had been transformed by success of a sort, and had become clearheaded enough to believe in their retailing business as a good provider, good enough to transcend caste notions of appropriate work—which, given their Brahmin heritage, meant absolutely no work! Dressed in starched, miraculously white, baggy Indian trousers and kurtas, the uniform of the local Konkana business caste (into which they had unofficially converted themselves), they were a running lesson in patriarchy. They made the loot, shoe-boxes full of it, and they expected the women to put the gravy on the table, and it had better be hot, and it better have verve and panache and zip so that the next day they could snap back to earning more dough, so that they might have more gravy with verve and panache and zip.

'What, *ré*?' said Uncle Eddy Baab, the eldest, entering that evening with the chup-chup-chup of chappalled feet and making his opening and closing statement.[*] Uncle Eddy Baab was an enigma wrapped in the green-checked lungi that was his domestic garb: he had appropriated a gloomy seriousness and made it a permanent feature of his sunbaked face topped by oily, greying hair. He never had much to say, and he said it in no time.

---

[*]   Every Mangalorean Catholic had an uncle named Eddy Baab or Jerome or Lancy or Wilfy or Leo, and an aunt named Mary or Mabel or Ulloo or Daisy or Dotty or Phulabai, just as every large north Indian family seems to have a child named Chotu or Chunni or Munni or Tikkoo.

Eddy Baab was followed by Uncle Eustace, who stomped in with crisply ironed grey trousers and smart and heavy leather shoes, which made their own statement. Uncle Eustace—with the bright-kid face and the young-man-about-town, brilliantined-hair—was the young 'un, the Hitler-moustached kid brother who had been sent to college by his Eighth-Grade (Passed!) brothers, and who, every morning thereafter at breakfast, ate bread and butter to announce to the surrounding Conjee-Eating Regulars his extra-planetary origins. Chomp on the thickly buttered slice in his right hand; chomp on the half-peeled banana in his left. Chomp chomp chomp chomp went his manual banana-bread processing machine. He ate bread and butter as if it were a political statement, a matter of national policy, biting into the soft, airy, thick, and hot-from-the-bakery-oven slices spread with soft yellow butter without inviting us children to share; that's why to this day I salivate at the very thought of bread and butter, and am doing so right now.

The next morning at breakfast, the odour of warm bread rising from Uncle Eustace's direction and mixing with the slightly dusty and acid smell of hot conjee and pickled green mango and the sweet smell of an overripe jackfruit in the corner, I made my announcement: 'Uncle, first in class, I have come. In Midterm exam.' And waited for the shouts of joy, the 'Shabash!' the promise of gifts, a bite of bread-butter-banana.

'Huhn, good! Shabash!' said Uncle Gaulbert, with his happy, masculine laugh.

'Huhn. I always knew you had a big head,' said Uncle Eddy Baab, suddenly revealing a mouthful of neem-brushed yellow teeth.

'We should put you on an elephant and parade you around the town,' said the deep-voiced Uncle Eustace, guffawing and displaying Pepsodent-white teeth. 'With a big hat saying "Number One Student".' And the other uncles obliged with diffident dutiful laughs at this display of 'humorousness' by the Educated One.

Maybe only real Dads could be expected to thrill at such news, to soar out of their chairs and lift one up in the air . . . my class-mates, even when they had merely passed, got presents of new clothes, stationery boxes, toys, sweet tins . . . .

That summer Uncle Gaulbert left the joint family residence for a new abode I never saw, with a new love, the result of having seen one romantic Raj Kapoor film too many; Hindi films, imitating Forties' Hollywood musicals and occasionally spicing them up with Chaplinesque socialist heroes, had become the Trojan horses of Western notions of romantic love. And Uncle Eddy Baab, propelled by prosperity, moved with wife and tots from the joint house by the paddy field to a large, cement-floored house in Jeppu. Compared to the rich greenery outside, the inside of the house was bare, its only decorative artifact being a large, Gothic wooden altar—within which, enclosed separately in their own glass cages, lay, from left to right, Mary, Jesus, and Joseph: the Biggies. This house became our chief holiday haunt for the next two years.

Arriving at 9:00 a.m. one Sunday, a vague hunger gnawing within us, a hunger piled up during five months of convent diet—sardine curry and spinach and gourds—we waited for the Main Event: the Sunday lunch. Since Aunt Esma's definition of good behaviour for children was, 'See No Evil; Hear No Evil; Speak No Evil; and Don't Move Until Told To, or I'll Thump You On The Head,' this meant four hours of frozen inaction in a chair, dull as a Hindi grammar class taught by a sing-song punditji on a hot afternoon just after a heavy lunch—an eternity that was endless, exitless, eventless, except for the noises that stole in from the kitchen: the breaking of coconuts, the scraping of kernels, the washing of vessels, the cleaning of rice, the rhythmic grinding employed in creating the masala of the day—excruciatingly recognizable sounds, combined with the sharp odours of ground turmeric and frying chillies.

At the unstruck stroke of the unspoken lunch hour, Uncle Eddy Baab, the man of this house, shouted from under his *Sunday Standard*, 'Is lunch ready?' and all of us children, including my cousins, strained for the answer.

'Fifteen minutes more,' Aunt Esma shouted back from the kitchen.

Sixteen minutes later, Uncle Eddy Baab repeated his question, adding a new and obviously insincere note: 'The children are hungry.'

When Aunt Esma finally announced her readiness, we were at the dining-table in seconds, trying without success to look casual.

At the unpolished teak dining-table, though anonymous custom decreed we help ourselves to the rice first, it was the soft mutton pieces* that we were really after. Arun and I watched from the corners of our eyes to dissuade ever so discreetly our competing fellow-tots from extra-large helpings, though our own helpings were the largest we could manage with impunity.

'Eat, eat,' Uncle Eddy Baab said, laughing. 'Fill your *poat*!'

He was in his boozy good humour, and didn't notice that Aunt Esma had simultaneously fixed me with a dirty look that said, 'Don't you dare eat too much!'

But I could never be sure my good luck would repeat itself, that another meal like this would ever come—tender mutton in a coriander and mint masala, sannan, a green bean *sabji* cooked with chillies, coconut, and raw cashew nuts. I wolfed down as much as I could bear, like a stray dog suddenly treated to a bucketful of wedding leftovers splashed onto the pavement.

The funny thing about being thin and malnourished is that you can, living in the world of the thousand-caloried, be called 'fat', because you have what appears to them a fat boy's or overeater's belly. I had acquired a pot belly—that is, a stomach which extended an inch and a half beyond my bare birdcage of a chest—which should have told them that I was deficient in Vitamin B. But my unscientific uncles found that a matter to tease me about. 'Look at your *poat*, I say. King Kong!' they'd say, Uncle Eddy Baab especially, and laugh. What would they do next: wait for me to go blind and laugh as I stumbled on the furniture?

It being Sunday, with Uncles Eddy Baab and Eustace home for the afternoon and in charge, the word 'holiday' lived up to its name. Uncle Eddy Baab, his insides soothed by spiced protein and country liquor, felt lax enough to let me have the *Sunday*

---

* The uncles, rather over-conscious of their Brahmin purity—diet being a function of caste in those days—ate only the best mutton and chicken, and refused to touch the downmarket and cheaper beef that my parents and other Christians ate. 'Who knows where those cows came from? Some people say the butchers buy dead cows at night . . .' they would say. (Their greatest contempt was for the local pariahs, who were reputed to eat crow meat.) They also steered clear of such Mangalorean specialities as pepper-masala, fried sheep brain, tripe coconut curry, pig's liver and intestine curry, sheep's head curry with ash pumpkin, and sheep liver and lungs in a coconut curry.

Standard—that cornucopia of entertainment and information that enriched our bookless world with the likes of Harold Macmillan, John F. Kennedy, Dagwood Bumstead, and *Bringing Up Father.*

I raced with my prize to the kids' room, and hungrily devoured it from cover to cover. The Kennedy titbits grabbed me first; but in those days, when I was as hungry for knowledge as a fat blotting paper was for ink, every scrap of information, every humble fact—from Jawaharlal Nehru's advice to the Burundians on personal hygiene to the starchy article singing the virtues of the humble potato—excited me and brightened my world. As did the hilarious knowledge, gleaned from *Bringing Up Father*, that American women called their husbands 'Insect!' and threw breakable objects at them. Those crazy Americans!

With the sun cooling off in the Western sky, we packed ourselves, eight of us, into Uncle Eddy Baab's tiny, hunch-roofed car for the one-mile ride to Milagres Church for Mass: oh the aroma of leather, plastic, and petrol in that 1955 Austin. Though it was the dull grey colour of my grandfather's faded coat, to ride in a car, to be even seen in a car—to be *suspected* of being seen in a car—was to provoke dreams of princedom, of wealth by association; and what a miracle it was each time when, after a tense minute of creaking persuasion, the car coughed to life and then moved.

But sorrow soon followed.

Shortly after the holidays began, my seventy-year-old grandmother had arrived from her daughter's house in Madras, planning to stay with Uncle Eddy Baab permanently. Thus began a strange bond between the younger generation—us, the quasi-orphaned brats—and the older generation, personified by my grandmother. We called her Mainn, and she followed our names with *puta*—son. Mainn's peasant hardiness came from having single-handedly reared chickens and cows and sold eggs and milk to feed her twelve children, of whom she had lost two to childhood accidents—one cobra bite, one unscheduled drop into an unwalled well, a healthy and normal death rate for that time.

Mainn had retired into a life of toothlessly mumbled prayers, with occasional breaks for the sniffing of snuff or the chewing of paan or betel leaves, which she kept in a cloth pouch wedged between her sari and midriff. She belonged to a black-saried sisterhood of widows and spinsters, some kind of cross between a senior-citizen sodality and a correspondence-course nunnery for those who wished to make a virtue of their necessity: their inescapable chastity. Her deeply wrinkled, rectangular face, muted by suffering and experience, and her weary but watchful eyes would occasionally light up in laughter or uncontrollable amusement, as when told that the recently deceased Prime Minister Jawaharlal Nehru, in a flamboyant act of sentimental patriotism, had willed that his ashes be scattered by plane all over India, to mingle with the sacred soil of the motherland.

'And everyone should hold their noses?' she asked.

'No smell. Fire destroys the bacteria,' pipsqueak-scientist Arun informed her.

'What is bacteria?' she asked, her sunken cheeks moving her paan to a different corner of her mouth as she spoke. And then, before anyone could explain, she said, '*Puta*, tell me when the plane comes. I'll run inside. I don't want Nehru's stinking ashes clogging my hair.'

'Ashes contain potassium. Good for you,' said Arun.

Mainn spent half her days walking with us to the town's dozen or so churches: magical oases, quiet, soaring, colourful, sad, cruel—the scene for daily breastbeating about the gory tortures of Christ and how each of us was *personally* responsible for those nails and thorns tearing into that bloody flesh, so weren't we ashamed and couldn't we stop sinning and hurting Him? Fat and bald priests in glittering costumes whispered furtive, magical Latin words over the host, as if guarding against its being pilfered by unauthorized agents of the devil. It was an impressive show, but in between shows Mainn often packed in a casual visit or two for a one-on-one with Christ: Jesus *loved* unexpected guests.

As she was the only adult around with time to spare for us, occasionally fishing small change out of her knotted handkerchief to buy us roasted peanuts or white peppermints or coloured lozenges shaped like miniature orange sections, we developed an unspoken bond, and the trio of septuagenarian widow and short-cropped under-tens was seen in all the religious hot spots of the town—until something happened to break my trust.

It was my bedwetting, which the adults tried to stop in many ways. To my shame, before all my cousins, I was made to sleep without my shorts so the servant might have one less item to wash the next morning. When this didn't shame me into stopping the unstoppable water of life, my grandmother tried a more ancient folk recipe: she smuggled in some raw rice underneath the mandri or dried-grass mat I was made to sleep on (instead of the usual cotton-filled mattress, which I might wet); the next morning, they fried the urine-soaked rice and tried to get me to eat it. The giggles of my young cousins made me suspicious, until a female one, who had a soft corner for me, confessed all, adding, to my sense of complete betrayal, that it had been my grandmother's idea.

I firmly refused the urophiliac, nitrogen-rich snack; however obedient and apparently meek, there was a line I would not be driven to cross. And once again, I felt utterly alone in the world.

It was only two years later (a brief fast-forwarding here), well after Quack Number Ten and Uncle Gaulbert's own home-made cures—whacking me, asking me to throw away the bedsheet, whacking me some more—that there was an unexpected cure.

It happened at the wedding of Uncle Eustace, who until then had intrigued us children with his marvellous possessions (a soda maker and a German Grundig tape recorder that reeled out racy Konkani songs) and his lack of an 'Aunty'.

Under the shamiana, a ceremonial tent made mainly of thatched palm leaves and festooned with coloured paper, mango leaves, and flowers, the overdressed guests, including women wearing all their resplendent gold jewellery and men wearing faded and shrunken grey cotton jackets and children in flowered poplin shirts and dresses, sat cross-legged on reed mats, their eyes popping in hungry anticipation of the Main Event. Which was to have food splashed onto their banana-leaf 'plates' by grown men in folded lungis, presenting their dirty, hairy legs for inspection as they hauled about large brass cauldrons of sorpotel or hot pork curry from salivating guest to salivating guest.

However, for the *portapon*—the day-after feast, for which a smaller band of about fifty lucky relatives and friends had been invited—Uncle Eustace decided on a classy touch of Western civilization: seated at two rows of long tables draped with starched white tablecloths, many of the guests, myself included, had their first *darshan* of brightly coloured paper napkins, which we pocketed as precious souvenirs, washing our hands at meal's end as usual.

There was no brass band. My uncles preferred to spend the

fruits of their commercial labour on more liquid pleasures, which included my first taste of beer: golden, sparkling, like nectar sent from heaven, and rationed out at about a glass per adult, half a glass per child, proof of age not required, just desire—and heaven knows a Third World country has enough pent-up desires to fill a galaxy.

And oh, the roast chicken: Indian chickens (or a fair number of them) are God's original chickens, fresh as the day they were created, having spent their lives roaming freely on the roadside and helping themselves to Nature's buffet of rubbish, the way God meant them to. You placed a morsel of this chicken on your tongue, and it slowly dissolved, all taste and no matter! The pure spirit of chickenness, Plato's Ideal Chicken itself!

All the while the Grundig tape recorder reeled out light-headed Konkani songs with German efficiency, combining with the aroma of the delicacies in the air to create a moment of paradise for the hungry, excited crowd invited to partake of this twelve-course meal, including dark brown mutton soup with ghee-fried onion pieces floating in it, spongy white sannan, sweet rice pullav, pork sorpotel, a beetroot and onion salad, and a maroon sweet-and-sour chutney. During a time when meals were milestones for me, this one would not be equalled for another ten years.

My uncles would joke later and wonder whether it was the beer or the chicken that had done it; but whatever the cause, I never watered my mattress ever again.

Bag Lady

THE YEAR 1960 was coming to an end, and even as America celebrated the election of John F. Kennedy, there were to be observed, at Saint Juliana's Convent, Mangalore, some very sheepish faces. For back at the convent, a very important event had just failed to happen. Somebody had forgotten to remind the Almighty that the world was supposed to end. So the tremulously awaited Doomsday had passed, with much prayer but without incident.

'See? Prayer works!' Mother Eurica gleefully exclaimed, next morning, losing her smile as soon as she noticed that a crow had chosen this propitious morning to fly into the class and shit on her desk.

Roly-poly Mother Eurica, whose cheeks were like tomatoes and eyes like blackberries, had recently succeeded Ottila the Nun as Mother Superior of Saint Juliana's. And God's failure to end the world as promised (a typically male thing to do—break promises), she felt, amounted to a loss of face for His retailing subsidiary, the convent. To counter the dangerous feeling of liberation that might result from this sudden absence of fear, and to re-open the windows of our vulnerability, Eurica—or Eureka, as we sometimes mispronounced her name—came up with an end of the world theory to end them all. She taught us geography, and with such universal and expansive scope that it included a map of the solar system which she spread out one day over the tiny, tripod-supported blackboard. On this map for the myopic were representations of the sun and its planets. The planets had been drawn larger than scale, so that the earth's circumference, for example, cut into the orbit of Mars on one side, and that of Venus on the other.

This, then, must be *God's plan* for the end of the world, she hypothesized, without using the word 'hypothesis': that differences in the orbital positions of the planets would keep diminishing, because of their different orbital speeds, until each planet crashed into the next in a simultaneous, universal explosion. Brilliant—and but for her inadequate education, which made our shaggy Scientist-in-Residence miss the fact that the map was not to scale and that there were millions of miles of empty space between the real planets, might not Reverend Mother Eurica have been a Reverend Mother Einstein?

At the time, I didn't have the facts either (I was eight years old and had no access to the town's two encyclopaedia sets, possibly of pre-Copernican vintage anyway) and the lesson made almost as powerful an impression on me as Mars or Venus would when they flattened Saint Juliana's Convent into a chapatti. From then on, I would look obsessively at the sky, my eyes peeled for any stupendously large object wobbling towards me like a fat and greasy and tipsy citizen of the heavens, like a bloated, avenging Sister Domina Mary; so that with the advance warning, I might bombard Heaven with my pleas for mercy.

It was a good thing the planets decided to stay in their God-given places, because suddenly, from Mom, came train tickets for our first visit to Calcutta and home in three years.

Oh, that first vision of Calcutta, with the ghostly, silver Howrah Bridge in the distance. The sights, the sounds, the million shouts that trooped into my senses as we came out of the ancient iron canopy of Howrah Station, trams gliding by almost within touching distance, hawkers and coolies and beggars by the million. The scene had the colour and excitement of a circus procession. A freshly assaulted Western mind might have described this super-dense result of India's copulation explosion as 'mere anarchy being loosed upon the world'. But I was eight years old, on my first visit to Calcutta. To me, it was love at first sight.

The trams mesmerized me. I would watch them cruise

confidently through a web of tram tracks. They were large, benevolent animals to me, love-spoilt elephants, with their tinkling bells, their self-confident magnanimity, the ease with which they bore their human riders. Their antennae seemed to bring out the music of the sky, and all other kinds of traffic—animal, vegetable, and mineral—seemed to scurry at their stately approach. I would have given up all the roasted channa that my father bought me that summer from roadside vendors for a chance to drift all day through Calcutta's streets in these gondolas of Calcutta's concrete-paved canals.

'How far can trams go, Daddy? Can they go to London?'

It was a silly question, I knew even as I asked it, but that was what fathers were for—to answer silly questions: Can a plane go to the moon? Can an elephant defeat a lion? Can a Studebaker go faster than an electric train?

And oh, the river. The Calcutta of my boyhood fancy was a garden city dominated by an enormous, muddy-blue river and an enormous, silver bridge. I would spend hours sitting on the river bank gazing at the other side, which to my imagination appeared to be a little topographical map, a miniature painting. In the river lazed numerous ships, mostly black, rusty and ancient, hooting at the city like dinosaurs with sore throats. It swirled majestically, this river, like a giant snake tickled by slithering ships, sweating port workers, hawkers selling roasted peanuts and channa, and the thousands of destitutes camping on the river bank.

On the road by the river, furiously rattling buses sped madly to such magical destinations as the Strand, Esplanade, Dharamtolla, Chowringhee, Kidderpore, Shyam Bazaar, and Dum Dum. Gloriously speeding buses, fast as the biggest locomotives. We secreted ourselves into the crowded buses sometimes, stopping off at Dharamtolla, where we pestered Dad for Kwality Ice Cream and Laughing Sweets and rossogollas and freshly squeezed sugarcane juice.

And Mom laughed and sang and prepared chapattis and puris and evening sweets, and Dad gave us piggyback rides (to ride him, to ride him, and oh to possess him, an urge greater than the urge for greatness or for riches). And on many a hot afternoon, afternoons slow as a loaded Dodge Fargo lorry running on adulterated kerosene, we slept on the floor under a creaking fan, the whole family in one room, side by side. For years thereafter, that summer of my contentment in Calcutta was my brief vision of heaven, my resurrection from death.

The holiday ended soon, and we were back in Uncle Eddy Baab's house, awaiting the school reopening. My brother Arun, a year my senior, had become eligible for transfer to a boys' school, and we'd be separated, I knew. And one day soon enough Uncle Gaulbert dropped in at Uncle Eddy Baab's house and said, 'Vijay, pack your trunk, quick quick, it's late.'

He drove me to a dusty, ancient, yellow-and-black house on a tree-shaded lane used by bootleggers to conceal bottles of the no-name-brand local cashew soro in the bushes. Stepping lightly to dodge the goat droppings littering the brick-red compound, Uncle and I climbed up the steps to the veranda.

'Say good morning to Granny,' Uncle said. He pointed to a dark, elderly, corpulent woman filling up a black wooden armchair, her loose flesh imperfectly camouflaged by her purple-flowered and greasy 'house-coat'.

'Good morning, Granny,' said I. I was a good feudal sort, trained by adult palms and fists to be serflike—like all Mangalorean boys from the age of four.

'I'm going, Lillybai, got work, so much work,' Uncle said, rushing out, leaving me to discover Lilly, and the limits of my tolerance, on my own.

Thus unwarned, unconsulted, unceremoniously, for reasons I was never to know, was I handed over to Lilly Coelho, the woman who would own me, who would rule over me with absolute power, for the next year. Thus began for me, until now a punching bag for the tricks and Divine Purpose of the Almighty, a year of awakening, of awakening to rebellion and to a consciousness of the thing until then without a name.

'Come on put your trunk inside now! Don't stare like that with your mouth open, you'll catch flies!' Lilly barked, the moment my Uncle had left, her smile revealing a shiny contrast of whiteperfect false teeth. It was a smile that seemed more threat than message of goodwill, and it developed in me an instant dislike for the droopy-breasted hag, for her black-tinged white hair topping an undersized coconut, for the mass of her shapeless arse.

Hardly had I been in my dark cell for fifteen minutes, meditating on my new condition, when Lilly appeared at the door. 'Now what are you doing in there, smelling your own farts? Go feed the goat! Just because your uncle pays me forty rupees a month for your boarding doesn't make you some big sahib!'

So 'boarder' was too poor a word to describe my role in this harmonic convergence of human beings, animals, and nature, for I was also her slave: among other things, I had to pick up fallen mango and jackfruit tree leaves to feed her goat (the otherwise un-Gandhian Granny believed like Gandhi in the special, nearly-spiritual virtues of goat milk). The resultant circle of being: I fed the goat; the goat fed Granny; Granny fed me. The goat pelleted the place with its black, lightly-smelling pellets consisting of goat-processed leaves; the servant girl, a thirteen-year-old from a village who had become tough as a donkey from being treated like one, kept sweeping the pellets; and the pellets, along with the ants, almost swept pellet-hating me out of the house (but where could I go?).

Somehow, I began to identify the goat with Granny, and every morning, as I sat at the dining-table for breakast, facing a glass of water containing Granny's lonely teeth, I had an eerie feeling, as if a loud bleat would suddenly issue forth from those false teeth.

A few months later, there occurred the incident by which my family came to nickname her 'Bag', after a hideous green plastic picnic bag which the nuns, with their remarkable taste, had presented to me on School Day. It occupied a special place in my heart, if only because it, aside from my clothes and a green-checked tablecloth, was one of my few pieces of property in this universe and my only potentially liquid possession. Yes, I will admit it: the poor think of money, usually peanuts. I was hoarding the bag for that emergency when it might yield a precious two rupees—a one-fiftieth down payment on an escapist train ticket to Calcutta.

The problem was: Lilly's fiscal antenna was sharp as a hawk's vision. The moment she saw my bag, she said, 'Give that to me. What do *you* need it for, you stupid buffalo?'

Thus did she requisition the property under her emergency powers for the domestic interest—that is, for fetching the smelliest fish, sardines and mackerels from the market. Saved her a good five rupees too as she didn't need to buy a bag of her own.

Soon the bag was too greasy, stinking, and decrepit to cherish as a part of me, and so was the fish-curry-stained tablecloth. When I reported this dispossession to my father the next year, hoping to be suitably avenged (hopefully with his army-issue rifle), he burst into hearty and rare hilarity, singing, 'Dear Granny, Dear Granny, with a bag,' to the tune, duly murdered, of "There's a hole in the bucket, dear Lisa, dear Lisa!"

Bag's own tune might have been "God Save the Queen!" For, though she was the princess of the darkness that was her nearly windowless, woodsmoke-blackened house, she somehow believed herself to be Westernized and sophisticated and, therefore, superior to 'Indians'. Like most Anglo-Indians and some older Catholics of colonial vintage, she praised the British Era and scorned Indians' attempts to rule their own country. Her chief claim to Westernization, though, was that every day she laid a turd in a tin can located in her bedroom. And every day, at a certain time—and without so much as a 'Hello, everybody, it's turd time!'—the servant girl, Yelloo, would carry the tin can or commode across the house to dump its contents into the squatting-type Indian toilet. And so, thanks to the ingenuity of this arrangement, did West meet East. The only flaw being that, thanks to poor house-planning, the turd had to make its journey through the living-room, dining-room and kitchen, leaving behind it an absurdly elongated cloud of foul vapours that hung in the air for the next hour or so, reinforcing the message that Yelloo had neglected to announce.

'A nice skinning will do you good. Now come, we're going to the Novena,'—a typical Bag pronouncement on a Saturday evening, skinning and spiritual enrichment falling under the same category.

Like millions of Christians in the former colonies who re-model themselves, torture themselves, and outdo themselves in their grim piety whilst their former colonialist masters skinny-dip in postmodernistic, materialistic, near-godless decadence, Bag also partook of Mangalore's heavily ritualistic Catholicism. Besides,

unless you were rich, church was about the only place to see people
and be seen, to have your new earrings and gold-bordered sari
commented upon. Besides which, she was truly a woman of faith:
like all of my tormentors up until then and for some time thereafter,
she was a devout and pious Catholic.

It would take me thirty seconds to slip my clean shorts up my
naked brown buttocks (I hadn't yet heard of the concept of boys
wearing underwear of any kind), button up my bush shirt—the
definition of 'dressing up' for me. Outside, a few score crows were
in orchestra, singing their farewell to the day as the sun sank below
the horizon. Tiptoeing through the dark living-room, I would
position myself at an angle to her bedroom and slyly watch her and
make monkey faces at her as she wrapped about herself the
traditional black, silver-bordered sari and white cotton blouse
which, in Mangalore, advertised widowhood forever. I would
watch her powder her dark face (a desperate search for whiteness
that often blights our lives), plant a ridiculous red hibiscus in her
little hairbun (in rebellious violation of the Unwritten Rules for
Mangalore Widows), and slip on four gold bangles.

Then we would be off, plodding on the up-and-down road past
Kirti Mahal and White's Shoe Store to Milagres Church, I trailing
bitterly. I hated this involuntary coupling of our fates. I was
ashamed of her tiny bun and fat arse, and felt like a goat with a rope
around its neck, a goat being led to spiritual slaughter. I didn't like
being force-fed virtue—especially not by her.

But it wasn't virtue alone that motivated the calculating Bag
into never missing the Novena, but rather Our Lady of Perpetual
Succour's promise of an unbeatable deal on eternity, a plea-
bargaining lawyer's wet dream: all penalties for past sins cancelled,
the penal slate wiped clean. And who could say . . . if you kept
collecting novenas, the impressed and highly-connected Mother of
God might even grant you, as a bonus, credit for *future* sins—a fully
paid up credit card for concupiscence.

And fearing God too—I was nothing but a bundle of fears
then—and still hoping to bribe His Mother into delivering me from
Bag, I would pray too, and pray also for credit against my
sins—being distracted in church, making monkey faces at my
superiors . . . .

But Bag had other ideas about how I could pay for my sins. How?

By peeing up.

Bag, you see, was a great believer in organic fertilizers, so like the servant Yelloo, I was advised, as far as possible, to direct my personal fertilizer—my liquid essence, now hers by virtue of commercial assignment—at the roots of the papaya trees and spinach plants. 'Why are you wasting your *sussu* in the kakkoos, dirty fellow,' she kept saying to me in the first month. 'Go make your water at the foot of the papaya tree!' Yelloo and I sullenly obliged, I slowly beginning to enjoy the open air, Yelloo defiantly flashing a bit of bum.

To improve the quality of my fertilizer, I was provided with free vitamins and protein in the form of nutritious ants (also the better to pick leaves for her goat with). Because hers was a mud house—and Indian ants take to old mud houses as ducks to water—every Bag dish crawled over with tiny red, and sometimes black, ants: *Protein and Vitamins, Live!* Or perhaps her culinary generosity was entirely due to her beastly eyesight, which failed to discern that her repasts turned out to be exotic Chinese rather than pedestrian Indian? In fact, she didn't even believe me when I, in shortsighted disgust at rice crawling with millions of live ants, one day summoned the courage to beg for something a little less alive to eat.

First she cackled in surprise at my impudence and uttered a truth much beloved of Mangalorean housewives: 'Ants improve eyesight, you don't know that? You need them for your big eyes! Now shut up and eat or I'll stitch up your lips!' (Yes indeed, I thought: they improve your eyesight so greatly that you can't even notice twenty million ants tap dancing over your riceplate, making your dish sixty-seven per cent ant, thirty-three per cent rice.) Then, her face growing even darker with anger, she followed with another gesture beloved to Mangalorean housewives: she slapped me on the head.

'For you, everything happens,' she said in Konkani with her apoplectic parting shot. 'Ants, pants, you find everything! Bull! Buffalo! Villager! Son of a kashti-wearer!'

Those last two epithets were born of her knowledge that my father was born in some dung-splashed village, and so, presumably, once wore the kashti or Vedic civilization's precursor to Jockey underpants or Le String Pour Homme. And so, a *villager* and kashti-wearer was he branded, he and his progeny, now and forever, as was the servant, Yelloo, who received an almost hourly string of abuses: 'Bull! Buffalo! Prostitute!'

Being too young then to understand her grievances against life—diabetes, false teeth, false bun, no man in her life to satisfy her intimate needs, no man except Jesus—my resentment grew, and one day flowered into defiant rebellion. 'I'll write to my Daddy and tell him everything,' I spluttered, having just overdosed on ant congee. 'I'll tell him to put me back in the boarding-house.'

'You can leave right now,' Bag struck back, with swift determination. 'I won't allow you to sleep in your room tonight. Buffalo! Out! Bull! Out!'

Put out of the house, like a cat that had peed on the sofa!

That night as I slunk back in from the devil-dark road and slept on the bare floor of the veranda, Bag through her loyal allies in the mosquito brigades of the mohalla crushed my rebellious spirit. The next day, looking like a convention of red bumps, my pragmatic side triumphant, I promised her my meekness forever.

My abject apology accepted, I was returned to my dark room. Dark, dark, dark. Dark days, dark thoughts—dark as an eternity without Jesus the Sacred Heart. Dark, mixed with the smell of goat milk, and (faintly exciting? erotic?) goat turd. Dark as never knowing your schedule, but just waiting for the next command or goat-flavoured errand. Dark as my depressing thought: two thousand miles separated me from my parents. Dark as never knowing for sure what's in the bedroom you sleep in night after night, because there's never enough light to be perfectly sure, and you must be content to smell the damp mixed in with *je ne sais quoi*. Dark as the statistics I find in a 1920s economics book I extract from a wooden packing case rotting in that room,* a book assigning to India last place in the world in everything.

But life in school, whenever I could catch it, had its charms. As for the *other* ten-year-olds, as far as I could see—and I couldn't see very far, precisely *because* of all that fucking ant juice clouding up my vision . . . . But as far as I could see, life, for the *other* boys in my class—the bastards—was a crisp, foot-long butter masala dosa laced with adrenalin!

---

*   The local method of garbage disposal was often to store something until it fell apart and disposed of itself.

Yes, the other boys were neck-deep in fun *now*—not on an instalment plan like myself, pay now and *maybe get it later*, perhaps in the form of megadoses of playing on the harp and singing the praises of the boring Almighty in Dull City, Heaven. And these other boys, as if to dramatize the nuns' point about the evil that lurks in the hearts of males, were worrying the veils off the Reverend Sisters' shaved coconuts! Perhaps the secret of their spirit, their jumping *joie de vivre*, lay in their domestic paradises, fully equipped with mothers or female relatives who fed them and adored them and washed their penises for them, as indeed most Indian mothers did their sons' until fairly late in the day . . . . Loy, whose father worked in Bahrain—where the streets, he told me, were paved with gold and Kraft cheese tins—but whose mother and two sisters, Fiona and Bittona, kept house here and looked lovingly after the family heir. Dayalal, living in a one-acre mansion with his cloth merchant uncles, seemed so well-fed his cheeks had bloom and fat enough, in themselves, to feed a poor family of six. And Justin, who lived with his mother and about five hundred toys and story-books and comics, bought by his doting, London-based father.

They all went back to real mothers, mothers who would wash them, tuck them into bed, call them sweet love names, even scold them with love, sleep with them, press their warm breasts against them, tell them stories or answer their questions while they fell asleep, feed them special delicacies hidden from their sisters . . . take them out to the Taj Mahal Hotel for coffee and laddoos and goli bhajjeas—energy to fire up their next day's pranks.

The pranks included filling the nun's newly built lavatories, the pride of the Apostolic Carmel, with stones, so the shit would stay up for eternity. And the last straw was when Justin, the untypically-daring prankster of my fifth-grade class, drawing inspiration from his *Archie* comics brought him by his father, developed a relish for catching girls and kissing them, while they laughed and shrieked '*Chi*! *Thoo*! Sister, Justin is doing dirty things!' Ah, well, boys will be boys, and will kiss girls within reach . . . . In an ideal world, a world without violence but without silly narrow-minded rules either, life will be full of stolen smooches, and those robbed, the possessors of pretty lips, would offer their loot with pleasure, I think now sadly, reaching into my past and letting my younger self reach out and kiss every girl within reach, erasing the Oliver Twistian idea of goodness that held me back then and scotched forever my chances of childhood happiness. Ah, kisses kisses kisses, I think, mourning those lost kisses. Surely I, first in class always, Solver of Math Problems Extraordinaire, could have provided some competition to Justin?

It was the precocious Justin who gave me my first English name for the thing, which had until then been no thing, a thing without a name.

'I lost my pen,' I said to Justin one day.

'You lost your *pen*?! Hee hee hee hee! Listen, everybody: Vijay lost his *pen*!'

A momentary burst of shame and understanding washed over my face, as it must have suffused the First Parents' when they bit into that cursed apple. But at least I now knew an English word for it: pen! (I would only discover 'penis' at fourteen—from a nursing textbook.) A splendid acquisition, because the Konkani word *mimi* connoted the microscopic organs of toddlers and *bitto* (related, it would seem, to the French *bite*) felt vulgar to me, even if it weren't already taboo, like every organ even remotely connected with peeing—balls, for example, which I and perhaps thousands of others imagined strained the urine before it exited your pecker. Until now, as when Leela and I spoke, I had used *yours* and *mine*. *Will you show me yours*? I suddenly felt adult: the proud owner of a pen! It was a pity that I did not connect it to a truth I had already learned: the pen is mightier than the sword.

In any case, it was now Justin the Magnificent, Justin the Hero, or rather Sir Justin Hero, who, having introduced me to a brave new universe of penmanship, lanced about a lot and delighted the girls with a preview of life's pleasures. When he had kissed his tenth (officially reported) girl, Mother Eurica decided that the will of God was being crossed. She decreed the phasing out of all boys, all possessors of *mimis*, starting with the higher grades, until the school was transformed into an all-girls' school, a *mimiless* void. A fortress of the distaff persuasion, of the cleaved sex, of the pink handkerchief and perfume gender . . . Petticoat Junction forever!

The Five Pillars of
Oppression

THANKS TO MY passing fifth grade that summer ('Bye, bye, Lilly Bai! Will never forget you!') the scene had now shifted a kilometre west of the convent to St. Stanislaus Boarding House, where I would be introduced to brotherly love, penis shame, and the five pillars of oppression.

   Important branch of an institutional empire that included St. Stanislaus Middle School, St. Stanislaus High School, the flagship St. Stanislaus College, St. Stanislaus Orphanage, St. Stanislaus Carpentry Associates Limited, and St. Stanislaus Pig Farm, St. Stanislaus Boarding House elicits from this adult narrator a respectful whistle. What a sophisticated, pure male prison! For unlike the high-walled convent, it had no walls. But then, what do boys and men need walls for? To keep out bands of marauding girls? Boys, like male dogs, are roamers. They invade others' territory and usually piss on it.

   Unless, like me, they have lost their boyness and inhabit a saintly netherworld, a no-boy's-land, a land where you piss on your own leg.

   It was a faded yellow, barn-like building standing on the western slope of Ignatius Loyola Hill, on a red gash of earth washed by the breeze of the Arabian Sea in the distance and the all-natural smells of the pigsty next door. On the upper floor, a dormitory and a study hall looked out beyond the palm-tufted fringes of the town towards the steaming horizon where the Mulki River flowed into the Arabian Sea. On the lower level, a dusty veranda with a few battered carrom tables adjoined a games room, a parlour, and a reading room—the walls haunted by group photographs of past residents, fuzzy but compelling records of undernourishment and piss-in-your-pants fear. Look at all of these through a romantic film of grease, dust, and consumptive breath and you have the St. Stanislaus Boarding House, home to a hundred hearts, two hundred lungs, and sundry battered organs raised on prayer, canes, bullock meat—and on the feasts of St. Ignatius Loyola and St. Stanislaus Kostka, masala dosas and shira.

'Girls' schoolboy, huhn?' said Father Edward, boarding-house director and middle school headmaster. 'Welcome welcome! We'll teach you discipline here. See that cane over there? The pillar of the Jesuit educational system, heh heh!'

Father Edward! Whose triangular, stubbled, chocolate milk face and thin muscular body radiated animal magnetism, whose milk-white cassock rippled angrily as he walked, whose high-pitched, always-on-the-brink-of-fury voice caused more quivers than Timur the Lame's battle plans. He rarely needed to use whole words, making do with the expressions and tone of one with years of experience driving buffalo herds to village fairs. He had a village voice, cured in the high Jesuit tradition of having to lead rude masses in prayer. Yet he also had an eye for the pretty young mothers of his students, and would use every possible excuse to demand of a student that he bring in his mother. When in this company, he could be as smooth as a parish priest trying to angle a donation from the local tycoon.

At first I was completely dismayed. Why had they sent me out of the Garden of St. Juliana's and dumped me thus into the *priapic* (their primary admission requirement was penile) St. Stanislaus's? Life around girls and women has a certain civilized surface to it, you must agree: recently-bathed girls in puffy blue skirts wearing flowers in their hair (oh, the smell of soap on a girl's hair and skin); laughter and silliness; their healing, soft smiles; the unisex, nearly-choral rendition of the sphincter-loosening school anthem, "We're the jolly girls of St. Juliana's!" Forgetting my tormentor nuns, I remembered, misty-eyed, the braided and bangled and earringed and fluffy-skirted Lola and Zuleikha and Ritu and Dimple, all of whom had had a soft corner for me, especially when they found that, despite my notoriously weak sphincter and physique, I always stood first in class and had never met a maths problem I couldn't solve.

All this I had left behind for a rough male world of swinging between trees, for the unsmiling canes of the Stanislausian lumpen Jesuits, for food slapped together by sweaty middle-aged males in shorts and sleeveless undershirts—a world in which life was nasty, brutish, in shorts.

It was the beginning of my future conviction that the forced segregation of the male and the female, by whatever logic—military or political, social or spiritual, sexual or philosophical—is a sin against Nature. That if you take women away from the human mixture, all you have left is . . . pigs.

'Boarding-house pigs!' exclaimed the day students on the first day of school, when they saw us, the boarders, bounding down the steep steps from the boarding-house to the middle school and joining the school assembly. And we smiled.

As if to stress our newly-piggish existence, Life, like a novice novelist, seemed to be getting its symbols straight: the boarding-house was famous for its pink or 'European' pigs (so-called because of the popular impression that Europeans rarely bathed), reared within sniffing distance of the dormitory. And oh, the padres were proud of their reputation for rearing the district's primest pigs—and without doubt the most profitable too because the porkers were fed the boarders' leftovers, costing the Jesuits virtually nothing! It was rumoured that the cooks had been instructed to cook to the pigs' taste, because the boarding-house was earning more praise (and rupees per kilo) for its pigs than for its boarders.

But slowly we realized that when the day students exclaimed 'boarding-house pigs!' they were referring not to the four-legged potential delicacy but the two-legged boarders, who carried about them an unmistakable stench like an Identification Document. The simple explanation for this Great Wall of Stench was that boarders of all ages, from seven to seventeen, had to wash their own clothes (to one stinking shirt add one chembu of water and a dab of 555 Bar soap; then beat the hell out of it on a granite washing stone)—which didn't happen very often. And cleanliness was the least of the boarders' worries, for they were unhappy as pigs without shit.

Except, maybe, for Adolf.

Adolf was the Bombay sharp who sucked up to the moneyed day-students and returned with the trophies of his flattery: aromatic, Indra Bhawan masala dosas, still hot in their banana-leaf packing, exuding an aroma of ghee and fried mustard. He would proceed to wolf down the dosas himself while saying to painfully salivating observers like me: 'Want it? Want it? Ha ha, greedy bugger!'

'You'll go to hell for that, Adolf! It's not nice!' I would shout back.

'Tell, tell, go to hell, ha ha!'

Though Adolf had a round bald spot on his head like Pope Pius XII, it didn't make him less snooty. 'I'm a Bombayite,' he'd crow—meaning he was better than 'Indians'. 'Indians! Don't even know how to make blades, man!'

But his chief claim to fame: he knew the *latest* English songs! Such as "Wooden Heart".

He seemed outwardly happy, but perhaps such happiness as existed, the happiness of life and boyhood seeping through, was a *perverse* happiness, because we were all part-time orphans. For it is an odd, even a queer thing: to have your father's place filled by gigantic bearded males in drag, before whom you are required to bow and say, 'Good evening, Father.'

But this was a world in which the queer was the ordinary, in which Jesuit padres played Pater to boys they hadn't fathered and never really would. They were the relics of a nineteenth-century Italian adventure that had climaxed with the college, a college now run by brown-skinned, white-robed heirs, oddities who stood out in the local market-place, their long white starched cassocks with trouser cuffs peeping out and their somber expressions standing out from the local coloured lungis and quizzical paan-chewing mouths. Standing out, if I may say so, like a dog's balls.

And yet, within the boarding-house walls, they ruled absolutely. Because they had perfected the System—which, unlike

T. E. Lawrence's wisdom, was built on five, not seven, pillars: bells, canes, penis shame, girl shame, and sports. And now, for the never-before-revealed secrets of this System:

THE FIVE PILLARS OF FOLLY AND SUPPRESSION

*A Case Study In The Management Of The Human Animal,
Ages 8-16*

PILLAR NUMBER ONE

BELLS

The boarding-house bells, hand-carried or suspended brass artifacts of various sizes, were the underpinnings of this System: they told you when to start anything and when to stop it; when to come and when to go; when to shower and when to shit. Their command was unquestioned and dictatorial. From the 5:30 a.m. bell that woke you (a minute later, Father Benedict the Prefect would walk through the dormitory with a cane and whip any still-sleeping bottoms; oh, the cruelty of forced waking at 5:30 a.m. in a tropical country, when all is blackness, and devils lurk about pillars, and hungry dogs with intestinal problems howl miserably) to the 9:15 p.m. bedtime bell, life was so perfectly structured into church visits and study and game hours that you never had to stop and wonder, 'What shall I do now?' The bells always tolled for thee.

The bells also did something else. Heralding our lives' most precious moments—breakfast, lunch, and dinner—their effect was Pavlovian. Thus did we salivate at the sound of any bell rung close to food time. For the boundaries, goals, signposts of our life were comprised of food; and our intellectual exercise was guessing the next meal's menu.

PILLAR NUMBER TWO

CANES

The police force of Jesuit canes—long, sexy, hard—supported the all-important bells. As perhaps the flute in seventeenth-century

Jesuit Paraguay, the cane (or *bodi*, or *danda*) was a sceptre, a symbol of the power of the local jesuitocracy. Every priest or brother,[*] regardless of his hierarchical position or his reputation, was known to have a cane concealed somewhere in his room or person, which he could produce within seconds when the ancient call of the Wild Man sounded within him. The Cane of Father Damocles, S.J., hung over the bottom of every boarder that disobeyed a bell. The cane's hiddenness made it awesome, endowing a mystic, erotic quality to those brief moments between the decision to cane and the cane's exposure. Not since the days of British rule, when a handful of Englishmen (five thousand at most?) rode a country of three hundred and fifty million, had so many quivering bottoms been ruled so completely by so few.

It was Father Edward who first made me dimly aware of why human beings often relish pain. He had caned me a few times in public, for 'talking in class'—an act of absent-mindedness no amount of prayer could cure me of. But when he discovered that I sometimes also topped the class, he began to praise me before school assemblies, once publicly holding up my fourteen-page letter to my mother as an example of writing style and volume.

And yet, neither this 'respect' for me nor his broader smiles inhibited Father Edward from what he considered his duty. The next time he caught me talking in class, he ordered me to walk to his office and fetch the cane that was to be the instrument of my punishment.

'Bring me my cane, please,' said he, almost like a lover. *Thou shalt know how I loveth thee by how hard I beateth thee.* The sacrificial lamb was after all a popular idea: Abraham and God sacrificing their only sons, Saint Jerome being deep fried . . . .

And I, yes, I obliged, bringing him the rod of my chastisement. How perfect the System had become, to co-opt its victims in its maintenance.

Still, better to be caned and loved than not to be loved at all. Father Edward was the first in a long line of Jesuit 'fathers' who supplanted my absent-at-first, then absent-in-his-ability-to-love father. And perhaps it was my yearning for such a father, and not piety alone, which made me send feelers above (the priests always

---

[*]   'Brother' signified a robed Jesuit one step below 'Father'; a brother couldn't say Mass, was less-educated, and often did the dirty work for the ex-Brahmin Fathers. However, the designation was apt, given that one of these brothers was caught redhanded and redfaced practising brotherly love on a boarder.

lived 'above', on the highest floor of whatever premises they haunted), conveying my interest in the priesthood. Perhaps it was also the promise of lifelong security, of awed nuns bustling about to feed and please their robed, male visitors—penilely gifted saints, direct representatives of Christ on earth! Yes, it was also the rich food, the promise of endless access to bread, butter, and bananas, glimpsed every time I passed by a priests' refectory and someone opened a door, that, despite the threatened vow of poverty, tempted me.

And then, I dreamed of being Pope someday. Why not? If I was first in class now, all I had to do was keep on coming first in every new class until I became first in the exam for cardinals and thus Pope! Of course the tonsure was somewhat distasteful to contemplate, and the requisite pot belly would take work, but the grub would be splendid, and the grandstand seat in heaven assured. Mom would be proud, and maybe I could get her a little flat in Rome . . . .

I would begin preparations right away by praying extra, saving up personal merit by reciting indulgences again and again ('Jesus! Mary! Joseph!' with seven years, was my favourite, being the best value in yield per syllable; what an ass one had to be to say a page-long prayer to Saint John of the Cross, say, and get a mere three hundred days in return!).

PILLAR NUMBER THREE

PENIS SHAME

Every evening at 6:00, when the bathtime bell rang, an amazing thing happened in this sardine-rich corner of the world, famous for producing tiles, beedis, nuns and nuts. Seconds after the bell's ringing, the three bustling hockey fields would be deserted. Two minutes later, there would be a hurried procession of fifty short boys, looking like little clowns with towels knotted tightly around their naked brown bodies, rushing down from the dormitory towards Bathroom Row, actors in a Third World opera called penis shame.

First a simple definition:

Penis shame: A psychological affliction, occurring mostly in the Third World, and especially former British colonies, in which males of the 'age of reason' and above feel shame at possessing a penis, and make every possible attempt to hide its existence from fellow human beings.

Now for a case study of an acute mass outbreak of this condition at St. Stanislaus Boarding House, circa 1962 (with appropriate references to the Indian Penile Code).

You see, in truth, one never exposed one's privates in this all-boy school; because every new boarder had either already earned his doctorate in the University of Shame (chartered by Queen Victoria and now a permanent fixture in this Country With No Locker Rooms, this late jewel in her crown) or would in no time. Not shame at anything anyone had actually done, but post-Fall, Garden of Eden-brand, *original* shame—one that pronounced the penis a thing of ugliness forever. Thus did we, green as we otherwise were, feel truly burdened by the *indignity* of our external plumbing.

Worse still, as we parentless boys grew taller day-by-day, our unreplaced shorts would grow shorter, and the danger of exposing our growing things grew, causing a great mental burden. (Underwear was still a luxury for the middle-school boy . . . but what an élitist complaint! How can you ever become a saint if you worry about underwear? Go look at the painting of Saint Stanislaus on the chapel walls. Do you see *him* wearing underwear?)

So now: How to protect oneself from shorts that barely exceed the length of a good-sized penis? In the tradition of the American how-to school, I lay out a step-by-step guide followed by us young boarders of the time, and perhaps many Indians and Pakistanis still living under Shame's absolute power. I give you, folks, **Poor Vijay's Guide to Not Showing Your Lingam:**

1) When peeing in the public domain (against a wall, say), geometrically manoeuvre your body into a shield against the X-ray vision of peekers.
2) Don't climb trees or walls; don't sit at any elevation higher than that of the masses.
3) In the dormitory—which, besides being a 9:00 p.m. to 5:30 a.m. snooze joint is also the Apparel Transition Centre—use the no-show manoeuvre:
      a) Unbutton shorts but hold them up through will power.

b) Tie a furtive towel around waist.
c) Wriggle: allow shorts to slip down to the floor.
d) Step out of them.
e) Do a little snake-dance to help your new pair
to climb up and clasp buttocks and privates.
f) Hold shorts with gravity-defying will power;
or, reach under towel with stealthy hands and
button up.
g) Let towel drop. Look, Ma, no penis!

PILLAR NUMBER FOUR

GIRL SHAME

A close relative of penis shame was girl shame, which often followed the daily enacting of penis shame, about 6:30 or so, when the sun was slowly moving over the Bishop's Compound and getting ready for its dip in the Arabian Sea. For some reason, this was just the time that, as the just-bathed boys walked towards the study hall, they would observe crossing the orange-lit playground below, possibly lost, hee hee hee hee a fem . . . hee hee hee hee . . . a bloody *female* of the species!

Simply, the facts about girl shame are these: Shame, redhot Shame blighted the poor boarder-boy who admitted the slightest association with the female sex—even historical, even with a mother! So stark and unforgiving was this rule that it made us try to pass ourselves off as motherless, sisterless boys. Ninety-nine point nine per cent of the time, the boarding-house was a pure male world in which visitors, except for cows and pye-dogs, were as uncommon as ghosts. But when, by rare chance or accident, a young female member of the human species passed through the grounds, we would tease the weakest among us: 'She's your sister! Ha ha! She's your sister!' To have gone further and said, 'You want to *marry* her?' would have provoked revolt even from the weakest. Yes, in this curiously sexless corner of the world, this boarding-house society born of the mating of muscular Christianity, Jesuit educational strategy, and temporarily motherless Indian boys, 'marriage' was a dirty word.

PILLAR NUMBER FIVE

SPORTS

True, the padres did occasionally try to impose the law of God on the boarders, only sparing the sportsmen. But when the reverends weren't looking, the musclemen ruled with the help of jungle law: brute strength, protection rackets, goondaism (sportsmen excepted).

So one day, inspired by *Sport & Pastime*, which filled my mind with Gary Sobers and Pataudi and Al Oerter and Bob Hayes, I decided to escape jungle law myself. Energized by the boarding cuisine, which regularly included testosterone-rich unnameable parts of bullocks, I threw myself into sports with the energy of a demon . . . .

I would be . . . a hockey star! Goodbye to the Age of Saint Juliana's Convent when one's objective in sports was primarily to stay clear of moving objects and people, to stay rooted to the safest spot until compelled to flee. Goodbye to the era of stones and paper-balls kicked past chair-leg goals in tiny and grim living-rooms.

And hello, hockey: a game in which two opposing teams, with opposing points of view but similarly crooked pieces of wood, attempt, by means of merciless bludgeoning, to persuade a ball to follow their own point of view.

Dear hockey mates: I want to hit that ball between the quaking legs of a goalpost, past shit like goalkeepers and backies, right up its arsehole. Oh, to be the choreographer of the hockey ball's sinuous dance, to direct it in a serpentine path past defenders I have outwitted, and then with a lusty shout to shoot the ball with unstoppable momentum into the goal . . . then to be carried high on the shoulders of my teammates, be embraced, handled roughly, thus reclaiming touch, the warm feel of another human body . . . .

But as Uncle Gaulbert always said, when stumped for a relevant answer, 'But life is different!' Life, in other words, is not kind to the physically flimsy, the emotionally abandoned, to former candidates for sainthood. Once, attempting an 800-metre race, I almost screwed up the event by getting entangled in the tape while one lap behind the leaders.

'It's time to tell them about Jackie,' said my editor, Pam Gardner, looking

at my manuscript. *She wore a thong bikini, which is a very distracting thing when one is sitting on Fire Island Beach and trying to edit a manuscript of a literary character. Especially distracting when one is faced with such perfect rear-globes as Pam has.* (Pam advised me to change 'rear-globes' to 'ass': 'You can't overdo alliteration. "Such a perfect ass as Pam has"—it stops the reader in his tracks,' said Pam. 'Like your ass does me,' said I.)

'About Jackie Kennedy? Now? Isn't it too early?' I asked, surprised.

'Always give them a little, tiny taste of what they're going to see later,' said Pam. 'Let them know there'll be champagne and roses, satin and lace, cake and ice cream—and not just padres and underprivileged Indian brats.'

'Roger,' said I—a silly thing to say, since her name isn't Roger. And I admit this wasn't a good way to work, let alone edit a novel—seagulls, surf, and steatopygous Thou beside me; what can I, weak soul, say except that I pretty much would have agreed to anything, that I would have handed her my artistic judgement on a platter? But who am I to complain, you approximately two billion envious Third World males, right?

Quickly, while she isn't looking, let me tell you about Pam, now my editor for all seasons, a magician with words, a magician with feelings, a magician at love—in short, the stuff a writer's dreams are made on. We had met a few months earlier at her office at the small, independent publishing house she worked at. And seeing her for the first time made my tongue fall out: blonde, silken hair that fell straight to mid-back, stunning, round green eyes, succulent Cupid-lips that you wanted so desperately to see in the act of sucking a lollipop. As she walked me up to her office, I following a step or two behind, I noticed the fall of her black silk pants, her hair swaying like a lazy pendulum, her buttocks waggling to the pendulum's timing. And her breasts: Help me, ye Angels on high, for her breasts were man-sucking magnetic fields, between which dangled a large, gold-encrusted ruby.

A stunning beauty of an editor who accepts your book and makes love to you! What more could a writer want? Ah, what a fantasy! you say. Come on, is that the truth?

Well, you tell me what truth is. Truth is a dull nine to five job, haemorrhoids, and being stuck in traffic that's going nowhere? Well, if that's truth, you can keep it. To me, what you call fantasy is truer than what you call truth.

Well, why are you telling me all this? you say.

In answer, let me tell you a joke.

A man goes to confession and tells the priest, 'Father, I am seventy years old, and just two days back my wife of forty years died, and yesterday at her funeral I met this beautiful young woman and I took her home and I shtupped *her seven times.'*

The priest says, 'Say seven Hail Marys.'

The man says, 'Father, I can't do that! I'm Jewish!'

'Then why are you telling me*?'*

'Father, I'm telling everybody*!'*

'Now stop staring at my boobs and telling horrid jokes,' Pam interrupted, pinching my bottom, *'and tell them about Jackie!'*

Let me tell you then that about this time I, an underfed ten-year-old from a country with 330 million (acknowledged) deities in its pantheon, had fallen in love, in a little-boy sort of way, with a man named Jack, and his wife, Jackie.

Maybe I needed a potent father figure, a mentor to replace my own disappeared father. And when I saw JFK (was it the cover of *US News and World Report*?) with his hard and erect and blue missiles facing up to the bad Russians with their also-erect but red-as-hell-fire missiles, I fell in love. In him and through him and with him I whipped the wicked Russians' and the naughty Cubans' arses and conquered the world. (Yes, whipping Commie arses was a big turn-on, this being long before I learned of Kennedy's over-supply of blondes, of secretaries on their backs on the Oval Office table, of even the idea of secretaries lying on their backs on tables of any kind. I only saw John the Potent, John the Dreamer, John with the Toothy Smile, the idealistic, heavenward eyes in the photographs circulated by the US Information Service in India.)

In my scrapbook, I lovingly pasted those early pictures of a young presidential couple at the helm of a country with a great dream—the only country, then, that could dare to dream. They captured my Third World imagination. The Kennedys, after all, did not belong to Americans or to the US Government alone . . . .

Forgive me, forgive me, I didn't understand that they weren't mine, never could be. I was just a frail, confused child who, having gotten a raw deal from my designated guardians, was a sucker for Guardian Angels, Fairy Godmothers, and the rest, see? Except that I read *Time* more than *Grimm's Fairy Tales*.

So, in a tiny, 120-page ruled exercise book, I created a novelistic President-king-adventurer-Robin Hood named John Kennedy, who, with a hundred horseborne followers, conquered the world, acre by God's little acre. John was pretty good with his fists and his sword, and he knew how to land a kick where it really hurt! And ooh, his horse: the great Bearheart!

And then, 23 November 1963. Blood spattered the Camelot of my scrapbook. Our newspapers, reeling with banner headlines, published special supplements. As if he had been *our* President.

For days thereafter, we walked about dazed. And I felt I had lost a family member, again, never recovering until I adopted Jackie Kennedy for a secret friend.

But that was later.

In the meantime, I survived by dreaming. The things I dreamed of: travelling to the moon, riding on an elephant, becoming a maharaja with the power to say, 'Off with his head,' flying in the air by flapping my wings, driving a jet-powered Studebaker at ten thousand miles per hour in space . . . .

But then there are dreams and dreams. There are dreams that you recognize as dreams even as you are having them. The Kennedys, Camelot, finding a pot of gold in a cave—they were dreams of this colour. But all that I dreamed of in my really real dreams that year was that my parents would come back to me.

II
ARTHA

Or, How to Succeed

Reunion

IT WAS AT the Mangalore Station, the forlorn and neglected terminus of a railway system that had been a staging arena or accessory to some of our lives' major events—it was on a dull and sweat-soaked afternoon in this tin-roofed station, sitting listless and forlorn on hard, green wooden benches, smelling a mixture of coal dust and diesel oil, that Arun and I waited for the return of our parents, dreaming of reunion and love forever.

The bell rang, sending a ripple of excitement and motion through the waiting crowd, which started to position itself at various vantage points, and to peep out over the edge of the platform. A few minutes later, a large steam locomotive thundered and hissed through the station, dragging a long line of haggard carriages from whose windows an anthropological variety of human heads stuck out in various attitudes.

A wave of passengers gushed out and were struck by a counterwave of coolies. And then . . . .

'Mummy!' I shouted, breaking into a run, almost crashing into a middle-aged woman carrying rolled bedding on her head.

Mother, her fair young face looking incongruous against her coal-stained green sari, her beige blouse having patches under her armpits where the perspiration had changed the material's colour . . . I ran to her first. And barely had she hugged me, when my clinging, big-headed younger brother, Anand, cried 'Mummy' and got back her attention. Yes he, a stranger who had monopolized my parents' love in the last few years, was now a question mark, reopening old wounds: why, why only him?

There he was: my sooty, dusty father, his bald, shiny head jerking, his soot-enriched five o'clock shadow telling of a lifetime of struggle, one leg of his trousers turned up higher than the other, as he followed the red-shirted coolies, human communist flags, who were trying sneakily to blend into the crowd and out of sight with his luggage.

Though we had called him Daddy ever since we could remember, some boarding-house teaser had mockingly retorted 'Daadi! Daadi!'—local lingo for 'beard'—when he heard me gloat, 'My Daddy is coming soon!' That killed 'Daddy' for us. And Arun and I, our imaginations catalysed by American comic books such as *Archie and Veronica*, and gradually alienated from the man who now ruled our lives, began to invent substitutes—Pop, Dad, Appa, Daddyji, Daddykins, Pater, Pitaji, Pater Familias, Morarji (he looked a little like that famous politician)—when speaking of him, out of his hearing range. In the process, 'Daddy' lost its (and his) moral high ground forever.

The trunks hauled up onto two bullock carts, the family following in a baked and battered taxi, cruising at snail's pace, we headed for our rented house. The house lay on a depressed piece of land lying at the confluence of two deep gutters that roared with water during the monsoons but were dry repositories for dead cats or crows at other times. The gutter's proximity made the house very damp and the surrounding earth as fertile as a Brazilian woman's armpit: full of tall grasses and crotons and creepers and moss. The papayas burst out of the trees and bent them with their load, while raucous crows pecked at a ripe one while it was still on the tree.

Inside the house, a perpetual twilit darkness ruled, the light bulbs being weak, windows small and sparse, the rooms cavernous and painted a dirty green.

But those last white-hot days of the summer holidays, what bliss they were. Bliss they were because of the fleshy, erotic presence of my mother, my Mom, Mummykins, Mater, my Mamma, a dream made real once again, fused back into our lives. Forty-eight kilograms of pure, sari-wrapped, elliptical joy: it was a delight to see her move, to watch her body in multiple motions, buzzing about the house constantly on missions that she seemed to invent from moment to moment. Still in her mid-thirties, she was conscious of her beauty and her unfaded bloom, of her very kissable, flaming red lipsticked lips, of the ripples they caused in this dull town. After seventeen years of dreary nomadic wanderings, of exile forced by marriage to a small-time soldier, it was good to be home, back amongst her relatives and childhood friends, who invited her to their homes like a long-lost sister, offering her tea and chuda and laddoos and chakkulis.

At home, the joy of our lives, of mine and Arun's life, was to be touched by our special girl, our Mummy, gently touched on a cheek or arm; to feel her kind smile of approval; simply her *being* and her being there, in the moments that she was at peace with the world. The joy was playing with her sari, attaching ourselves to it and following her like a wagon does a locomotive. Even if we had to say Choo Choo Chuk Chuk ourselves—with some feeling of silliness, of course, trying to recapture those magical times when we had been tiny enough to say Choo Choo Chuk Chuk without thinking ourselves particularly silly. The joy lay in tickling her feet while she 'rested' on her bed, reading her *Eve's Weekly* perhaps—tickling her just to get a reaction, any reaction, like 'Now stop that!' 'Enough enough!' A reaction that told us she was alive and breathing, and that her existence made ours possible. It was like the satisfaction you felt at discovering that your heart was beating. The joy was to sleep in her bed and have her soft flesh graze you, because her small bed made such liberties possible and inevitable.

The softness had been bred in her by her sentimental past, her tender mother, her Mamma. 'I was three years old then, *tiny* I was. And Mamma used to carry me. And I would point to a picture of the Sacred Heart and say, "Give me Jesus' heart, Mama, to eat." Ha ha, Jesus's *heart* I used to ask for!'

Good old gourmet Mummy, who even at that tender age loved that Mangalorean delicacy—sheep's heart curry—so much that not even Jesus's sacred organ escaped her eyes of desire. That memory was tied up with a poignant one: that of her mother's early death, survived by eight children. The youngest was two years old at the time, and pious relatives comforted the children with, 'Isn't it nice to know you have a mother in heaven to watch for you, wherever you are?'

At more cheerful moments, in a voice that slowly bubbled, she would tell us about visiting her paternal grandfather. In the 1930s, wooden-wheeled bullock carts were the way to go places. Bumping along on mud roads at the lofty speed of 3.5 miles per hour, fearful of tigers that might pounce from the roadside jungle, the cart took two days to get my mother and her brothers and sisters to Mulki, where they spent their summer vacations.

'My grandfather—Mulkicho Aaab—' she began; and we sat down at her feet, mesmerized. 'He worked for a *rich* Englishman named Forrester: Aaab was the manager of his estate. Mr Forrester, he had a spinster sister who must have been a partner.' The spinster sister, it turned out, had nothing to do with the rest of the story, her existence being just one of those delicious details that seemed to define Mr Forrester, and through him Aaab.

'Mr Forrester liked my grandfather so much, he used to send him cigars—*fine*, *perfumed*, *English* cigars!' Mom continued, proudly, as if by extension she herself was entitled to bask in the warmth of the great Mr Forrester's approval. 'Every morning Aaab called all the little ones around him, and as we sat down beside him and massaged his legs, he would ask, "What do you want to *eat* today, children?" And we children would bicker loudly, shouting a variety of names—till we finally settled for masala dosas or godachi mutlin or patolio or just god panpale.' Aaab's culinary largesse, his democratic behaviour in ascertaining the gastronomic will of the people—that was the story; that was, in Mummy's hungry-child eyes, what had destined him for immortality.

But at summer holidays' end, when the pouring rains and muddy waters dampened everything in sight, and my magical Mummy was transformed into a harried housewife and Dad began losing his shirt over every spent rupee, our short reunion party began to wind down.

With Mummy, the eternal relationship with a sweetheart I had fantasized about from a distance . . . vanished, when faced with the real thing: the love of one tired and often irritable mother divided erratically between three hungry children; one husband who kept saying, 'You have such a long tongue, Lena! Long tongue means—long long long!'; relatives who dropped in on food-tasting or intelligence-gathering visits ('So what did you all eat for lunch yesterday, baa?'); and an old father who dropped in at odd times to sermonize on obedience and duty and other virtues enjoined upon the faithful by *Reader's Digest* (she sometimes responded irritably by giving *him* advice, which startled the patriarch into a sheepish look, as if of Mahatma Gandhi being ordered to wash behind his ears).

As for Daddyji, he found that a monster called inflation, heightened by the shortages caused by a killer famine and a Pakistani war was devouring his life's savings, transforming years of constipated self-denial into one little pellet of goat poop. He began to see every cause of expenditure as a mortal enemy. 'Money, money, always asking for money, where from to get money?' he would grumble. And stumbling one day into an unheard-of bargain for an overstock of boblen—white pumpkins—he succumbed. One day, a bullock cart arrived at our doorstep, unloaded a one hundred-and-twenty boblen, then disappeared.

While Pakistani planes rained Indian towns with American bombs designed to defend the Free World against evil Russians, my father, that son of an American bomb, rained boblens down on us.

Somewhere I had learned that food equals love, equals approval. So what about boblens?

Some things were food, others were not. Rice was not food, for example. Rice was what you fed to chickens. You also fed it to people in the hope that, by stuffing their bellies and dulling their appetites, they might be too comatose to ask for real food like beef, chicken, biryani, bananas, bread pudding, mutton cutlets, poulet au roti.

'Only boblen?' I asked sadly, day after day, rushing home from school to see what was for lunch, finding the unchanging lunch menu to be boblen curry and rice; boblen curry and rice; boblen curry and rice.

'When I was a prisoner of war, I survived on stolen scraped coconut,' Dad retorted. 'I would have given my life for simple rice and boblen curry.'

'Well, *we* are not prisoners of war. So why stuff *us* with boblen? You didn't capture us! You only gave birth to us!'

'You don't know the meaning of difficulties,' said Pop, upset. The veins in his forehead swelled, and sweat drops glistened on his dark brown temples. 'When you're on your own and *starving*, then you will realize.' And then, to Mummy, 'No gratitude, these children. If you give them your own blood, they'll say it is sour. If a stranger pees on their legs, they'll say it is warm.'

So King Boblen ruled the household, except on the days that sardines or mackerels were selling dirt cheap, on Saturday nights which seemed to call for chapattis and mutton cutlets, and on Sundays, the perfect occasion for a cholesterol-dense beef biryani.

Ah, Mummy's biryanis: yellow from their density of spice, cooked in a large aluminium pot with burning coals placed atop the lid, which was beaten and misshapen enough from decades of use as to let ecstatic gusts of flavour escape to tantalize and trouble the house's already excited and impatient residents.

And mutton cutlets, their surfaces almost black and crusty, yet soft and steaming within, the meat grainy and mildly chewy—our hand-operated meat grinder didn't grind too fine—with onions and coriander and green chilli bits peeping out from here and there. A concentrated taste of beef or mutton—tangy, slightly acid, slightly bitter. You let your molars crush the minced morsels and the sensations exploded across your palate as if a shower of rose petals had fallen over the taste centres in your brain.

In the absence of love, real love as practised by its famous practitioners, food had become the measure of love.

And it fell short. So I began to look for love elsewhere, such as in moojik-the-phood-of-love, and in the feminine adulation I hoped my harmonious charms would bring. Since the time I stopped singing 'A five and a six and a kiss me quick! A kiss me quick! A kiss me quick!' to please Aunt Meera, there had only been endless "Kyrie Elei-son"s and "Adeste Fideles"es at the Jesuit boarding-school. But recently, I had become enamoured of Cliff Richard whining "Summer Holiday", and Elvis Presley crooning "Jailhouse Rock". The picture of a country where even prisons were such ecstatic places, with jailbirds dancing and saying cute things to each other: it made me fall in love with America all over again. I wanted to project myself into that utopian world. I begged my father to buy me a second-hand, Spanish box guitar.

'You'll become a hippie,' he warned, forgetting his own post-War interlude with a violin; the music had been squeezed out of his soul by recent events.

'What, is it magic or something, the guitar wood, to turn me into a hippie?' I retorted. And I thought: Anyway, nothing I do makes any difference to you. Last time I came first in class, you said not a word of praise. Just 'Oh!' Only when my cousins achieve something will you mention it.

But he bought the guitar to get rid of me, and I was soon taking guitar lessons, hoping soon to wow large crowds of admirers, like the new-fangled all-male musical groups that had just become the rage. Their members, attired in 'drainpipe' trousers, pointed shoes, broad belts, shirts unbuttoned to their belly buttons, serenaded posh Mangalore weddings and First Holy Communions, sometimes singing such unintentionally funny numbers, (for these obviously heterosexual males) as "To Sir With Love".

At home, while Dad was away at work (working as a ticket-seller in a private long-distance bus company to pull in a few hundred), and Mom in the kitchen, I would escape to the seclusion of their dimly-lit bedroom, draw the dirty, green curtains across and, with a rock-singer-to-be's determination, croon into the curtained sunset such heart-throbbers as: "Gotta Funny Feelin' That I'm Fallin' in Love with You", "Living Doll", and "Jailhouse Rock".

Paradoxically for a singer, I had been in hiding for a few months now. Because, about the time I turned fourteen, pimples and tiny oil wells had burst all over my face, making it shine like a pink moon, making viewers gasp at a hundred paces. And Indian films, almost all love stories depicting the interval between the acute desire and the lachrymose happilyeverafter, only featured heroes with baby-smooth skin and baby-photo competition beauty. Pimples were the enemy, then. So began my pimple wars, my implacable hatred of bacteria, and my tortured efforts to keep out of sight of the girls I admired and fantasized about. What a world, when a stupid skin condition drives some people underground, forcing them into subterranean lives out of the reach of sunshine, flowers, women.

I tried especially to hide from Wet Dream Girl Number One, whom we called Golden Hair—a mysteriously red-and-gold-haired neighbour (an albino? a beneficiary of old Portuguese mischief? There had been a Portuguese outpost ten miles outside Mangalore at Feringpet, the military outpost of *phirangis* or foreigners—also called the Town of Syphilis, because the Portuguese had brought syphilis in). The magical Golden Hair often floated past our house to church, her buttocks making the roses on her well-starched Kuwait-bought skirt sway hypnotically as if in a gentle breeze. Heart thumping, I would dash behind a tree or duck into a by-lane the moment I saw her walking towards me. At weddings, where sex-starved young males took advantage of the mildly permissive atmosphere to chat with girl cousins and exchange sly smiles with their cousins' female friends, I hid out in man-dense corners, or occasionally behind a clump of cacti or crotons. Nor did I join boys my age who loafed about the fringes of the local girls' college in groups, mostly ogling but occasionally picking up smiles and words of encouragement. Instead, I spent the saved time peeping out the windows of darkened rooms and looking up medical books for pimple panaceas.

A fat-free, fruity diet plus globs of tetracycline were what the books suggested.

'All nonsense, these books,' Dad retorted. 'My pimples were big as borams, and I spent not a paisa on my face. They just disappeared one day. And then I became handsome.'

'In your time they didn't have penicillin either. So I shouldn't use penicillin to save my life? You worry only for your money—not for me!'

'If you are not happy in this house, leave right now! Learn to feed yourself! When you are starving, you will know how hard life is.'

'I'll become a millionaire!' I said, adding silently: *and I will shower hundred-dollar notes on your bald head from a plane to prove it to you!*

'Yes, you'll become a millionaire—when a bull gives birth to a calf.'

'I'll show you!'

Curiously, it was thus that Pop provided the coals that fuelled my ambition. I wanted to prove him wrong, and Mummy (years before, when she had been proud of me) right. To feed oneself wasn't a worthy goal. I would feed myself *and* thousands.

Low Living, High Thinking

IT WAS A turning point. I would leave my low life and family behind and soar into the jet-setting world of Beechcraft and beach houses on the Riviera, of Pontiac Bonnevilles and cheese and uplifting thoughts, the international world of limitless opportunity opened to me by *Time* magazine.

I began by writing to Jackie Kennedy, whom I had secretly admired as my hero JFK's wife, and now for her own self, for her grace, her beauty—her millions. I wrote:

Dear Mrs Kennedy

Greetings, Esteemed Madam. Let me introduce myself.

My religion is Roman Catholic, like you, and I read about you in *Catholic Digest*, about what a brave lady you have been after the death of my Favourite Leader in the World. I am 15, and I have a great fascination for America. For Marlboro Country. I can easily be found boasting about the USA to my friends and no wonder I am nicknamed 'Mr Vietnam' or 'Johnson's Son-in-Law' or 'American Spy' and so on. This is because I read plenty of American magazines and books like *Time*, *Life*, *Reader's Digest*, and frankly speaking, I may know more about your country, its statistics, etc. than many Americans do. And I assure you I am not satisfied with our Indian government's policy in Vietnam because it is too pro-Communist. (It should warm your heart to know that there is at least one Indian who will fight the Reds till he is dead.)

Incidentally, I read once that Americans have 50 times the food available to the average Indian. I suppose, since your stomachs cannot be 50 times as big as ours, that much of it gets wasted. If so, would you ask one of your servants to mail me some of your surplus cheese? I ask only because waste is a sin against the Almighty, and I wouldn't like you to endanger your noble soul.

Your devoted admirer,

Vijay Prabhu

P.S. I also collect stamps, and have about 2,000, because of my lovely fantastic Aunt Meera. You must have over a million, I presume? My Aunt Meera also gave me a Swissair World Atlas, and I have memorized the populations of most of the world's major cities. New York, Number Two, population fifteen million, no?

Jackie's silence upset me at first. But then, she probably had millions of Indians and Americans and Chinese writing to her. And foreign stamps were expensive, and probably added up. Besides, the American medical textbook had forbidden cheese to the pimpled, and her secret agents must have advised her to maintain a diplomatic silence in the interests of my health. So I forgave her, and continued to love her and occasionally write to her.

At the new rental house we had moved into, in a suburb of Mangalore called Pump Well, the action was heating up.

'He was saying he will make millions,' said half-pajamaed Dad sarcastically, chap-chapping out of the old brown tiled house and towards a broad and muddy fake well, in which, every monsoon season, a gutterish mud solution from the heavy rains collected, water not fit to wash a pig. 'Now let me see how many millions of buckets of water he will carry.'

The brass heat of the late summer having dried up the well with the good water, we were carting buckets of yellow water for our baths (tap water is too expensive to use merely for a bath, said Dad).

These jarring notes, coming from the mixing of two irreconcilable spheres, from two different centuries, were now a daily occurrence.

In addition, there really *was* jarring music in the air. On this typical weekday morning, as we waited for Mom's aloo parathas, Radio Ceylon—that beacon of hope and pop and Jim Reeves for India's Anglophile or phoren-inclined set—blared at a volume that was destined to provoke a psychotic outbreak. In an uncharacteristically extravagant gesture, Dad had recently purchased an upscale Philips Maestro Radio. Wrong move. Because music didn't have enough charm to soothe the chaos within him. Especially the music which his children, suddenly energized by the announcement of a Beatles number, screamed in dissonant discord, misunderstanding the Beatles' forked-tongue white-man speech:

> *She's Gatta Tikky-too Ra-Hight*
> *She's Gatta Tikky-too Ra-Ha-Hight*
> *She's Gatta Tikky-too Rite*
> *But She don't Care! [4 to 7 times]*
> *Whoa Piggy don't Care! [Last line]*

Three voices screamed thus, while quick-fingered I also strummed a guitar missing its G string. Meanwhile, Pop thudded up and down the veranda in Hawaiian chappals, barechested, in green pajamas, the drawstring curled into his belly hair, murmuring imprecations at whosoever's failings happened to occupy his consciousness at that moment.

At this moment it was the water.

'Who left the water running in the bathroom . . . silly fellow?' shouted Daddyji.

'I,' said I, resisting the temptation to add: *with my bow and arrow*. An irrelevant phrase, but it invaded my brain nevertheless, like an endless locust storm of irrelevancies weighing down on my brain and keeping me down.

'Water, water, everywhere, not a drop to spill!' responded pajama-clad, also-barechested Arun teasingly, his hand massaging his belly with the supposed ayurvedic intention of 'loosening' his constipation.

'Last time the water bill was twenty-five rupees. What you think, we are like the Pintos?' Dad continued, still irritated, and disconcerted by Arun's flippancy.

The Pintos were local millionaires, coffee estate owners. Daddy had come home with the news, which he recited again and again, marching up and down: 'The Pintos are worth seventy-five lakhs! Big people!' Almost like an accusation against us. Every couple of weeks, there would be a new estate bozo—Saldanha, Coelho, Kamath—and new figures of net worth. Until there came a time when I could have recited a *Fortune* 100 of Mangalore if asked.

'Don't worry. I'll pay back your precious water bill with interest!'

'Yes, yes, everything you will do. Sitting at home with legs up reading the newspaper. Such dynamic sons we have, Lena! What good did we do to deserve this luck!' he said, his worry-disfigured face breaking out in a pinched laugh.

It was unfair, I thought, Dad's habit of lumping mine and Arun's faults together and blaming each of us for the sum of them. As for sitting with the legs up while reading the newspaper, that was Arun's specialty. And for a simple reason: he found it more comfortable to fart that way, besides finding it an expressive way of telling the world what he thought of it. Whereas I, cut off from our natural heritage of pride in bodily functions, would sneak off to an unpopulated corner and then dance about the place to dissipate the poison.

I was putting a piece of polo—a fluffy white rice pancake fermented with a little toddy and then fried with Dalda—in my mouth, when Arun said, 'Ah, I just got a lot of shit.' And then, patting his belly approvingly, 'My stomach is empty. I feel fine.'

'Loose talk!' commented Dad, passing the dining-room and overhearing Arun. 'You fellows—you will never pull on in life!'

For Dad, the summit of human achievement and the *raison d'être* of human existence were encapsulated in the words, 'to pull on'—'pulling on' being a blessed state whose chief feature was managing one's life with the least amount of money, besides making regular and productive trips to the bathroom.

And all the while, secretly fearing that we were comparing

him unfavourably to his more-moneyed brothers, he countered with a front of Gandhian simplicity, saying, 'In my whole life, I haven't wasted a single paisa on unnecessary things!'

Yeah, toys for his kids, for instance. No toy, ever! He was hoarding money to outlast a future Japanese occupation.

'I don't expect *anything* from you,' he continued, '*It is enough if you feed yourselves!*'

Feeding oneself: that was all there was to life.

But maybe, I thought later at one point, projecting my own too-male mind onto my father's—maybe he had his own justifications for the kind of man he was. To see it one way: he was the donkey of the family, putting in ten hours a day to feed his endlessly demanding brood. *A few sad fucks in the dark—and he was stuck for life.** *What an unnaturally high price, what a whopping punishment for an only-too-human crime!* Yeah, a man takes a little joy for himself, a little joy in the dark, on a cold or sweaty night, and he's slapped with a gigantic, everlasting ticket that says: Duty! Sucker! Forever!

It was Christianity that, in effect, made people despondent thus. Because it told them *that THIS was the only life*, the only life you could sink your teeth into, *because after this life there would be only a boring eternity of playing Follow the Angels: yes, imitating those*

---

*   Yes, I imagined later, reading Vatsyayana's descriptions of the sexual predilections of women from various regions of India, and projecting my own sad frustrations and dim memories of noises in the dark coming from my parents' bedroom: this country had gone from something of a Golden Age of *The Kama Sutra* Knowing to a Dark Age of Unknowing. Indians now produced fifteen million babies a year, or more than the entire population of Australia, mostly fucking in the dark, for perhaps one three-minute session a week, (national holidays excepted) with most of their clothes on—attire suitable only for the standing fuck position—often thinking of the act as filthy, a dirty duty to posterity. With conquest and suppression (with monotheistic, intolerant, Middle Eastern and Victorian moral systems) had come puritanism; political colonization had made them lose sovereignty over the little territories between their thighs; poverty, shame, drink, a lack of privacy, and centuries of patriarchal and paternalistic withholding of knowledge from women and lower castes added to this inhospitality to sex.

And yet, the naked truth was that this sperm and these eggs, often spat out so shabbily, were vengefully productive and fertile, populating the country at such breakneck speed that even the Chinese were beginning to get nervous.

silly fairies, flapping wings and plucking harp strings. If you wanted real fun, real, he-man fun, this was the life to do it in: whether womanizing, drinking, or pigging out. What a *pirki* you had to be to play angel in this life too.

'Isn't the omelette ready, Lena? What's wrong, waiting for the hen or something? I've been warming the bench for half an hour!'

Dad, prohibited from lust by his forbidding religion, was trying to salvage at least a bit for himself. His financial security. His gastric range. Mom, officially the Chief Arbiter of Portions, knew enough to give him man-sized portions, to cook special, fluffy, onion-and-chilli omelettes for him and only him in the evening with his chapattis, because he *needed* them, because he *worked so hard* (when Mom spoke in *italics* you would do well to keep your ears pricked and your mouth *shut*). And his evening shot of 'medicine'.

Yes, medicine for his condition of donkeyhood.

Thuk! Thuk! Thuk! (Mixed in with Caw! Caw! and Cocococo!)

Someone was knocking at the door. Which was a very silly thing to do, because the diamond-patterned bamboo door made only an inaudible thuk! when you knocked at it, like a crow's egg dropping on a pile of wet leaves—a sound drowned out by the cawing crows and the irascible fowl population just outside. So after a while, forty-year-old, lean-and-weary Uncle Everest just walked in, saying, 'Vijay! Arun!'

Uncle Everest, in faded, unwashed, loose khaki trousers and a hand-me-down cream shirt from a *younger* brother, its collar past redemption. His hair like the feathers of a wet crow, his expression just as desolate. His pencil moustache camouflaged by forty o'clock shadow. His eyes rat-like and furtive, chewed at in their corners by shame, guilt, envy, and defeat. And lyric poetry.

Arun and I would end up like Uncle Everest, my mother's cousin, Pop had prophesied. Like Uncle Everest, once a reader of *books*—real books, not newspapers!—and respected around town as the *mando* or brain of the family, junior college or Intermediate-Passed, now a pitiful near-beggar to whom society threw its crumbs with disgust? It frightened us, and yet we felt sorry for the man Pop had lumped us with, as blackbirds of a feather. Here was at least one relative less blessed than we. Ever since the day when, in a fit of temper, he had smashed his father's face into his plate of steaming morning conjee, giving the patriarch's moustache and nose and eyebrows an unbargained-for coating of conjee, he had lost his job and his life had raced downhill. Recently, his younger brothers, having grown into Dara Singhs, had chased the thin and anaemic Everest out of the house, forcing him to move into a miniature shack next to the smelly outhouse. After that, Everest had to depend on his large network of relatives and family acquaintances, and on the strong but fading Mangalorean tradition of hospitality, for his meals.

'What's for lunch today, meat, fish, anything?' said Everest, his atavistic, amoebic brain driving straight to the food point. 'I was late for Casimir Souza's wedding reception. Catholic Club. Only got a piece of cake. Meat puffs were gone.' Everest had been crashing wedding receptions for so long (successfully, because it is considered bad luck to turn someone away from a wedding, whether invited or not), had acquired such seniority at that practice, that he had come to the stage of feeling righteously indignant if he wasn't served the full course: sweet red wine, dark brown fruit cake, meat puffs, saat, sweet yellow boondi laddoos, coffee, badam halwa.

'I'll serve. Wait,' said Mom, in a long-suffering tone. While I thought: meat puffs. Scrumptious, crisp, hot meat puffs with onions and curried mince inside. I'd be disappointed too.

Everest was now the bleak sheep of the family, the very mention of his name bringing forth awkward smiles in our typically stiff family gatherings. Despite his insistent complaints that life had cheated him of his due, and he quite blameless, this once-respected Intermediate-Passed Lover of Keats and Shelley was bombarded with advice by his brothers, uncles, aunts, and distant cousins—and occasionally, his teenaged nephews. This free advice would cover every possible subject: from cutting his hair to repairing the hole in his pants to saying a quick, formulaic prayer to St. Bartholomew, Patron Saint of the Unemployed. To his eternal dismay, Everest attracted advice like elephant shit attracts hungry flies. Most of the time, this advice was not even specific and relevant, but General Wisdom: the platitudinous heirloom of a preachy Mangalorean civilization. However low your absolute position in the universal scale of success, so long as you were one notch above Everest, you had the right to aim General Wisdom at him.

'You must pray too. Not praying, so all these bad things are happening to you,' said Mom, dropping—plop plop plop—a few pieces of her Beef Pepper Roast, the pieces cut flat and soaked in a black pepper gravy, onto Everest's plate.

'What shall I say? No Mother. Mother is gone,' said Everest abstractedly of his forty-year-old motherless state, which in times of stress he blamed for all problems, physical, spiritual, and international.

'Do you eat a balanced diet?' said Arun, contributing his own share. 'Do you?' (Arun didn't even know he was being funny: as funny as American AID officials explaining balanced diets to starving Biafrans.)

'Enough, Arun, don't talk,' said Mom. 'Study, go.'—'Study go' being the ultimate retort that adults used to shush children.

'Sprouted green gram,' said Arun. 'Eat it the first thing every morning, with one gooseberry for the digestive enzymes. When your stomach is at its most efficient. Low cost protein, needs no cooking!' Arun didn't seem to realize that Everest didn't care for the lowest-cost solution around.

'He's practising to become India's Minister for Nutrition, Mom,' I said.

'You shut up,' said Arun. 'Or you'll get one whack on your bean.'

Ah, Arun. Must I tell you about him?

I don't want to. He was a presence at breakfast, lunch and dinner for most of my childhood life, I admit. A competitor for space. He was a fact of my life. Like morning shits. Like muddy rainwater splashed by passing lorries

But he was not a brother. Just as the relationship with my grandmother had a few years earlier, brotherhood too had died for me. It had died the day in the convent, I being eight and he ten, when he joined a group of tough kids in throwing stones at me. Kids who had simply chosen me as Victim of the Day because they needed one. Brothers should be protectors. This brother had been a coward: he found it expedient to join with my tormentors instead of protecting me.

For years after that, he used his muscle power to control me, to make me cry, to keep me down. That's why, when my little brother Anand came on the scene, along with my parents, I could never feel a special emotion called brotherhood for him. Brotherhood? What's that?

In fact, the funny thing that I would discover about life is that one never finds love and grace and kindness in the expected places. At least for me, it always came from the most unexpected places.

Anyway, I was a lanky fifteen now, bicycling three miles each way to high school. He couldn't whack me again. Though he still yearned for the old days of absolute power.

'My bean? Or your smelly bean gas?' I retorted.

'You're spending hundreds of bucks on your pimples,' Arun's voice, having escalated quickly, hit my most vulnerable spot.

'You're spending hundreds of bucks on your flute,' I shot back hotly. 'Flute' was the word I had invented for the remarkable source of his musical farts.

At which Arun landed a Dara Singh right on my nose, drawing out a trickle of blood, and leaving me momentarily dazed.

'Leave the house now!' I shouted, suddenly authoritative, decisive, imperial. 'You have no hope! You're doomed! You can't earn a living, you'll come begging to me!' It was the domestic wisdom, distilled from his customary difficulty in passing exams, that he would be a failure in life—or at least the most outstanding failure of us all, since Dad often declared we *all* would be failures!

'I've not *given* you a blow. I just touched you. Shall I give you a real blow and show you how it feels? I could kill you in one blow.'

'Oh, yeah? I'll get the whole town to know that I live with a killer. Kill me now? Then your only hope is to surrender yourself to a lunatic asylum—immediately—so that you may stop committing further crimes! Or fly away to the Windy City!'

He gave me a blow, and I blew hot air in return. I realized I didn't yet have the courage to hit him back. My time would come, I told myself. I didn't then see his side, of being an elder brother who felt cheated by the genetic lottery, who had to suffer in silence and be in my shadow while I won academic prizes and attention. I simply saw him as someone to avoid modelling myself after.

As I did Uncle Everest, a genetic premonition of disaster and starvation. For it scared me, even the slightest chance of Dad's prediction coming true: my ending up like Uncle Everest. I would become an engineer or a doctor, I decided. No begging for me. I began to prepare mentally for my entry, in a month or two, into the hilltop college that sniffed snootily at the Arabian Sea.

St. Stanislaus College, run by Jesuits, had once been a prime disher-out and exemplar of Macaulay's masala—a British policy, instituted by Lord Macaulay, to create Indians who were brown in colour but English in thinking so they could serve as intermediaries between what the British decided and what the natives thought they wanted. But independent India had gone in a big way for professional colleges, and I had been weighing the only two choices considered worthy of the high school cream: medicine or engineering. The choice between *these* two, according to the crude sub-wisdom that fell my unprivileged way, really hinged on whether your preferred route to fat-cathood lay in working with bodies and asking people to take off their clothes, or in working with stones and machines and drawing a lot of diagrams and tightening a lot of bolts.

I cast my lot with medicine. Chiefly, because I hadn't yet seen a naked woman. *Yes, I hadn't seen fifty per cent of humanity in its pristine, unencumbered state*, and I was excited by the power over the human body exercised by the antiseptic, white-starched medical aristocracy. So I joined a class of sixty males as sexually aroused as I at the prospect of acres of naked skin on the horizon—at this promised entrance to a forbidden world, a powerful freemasonry (thus did puritanical India gradually build a huge bank of medical manpower, large enough to flood the West). And despite a bowdlerized syllabus and modesty-cloaked teaching, the boys managed to extract from the lecturer the admission that the tadpole had a urethra and the frog a cloaca—and yes indeed, a cloaca would be called, in more liberated circles, an anus. The naughty, naughty frog! Which led the animal kingdom in its uninhibited sex life! Which paraded its cloaca for the whole world to see with its *naked* eyes! Giggle, giggle, the class went as the teacher—forced for his livelihood to pander thus—broke into an embarrassed smile.

But by the middle of my pre-university year, relations with my father had deteriorated into such bitterness that I had little hope of getting any assistance from him for my medical college fees. By then I had become jaded with frog-sexuality and amoebic love tricks anyway. So I eased off the exam rat-race and frittered my energy away in chasing aphrodisia outside the biology syllabus: foreign movies, in which lately the characters itched to shed their already-minimalist clothes, one cinema poster describing its offering as 'plenty of nudity . . . cheerful display of female flesh'.

And four months later, I let an imperious judgement from the eccentric Father Wilfred Shenoy, S.J.—a padre who for some reason, perhaps because of a deficiency of vocabulary, called me 'philosopher' and declared my 'intelligence' was not destined to be wasted on Science—*Thoo!* Pftooey!—sway me into joining the BA.

If Dad needed another confirmation of his son's worthlessness, this was it. As even a roadside hawker of diseased mangoes in this educationally savvy town knew by now, the Bachelor of Arts degree was the ultimate stamp of the *bekaar* or social reject—a worthless, terminal diploma on the low road to unemployment.

But I would show them. I'd become the editor of *The Illustrated Weekly of India*—a savant and ex-officio Philosopher Laureate of India, one whose job description entitled him to pronounce with sneering finality his opinions on all matters within the Milky Way. Shortly after, I would become Assistant Editor of Britain's *Punch* magazine, which had now replaced *Reader's Digest* in my mind as the zenith of human wisdom. I imagined myself sitting across a sofa from Big Boss Alan Coren, exchanging jokes about popes and women's underwear.

But first, there were more urgent priorities. Such as: what exactly was this joy that women were supposed to bring into the world? It was still, for me, only a hearsay, theoretical joy, as theoretical as the speed of light or the expanding universe.

Because *I*, despite all my pretensions to knowledge and intelligence, despite my fustian and sweeping essayistic forays, *didn't really know*. I didn't fucking know! And if I didn't know that, I didn't know *anything*.

Prometheus Unzipped

IT HAPPENED AT the end of summer following my fourteenth birthday. The afternoons were still and lulling; in those final days of the summer holidays, I usually took a short nap. On one such afternoon I woke up to find that a great dark mass of clouds had arrived and obliterated the sky, the merciless, endless rain accompanied by a wind that threatened to topple trees, tear off tiled roofs, wash the world's human dirt and its mucky civilization away. It was water, water, everywhere, as a windy, slashing rain wet more than ankles, more than knees, more than thighs. Umbrellas whirled and flew down the road, passing lorries splashed mud at passers-by, torrential rains deluged the town and the earth itself, until we felt like helpless fish swirling about in a universe full of water.

It was the kind of weather that usually precedes a happening of momentous, planetary importance, and it just so happened that a morning about a week after that burst of nonstop monsoon, when a break in the black sky had opened to reveal a delightful morning sun, Dad approached my bed on the veranda of the Pump Well house.

'Get up, getup getup!' he said, his voice like a dog emitting a surprised cough. 'It's seven o'clock.'

It was Dad's military aspect carried over to domestic life: early rising was the key to discipline and virtue and a job to feed oneself with, and late rising a guarantee of vice and permanent unemployment. To see us horizontal thus when he at fifty-six was up and shit-shave-shampooed and feeling his oats—it maddened him beyond bearing.

'I can't get up,' I said matter-of-factly, watching my agitated father framed behind the netting, barechested, wearing only his lightgreen-white-and-brown pajamas, looking almost as if he should be thumping his chest and bellowing, 'Kreegah! Bundolo!'

'Why not?' he growled back, angrier.

'Don't you understand?' Now *I* was angry too. 'I'm a teenager now!'

'So why can't you get up? As if we were all not once teenagers! So did we sleep in bed all day because we were teenagers? We had to get up and milk the cows!'

The cows and my poor dim father would have to wait a long time, I thought. I just *couldn't* get up today. Because this morning, about the time that our domestic cock, Bimbisara II, crowed thrice, the world had changed for me. Like Byron waking up one morning to discover he was famous, I woke up on that sunny morning of my fourteenth year to discover that my most unassuming member had tripled in length and was pointing unaccountably heavenward. I tried disbelief; I tried patience; I tried beating it into submission. When all failed, I rushed to the bathroom wrapped in an evidence-hushing bedsheet and proceeded to examine every aspect of what I regarded as a medical problem of historic significance. And then, failing to persuade it to retreat like a nice fellow, I had dashed back to my bed and snuck under my bedsheet, and wild elephants couldn't drag me out of that bed just right now.

I hate to sound as if I have a chip on my shoulder about a bulge in my pants, yet what a pain in (the vicinity of) the nuts it became for the next five years! I'd have given anything, in those years, to read a treatise on Erection Management: how to negotiate undesirable hard-ons in public, and how to tell your father: 'I can't get up right now, Dad, because I have a hard-on the size of the Octerlony Monument, and I wouldn't like to upset any furniture.' I'd have given anything, too, to know that, in the right circles, a hard—especially a stubbornly hard—penis was no liability, but quite the contrary. Given the primitive worldview I had inherited, given that I didn't understand the biological purpose of this unannounced, awkward swelling, an erection seemed to me one of the less successful aspects of God's creations, besides also being inconvenient and terrifying.

Consider: an erect penis is almost always incongruous, it does not belong; it is a homeless, stateless, parentless, pointless, extraterrestrial creature. Michaelangelo's David is a work of art; but give Little David an erection, and Florence would become the laughing-stock of the world. An erection arrives like a bolt from the blue; and arriving uninvited, it stays as long as it jolly well pleases, or until well pleased.

In a more natural society, this would of course be a simple act of nature by which a fellow's tool announces its desire to come out of its relative seclusion and claim its rightful place in the biological order. It was my living in Mangalore, India, at that time that made this first erection—and the sexuality that came with it—so catastrophic. What a mess our country has made of its sexual frontier, riddled as it is with thirty-year-old males who are sexual *bacchas* compared to Western fifteen-year-olds. The Indian energy crisis: how much of it is misspent, misdirected, unspent and therefore imploded sexuality?

Almost a year after my first hard-on, there came to universal astonishment a hyped-up sex education lecture by Father Bernard in tenth grade: a pseudo-biological lecture that launched into rhapsodies about God's spiffy devices for human continuity, oh, the beauty of His purpose, and ooh the purposefulness of his beauty . . . . But what about bollock-naked, sweaty sex? Not *one* item of cold information, not a single naked-as-a-jaybird fact.

Consider this: I, a semi-urban, moderately literate Indian, took one of the most roundabout paths to the discovery of sexual knowledge ever recorded in human history. What a one-hour reading of a straightforward, illustrated, no-holds-barred, keep-your-airbrushes-in-your-bloody-pocket-and-spread-'em sex manual might have told me, it took me an average of two days a week for *seven years* (or the combined lifetimes of two frogs) to discover. Seven frigging years in which I could have probably discovered the Theory of Relativity—or at least *understood* it! And by the time I *did* discover it, the apple of knowledge had acquired such cosmic value and significance that it didn't seem worthwhile to stop learning about sex; I had become an unpaid, professional sexual sleuth, probing the frontiers of carnal knowledge for humanity.

But before I reveal that extraordinary route, I have a gripe to unload. It is about social hypocrisy, and what a terrible—though occasionally joyful—burden it is to be a man. And how it is almost easier to do all the things society expects you to do than it is *not* to do all the things society expects you not to do . . . .

But first: To the catalogue of terms such as childhood, puberty, adolescence, adulthood, and menopause, I bequeath a neologism indispensable to understand men: penishood. (Step aside, Freud, though I know you're now wracked by penishood envy.) Penishood is that period of a man's life commencing sometime after puberty when he begins to be ruled by his penis and its activities, its needs, its perceptions of life, its fantasies, even its moods (such as dejection, elation, stubbornness). In most men penishood is ended by marriage, ambition, sexual disenchantment, fatigue, transfer of interest to a new pursuit, or the mellowing hand of Time; in certain asexual, repressed, or hermaphroditic types, it never begins; and in a few, it never ends.

To the groan of a bloated English language complaining of word-punishment, I respond: By their uses shall ye judge them! Because words, like penises, are justified solely by their use. (To digress: If I were God, I'd retract the penises of all celibates and transfer them to the involuntarily impotent: penises would be 'that one talent it is death to hide'.) Of course, I use 'use' in the broadest sense to include play. For words—like penises—are meant to play and have fun with, not to be feared, quarantined, banned, tabooed, kept at arm's length, driven underground. Tool, bishop, pego, truncheon, ladies' delight, John Thomas, and other synonyms for penis—if these words, used properly *and* improperly, don't give you delight, then probably an actual penis never will. 'Play', as in: Pumpkin, Pumpkin, peter eater.

How else to describe this period, during which all of a man's decisions serve to advance his phallic interests; when his truncheon is a rampant despot to which the will, the flesh and the intellect are slaves and instruments; when the entire universe is nothing but an infinite possibility of spaces and enclaves that will accommodate and succour his pecker? Yes, a word whose understanding cannot but make women more compassionate toward men. Central in the understanding of a man's life, thoughts, motivations, values. Of a time when the penis is king—Ay, every exaggerated inch a king—even if often without a kingdom. Could one conceive of a history of France without Napoleon or Louis XIV? Yet how many autobiographies and novels pretend their male protagonists hadn't even heard of a penis, much less possessed one?

Not that I discount the emotion of love as an emotion apart from the sexual drive. I am big on love, as will be revealed soon in a chapter entirely devoted to pure, all-natural, vitaminized love (at the risk of having the macho brigade desert me, I will confess that I saw two of the world's most romantic movies, *Romeo and Juliet* and *The Sound of Music*, thrice, misty-eyed every time). But my wise elders had by this time deeply convinced me that the human pissing equipment was 'filthy'. In my mind, therefore, love was a totally different animal from the dirty snake that was now rearing its head . . . .

For the next twelve months after the birth of my manhood, I merely staggered around the town in fear and trembling and tent-like pants, too embarrassed to consult a doctor or confide in my friends. Then one day, restlessly looking for something to read, I stumbled upon an old nursing textbook left by a previous resident in the space between the matted straw ceiling and the tiled roof. Locking the door, I feverishly discovered, buried in technical jargon, a chapter of stone age obstetrics that told diagrammatic tales of the breech delivery and gave macabre views in cross-section of the female and male reproductive systems including what it called the pudendum. It was my first, faint understanding of what women had under their clothes, and men under their skin—fore and aft. Until now, my idea of a woman's vital centre had been formed by a momentary vision of a convent playmate's dividing line that disappeared beyond the horizon of her half-lowered chaddi's elastic and so limited my horizons of knowledge. Though the diagrams' clinicality might have turned off a blind man, they cleared up some of my absurd misconceptions, one of which imagined breasts to be extended lungs that enabled women to breathe longer during a fight.

But beyond all it was the words, and the diagrammatic

suggestion of pubic hair, that were as explosive to me as the Hiroshima bomb, that changed *my* world more than the theory of relativity or Archimedes' discovery ever did. I read through the chapters dozens of times, my fascinated embrace of illicit joy and my sense of having reached a smutty, moral nadir each topping the other. For weeks thereafter, 'pudendum' reverberated through my brain like a loose cannon ball.

And what a powerful dimension to knowledge the pubic bush gave; it was like a curve that bent my fundamental space-time. When belly whiskers came into my life, God and fifty tons of painfully-accumulated religious baggage whooshed out the window (Founders of future religions: Accommodate pubic hair, will you?). How extraordinarily complex the question had become: a forest with dark and dangerous and unlimited possibilities.

One day, when I could bear my new half-knowledge no longer, I biked furiously to the house of Uncle Eustace—the one who had accumulated a large library with the help of *Reader's Digest*, American penfriends, and others—and, confessing to my aunt a sudden urge to improve my fifteen-year-old mind, slipped into the library room. This was the library that had, with its glossy imported *Reader's Digests*, given me an unquenchable yearning for America, the land where Campbell's Cream of Chicken Soup boiled in every pot, and lowly dogs and cats were served with Purina delicacies that I'd have said a million woof-woofs for. Chicken soup was far from my thoughts as I took out Volume 2 of the *Reader's Digest Great Encyclopaedic Dictionary*. 'Pudendum' was defined as 'female organ of generation'. I shelved Volume Two, took out Volume One, and looked up 'generation'. Not much luck. I tried 'nude'—because that's what one must be if one displays one's pudendum. No luck still. But, following Sherlock-like a trail of 'sex', 'reproductive system', 'love', 'pubis', 'puerperal fever', and so on, I greatly expanded my vocabulary (and temporarily, my lingam), arriving finally at such thrilling discoveries as 'vulva' and 'clitoris'. I had already seen most of these words (and their artistic representations) in the nursing book, so my thrill was merely to realize the words were there, accessible to me; that I had *found* them; and that they were not merely a figment of the nursing-book author's imagination, but had been verified by good old *Reader's Digest* itself.

None of these words, by themselves, actually told me very

much about what actually happened between men and women; they suggested the primitive architecture of love, but not its thermodynamics. Yet, the mere fact that these complex systems *existed* within our trousers and skirts made me deliriously happy. It also increased my interest in the recent tide of Western novels whose jackets displayed women in various states of suggestive undress—a plague of forgotten or missing buttons seemed to be abroad—their faces hot with desire. This was also the time the James Bond films and their imitations had begun to splash suggestive posters on town walls, showing Mangalore what it had never in its three-thousand-year history seen before.

But ah, yes, it was the *Clean* Literature Drive, organized by my half-patron Father Wilfred Shenoy, that gave me my first peek into a brave nude world of salacious literature.

Father Wilfred was an unusual priest, inbred with a missionary fervour rare in the Indian Jesuits of the time, who, unlike Father Wilfred, believed that any labour other than teaching (or preaching down from the tips of their noses—the same thing) was too low-caste for their exalted tribe to stoop to. Somehow, Father Wilfred had chanced to hear of a tendency in world literature towards falling moral standards. So he determined to pre-empt the corruption of Mangalorean youth and their domino-like falling to Ho Chi Satan by capturing their hearts first with his gloriously clean and wholesomely entertaining literature.

Unfortunately, he was too otherworldly to realize that this immoral Western literature would have, in the normal course of events, taken at least five more years to reach the tightfisted intellectual backwater that was Mangalore, where people would rather spend money on masala dosas and laddoos than on a book, where people bought even textbooks only on threat of being failed, where the only English bookstore in town sold books of pompous quotations and weak jokes, and study guides, and assorted self-improvement manuals from the Dale Carnegie school. Further, he was too innocent for the crafty publishing barons of New York and London. When he opened the cartons of books that he had ordered by the metric ton, and had them spread out on the display tables, his commandeered volunteer salespersons could barely stop reading to attend to customers with urgent expressions on their faces and suspicious bulges in their crotches. Thanks to him, a whole new soft core paperback world had been opened to us! Harold Robbins, Ian Fleming, Mickey Spillane, John O'Hara, Henry Miller, Erskine Caldwell! Covers with half-dressed women (I always saw the glass as half-empty), legs spread in a most un-Indian fashion! Books about people who were doing it! An elephantine shot of testosterone for those whose acquaintance with Western literature had so far consisted of *expurgated* Shakespeare and puerile abridgements of George Eliot, force-fed by frustrated drones.

'But, but . . . ' sputtered Father Wilfred, whose last acquaintance with a Western novel had been some pious soporific by crusty old Pearl Buck. 'These are reputable publishing houses. Corgi, Black Cat, Midwood. I thought they would send me *uplifting* books: quotations, Keats and Shelley, nature, science, space travel, general knowledge, *literature* . . . .' He hadn't known that the line between good books and bad books had recently blurred, with *Lady Chatterley's Lover*, a novel about no-holds-barred all-natural fucking, having been recently admitted into the high church of Great Art. It was too late to return the books; the customers, the People in all their assembled majesty, were already beating down the doors. And who in the mouse-poor Society of Jesus would pay for the overheads already incurred if he didn't make some profits first!

Nay, I blame ye not, noble Father Wilfred, S.J. On the contrary, I commend ye greatly for helping re-open a mind that some of your brethren of the cloth had so efficiently closed. And in any case, soon after your momentous exhibition ended, I was whetting my newly-acquired appetites and devouring further examples of these literary giants at my friend Shekhar's house.

•'So you've taken good advantage of the Clean Literature Drive, what?' I asked Shekhar, who had well-thumbed copies of Mickey Spillane, James Hadley Chase, Ayn Rand, and T. Lobsang Rampa spread out on a side table (his *mother* read Ayn Rand and T. Lobsang Rampa, as did most mid-level snobs, because it somehow excused the fact that they also read Harold Robbins).

Tall, jean-butted Shekhar and his bob-haired, noseringed Renaissance-woman mother, living in an old mossy-tiled house surrounded by a small orchard of sapota, pineapple, jackfruit and mango trees, kept a liberal, open house—a pop-culture salon to which I had a fourteen-hours-a-day, seven-days-a-week pass, especially after having expressed admiration for his rendering of the song "Summer Wine", which I thought especially convincing since he had never tasted wine of any kind in his entire life, just toddy and beer and local hooch. I'd just amble over to his place, and if he wasn't in, I'd sit down and peek into his stupendous collection of bound comics, dusty paperback novels, or 50s' issues of *Look* and *Saturday Evening Post*, strum melodies like "36-24-36" and "Apache" on his guitar till I was bored, or just chat with his mother.

But my recent obsession had been limited to breathlessly scanning American paperbacks, hunting for their miserably ungenerous sex scenes (as a speed-reading technique, I tell you, this leaves Evelyn Wood and Tony Buzan light years behind!). This was my introduction—backdoor and illegitimate though it might seem—to modern Western literature, extending a skimpy academic acquaintance that had stopped with Dickens and George Eliot and John Keats. (There had been only one experience combining the classics and sex. Poor dead Keats in your bloody grave, hear, oh hear my confession: So desperate was I for erotic fuel that I must have been the only person in human history to have shot his wad reading and re-reading your poem, "The Eve of St. Agnes"—a presumably literary experience, which had become for me a most ennobling and edifying erotic experience, as I, provoked by these lines, imagined Madeline in the buff in those good old panty-less days: '*Loosens her fragrant bodice; by degrees/ Her rich attire creeps rustling to her knees.*') (And dear reader, if you must shoot *your* wad now, you have my blessing and Keats's—remember it is a high literary tradition. And perhaps years after my death, my birthday will be celebrated all over the world as International Friends of Keats Wad-shooting Day, resulting in communal orgies of onanism not rivalled since the days of the Roman Empire.)

I had sped thus through countless novels, uninterested and oblivious to plot, eyes slowing to normal speed only at the promising pages—usually towards chapter's end or the book's latter middle—where someone, it being bedtime or bathtime perhaps, might undress and expose something, and someone else might venture further and do something to that exposed something. Nine times out of ten, I would be frustrated by the cliché 'He cupped her breasts' (such a favourite of American novelists, I wished some flying saucer would hit them) climaxing the purported love scene—because, dammit, breasts were no great shakes for a prurient Indian used to displays of public breast-feeding.

But Shekhar's literary offering on this particular day, the priapic *Peyton Place*, so overflowed the usual suggestive cups that I had to reposition my tight pants and Bhim underpants to ease the constriction on my engorged cock. Just then Shekhar, who had disappeared into the kitchen a while ago, re-entered the room and asked if I could just stand up for a moment so he could open the cupboard behind me. I stood up slowly, bending awkwardly to conceal my excitement; but Shekhar and his friend Mick (an easygoing layabout whose signature phrase was 'Behave yourself', followed by a cackling laugh) noticed the tell-tale and uncamouflageable bulge and burst into interweaving waves of laughter—one starting when the other stopped, and vice versa—for the next five minutes. And though I knew they knew, and they knew I knew they knew—the subject of erections was too hard for me to mouth, the discovery of my particular erection too shameful to own; so I hid behind my feigned obtuseness.

About a year later, following a trail of *Tit Bits* magazines that used to appear and disappear on Pop's bedside reading-table, Pop hiding them or looking very seriously engrossed in investigative journalism whenever we spotted bared tits or thighs on them, I chanced upon a lending library. It was a ten-cubic-foot establishment in the bazaar section of town, wedged between grain shops and stainless-steel utensil dealers. The owner was an unlikely, traditional-looking, lungi-wearing lapsed Brahmin (oh, what a lapse was there, my countrymen!) named Padmanabha—the sort of chap who would be the proud owner of an exotic lingam rather than a pedestrian cock. Padmanabha's chief means of bringing home the bacon was to lend, under the table and at steep hourly rates, pseudo-photographic books of meaty shots imported from various advanced, high-protein civilizations. Indeed the books, with titles like *Figure Studies Number 4* and *Photographic Technique Number 3*, purported to be expositions on photographic technique and probably were quite legitimate if that was what you were looking for—but I *wasn't*, dear reader, for I didn't even possess a toy camera! But these books, though a welcome introduction to a new world of open-air shamelessness, infuriated me by their sneaky use of shadows, crossed legs, and an occasional guitar to hide the things that really mattered. (Music ought to have been the food of love, not its enemy!) Book after book would disappoint me; yet I would race back within minutes to Padmanabha's 'library' to borrow the next book, bike breathlessly to the nearest deserted street, stop the bicycle and support it and myself on my toes without getting off, ignore the stink rising from the surrounding gutters, whip out the book, and flip furiously on, hoping with bottomless optimism to catch the one page or photograph where the napping photographer's shadow machine had failed to camouflage the prized netherlands. The lesson this taught me (yes, silly me!): women were reluctant givers, playing hide and seek with their assets, capitalistically manipulating them for maximum returns.

Indeed, what an enemy of Pure Knowledge this thing called feminine modesty had been until now; what an army of NORAD-shaming hands would spring to its defence at even the flimsiest danger of exposure. On the other hand, there were the ravenous and polymorphously perverse heroines of the Paris-published Traveller's Companion series of novels that Padmanabha also lent me. Their giddy ebullience, their riotous energy, their penetrating prose! In them I began to understand Carlyle's definition of man as a tool-using animal. In one such book, which I believed more Nobel-worthy than crusty old Pearl Buck, stark-naked characters of both sexes raced, not on horses, but on the stark-naked backs of other, whip-propelled characters of mixed endowments. How much more zest than those tired American offerings—the Midwood Classics—in which fun was only do-able in three combinations: organ-organ, mouth-organ, and hand-organ.

Yet, despite India's oppression then, at this fag-end of the

1960s, a revolution of sorts was brewing at the fringes of our colossal society; Sex had begun trickling down from the upper classes to the upper-upper middle classes—in India, fucking had been until now the sport of the rich. At the town's poshest three-star hotel and Temple of Hedonism, Moti Mahal, striptease cabarets had opened to packed crowds. The dancers, usually with two-syllable names like Mona, Lisa, or Binky, spent most of their performance doing a pseudo-arty cross between belly dancing, twisting, and advanced stomach-ache; but I heard that when the lights darkened for their final, thirty-second climax, the dancers would partially—and on rare occasions, completely—strip. Rumours circulated that on occasion a spectator would manage to yank off a conservative artiste's G-string or finger its contents—to the chagrin of the management and the uproarious, tumes-cence-flavoured laughter of the audience.

All this new knowledge charged the air, gave new meanings, new tumescences, to things. Suddenly, I beheld a Mangalore filled with women who had extraordinarily complex devices—yonis, the keys to my pleasure!—under their skirts and saris. One night, passing through the dining-room on the way to the bathroom, I noticed the sleeping twelve-year-old servant girl's skirt had ridden up over her belly. Making seven more trips to the bathroom that night, I had observed with fascination the faintly smiling face with its expression of Eden-like peace, (like Modigliani's *Reclining Nude*, I think now) coupled with a belly and pubis completely devoid of hair (quite unlike Modigliani's model). The act of observation had given me great scientific and aesthetic pleasure, but it had thrown my recent knowledge of pubic fuzz in doubt.

I could bear my state of half-knowledge no longer. The lending librarian, for some time now, trusting me as his regular customer and major source of income (the money I had borrowed from my uncles as a capital investment to improve my mind), had been lending me black-and-white photographs which he fished out of a secret hiding place—they were illegal as hell, three years hard labour minimum. In these stark mirrors of naked truth, shadows no longer lurked around the behinds of women, like an unwelcome supporting cast. The models were mainly Western or Oriental, except for a few Indian aberrations who looked like surprised cows. Many of these models didn't just stand there; they did it, with each other. This was the final, black-and-white proof that I the now-eternal sceptic and illegitimate son of Bertie Russell had been waiting for, that *it* was *do-able*! And do-able not just by exotic foreigners from countries that had invented hot dogs or sent men into space but also by otherwise-inefficient *Indians*!

Returning Padmanabha's paper beauties one day, I asked him, 'Do you, er, er, know of a place where I could do it?' I pointed to a group of photographs bound in a rubber band to make my point.

He surveyed me quietly, then smiled, as if to say: You have proven a good *shishya*, a worthy pupil. Now go and fornicate in peace.

He said: 'It? *It*? Ha ha. So you wanting to be discharging in a vulba? You wanting a lady for enjoy?'

'Ahem, yes,' I said, embarrassed as well as amused.

'I hope you will like it surely. Now carefully listen: Go to the Green Star hotel, ring backdoor's doorbell, and say to the answering fellow: "*The moon is round.*"'

I bicycled madly towards the hotel, overtaking bullock carts, fellow cyclists, purring private city buses that snacked at clumps of commuters while staying poised to spring forward at the approach of a competing bus. But I saw nothing, merely groaning at the pain caused by my insufficiently elastic erection within my extremely punishing underwear, now brutalized by the dynamics of bicycling. The lungi-clad man answering backdoor's doorbell saw the bulge in my pants and didn't even wait to hear that the moon was round. He led me through a corridor lined by green plywood cubicles, and into a cubicle where two chocolate-skinned women clad only in coarse petticoats and blouses sat on a thin mattress atop two joined benches. They smiled craftily.

I chose the fleshier one, passing on the one who looked like she hadn't eaten all week. For it was going to be a question of energy today, of being able to satisfy all of my pent-up demands without demanding refreshment breaks. She was a long-haired, full-lipped, chubby-cheeked, languorous quasi-beauty from the state of Kerala—speaker of a language I knew not one word of. We went to the next cubicle, where she proceeded to squoosh down on the narrow, spartan bed, under a squeaky ceiling fan. I took off my trousers and sat beside her in my underwear. We smiled at each other for about a minute, while she tapped one foot on the floor to some unheard melody. This was getting nowhere, so I gestured that I would like to inspect her merchandise ('Look before you leap' leaped at me). Reluctantly she lay back and lifted up her pink petticoat, as if my demand were freakish; and in the dim light of the room, I pieced together my first aerial view of the hitherto-hidden treasures of a live, grown-up female of the species. I still remember being surprised by amplitude, wetness, darkness, hair, aliveness, a strong, wickedly enticing smell. So this was a woman! The sanctum sanctorum.

My primal sense of sexual etiquette told me I wasn't permitted to look for more than a few seconds (I added a sixty-second grace period), and that some get-acquainted foreplay must follow. Accordingly I lay on the crowded bed with one arm loosely wrapped around her, partly to keep my balance I suppose, and stared at her for another two minutes. She still had her blouse on, only two buttons off, but enough to confirm for my benefit: *Her moons were round*, and gorgeous.

Time to begin the main show: removing my underpants. This accomplished without any major PeterSellersian disaster, I lay on top of her with my choice-but-inflamed portions over her choice-but-unperturbed portions. Did someone now open her ruby lips to beg the voice and utterance of my cock? No. In a total denial of my fantasies, we lay motionless for a further two minutes. *O damp, tangy, salty, fruity woman! A dish fit for the demigods, and I reduced to salivating inertia.* The culprits, besides the linguistic Berlin Wall that prevented the communication and erotic flirtation that I believe helpful, if not essential, to good sex: ignorance, tension, numbing excitement, guilty fear—any moment now a police raid.

Tat! Tat! Tat! A knock on the door. She answered, man said something, she returned and gesticulated to say: *Time's up!*

Suffice it to say that I came out of this with my cherry and my erection in their original unwrapped condition. My ladies' delight had delighted not; nonetheless it had been a giant leap-in-place for a virgin. Of course I couldn't be sure that God would take as clinical a view of this: so I dashed for the confessional and made a clean breast of what I hadn't done.

How to Succeed

THE CONFESSION HAD taken place on the very evening of the afternoon in which I had failed to unburden myself of my cherry. Heavy-handed Catholicism had seized upon my sinning frame with Inquisitional power; within an hour, I had rushed to Jeppoo Church, a Portuguese style structure coated with dark-green moss and peeling yellow paint. Choosing the oldest and possibly the most deaf priest in the saint-rich church, I had confessed, shyly and mumblingly, my inept sin.

It was 1969, the year Neil Armstrong stepped on the moon for us all, for Indians and Papuans as well as Americans. The year in which Mangalore cinema theatres exhibited *Casino Royale*, *Shatranj*, *The Good, the Bad and the Ugly*, and *Operation Lovebirds: Story of Secret Agents . . . Sexy Agents . . . Super Agents . . . and Kissing Agents*. And at last, in an achievement that to me equalled Neil's, I had suddenly understood. Kneeling at that confessional, I had suddenly understood the mysterious Big Three questions that my Konkani Confessional Guide had put to me during seven years of innocent and puzzled childhood:

> Did you see *halshik* things?
> Did you do *halshik* things?
> Did you think *halshik* things?

What could they possibly mean, I would wonder as a child. If I did *halshik*, or dirty, things such as pick my nose, or *think* about playing in the mud, how could that be sinful, rather than merely unsanitary? Now I not only understood but could answer these questions with an unqualified yes!

Yahoo!

Understand, please: I still feared God and the doom of my immortal soul. So scared was I of what I had done, of that woman's dark, sweaty jungle that had barely touched my own, that I never again bicycled within a mile of that hotel. But, ruled by a force that was more stunningly powerful than a confessional guide, I couldn't stop being obsessed by sex: that three-letter synonym for sin. Days after I made my confession, I returned to my pursuit of carnal literature.

I felt now like a lost, fallen soul, beyond redemption forever. When I tried to pray, a strange voice within me, like a rude telephone operator, interrupted the lines and addressed God directly, though illegally, on my behalf: 'Who are you? You are an imposter! Leave me, you who call yourself God!'

'Even if I make a mistake, *don't* help me,' the voice said to God. 'I don't want your help. If I sink, I sink alone. All these years, when I asked you for your help, *where* were you? Eating biknas?'

It was this sense of being forever damned and beyond redemption that made me act perversely, even angrily. I found for the first time that I could resist the urge to do good, and for no particular reason. Noticing a fallen teaspoon and on the verge of picking it up, I would pass by defeatistically thinking, 'Lost. Anyway my soul is lost. So what does it matter? Never mind.'

What speeded up my Fall from grace, my complete escape from heaven, my descent to earth and earthiness, was life on the home front.

The rented house we had moved into the previous year in a very minuscule act of upward mobility, hid in a section of Jeppoo so dense with coconut, mango and jackfruit trees that it was often hard to tell the time, and a fruit-flavoured late-afternoon, siesta-like mood hung in the air for most of the day.

At the end of a narrow, unpaved lane through which only a man and a bicycle could pass simultaneously, you opened a faded ochre iron gate, and entered a small compound, a sunlit clearing occupied by a lightly mossed eggshell-coloured mud house in dirty brown shorts. You walked over the crunchy mud and pebbles, past exuberant and sometimes riotous red roses, marigolds, bluebells and crotons on either side, and rang the doorbell, which gave a muffled animal cry: Aaark! A minute later, a harried woman in a sari, hurriedly uncombed hair, sweat droplets on her face, would open the thin wooden door and smile weakly, just a shade defeatedly.

'Yes?'

It was my mother, and she would show you—if you looked respectable enough—into the house where I lived in the embers of my teenage years. In the tiny living-room, a disorderly assembly of furniture would greet you: a blue plastic-covered sofa and four wooden chairs on which lay anaemic, crumpled green cushions like vagrants on a park bench; a wooden table with a few pens, a table calendar, books. Occupying a strategic high point on the wall opposite the entrance door was a lemon-coloured picture of a blond boy Jesus, eyeballs recklessly upturned, the head wearing a vaporous, yellow halo; below it a banner of red letters on white demanded: GOD BLESS OUR HOME.

Stepping through the door, you'd find yourself in the primordial darkness of the altar-room-cum-part-time-bedroom, dominated by a Gothic wooden altar. A pint-sized, red-robed statue of a brown-haired Jesus stood glumly under the centre arch, flanked by a maroon St. Anthony and a blue Mary under each side arch, both stonefacedly grim, as if protesting their damp and dingy confinement.

To your left now lay the tiny paternal bedroom, a badly-lighted cave piled with the furniture and material possessions—including some calorific possessions—of the Prabhu family. At the present moment, on a September afternoon in 1969, it also contained one horizontal Mummyji, trying to snatch her pre-lunch maternal nap.

At which point Rukmini, the pigtailed eight-year-old pigmy of a servant girl with coffee-coloured skin and bright eyes always on the point of smiling, burst in and reported thus to Mrs Mummyji: 'A cow has entered the gate!'

Mummyji: 'Drive it. What do you have to tell me for?' She paused, and then followed with: 'I'll drive you too with the cow! Let's see. I'll find out what you're doing!'

Rukmini, like most of our other short-lived servant girls and occasional boys, didn't actually increase domestic productivity or give Mom the eternal rest she so craved (even though she did ultimately drive this particular cow away). But she gave Mom a role to play, a role that was as important as being Mrs Mummyji: she was the director, producer, and star of an endless soap opera called *Me and My Hopeless Servant Girl*, with songs such as "Oh What a Messy Morning", "Poor Directing I", "You Say Potayto, I Say, Peel 'Em", "With a Servant Girl Like You", "Now Sweep that Chicken Shit", and "When Chapattis Are A-frying, I'll Come Yelling Back to You".

Mom's other starring role was in a poultry production (in association with Cock a Doodle Doo, Inc.). Yes: while Pop defended his savings, Mom became Defender of the Hens. At any given time she ruled over a colony of at least three hens and a cock, arguing that it was cheaper to grow (lay?) your own eggs—despite an actual yield of about an egg a day—while we ungrateful egg-eating kids blasted Mom with newly learnt theories of the economies of scale, according to which three hens were a drain on the household economy because of their disproportionate use of management overheads. But our real grouse had to do with the tendency of the hens to sneak into the house at the slightest unguarded moment and shit on chairs, tables, the floor, our shoes—and on occasion, perhaps in an outburst of good manners, in the toilet. This tendency, besides prompting us to rename our house the Brown House, 1600 Hen-sylvania Avenue—was a greater catastrophe than might appear at first sight to the holistic, natural fertilizer lobby. For instead of a Pursuit of Truth, a Quest for Meaning, a Search for Identity—all those building blocks of True Greatness (Note this, ye historians!)—one's major purpose in life became the Avoidance of Shit. The Prabhu children's potential contribution to civilization was lost forever, because they were scarred by the fear of stamping, sitting on, getting one's hands into hen shit.

It was a half hour before lunch, time for Mom to put the final touches on her culinary production: daalicho saar or spiced lentil soup, bazale bangde—lean, young mackerels marinaded in a red chilli and vinegar paste and fried in coconut oil—and guzo, unripe jackfruit cooked dry with coconut and chillies. Waking up, still

under the influence of her recent horizontal state, she waddled into
the poorly lighted, greasy, soot-black hole that was the kitchen, all
the while finger-combing her unruly hair. (When she was bad, she
was bad bad bad: hair falling down over her unhappy, unwashed
face. I confess: I wanted an edited Mom, a Mom without her faults.)
I, let off early from college (in celebration of Saint Stanislaus's
victory in the district kabaddi championships), hungry and
restless, prowled the kitchen sniffing around for food and
conversation.

Which probably wasn't such a smart thing to do. Because,
despite all her apparent harmlessness, her fuzzy air of universal
benevolence, Mom was, or had now revealed herself to be, a verbal
guerilla, a master of the unexpected, unmerited, and
illogical—therefore deadly—squelch. (Her illogic was all the
stronger because it imagined itself Einstein.) Anyone else who
opened his mouth in this house did so with a smell of danger as
unmistakeable as the smell of a red chilli fallen into the coal stove.
Because, though Mom was always trying to snatch a few moments
in which she could be horizontal, always claiming to be in a
semi-permanent state of no-energy equilibrium, this didn't apply
to one extraordinary instrument: her tongue. Her tongue, when not
in hyper-use in managing the servant along always-critical paths,
lay in wait for an opportunity to strike at the higher intellectual
echelons which condescended to her uncompleted high school
education.

Simultaneously setting the table and shooing off an intrusive
housefly, Mom said of Cecilia, a distant cousin, 'Nine years old and
she still wets her bed. Her mamma told me.'

That old chip on my shoulder. I had recently been lapping up
endless psychological wisdom from Mom's *Eve's Weekly* and
Femina, both of which devoted a quarter of their space to the
subject. Was it that women, being the weaker sex (as unenlightened
I picked up from the literature of the time), and naturally weaker
in the head, needed this extra psychological insight? Or was it their
having to put up with their boorish and unliberated men, boozers
full of bad breath and bad vibes and bad karma? In any case, I had
quickly become a better student of *Eve's Weekly*'s lessons than my
mother.

'It's a form of rebellion, I tell you,' I informed her sagely. 'Because of some anger or grievance against the parent. Maybe lack of love or something material.'

'Yes, everything you blame on parents. The children have nothing to do. Only parents are bad, right?'

Frustrated and annoyed now, I said, 'Look, Mom, facts are facts.'

'Facts! Yeah! First you were so *bad*. Now you've become a saint and are telling *me*. When you were causing so much trouble, that was not a fact.'

'No, Mom, that's not the point. This is Psychology! It's been proved!'

'Yeah, every time parents are bad! Children can do anything they like.'

'But Mom, the psychiatrists who say this are themselves parents.'

So it went for four more years: I, the new convert to Knowledge and Enlightenment, trying to guide my parents out of the Dark Ages. In four years, she conceded exactly zero point zero points. Aaarrgghh!!! Why is it that wisdom, on whatever subject, comes to us too late to be of any use?

In the altar room the family would gather nightly for the evening rosary, their voices a curious mixture of sadness and defeat, aggressiveness and questioning, indifference and exhaustion. *Hailmairrry fullo'grapes, the Lawdiss widdee . . . and Blessdis da Frootathywomb Jesus!*

It had been the same tableaux for years, as it had been since the beginning of time.

'Vijay, come quickly, rosary has started!'

Yeah, and what had it done for me? After my parents used up all their energy in the rosary, they had none left for their children, I thought.

Religion—it only makes parents cruel. There's so much misery and punishment and torture in it—hell and crucifixion and guilt and so on—that it squeezes you dry, making it hard to love and laugh and be whole and kind to your fellow-humans afterwards.

Also, it tells you sex is wicked, and if it is, why did God give me a body?

How religion had usurped my life! I wrote down a rough tally of my achievements in the last sixteen years of life:

Trips to the beach—4
Trips to the mountains—3
Picnics to a rural setting—5
Visits to any park—25
Ice Creams (estimated)—45
Rosaries—5,500
Masses—3,700
Hail Holy Queens—5,600
Hours spent on my knees praying—12,500
(Of above total: hours spent bare-kneed
    on abrasive surfaces—6,300)
Hail Marys plus assorted ejaculns—265,000
Hugs (including half-hugs)—7
Full-sized books read—11

What a loss of precious, redblooded Life! Sixteen years of prostration before the Cross, of begging forgiveness, of repenting sins I had never committed, never (given my half-famished body in various boarding-houses) could even have summoned up the energy to commit. I had been the victim of a cosmic ripoff. At age sixteen, I had woken up. And so at age sixteen, my life had begun.

But those who move from fervent, tremulous religious belief to complete non-belief don't usually do so overnight. Instead, they pass through The Six Stages of Unbelief (many more are grounded at the second or third stage), which will be explained at further length in my soon-to-come book, *Pandit Shri Vijay Prabhu's Guide to Life, Financial Security, and Endless Orgasm*:

1. They accept the message and messengers lukewarmly, sullenly, letting their unresolved doubts lie.

2. They accept the message, but scorn the messengers.

3. They accept the message only in its distilled, universal essence.

4. They question the message, ask many, many questions.

5. They discard the message, and look at other messages.

6. They discard the question altogether, and realize it just doesn't matter, that the question was just a linguistic sand trap, just someone's idea of a joke—that life is too short to be spent in pursuing questions that are someone else's invention.

And so I moved, very slowly in the next few years, from Complete Knowledge to Complete Scepticism and gradual Indifference. For how could I, after sixteen years of fervent, soul-twisting, spirit-squeezing belief, reject my whole past life as a mistake, as a waste, as a cosmic practical joke?

'This is a wicked book,' Arun said, pointing to a book prescribed for his English class. 'Father Maximus told us to pray to Jesus before and after reading it.'

'Which book? What? Show, show me!'

Thus did Arun introduce me to the writings of Bertrand Russell. Russell's unassuming paperback *Let the People Think* had apparently been slipped past the watchful attentions of the too-moral majority, by some gentleman with rare moral courage, into the university's degree curriculum. The eye-opener for me was an extraordinary essay called "An Outline of Intellectual Rubbish", which among other things ridiculed the nuns who, to foil a peeping-Tom God who might pierce through concrete walls to gaze at their nakedness, wore raincoats while taking a shower.

Thus did this philosopher laugh the knickers off the prim and proper Mrs Grundy-like religion and social archaism I had been brought up to believe in, and with a sexy and unwavering logic dismantle step-by-step its hopelessly gargantuan edifice. I had lately begun to suspect that the God on whom I had pinned my hopes and my life for the last sixteen years had done only one thing right: person the world with beautiful women; now I discovered that He didn't even exist.

It was a few more months before the book became to me what it became: a gift, to a half-blind man in a garden, of a pair of corrective glasses. My first reaction was that Russell had to be a wicked man; there had to be something wrong with his claim that there was no God. But, by God, what he was saying about the nuns, those holy icons of my childhood, seemed to make a lot of sense, as did much else.

How Russell's plea for the scientific method, for rational thinking, and for scepticism stormed my hitherto religion-nurtured brain! I began to see things with gradual, and soon, astonishing, clarity; it was as if the universe had unlocked to me its secrets. I was slowly able to put distance between myself and religion, and to speed in my imagination to a never-never land where men and women wore no clothes and fed each other grapes, vegetable and animal.

Sex was OK, I knew now. Russell had proved it in his own life! For here was this man, Russell, who, hitting the Sixth Commandment for a sixer, had had four immensely satisfying wives and at least as many immensely satisfying affairs; and the clarity of his brain seemed to have suffered not one jot. Nor did he, though this was hardly his exclusive occupation, seem very tired; he sounded, instead, like the prophet of a New World.

I could now feel the unending supply of fresh air, on a wide-open African plain, that was the freedom given me by the philosophical attitude of scepticism. Building on my own passionate yearning for fairness and generosity as a child, I could arrive at Russell's few—very few—fundamental beliefs: the immorality of war, the possibilities of improving human society, the brotherhood of man, and the necessity of a world state. (In other words: Love Thy Neighbour. Ah, what an illusion all progress is!) I would be an incurable romantic.

This was when I mailed my last few 'holy pictures' to the Pope with the following letter:

Dear Mr Holiness

Please find herein all your holy pictures, returned with thanks.
Sincerely,

Vijay Prabhu.

P.S. They don't work. Also, please strike me off the list of candidates for Bishop of Mangalore. And say hello to Him for me.

Ah, you say. You were cruel, you were shallow. God made you, and you just gave Him the pink slip one fine morning, like a big heartless estate owner lets a lazy coolie go. Rationalism—this isn't about rationalism, it is about faith.

But I did give God and faith one last chance. A few years later, in a moment of combined financial and theistic weakness, I bought a lottery ticket, Rupees Five Lakhs Bumper Deepavali Prize, and prayed to God one last time: If you really are up there, show it to me by giving me this money—of which I'll give you a ten per cent commission—and all will be forgiven. Just cough up, and I'll believe in you once again. Well, God screwed up once again, and fair is fair.

So I take you now to the scene, on the top of Loyola Hill—stones, red mud, blue sky, sugarcane juice-stalls outside the gate—in the granite College Main Building, in the compulsory Religion Class. A year after my first encounter with Russell, Father Liphord is holding forth on the Five Proofs for the Existence of God. Proving to us, raucous lumps of testosterone, how far we had travelled from the time when the very idea that God's existence might need proof would have been heresy.

It hadn't been Father Liphord's year. One of my classmates, Jocelyn Rego, had become a living legend when, informed by Father Liphord of his expulsion from the hostel, he replied simply, 'Bloody Bastard Bugger!' *The three B's, triply fortified from being uttered together! The Big B's all uttered in unholy proximity to a Man of the Cloth, the Personal Representative of the Sacred Heart!* In combination, this had to be the Fat Boy of curse words, enough to blast Father Liphord's holiness out of this sad hillside of Loyola.

And now, this wasn't to be Father Liphord's day.

'Father, I can give you seven proofs for the non-existence of God,' I said suddenly, standing up.

'What . . . ' the colour had drained from his face, as assorted gasps and semi-guffaws died down into an expectant silence.

'Yes. Proof Number One: As Russell writes, "Pathetic and very terrible is the long history of cruelty and torture, of degradation and human sacrifice, endured in the hope of placating the jealous gods." Despite being all-powerful, God encourages cruelty and torture, or at least allows it. So God is either not all-good or not all-powerful. Therefore, he is not God.'

'What rubbish!'

'Proof Number Two: If the world is controlled by God, and God can be moved by prayer, we acquire a share in his omnipotence. So God is only semi-potent. So God is not God.'

'Out!' There was laughter; the class seemed to be unravelling towards chaos.

'Proof Number Three: You can't bear to listen to a proof of God's non-existence. Therefore you fear God may not really exist. Therefore God does not exist.'

'Out of the class! At once!'

The emptiness that came into my life with the crashing-down of the entire, interconnected edifice that had been my belief-system had somehow to be filled. That's the trouble when people build watertight, complete ecosystems around their ideologies. There was a Catholic philosophy for doing everything: they had had, after all, two thousand years and incredible resources, millions of under-employed monks with itchy brains and itchy fingers. I was sure, if one looked hard enough in the Catholic canon, that one could find a teleological treatise on the meaning of shit.

A void opened in my life. I had lost a consuming passion, a faith, a centre. I was a believer, but I had nothing to believe in. Russell had clarified the world for me, perhaps too much so. Every rule that the Great Forbidding Society had laid down for me became automatically, *ipso facto* suspect. My rule-givers had fallen flat on their faces; now I had only a quest, and no rules.

Then, I had come across these brave American books with their evangelical, almost mystical faith in success. Success came from faith in oneself, just as, earlier, salvation had come from faith in God. If only you believed, all things—*all* things—were possible. *What a Christian way to make a killing without the Christian disadvantages of pain, boring prayer, and sexlessness!*

It was inevitable, given all that had gone before, that I soon began to look upon the lack of money as the root of all evil: the roomful of hated boblen, battles for dermatologists' fees, and the dim recognition, becoming increasingly brighter like a petromax lamp in the process of being pumped, that not even girls with glasses would make passes at the ill-coutured, now that drainpipe trousers and fanatically gleaming needle-pointed shoes had begun to raise the sexual temperature of Mangalore. And finally, Pop's contemptuous prediction: 'You will starve.'

So I hatched an elaborate plan: to make my first million by the time I was twenty-three, and ten million by age twenty-eight (so long as one was in the business of raking in millions, there was no sense in being modest). By age thirty I'd become a philanthropist, buy myself a Boeing 727, and retire. In six months I'd have a motorcycle, putting me on an even footing with the town's Casanovas: medical students whose plutocratic families had bought their spoilt brats' way into the local medical college, which had pioneered the open-market auctioning of medical seats in return for large 'donations'—daddy-bought licences to kill, on occasion, for many of these brats would take years to pass their exams. These dark-glassed and cigarette-lipped would-be studs sputtered about Mangalore's roads at high speeds on their noisy mechanical horses, Royal Enfields and Jawas, spewing smelly smoke into my daydreams.* But now, within six months, I'd have the motorbike, *and* some of the best dermatologists.

How? you ask. The game plan, pliss, O Learned One?

First of all, I'd sell fifty anecdotes to *Reader's Digest's* "Life in these United States", which paid a fortune—$200 or twenty times the monthly salary of a local coolie—for each anaemic and silly joke

---

* In Mangalore, the medical students, long before any other group, tended to be very lucky with women—many of whom, in Mangalore's conditions, were sex-starved, but dared not admit it (or oftener, didn't know it themselves, until an ungloved, investigating medical finger—gloves being a luxury in those hard times—stimulated a rather exciting discovery). Maybe, I assumed then, that the medico's special privilege came from the fact that once someone had been known to see a woman's—any woman's—sanctum sanctorum in well-lighted detail there was nothing left to protect him from. No more need for hypocrisy, therefore.

about dogs and grandmothers! These jokes, manufactured by my universally empathetic brain in Kankanady, Mangalore, would be mailed from Beulahville, Ohio, by my American pen pal Bertha.

A blonde girl with shining, silver-rimmed glasses and blurred, pale-pink face and rather touching notions about India ('Gosh, it must be dangerous living there with all those snakes!'), Bertha had been dumped on me by Shekhar, by now already onto *real* women. Her earnest letters blurted out the correct anti-war views appropriate to 1968, while I patiently explained to her (ah, these dim Americans!) the importance of Uncle Sam standing up for world freedom and making keema or mincemeat of atheistic Commies. For, with the help of *Reader's Digest* and *Time*, I had simply transferred my vision of heavenly justice to a temporal one in which America, ruled by the Spirit of John Kennedy, was the sword of universal justice. Justice was still a foundation of my worldview, see?

Also, I sometimes practiced on Bertha (with little success, but just for the practice, folks) my budding arts of literary seduction. I also got from her a lock of her blonde hair, which I carried with me in an envelope wherever I went, like a powerful charm—a piece of an indestructible blonde goddess.

I would write to Bertha in the hip style that I gathered from *Archie* and comics satirizing hippies, and that I imagined American girls dug:

Hello, Old Girl

    Well I'm just seventeen,
And you don't know that I'm IN
Digging girls n' cheese, just way beyond compare
So how could I write to another
Oh, when I strum write and keep long hair
    I don't remember seeing a girl with green eyes, Bertha, except in the movies. So I'm sticking to you, babe. Please be my pen-gal.
    Peace. Love. And may your old man give you lots of bread.
Bye, gotta split to my pad now.
    Yours,

Vijay Prabhu.

Anyway, Cool Bertha of Ohio would dig being my co-conspirator in this scheme to lighten the *Reader's Digest* cats of spare imperialist bread, she contributing the notarized veri-similitude, the claim they had really happened in Beulahville, Ohio (what's truth and time but a consensual illusion anyway, like the 'value' represented by paper currency?). After taking care of Bertha's twenty-five per cent hush money, I'd still have plenty for the bike.

As for the novel bringing me my first million, my immediate inspiration was Saul Bellow's *Herzog*, of which a used, tattered copy somehow became the first piece of Nobel-calibre fiction to fall into my hands. At that time, and for long thereafter, my reading list was mainly determined by the used books blindly purchased for one or two rupees each from assorted dusty pavement-bookstores when I visited Bombay to consult pimple specialists (about twenty Perry Mason novels borrowed from a local lending library were the only exception). Books in English by Indian authors—I didn't consider them worth the horrid paper they were printed on. My generation, having been repeatedly and sadistically exposed in school to bad poetry by Toru Dutt, pompous, lofty bunk by Tagore, and sermons on Truth and goat milk from Gandhi, had no patience with Indian writers of those times, their stinginess, their piety, their pinched view of the world, designed primarily to deny the existence of their peckers. Piety, piety, piety—good Lord, we didn't want it. What good had three thousand years of it done India?

So Liberation came from the West—at the moment, in the form of a crazy novel about a horny nut writing to VIPs as well as other crazies. So the beautiful ravings of a lusty madman (Herzog, Bellow, what was the difference?) could earn a $10,000 prize plus stupendous royalties?

To be a great writer, then, one had to be somewhat bananas; and it certainly helped that I was already halfway there (propelled by slow-poisoning mad-dog juices), as some of the jottings in my notebook seemed to suggest:

- One of the first things I'll do when I reach America will

be to sit all day with a phone in my hand and say 'Hello' and 'Damn you' to hundreds of people.

- What a lot of firewood and coal they must be using to keep hell burning! God could give us some of that, instead of wasting it. So what if hell is a few degrees cooler? God will have made his point.

- If only my ideas were like piss and I could wee-wee them from atop a cloud onto the heads of people—then they'd take notice. They'd have to. On the other hand, since I don't have that many ideas, maybe it would be better if my piss—which I have lots and lots of—were like ideas.

There was only one missing element, as I gathered from *Herzog*, *Peyton Place*, Harold Robbins, John O'Hara, William Goldman, Ian Fleming (and a couple of years later, John Updike's *Couples*, which added fuel to my American Dream by convincing me that in America, a good hard man, if not hard to find, was at least pretty good to find), and the other great Western literature that came my way. To write in a million-copy style, one would have to know lots and lots of women. I mean really, deeply know them. It was simply a matter of artistic commitment, of technical knowledge, just as a doctor studies cadavers, an engineer buildings, an Idahoan spuds. It didn't hurt, of course, that I would enjoy it immensely. So I set myself a sub-goal: I would make love to at least one hundred women, of at least ten different nationalities, and one of them a world-famous beauty, by the time I was thirty. Ever since I had read Russell, four wives seemed to me something of a given, something of a decent man's fair portion—the prerequisite for being taken seriously in intellectual circles. And if four was a given, who would quibble if I asked for a few dozen extra?

Money began to flow in a month later—not from *Reader's Digest*, but from essay competition prizes, and commissions received from selling the most subscriptions to a pseudo-saintly magazine—a most unbecoming occupation for a budding agnostic but it happened to present itself just when I wanted to show myself I could do it, do it, do it, even if it meant using emotional Mafia tactics on my friends (such as: 'Do you think our friendship is not even worth the price of this magazine?' 'If I were to be run over by a bus tomorrow, will you still be glad to have refused me?').

The women—being perhaps the most expensive and angst-inducing members of my list—could wait, I decided, while I first met my minimum needs: in my younger days, these had been chickeys and laddoos, then stamps, masala dosas, and chuda, and now they were cheese, doodh pedas, high-protein mutton cutlets and patties at Woodside Hotel, Vegetable Petrograd at Komal's Cream Parlour, success books, black-and-white anatomical studies, compendia on self-and-penile improvement. I had already begun to live like a successful man. Why bother fighting with Dad for money?

Ah, how sweet success is!

Love in the Region of
Filaria

ONE NIGHT IN September 1968, after a day in which rainwater had washed the sky, the stars, and the trees and rooftops of Mangalore clean, I fell in love for the first time. And I loved her like my mother's most stunning creations, like her vermicelli payasam dense with boiled raisins and cashew nuts, like a month's share of evening sweets (greater love than that hath no Indian).

Ah, love: This is a chapter for the ladies, and for all those who find any fifteen-minute period worthless unless they have dropped a tear during it. I confess: perhaps my clarity of mind was not always with me. Blame it on a diet low in red meat, a life devoid of crucial macho prerequisites of manhood such as rape, pillage, and hunting down with my bare hands: but once upon a time, I was a mushy-head who liked, once in a while, in secret, to cuddle up with a good, romantic book; I was a light-headed teenager whose eyeballs misted at repeated viewings of *The Sound of Music*.

Her name was Deepa and she was a glowing fifteen and her eyes sparkled and her hair had an electricity that, as she sat on the steps of the front porch in the sun languorously combing it, scorched you from a distance of fifty yards.

But before I tell you more, a little background on my romantic education and the events leading to that night.

Having grown up in a corner of the world where for at least the last couple of millennia your parents had told you whom to marry, and where, outside your marital bed, you were supposed to behave as if the opposite sex left you completely cold ('First finish your studies; then about girls and all you think,' Mummy used to say in my *late* teenage years when it was already obvious that I was crazy about girls), Love-and-Romance was not an object that occurred in Nature. So I had formed my first idea of it wholly from the Hindi films that comprised my early celluloid world. The Jesuit priests who had once shepherded us students every month to the local Hindi theatres believed the kiss-proof but idiotically romantic Hindi films to be morally superior to those early-Sixties English films with their steamy kissing and sexual innuendo. Long before I became conscious of the existence of sex, therefore, I believed that men and women behaved inanely with each other, danced around trees, sang enchantingly while they did, and called it love.

And now, in my sixteenth year, I had for two years felt similar urges to dance around trees and be inane with the girls I saw; but these feelings were so cocooned in High Virtue that Mary, Mother of God and Star of the Sea, would have cheered wholeheartedly and given me honorary membership of her exclusive Sodality. Embraces, chaste and symbolic kisses, dreamy looks, walking hand-in-hand, watery smiles—that's as far as those reveries went. Sex with *them*? I'd have been mortified.

That was when Deepa, sister of my childhood classmate Shekhar, came into my life. One day, as I sat in Shekhar's drawing-room on a sofa fashioned out of benches and pillows, amidst green walls hung with old calendars, inhaling the typical smells of the ultra-liberal Brahmin household (tulsi leaves, incense burning in the idol room, rassam for the parents, fish curry and beef pepper fry for the family heir), Shekhar's greasy copy of *The Carpetbaggers* by Harold Robbins clutched in my hand, Deepa walked in daintily, in rubber slippers. In her hands was a stainless steel tumbler full of sugary, pale grey lemon juice for me, squeezed for me probably with her own fingers, for it was a necessary feminine virtue at the time for middle-class girls to 'help in the house', any house.

'You have met my sister Deepa before, haven't you?' said Shekhar, who at around age fifteen-and-a-half, had suddenly transformed himself from a stone-throwing goonda to a near-perfect teenage brown sahib who knew how to use a fork and a knife and formally introduce persons of the opposite sex.

'I think I saw her a long time ago,' I said. 'She looked younger then.'

'That's because she *was* younger then,' laughed Shekhar. 'She was studying at the Coonoor convent. Now on she'll be going to school here itself.'

It was Deepa's last year of high school, and since I passed almost all my leisure time now at Shekhar's house on Filaria Road—so nicknamed because of its density of residents whose legs had tripled in size courtesy a filarial mosquito relation of Charles Atlas. And I was always seeing her walk in and out. She spent so much of her life clad in her school uniform—starched, pleated blue skirt, and puffed white blouse tight enough to hint at breasts that made me secretly, unconsciously quake—that I couldn't daydream of her out of that uniform, the blue skirt that fell to her knees, and sometimes rode slightly above them, revealing thighs the colour of imported, American PL 480 wheat, wrapped in a thin, erotic jacket of baby fat. She had indolent, dreamy, almond-shaped brown eyes, and a distant, shy smile. Her cheeks were mildly chubby and pinchable, dimpling when she smiled; her skin a smooth and lustrous light brown, proof that she bathed using Rexona Soap with Secret Cadyl.

At first, hearing the tinny-tinny-tinny-put-put of my Hercules bicycle sliding down the laterite-littered lane and then the drive from the gate, Deepa would come out, her hair bath-fresh and slightly oiled, knotted in a single, conservative braid with a few stray hairs flirting with her forehead and temples. Letting my face register imperceptibly on hers, she would call out to Shekhar, 'Vijay has come!' and disappear into the house's bowels by the time I had walked up the steps.

But lately, as if acknowledging the approach of adulthood and her drawing-room role, she had begun to smile and say, 'Come in.' Occasionally, she sat around and listened silently to a conversation, smiling only at an especially outrageous joke. Once, when I came in, her hair was still wet from a recent bath and—I don't know why, I had never had this urge before—I was swept by a sudden desire to towel it dry for her. To towel it and towel it and towel it—to protect her from something as common as a common cold—and then maybe to towel those little droplets on her long eyelashes, and the light down in her armpits . . . .

Then came her sixteenth birthday party, for which I was invited.

It was already dark when I arrived, but Shekhar had switched on the outside sixty-watt bulb, which dimly lit the gate, an old black dog, and the granite-and-mud pathway. As my sandalled steps sounded through the curtained door and the half-open windows, the chatter from within the house screeched to a hush, and Shekhar called: 'Who is there?'

Gently prying apart the faded green curtains in answer (while concealed bells tinkled in musical approval) I stuck my neck in like a newborn chicken peeking out at the world, only to see other similarly outstretched necks from the living-room nodding in approval and relaxing: the noseringed, long-skirted forms of Sundari, Sarita, and Uppama, and the better-appointed forms of the two Singing Sisters, all schoolfriends of Deepa.

'Come, Vijay,' Shekhar in his dark jeans and dark blue handloom shirt said amiably, like a young Clint Eastwood in rare good humour. I walked in unsteadily, smiling sheepishly into the haze of appraising and mildly disapproving gazes, sandalled left foot forward, and then the right gently following, rustling my soft cotton psychedelic trousers along with it. Looking for the Girl of the Day, I spied her sitting anonymously in one corner, dressed in a dark green-silk kurta pajama, her long black hair in a single loose braid draped flirtatiously over her left shoulder and breast, smiling shyly like a little girl playing hide-and-seek, caught hiding in a really clever place.

She stretched out her featherlight, cream-soft hand, which I bashfully squeezed, ever so lightly and tenderly, as if a ripe Hyderabad grape were nestling in her palm.

'Happy Birthday,' I croaked weakly, while really hoping I could hold her in my arms and sing, six inches from her face, head slightly angled, 'You are sixteen, I am seventeen . . .' from *The Sound of Music*.

Mechanically, with a shyly whispered, 'Thanks,' she accepted my gift: a candy tin painted with nondescript red flowers—Parry's Assorted Sweets—on whose silvery back Shopkeeper Aboobacker Moosa had crayoned in the price, Rs 3.45, in thick red numerals. (The shame of that shouted-out price, coupled with its fiscal insignificance and my carelessness in leaving it on, would haunt me for months, 'El Cheapo!' reverberating in my brain.) Walking over the tiled ochre floor of the green-painted room, I squeezed myself between well-tailored and laundry-fresh Neelakanta Reddy, the Neighbourhood Medico, and the wall on a comfortable bench over which a flower-printed bedsheet was spread.

'We were waiting for you,' said Shekhar's wickedly bright-eyed mother flashing her let-me-get-it-off-my-chest smile, her I'll-put-it-plainly smile. As if by my twenty-seven-minute delay, I had held up the entire assemblage of worthies.

'I'm so sorry,' I said rather blushingly in my you'll-get-used-to-it smile, my I-hope-you-don't-mind-it-more-than-you-should smile.

The conversation steered away from me now, as the two Singing Sisters, well-padded Bombay-sassy girls with short, insouciant haircuts, launched into their act. Sister Number One, parking her nicely-rounded, tight-skirted fanny on the piano bench with a quiet psshhhh audible only to microbes, banged a few horsey, galloping chords on the old piano, waking up its ancient strings with a jolt. As the horse picked up a steadier canter, the two horsey sisters began with a throat-and-nose-clearing 'Um!' and then,

'MIS-SUS-AP-PUL-BEE!'

I almost jumped off my seat in surprise, as the shrieking sound and a thought hit me: Apple-cheeked! That's what Deepa was. Even though apple-cheeked beauties were rarely to be found in India, outside Kashmir and the northern hilly regions, apple-cheeked she potentially was, with a slight stretch of the imagination, say like seventy per cent.

And I'd tell her she was apple-cheeked, that to me at least she would always be the definition of apple-cheeked. And she'd smile her shy, honorary-apple-cheeked smile. And then I'd remind her of that class essay she'd written, and which I had accidentally snooped on, in which she had described, in her unforgettable prose, the 'swish-swishing' of leaves. And chuckling, I'd swish-swish her waist-length hair for her. And laughingly we'd kick a few swish-swishing leaves into the mouth of a waiting goat with a swish-swishing tail. And then we'd swish-swish into the sunset, laughing and singing, 'MIS-SUS-AP-PUL-BEE!'

But when?

One of these days I'd visit her at a time she was alone in the house. Faithful to her upbringing, she'd ask if I wanted water or lemon juice.

And I'd say, 'You know what I've come here for. It is not lemon juice.'

And she'd say, 'Fine then. I'll get you water.'

And I'd roar in laughter, saying, 'You little apple-cheeked strumpet!' and squeeze her in my arms, and bite into her neck, no, I mean, implant a tender kiss on her rosebud lips . . . .

'I don't know when they'll come, those band-fellows,' someone said, breaking into my reverie with a Kerala English accent and a voice in need of Strepsils.

'They' were the guitarists from the top local rock band, The Mean Schemers. I didn't want them to come, those unctuous, versatile, quick-fingered, talented snakes, tight-panted and smooth-pelvised to perfection, who could rock 'n' roll, twist, sing, strum, and *make* girls fall in love with them. After all they were used to performing on a stage before thousands, belting out wickedly energetic songs such as "Bad Boy" and "Satisfaction", making teenaged girls go weak at the knees, making elderly, frustrated *matrons* go weak in their arthritic knees, making *me* go weak in my knees, booting the syrupy "Edelweiss" and "You are Sixteen" out of my head and into the musical gutter where they belonged. Thirty-year-old oldies, they; they had no right to compete for these sweet sixteens! I would die fighting to defend my lambkins from these ageing wolves in sheep's clothing. They better know that they are old men, old old *old*; they better keep off the sweet-sixteen grass!

Gazing at Deepa in soft focus, from a safe distance, I dreamt that the two of us were dancing alone, alone in the whole wide world, while a soothing "Those Were the Days, My Friend" played on the stereo, misting our eyes so full of calf-like love.

What really happened was that I sat out that evening, past the arrival of the middle-aged rock singers and their posturing, almost until the end—when, egged on by Shekhar's mother, I walked up to Deepa, said gruffly, 'Coming?' and whisked her about for a clubfooted but divine dance, dreaming of a love sealed forever.

Damn! What had happened to my tongue? I had been so ecstatic at that little touch of her delicate hands on mine, the closeness of her perfume; I had been so happy with so little, that my tongue had refused to move—making me fear I had looked like an idiot to her. Besides which, our feet had stumbled into each other's a couple of times.

I was embarrassed and in time, my wordless hopes, the fantasies of towelling dry her hair for her and all that, died down as they usually did. Apple-cheeked beauties, even pseudo-apple-cheeked beauties, were not to be won with Rs 3.45 tins of Parry's Sweets, for godsake; they were won with elephantloads of emeralds and rubies, with chauffeured cars and lassi-bearing servants, and above all with a Poppy who was rolling in dough, who had *karodpati* tattooed all over his Indian whisky belly. And so, was it love, Love, a near-hit, or a near-miss? Or was I just in love with love, needing it like the devil needs a hiding, latching onto the nearest thing with a thatch between its legs instead of a pendulum? In any case, courage: I was soon to shoot out of these maudlin, preadolescent cloth diapers and grasp at something more substantial, something with more red meat in it.

Still, I asked myself: what *was* the missing element in me? What was it that made girls rush after certain *other* guys desperately trying to feed them grapes—making male pursuit unnecessary? Because male pursuit sucked. Because I detested *work*—the labours of love. Because, in any case, it was always the girl who made the decision (Yes, in Mangalore circa 1968, yes indeed). Though girls laughed at my unexpected humour and made perfunctory, unintelligent comments about my 'intelligence', they reserved their powerful crushes for a host of other less-qualified mortals.

Slowly, my fumbling investigations led me to identify the twin villains: my scrawny body and my tongue-tied state. But not to worry: soon, I'd have a body built like a brick outhouse, powerful enough to push and kick-start the Royal Enfield motorcycle that would shortly arrive and help me—barroomm barroomm! phutphutphut!—zoom into the hearts of Mangalore's pretty wenches.

The Road to a
Woman's Heart

IN THE BEGINNING, long before the fitness craze and muscle-bound best seller lists, long before I was bitten by a love bug or even dreamed of joining the motorcycle racket, there was my body, a thing of shreds and patches, a build-it-yourself toy put together by a squint-eyed Creator. It was no more than a vehicle for my journey through this world: it was no flagship, no status symbol, merely something that would do, a no-frills model that would cough its way to the next petrol pump. A genetic disaster it was, admittedly, but what did I care? I lived entirely in my head, and in my soul, praying for my tormentors and dreaming of a heaven in which my wings would pack more raw horsepower than those of others.

There were times that I did care, I must admit, especially whenever I had to take another lesson from the school of hard knocks—that is, knocks on the choicest portions of my anatomy from assailants and microbes of all sizes, sexes, and ages. At these times I consoled myself with the thought that when I became famous, they would apologize; and if they didn't, my bodyguards would persuade them to.

But now at seventeen, once-bitten by love, I had suddenly graduated to a can-do mode, success books and Bertrand Russell having liberated me from my former fatalistic and otherworldly thinking, which had once translated punishment in this life into reward in the hereafter. The specific provocation for the muscular line of self-improvement, though, was a series of well-aimed ads in the English-language periodicals of the country. It was an amazing campaign (unheard of in Spartan, Gandhian India), *for an exercise machine!*—more precisely, a fancy steel spring with blue plastic handles—called Bullworker. The ads ridiculed my skin-and-bones body, recommended I go in for a new model, and 'guaranteed' I could become 'a he-man with rippling biceps, brute strength, and a V-shaped body.'

'Bullworker is for bulls,' said Dad. 'What you need is a student-worker, ha ha.'

'A pimple worker,' said Arun.

'A body transplant,' said Anand, who had just begun to brandish a wit of his own.

That, and the outrageous price Bullworker was levying for a mere spring, ended that episode.

But it was another ad, appropriately placed in numerous American comic books (which exercise an influence on Japanese men and some Indian men well past the alleged age of reason), which actually hit my sore spot with somewhat more effect, eventually doing me in. In this ad a fellow named Charles Atlas promised sand in the eyes for the weakling, but bikini-bursting beauties for the brawny. Love and fortune favoured the ox-strong: that was the ad's fascist philosophy. I was certainly no beach bum—unless 'beach bum' was someone who wanted to leave behind him footprints in the sands of *Time* magazine; but after years of resisting the ad's message, my recent pubic flare-ups had brought home to me, in a moment of epiphany, the realization that bountiful beauties were more fun than books by a wide margin (and my temporary reading preferences only worsened my problem by spreading the raging fire in my loins into every single unoccupied brain cell). The time had come to steer my life in a muscular direction—in the cause of Love. Thus began my bodyssey.

But before catapulting my father into shock by an unprovoked mention of eggs, meat, and milk, I would try a last-ditch cerebral approach from one of those American success books that sell so well in failure-prone India: *Think and Grow Strong* by one Vincent

H. F. Purblind, who had graduated from the selling of insurance to the writing of self-help books. The book counselled auto-suggestion to achieve any desired goal. 'Day by day, in every way, stronger I get, and stronger I stay,' I faithfully murmured to myself three times a day after meals; then smiled into the mirror. The strain of this mantra drained me, and a month later I was weaker than ever. Now I had my cleverest *thought* yet: I fed the book to the neighbour's goat, thinking, 'Confucius say: Better a well-fed goat than an ill-thought man.'

'An egg a day is bound to pay,' boomed my first professional human adviser, a massive discus throwing bruiser called Bholaiya Shetty, nicknamed the Human Rhino (who, it was rumoured, liked reading Nurse Romance fiction in his spare time). Bholaiya offered to shake my hand after giving me this piece of advice but I begged off.

Might not 'an egg a day' seem more persuasive to my cost-conscious father than eggs, meat, and milk combined? But my father's knee-jerk reaction was the blanket economic conservation approach: whatever I asked for, he was against it. 'Eggs in *summer*? You'll get burnt, you egghead!' Pop retorted. He suggested instead that I drink the coolies' tonic: conjee water. Conjee water, the starchy water left over after rice is boiled south Indian style, has a mythic reputation in certain circles for its body-building qualities. But after downing buckets of conjee water for a month, my bloated stomach announced, Gandhi-like, its non-cooperation movement.

Pop suggested I step down from my conjee high and physical low by *working* like a coolie, such as by watering the garden (lifting buckets of water from the well and carrying them to the trees). I returned the suggestion with thanks, explaining that I preferred the advice of specialists.

The next specialist I consulted was my friend Narayan, a confirmed bachelor of science, one of those zealots who walked about with a slide rule behind his ear constantly measuring things and making complex mental calculations. 'Conjee-water? Pooh! It's only starch! Protein *builds* you up. Eggs, though, don't have the right amino acids. You need *meat* to put on meat: half a kilo every day.'

Since my domestic ration of meat was closer to 100 grams a day twice weekly, I raised the desired meat capital by using my current fund of goodwill with a brother and three uncles. Arun gave me a 'loan' of two hundred rupees, but of the uncles only Uncle Gaulbert coughed up a small donation.

Then I discovered that the typical lumpenrestaurant's serving of meat, described in a curry-stained menu as 'one plate mutton', consisted of two two-ounce pieces of bone surrounded by skin, gristle and a few fugitive molecules of meat. This famished duo floated forlornly in a sea of gravy: in Mangalore, spices are cheap, meat is not.

I called the waiter: 'Only this much meat?'

'You want one more plate?' said the lean, scurvy fellow in khaki shorts—a *garçon* with hairy thighs—raising his right eyebrow without dislodging the pencil behind his left ear.

'Only this much meat for *three* rupees?' I shouted back through the restaurant's clatter of aluminium dishes and bellowed orders.

'Three rupees for meat *and* curry, sir.'

'OK, a deal: would you exchange all that curry for another pure, *boneless* piece of meat? I asked for meat, protein.'

'We don't serve "protein", sir.'

'Only bones, I suppose,' I barked.

If I'm destined to lead a dog's life anyway, I might at least do it like an upperclass dog, I thought. So I made a few trips to the somewhat-more-expensive, newly-opened Hotel Woodside, where people ate in a dark hall, darkened almost to quarter-moon dimness in the cursed fashion of the time. An ashtray, a saucer with grains of saunf, might be on the table. Faces were dim, withdrawn. The shadows hid faces, hid grease and dirt, hid guilt. Booze had sharpened the eaters' appetites and dulled their judgement, making their voices hoarse, their laughter appropriately raucous or girlish. Ordering a plate of delicious mutton patties for six rupees, I sneakily devoured half a bottle of tomato ketchup, from a red, plastic bottle shaped like a large tomato. Supplementing my expensive protein with large quantities of free carbohydrate and Vitamin C was my tiny contribution towards reclaiming capitalistic superprofits on behalf of the masses.

Having munched up my month's allowance in patties, I confessed my doggone experiences to my close friend Shekhar.

'You've got it backwards,' he said. 'Exercise first, eat later. Come home—I have a small gym.' Shekhar's 'small gym' consisted of a collection of small red bricks (hijacked from a building site, needless to say) which he used as weights, and a pair of rusty hand-springs. Here I did a three-month penance squatting precariously while balancing bricks in my palms, trying to compress a spring that wouldn't budge, becoming in the end an ache-wracked phantom, wondering: would I vanish before my aches did?

When I took someone else's advice and started taking anabolic steroids to see if that would jump-start my system, my bespectacled friend Vishwanath, nicknamed 'Gandhi' for his devoutly anti-Western opinions and his trademark white homespun trousers and kurta, entered the picture.

'Never take Western drugs,' he said ominously, 'they are very *strong*.' The 'strong' was uttered to mean 'depraved'—an appropriate stance, because Gandhi had made a virtue of *weakness*. Then, appealing to the pervasive tendency to confuse medicine with secret herbs, he suggested instead an ayurvedic tonic-food. His uncle had switched to it directly from mother's milk, and had gone on to win the 'Mr Calcutta' body-building title for the best physique in the East. 'You know, the British weakened us with their drugs, then conquered us,' he added grimly.

'Then the tonic-fed Indians drove them back,' I joked, to his displeasure. Anyway, Mr Calcutta was worth the fourteen-rupee price of the tonic.

A month later, and twenty-eight rupees poorer, I was still Mr Myself.

This was when I ran into the rowdy-maned uncrowned college philosopher Sankara, walking down the college hill, his eyes staring distractedly into the blue yonder: a fellow stoop-shouldered as if borne down by the weight of the meaning of life, and who in his wise thinness so underpopulated his billowing grey pants as to be accused by the college's Marxist fringe of unsocialistically hogging space; yet, one who regarded me as a heart-to-heart friend with similar interests—and chest measurements. Sankara, who was not just a true descendant of Manu, but one who showed it in his face. Sankara, who was in the habit of making obscure pronouncements quickly, in a high-flown British accent, and then smiling a cat-like smile, as if his immortality had been assured by the preceding statement.

Sankara took one look at me and resolved to save me, to return me to myself. He explained, quoting Kant in a way that no one could replicate, how pure reason demanded pure brain; how a huge physique would make me physical, not intellectual; how it would curb my free spirit, steal blood and nourishment that rightfully belonged to my brain; how the greatest intellectuals were thin intellectuals; and so on and on, launching into his Critique of Pure Muscle.

'Listen,' he said, administering the *coup de grâce*, 'all Immanuel Kant did was walk; Bertrand Russell, Einstein, Shaw, Joyce—all were walkers who would never have consented to being photographed with a steel spring, whether it had blue handles or not.'

'Really?'

'Gandhi, Jesus, Rousseau—were they famous because of their muscles?'

'No.'

'Did the Buddha have great biceps?'

'No.'

'And Confucius outstanding pectorals?'

'Never seen a picture of Confucius,' I said.

But he certainly had a point. In human affairs, words were everything. Language was power. (And besides, life was too short.)

I decided I would become such a wizard with words that girls would fall for me like mesmerized cobras before a snake-charmer's flute.

But this worship of words led to an unexpected result: I gained a mentor named Father Maximus, who would shape my fate like few others before or since.

It happened shortly after I laid my hands on a book called *Thirty Days to a Better Vocabulary*. Suddenly the richer with words like 'hiatus', 'factitious', and 'cacophony', with no possible ways to use them in Mangalore, I unloaded my newly learnt vocabulary in a piece about manners:

> Egregiously taking advantage of the hiatus in general ruminations, the factitious codger launched into a cacophony of indiscreet coughs.

'Amazing piece,' said one of the priests when he saw me next. 'You must be a walking dictionary.'

It tickled me no end, the thought that the English language, in the hands of a linguistic Genghis Khan like myself, could sound so sophisticated to the literary numskulls inhabiting the surrounding plots of earth. Fed on A. F. Gardiner, Macaulay, Charles Lamb, and a freak *Shortest Oxford English Dictionary*—missing all pages from 'Pest' to 'Roguish'—my wordly goods exploded across the district, winning essay and debating competitions. The judges felt foolish before the obsolete words I had mined from the *Shortest*—words they were too lazy to look up and discover to be obsolete.

By now I had read Oliver Goldsmith, and tried my hand at a little curmudgeonly writing (in an article for the college magazine about a local city bus ride):

> In the bus whose capacity was officially stated to be thirty-eight, no less than eighty-three people were stuffed. The conductor was cramming more and more people inside like a washerman stuffing his bag with laundry. Anybody who raised his leg could never hope to place it on the ground again.

I had almost forgotten about this so-so piece of gas when . . . .

'*Anybody who raised his leg could never hope to place it on the ground again!*'

It was Father Joseph Maximus, S.J., the chap among the fathers most likely to be seen with a good book, and the unofficial Literary Field Marshal of the college, standing by the melancholy, red-robed Sacred Heart statue in the college veranda. He was speaking in mock-declamatory style, repeating the line from my essay as he doubled over with laughter, holding his stomach.

Father Maximus—his face a rosy, almost rummy mixture of St. Ignatius of Loyola and Timur the Lame, his expression alternating between dramatic hushes, scornful snorts, and volley-like laughs, his eyes looking down from a sloping face that began from a high retreating hairline of a head held too high—was my intellectual mentor. He had told me my writing needed style—which was like informing a Neanderthal that his cave needed ambience.

'Style? What is that, Father?' I had asked.

'Read Lytton Strachey's *Eminent Victorians*. The bible of style.'

Oh boy, I had thought. And of course, daunted by the library's contortionist requirements for aspiring borrowers (choosing a single book from a decrepit catalogue and placing a requisition between 8:45-9:00 a.m. only, and picking it up between 4:45-4:55 p.m. only), I hadn't.

Had he found my style eminently un-Victorian, I wondered now, as he repeated the quote and laughed uncontrollably again, blood rushing to his now-pink, robust face.

Then it dawned on me that Father Maximus had placed another, unexpected feather in my cap: *a sense of humour*!

Thrilled, I played tricks with my creation: Anybody who raised his foot was guaranteed to put it in his mouth! Anybody who raised his foot would sooner or later have to foot the bill! Anybody who raised his foot would one day have to send it to college! The English language! I loved it for being so funny, so malleable, so *mine* . . . .

And yes: after all was said and done, and after all the nationalistic pieties were uttered—*English ruled the land*! And anyone with the balls to pretend he owned it could go far far far.

I went far that year, bringing home to my college gleaming cups for my sage thoughts about politics, morality, world peace, and the need for public toilets.

And I was proud because Father Maximus was proud of me.

After all, Father Maximus was more than my intellectual mentor; he was a friend, father, and lending library—with no tiny, dog-eared slips to fill out, no complex catalogue numbers to jot down. On the creaky wooden floor of his dusty, cobwebbed, crucifix-decorated room, usually containing a lizard or two on the walls in the act of chasing flies, towards an area hidden behind a screen, there arose an intellectual Himalayan range: irregularly piled copies of *The Illustrated Weekly of India, Time, Life, Look, The Sunday Telegraph Magazine* of London. If one was researching an article on the Student Revolt, say—and one was always writing articles on the Student Revolution in those days, whenever one was not writing essays or speeches on "Why Mangalore Should Have Coeducation/A Swimming Pool/A Radio Station/A Five-Star Hotel/A Public Toilet"—the place to go was not the hopelessly bureaucratic and mercilessly censored College Library, run by vaguely disgruntled ex-peons trying to pass off as literary prison guards, but to Father Maximus's room.

'Tell me, these topiwallahs, in thirty years of independence, what have they done!' he might say, with a scornful laugh. And I would listen, hushed.

No wonder many of us intellectually undernourished college boys had the habit of following him, hoping for astonishing insights, spectacular bits of wisdom; for we were green, and he had this manner of delivering the most banal opinions as if they were the last word on the subject.

Categorical, muscularly delivered opinions such as, 'To read *Reader's Digest* is to have a worldview.' For me, a teenage boy from a town that practically did not exist on the world map, he was the supreme arbiter of journalism, style, literature, and universal knowledge. His pomposity and grandiose expression made him a star in my one-watt world, and like a humble disciple I picked up the droppings of his wisdom and glued them into my brain.

A string of essay prizes netted me over two hundred rupees, and another thirty came from the *Deccan Herald* for a piece on nuclear-powered five-star coed colleges with swimming pools, but it was not enough. Bertha had informed me that my jokes for *Reader's Digest* hadn't met with quite the thunderous reception I had expected.

A year after the launching of my Great Plan, I still had no motorcycle, no Boeing 727, but only a debt-to-assets ratio that would have scandalized the World Bank. But maybe I could laugh about it, I thought. After all, my sense of humour had been certified by Father Maximus, no less.

Domestic Bliss

ONE HOT MARCH afternoon in 1970, well after the relentless summer sun had begun to brown the now-parched landscape, I was called into the chambers of Father Ivan the Principal, called Princey for short, though his head was quite long (and his cock probably micro-short). Whenever I had entered through those blue swinging wooden doors, on the rare occasions that I had to, it had always been with a slight tremor: quite unlike Father Maximus, Father Ivan was a cold technocrat whose smile, like his hairy face with its moles and deep eye shadows, had been arrested before reaching its full evolutionary potential. Responsibility, rectorhood, was like an oppressive weight on his limited skull, forcing his brain cells to move out into other parts of the body, puffing up his chest, for example. And he walked as if he expected page boys to follow him and hold up his cloak. Or preferably, the college's lecturers and professors—one of whose request for a leave of absence to be present at his own wedding he had turned down with a scornful: 'This sort of thing should be done during the holidays.'

'You have fifty-seven per cent attendance in Political Science,' Father Princey said bloodlessly, explaining I needed sixty per cent to go on to the Second Year BA.

My head spun as I squeaked: 'But, Father, I have very good attendance in all the other subjects. And I still stand first in my class.' Caught! Betrayed! Impaled on a papal prick, on the papally long sceptre of authority!

'Rules are rules,' said Father Ivan. 'I can't make an exception for you.' I could see in his face now the ill-concealed contempt of the Guaranteed Saved for the Damned Sinner—which I had proved myself to be by daring to cut classes.

'Father, it's only a college exam. Please . . . ' I said, sensing that the time for reasoning was past. *I have brought you gleaming trophies! How can your superior conscience approve fake attendance for athletes, but not for intellectual achievers like debaters and essayists?*

But I said nothing: our culture taught that it never paid to argue with a superior; in Hindi films, the usual way to mollify an enraged superior was to prostrate oneself, kiss feet, kiss the dust. Nothing was as disastrous as argument. I might as well have argued with a roaring lion. Besides, I suspected the complete futility of protest: the Seven Proofs for the Non-existence of God, that was the real reason I was being kept back, I was convinced.

'Don't be a nuisance, Vijay,' Father Ivan said.

And that was that. That afternoon, my name was one of two on the notice board—chosen, from the entire college, to repeat the year.

Thus did this messenger of God hasten my secession from the True Faith (within a matter of days, I had rocketed from the second stage of unbelief to the fifth stage), losing forever the most promising candidate in Indian history for Pope. Or else, why have a reasoning human being as principal if a rule-book suffices? And why should the class's brightest student have to listen to the same warmed over oompah for one more year when all the rest, sitting in class like mentally challenged sheep, moved on in life?

But to my own father, to my flesh and blood and gene-giver, it was simply that I had stained the family honour. Shame. A year in life, never to be got back. A failure, as surely as he'd predicted I would be.

OK. Bursting with the suppressed artistic desires of many years of boarding-house confinement, suddenly tasting the freedom of movement conferred by a bicycle and grown-up trousers, I had seen many movies that year on class time, had conferred with many Hollywood Muses. *The Sound of Music* with its syrupy music, its treacly romance; 007, and the Bond copies: *Assignment in Bangkok, OSS 117, In With Flint*. Some of these at the famous Balaji Cinema where, in an ironic outburst of 3-D realism, a customer absorbed in a sci-fi horror movie about giant rats had

had his shoes nibbled at by the theatre's own rodents. But in my defence I must say I got more from these holistic, celluloid essays on life than from the capsule-formatted lectures, designed for mental defectives. Lectures such as: 'Philosophy of Marxism consists of—write it down!—1) Dialectic materialism 2) class war 3) dictatorship of the proletariat . . . .' So simplistically delivered as to be useless knowledge, as useless as the weight, dimensions, and calorific content of lion shit.

Well, maybe I had courted danger by being seen with the evil guitar, letting my hair grow wild, wearing a psychedelic shirt and micro-checked cotton pants; this garb had once provoked Father Princey's scornful remark: 'Hippie!' But if these were crimes, the punishment was disproportionate: a year of one's life for seeing three showings of *It's a Mad Mad Mad Mad World* and one of *Carry on, Cleo*?

I heard that the Registrar of the University, an exalted functionary decorating a chair in the faraway city of Mysore, could 'condone' my attendance shortage. A 'pilgrimage' there might do the trick, especially if accompanied by the principal's letter of recommendation or a doctor's certificate. But the principal contemptuously shot down my suggestion, and Dad scorned my request for bus fare.

Or, as my childhood guardian Uncle Gaulbert would have said, 'But life is different.'

For six years now, Uncle Gaulbert, an idealist and the most magnanimous of the uncles, having a special affection for his ex-charges and believing in the educating power of money—of its being a kind of Vaseline that eased your passage to adulthood—had been a monthly source of 'pocket money' to me and Arun, starting with fifteen, and later, twenty-five rupees in return for accurate, ledger-style accounts of how the money had been spent: *To Peanuts (March 15): 0.35; To Pencil (broke, March 21) 0.15, To Movie (educational, March 23) 3.00, From Uncle (April 1): 25.* On the first of every month, Gaulbert would deliver unto his salivating nephews the moolah, along with some spirited advice about Life (coconut feni was the choice spirit, with Indian-made foreign whisky running a distant second). In his late teens, looking for a job in Bombay, he had slept in the streets. The same as earning a Ph.D. in Life. There wasn't an authority on Life within a radius of fifty miles who could match him.

Arun and I, our expressions always awed and respectful and our ears cocked, would gobble up every word of Gaulbert's discourses on Life ('Really?' 'Oh!' 'Che Che!') while meditating concurrently on the multi-course lunch that Aunty was serving in the next room. Mutton korma, pan-fried Bombay Duck, fried chillied brinjal, freshly-churned buttermilk. And tiny, debaale plantains that melted in your mouth like sweet, warm butter. I had been compensating for my deprived taste-buds and my ceaseless adolescent need for nutrition, for solid meat, for mutton still exuding the flavours of the slaughterhouse, by paying him frequent mealtime visits—counting on, despite my slight shame, the mandatory Indian tradition of hospitality that would fill my stomach, fill out my muscles—unlike the boblen and sardine curry and parboiled rice that was standard home fare. But our country's renowned hospitality operates along a class band that does not extend beyond about three rungs below one's social class. I recognized my new social leprosy, the still-hot brand of failure on my rump, when my aunt formally suggested I stop my mealtime social calls.

'It's not proper, when you have a home of your own,' she said. In other words: Eat your just desserts, not ours.

Banished from my second home, and already self-banished from God the Father's, and thus realizing I was stuck with my own father, like it or not, I fell into a deeper despondency.

A Fallen Angel! A Repeater! My friends, touched by caste notions of social correctness, scampered off now at my approach. At home, the failure was a signal for Dad to resume a decisive and aggressive ascendancy in the Battle of the Generation Gap, a battle he had unilaterally suspended after my disconcerting barrage of recent essay competition victories.

'I am not the Melvin Prabhu of yesterday!' he shouted, walking in the door a few days later. 'For three years you have gone on with your *evil* behaviour! Now I'll teach you! Belt you mercilessly if you want to stay in the house.'

I responded with Gandhian passivity but that only irritated

him more. And every evening, as his daily dose of country brew soaked in, he grew louder and more sarcastic.

Finally, one night, I hit back: 'I simply missed the *wrong* classes! Had I only missed classes evenly in all eight subjects, I could have missed many more classes and stayed well above sixty per cent. It was just bad strategy: like Napoleon's invasion of Russia!'

'Evil fellow,' said Dad, looking up from his glass of feni, his cranberry eyes gleaming with hate.

'Oh, stop talking now!' Mom said to Dad. 'What's the use of repeating over and over! Pye-dog's curly tail, if you place it in a pipe, it won't ever get straight. Anyhow, it won't hurt *him*. These children—they don't care!' Another of Mom's infuriating tactics: in the guise of asking Dad to stop, she would add crackling new firewood to the fire. And coming from her, my one-time special love and partisan, it was betrayal.

The pattern continued about twice weekly: rosary-drink-fight. The pattern itself was a rosary of its own, I noted (being not yet confident that my writing was deserving of a notebook of its own, I jotted my inspiration in the one-inch margins of a used Chemistry workbook); if you walked the streets of Mangalore at 7:15 p.m., when it was completely dark, you heard the shrill racket of the Daily Rosary emanating from the Christian houses. If you walked past the same houses at 8:15 p.m., you often heard loud abuse. The link, hard liquor intemperately consumed, was a habit made acceptable and fashionable by the foreign powers, to make the swallowing of a harsh foreign religion easier. Pork and moonshine had become the most visible symbols of the culture, resulting often in alcoholics, wasted men, abusive men, unforgiving men, physically devastated men.

I thought of running away from home, smuggling myself via a smuggler's dhow or ancient commercial boat into the Persian Gulf and a high-paying clerical job, emigrating to Canada or the US, where waiters reportedly earned fabulous sums—fabulous at least when I translated them into rupees, not knowing enough to deduct the equally huge dollar costs of living. With the savings from waiting tables on rich Americans, who flung wads of cash about the way the Caliph of Baghdad once scattered jewels, I would soon be independent and write my book in peace.

That was when I wrote my next letter to Jackie.

Widow of my slain childhood hero, canonized now in worshipful articles in *Catholic Digest* and even *Reader's Digest*, she had so many millions, it probably drove her accountants bananas just trying to count them. On my best blue airmail paper, I wrote:

Dear Mrs Kennedy

It's me, your Indian connection, again. And I stand today on the edge of a new frontier: being kicked out of my house.

Please reply. I cannot live with my egregious father any longer. I ask for freedom: to come to the USA and work as dishwasher, waiter, butler, anything. I can even work for you.

It will be easy. Because I already know *everything* about the USA. The 50 states and their capitals, by heart. Have one of your agents test me. I know not only of LSD, but of the psychological and medical aspect. I know of Hughes and Getty and the Rockefellers and Charles Mott and Dewitt Wallace, etc. And music: Herman's Hermits, the Beach Boys, The Monkees, Chet Atkins.

Can you lend me money for the ticket? It's less than the interest your millions earn in one second, probably. One hour, at most. (And a lot less expensive than sable underwear: ha ha, only a joke, I cannot help joking sometimes—like your late and revered husband.)

In return, you can use me as you wish!

But I ask you: ask not what an Indian can do for you; ask what you can do for an Indian who admired your husband and wrote a short novel about him (it got lost). (And of course the other kind of Indians, Red Indians, did a lot for you—they gave you their entire country, right?)

Of course if you don't wish to use me, I will make the best of my three years in the USA. Get experience, return to India, start a small magazine. Counter nefarious communist propaganda. Start a philanthropic business distributing high-protein food and cheap vegetables to the masses, so they can be intelligent and well-fed enough as to resist Communism.

Please reply. You *have* to be kind enough, this time.
Yours faithfully,

Vijay Prabhu.

Naïve, perhaps, but it had become essential to my psychological survival at the time: a naïve belief in the kindness of strangers. And a view of the world in which intelligence was rewarded: sweets to the sweet, prizes to the bright. And Americans—didn't the newspapers and the USIS publications proclaim it?—Americans were the kindheartedest people in the world, in human history, and Jackie was their living saint. Jackie would be grateful for my gift of a few moments of laughter, would reward me with a prize: an airplane ticket. Maybe a first class ticket.

But another unconscious influence on my letter-writing style: the insouciant, cantankerous letters that Herzog, in Bellow's novel, wrote to famous world figures, living and dead. Guffawing at their lunatic wit, I translated insouciance as charm.

Bicycling to the post office on my Atlas bike, I was suddenly charged with hope, the dream of a new life. The evening sky over the Kankanady Maidan where boys played a loud game of rubber ball cricket was a tangerine gold. I proceeded from the post office to Indra Bhawan, a small Udipi restaurant, for a masala dosa and coffee—a toast to my new life. After all, how many of Jackie's correspondents, millions though they be, had written novels about her husband *and* were so knowledgeable about America?

Summoning one of the thin, waif-like waiters who haunted the place and called each other 'Bhattare!' I soon got my dosa, which I attacked in typical south Indian restaurant style with *two* stainless-steel teaspoons. It was crisp and delicious, with just the right mix of brownness, ghee, and urad daal. Sipping my coffee across from a mud-faced coolie and grease-stained autorickshaw drivers (an empty seat was an empty seat; no one dared claim a whole table to himself in this class of restaurant), amidst cries of '*Three more masalas!*' and the immediately answering '*Chhhhh chhhhh chhhhh!*' of batter squealing on hot griddles within, newly-energized I wrote to my pen pal Bertha on my airmail pad, which was balanced on my lap:

Dear Bertha

Congratulations and thanks a million for your marvellous, fantastic, gorgeous, exhilarating (I can say little even with my gargantuan vocabulary) letter. It was so titillating that my face

muscles yearned to denude my teeth (pretty as they are). I had
to hide myself lest I be suspected of psychosis.

Now that we have once again 'met', after our brief
misunderstanding, let us not separate again. I may write
something of a controversial, silly, gauche or offending nature.
But don't jump to conclusions unless you're absolutely
convinced of my psychopathic credentials. The offending word
or phrase may be a malapropism, or the victim of my flagrant
fiddling with the mighty English language, etc. etc.

The greatest reason why I adore you is your magnanimity. (I
hope I'm not making you chase a dictionary. The word means
large-heartedness.) If all people were like you, there would be
no wars, no misery, no poverty. And of course your
above-average intelligence, which makes you my type of gal.
Forgive this adulation, but it's good that I tell you, you won't
have me suppress my feelings, would you? Praised be God that
linked our distant souls.

Oh, by the way, until the *Reader's Digest* loot comes in, could
I ask you for a small loan towards my ticket to America, which
I will repay you when I get there and start working . . . ?

Yours most affectionately,

Vijay Prabhu.

I waited for three suspenseful, gradually gloomier months.
But not one reply from Jackie. And Bertha had angrily jettisoned
me because of my recently-conveyed insinuation that she must be
bathing in champagne financed by my *Reader's Digest* sales (how
could it be that not a single one of over a hundred truly *hilarious*
jokes, only fifty of them about pooches and grandmaws, had made
a hit with those jokers?). I was so dejected and so angry, angry that
all my desire for love and friendship had come to nothing, that one
day, simply picking up a name at random from a list of penfriends
in some magazine—a Margaret from Idaho whose hobbies were
'swimming, dancing, and going to the beach', I wrote:

My not-so-dear Margaret

This is to tell you I hate you. I hate everything about
you—though I don't know you from Adam. I have included my
name and address inside; only because I wouldn't want to write

an anonymous letter. But I don't want you to write to me. I already know you hate me, so why bother to tell me about it? So we close this affair immediately, with your permission.

Let me emphasize again that there's nothing personal about my hate for you, since we don't know each other. So try not to feel too bad about it. I say 'too bad', because you'll certainly feel at least a little bad (however little that be).

You might feel: 'Let's see what happens. I'll write.' Please resist the temptation. Determine to gather some will power at least for once. You might think this is a gimmick or a provocation. I say, 'OK-doke, think what you may; but for Heaven's Sake, don't reply.'

Yours sincerely,

Vijay Prabhu.

And I abandoned hope of overseas solutions. There was no Santa Claus or Santa Clausappa—*never had been, and never would be for poor Third World kids!* I would have to do it myself.

Anyway, I was a changed man now. Father Ivan's injustice had ignited my inner fire, had liberated me from the automatic deference to authority that is an Indian's lot. And whereas Darwin had lost his faith when he lost a young daughter, I had lost mine when I lost three things: my parents (or my trust in them), my cherry (or half of it to be precise), and my faith in clerical authority.

Quoth the raven, Nevermore! Nevermore shall I let pompous, prissy padres hold me in the palms of their hands and squeeze the jism out of me, drop by drop. Nevermore shall I be buggered by the mediocre and the little of heart.

As time went by, I got bolder, more openly irreligious. The domestic fights grew more rancorous. And one day, Daddyji demanded I leave home.

In our diploma-conscious country, that would have meant that my life, for all practical purposes, was *khatham*. That I would have about as much of a future as a pig turd. The thought sent me reeling.

I told my story to one of my adopted fathers, a Jesuit priest who occasionally asked after me and told me comforting stories about America. He gently summoned Pop, Mom and me to a conference on the high Jesuit hill, in the lofty Jesuit tradition. My father had grown up believing even a priest's shadow to be blessed and sacred. When an occasional priest visited the house, Dad behaved like a dog reunited with a long-lost master. And the *Jesuits*: their intelligence and education and *wisdom* had no parallel in his mind. He had no choice but to agree. Besides, he was certain the padre would be scandalized when told of my sinister behaviour, and that he would put his priestly seal on my damnation.

Father Alphonsus D'Cruz: long head, grey hair, idealist, soft. The hectoring tone, when Jesuitic duty absolutely demanded it, was briefly put on, and could never be mistaken for an integral part of his soft, contemplative whole.

At the 'conference', one Sunday in October 1971, we arrived separately, walking up the college hill in the afternoon sun, like combatants ready to get their best from a UN-mandated peace conference. In the St. Stanislaus College parlour, a god-blessed quiet hung in the air. A bible sat on the table, imperialistic *Catholic Digest* and paternalistic *Don Bosco Magazine* on a side table. Our two sides positioned themselves so as to catch the first glance from the arriving Father D'Cruz, hoping thus to gain a subtle psychological advantage.

Father D'Cruz arrived with a rustle of his starched cassock, and motioned us to sit: my parents subdued and awed, I nervous yet mildly gleeful of my secretly anticipated victory, aware as I was that the padre's Western 'enlightenment' would work to my advantage.

Father D'Cruz had droplets of sweat on his forehead and upper lip as he began, 'First, Mr Prabhu, you tell me your story.'

Dad, in a querulous voice, complained of hell in the house, of 'no respect', of misbehaviour, his indignation climaxing with the scornful report: 'He says he is a teenager. We were all teenagers. Does that mean teenagers shouldn't behave?'

'Well, in what way does he misbehave?' asked Father D'Cruz.

'Shouting. Not saying prayers.'

'I told him that saying "Hail Mary" fifty times every day is not necessary,' I interjected. 'Mary *knows* by now, if she has any sense in her, that she is hail and holy and full of grace. She doesn't need poor little me to tell her that. There are much better ways, in deeds, for me to please her.'

Father D'Cruz must have sensed that I was too full of incendiary rebellion to back down.

'Teenage years. They are very difficult times. Hormonal changes, you see. There must be some give and take, Mr Prabhu,' he said.

It was as if someone had let air out of his bicycle tyre. 'But it is his bad behaviour,' he said, finally.

'Hormonal changes,' repeated Father D'Cruz. 'It makes them very emotional. You shouldn't get too upset about it.'

'And what about his guitar?' asked Pop, who commenced a new diatribe against my depradations. 'Wasting his time. In our day, it was different. I had to walk twenty miles to school. Without shoes. On *jully* stones.'

'Ahem,' Father D'Cruz said, gently trying to bring my father back to the subject.

Daddyji was wrong about the guitar, which I had already banished from my life forever, taking the platonic view that music was an enemy of my intellect, of my dreams of achievement. But I let him carry on.

'So can I not have a little peace in the house? And respect? These youngsters, they have no respect. The other day, when I refused him money—he wanted to buy some pimple cream, what pimple-shimple cream, I used *nothing* when *I* was young, I told him. So he said, "Why did you produce me?" I don't think there is a single child in the whole world—not even in America, there they don't care of course, all those hippies and all, immorality they have, still, not even in America—not a single child who has said to his parents, *"Why did you produce me?"'*

'And you, Mrs Prabhu,' said Father D'Cruz. 'Do you have any feelings about this you want to share?' Father D'Cruz playing 'Sensitivity' games, the How-do-you-feel-here-and-now jive he probably learned during his two-year American jaunt.

'What to say, Father, we are so *sad*,' Mom began, her voice and face drooping as she fiddled with the end of her sari. 'Vijay was my favourite boy at one time, until he hurt me. Hurt! What words. Such a loose tongue, just because he had a com*mand* over English, *First First* in English and all that. But never *thought* before he said things. I do so much for him—remind him to study, to pray, to eat. He's so absent-minded, he even forgets to eat sometimes. And I pray for all the children, but him specially. But does he care? Appreciate? No appreciation, that's the trouble.'

'Ahem,' said Father D'Cruz.

'What do they know, how difficult it is to be a mother, all worry worry. Every night, Melvin whispering in my ear, this problem, that problem, no money . . . .'

'Well, that's not the point, Lena,' Dad interrupted in his slightly annoyed, muted but authoritative tone. The talk was drifting into dangerous territory: *his* behaviour. When they got home, he would have to give her a special tongue-lashing, double the daily dose. 'The point is, Vijay's *behaviour*.'

'Ahem,' said Father D'Cruz.

Ultimately, his priestly cloak soothed and calmed my agitated Popkins, who suffered respectfully but uncomprehendingly through Father D'Cruz's new-fangled point of view, his protests growing softer in the presence of the Personal Representative of the Lord. He finally agreed to grant me a cease-fire and temporary tolerance because 'Father D'Cruz had advised me to.' The word of a priest—its holiness, its supreme, God-speaking-through-his-representative sanctity—had finally, and ironically, come to an atheist's rescue.

Kiss Kiss Kill Kill

AT THIS POINT, the plot broadens. What my Dad didn't realize was that he was fighting History—which, thanks to *Time* magazine, had recently descended on sleepy Mangalore, and may or may not have been trying to thrust greatness on some of its residents. Unfolding events and newly-hatched ideas from America, France, and England, notions so newborn their eyes still had gum in them, were packaged and glossed in scintillating, inimitable *Time*-style prose and being sped over land and sea to the dusty, decrepit, disarrayed college library and to the mosquito-ridden District Central Library every week to be lapped up by the likes of lanky, lozenge-sucking Vijay Prabhu, 19.

Mangalore at this time had barely begun to digest the first two decades of the twentieth century, and the sudden avalanche of *Time*-borne ideas resulted in much heartburn and indigestion. Dodging blobs of cow manure on the road, we chewed on Mao Tse Tung's words, 'All reactionaries are paper tigers.' Wriggling into our khadi or handloom skintight pants purchased with parental bread, we meditated on Jerry Rubin's, 'Until you're prepared to kill your parents, you're not really prepared to change the country, because our parents are our first oppressors.' Throwing stones at a ripe mango hanging over the roadside or at a stray dog, we pondered Stokely Carmichael saying, 'Violence is as American as cherry pie.' Cheering at Clint Eastwood plugging holes into the bad guys in *The Good the Bad, and the Ugly*, we unconsciously digested Che Guevara's words, 'The true revolutionary is guided by a great feeling of love.' Joining a lowly crowd excitedly gathering around a bear dance at Dussehra, we thought of Germaine Greer saying, 'Revolution is the festival of the oppressed.'

Still, Pop had only to fight his son Vijay and History. And after all, he had already fought—well, surrendered to—the vicious Japanese.

I, on the other hand—in the next two years—had to fight Daddyji, follow History without quite bumping off my parents, find my revolutionary impulses, find Love (and sex, which I had recently put on the back burner so I could devote all my energy to ambition and Destiny and showing Father Ivan what an ass he had been), discover and fight class consciousness, find success and a vocation, and above all, *show* Dad and, even though I didn't know it then, get back his love. And all of the above I had to do on a measly budget of twenty-five rupees a month—my credit at the time having reached a point of no return.

All in all, a difficult, complex, heady time. India would soon be liberating Bangladesh and winning its first decisive military victory in a few hundred years. History was on the make. Two years encapsulated in the title of a spaghetti James Bond imitation flick that I saw that year, *Kiss Kiss Kill Kill*.

I needed a plan. And briefly, I experienced a resurgence of the success mode, impelled now by Dale Carnegie's *How to Win Friends and Influence People*, a dog-eared copy of which had been given to me by an unpopular uncle who did neither. A resurgence of my too-great faith in books. Starting with the Bible and culminating in *The Kama Sutra*. The story of my life.

I also landed one book that, helping me improve my personality, taught me the correct way to laugh a pleasant, confident laugh that would win friends and attract women: HA ha ha! (stress on the first aaaaa 'ha'). Not 'Ho ho hee' (feminine, erratic brain functioning), 'hoo hoo hoo' (silly), or 'har har har!' (sarcastic, uppity), or 'hee hee hee' (ultra-wimpish), or 'ho ho ho' (Santa Claus, demented).

Among other things, the new and burning desire to rocket out of the lowly prison of my existence made me write brash letters like this one, to a senior executive I met in an ancient First Class carriage, I having won a Railway Essay competition and a free pass. A pinkfaced, beefy Brit who had opted to settle in India after independence, this fiscal heavyweight had paid his homage to

Intellect, Youth, and Virtue by buying me a banana-leaf packet of mutton biryani while the Pandyan Express hurtled senselessly from baking Madurai to steaming Madras.

Dear Mr Higginbottoms

You are the topmost dignitary I have ever met. Period. All my life (my life really began at sixteen, so that makes it the past three years), I have been reading about success in success books; but now I've met a real, *live* success story. To earn 3,000 bucks a month, while most ordinary wretches earn 300, you must have had a lot of persistence, endurance.

I myself, Mr Higginbottoms, have changed drastically because of a personal tragedy, which filled me with determination. I've learnt a lot. I love life now. I could slap somebody—even you—just now on the back (if my arm was long enough), roaring, 'Hello, old boy! How are you!' without fear of being misunderstood. In fact, in my college, I now regularly slap the backs of 1) the tallest 2) the heaviest 3) the cleverest boys.

Mr Higginbottoms, I'm *going* to succeed. Greatness summons me, and many factors are going to help me: my study of *Time* Magazine, for example, and you, for example. It falls to your lot to lend me 400 rupees for the medical costs (pimples, body-building), books, et al, which I really can't spend too much time on, because I am an agent of History. Even if you think I need a psychiatrist (and I need one for some other reasons anyway), I have confidence that you'll take me to him—at *your* expense. For History does not stop for you and me, for our deliberations. Like the Pandyan Express on which I met you, History has places to go.

I humbly suggest, Sir, that if you send me 250 down and 50 a month for three months, you'll be doing a great favour to me and to human progress.

By the way, thanks for the biryani—the most delicious I have ever eaten. Especially, ha ha, because I didn't have to pay for it.

Sincerely,

Vijay Prabhu.

Of course the letter now seems a piece of strained flattery. And maybe indeed, Life, by administering some sharp shocking shocks to the poor and the weak, tells us that we need to flatter the powerful and the rich to survive—and sometimes just to have a slightly better meal than the one that falls on our plantain leaf, or a few laddoos for dessert instead of none. But we from the short dark sullenly rebellious south India, we are never quite able to pull it off. The average south Indian has a hard enough time keeping his lungi up: he's always folding it, tightening it, loosening it. It's a precarious thing, this lungi of his. He has no time to think about flattery, the right dose of it, the right increments of it, the right angle of approach to your big fat overprivileged boob of a victim. *Makkhan* flowed rarely from our mouths, partly because we were far away from Delhi and the paths of invaders, and history and Central Asian horsemen hadn't buggered us as much, and our egos were not that elastic. If at all the south Indian wanted to please or otherwise insinuate himself, he simply smiled slyly, and didn't make his true feelings towards you known—such as, that he'd like to tear you apart limb from limb.

But I saw it then not as flattery, but as rendering due appreciation to the fine qualities and achievements of a fellow human—a trait Dale Carnegie had told me was indispensable for success in life. If Dale Carnegie, millionaire American and super-author thought so, who was I to think otherwise? I worshipped books. Book wisdom was sacred to me.

As it turned out, History decided for the moment to work not through Mr Higginbottoms, but through an act of Father Maximus, thanks to which I kissed fifty girls, most of them young and tender and heartbreakingly beautiful—and many of them commies (which means their kisses had extra soul)—in a space of about sixty minutes. (In fact, the next few things that happened—my meeting with the most important woman in my life, my radicalization, and the freeing of my speech—all interrelated—all had indirectly to do with Father Maximus, as I'll explain.)

For the red-blooded and anti-Communist Father Maximus, in addition to his curious habit of quoting *Reader's Digest* and Gibbon (more often the former), also did some kind deeds for the young and horny men of Mangalore, on the side.

'Babes,' said Dilip.

'*Chedwan*,' said Subir, using the Konkani word for girls.

'Dames,' said Arun, smacking his lips.

And we loved Father Maximus, because he'd arranged for us goofy, girl-starved boys to meet St. Agnes College counterparts in specially-organized seminars on momentous current issues.

Which made Father Maximus, in our adoring eyes, the personification of Knowledge, Enlightenment, and Modern Man. Absolutely alone among the male priesthood of the time did he regard post-pubescent girls not as vials of temptation but as containers of much that was admirable and—yes, laughable. But only mildly laughable, like those quaint jokes about feminine tongues and female vanity that peppered the local Lions Club circuit and milked girlish giggles from plump, curd-devouring Kanchipuram-saried matrons; for this was a man who believed in the civilizing effect of an encounter with the female of the species.

What happened at these meetings, during supposedly serious discussions on grave matters such as Indian poverty, politics, violence? Tall, slim girls in saris and fair or dark-and-powdered faces. Girls named Darlene and Irene and Shanti and Geeta and Juliet and Gisella and Minnie and Frannie, their mascaraed eyes as bright and hungry as a newborn babe's, their hair plaited and pinned or cascading down in rich, gleaming black waves. A few fashionable girls in bobcut hair and bouncy, frilly dresses, with the sexy upperclass habit of always seeming to be amused in company. *Christian* love. Honest. For it was love in the course of which not a single sperm got within writhing distance of a single ovum.

Things happened at these meetings of the Christian Students Union: bullshit art; political education; growing confidence; personality; balls. And, at a 'leadership camp' in Tirunelveli, near Madras, a historical materialist named Maya Monis Bhat—'Bhat' being the ancestral Hindu family name she had recently reclaimed.

In the long, bare-walled dining-room, about a hundred campers were wolfing down beef curry at lunch time (whenever they were not serving sardine or mackerel curry, Christian hostels always served beef or bullock meat, for the simple reason that beef in cow-worshipping India was five times as cheap as mutton).

'Please pass the un-pickled pepper, er, what's your name?' I said, trying to disguise the thumping of my heart.

'Comrade Maya Bhat.' Her smile was weak, as she regarded me, as if in a trance. Her most stunning features were her translucently light-brown eyes, dark bushy eyebrows, pouting brown lips, rough, bewitching, just-bathed hair, lightly coconut-oiled. A nose slightly longer than warranted proclaimed intelligence, and a solitary red pimple hinted at a repressed sexuality and enhanced the charm of the rest of her.

So she was completely in it: Marxism. Admittedly, in those days, it was hard to be a young and patriotic Indian, a person of heart *and* brains, and not to believe that only guillotine-style politics could purge India of its Number One curse: corrupt politicians. Who, as our Lincolnian joke went, were true democrats: they buy-ed the People, off-ed the People, and far-ted at the People.

'But you mean *Chairman* Mao, don't you, not *Comrade* Mao?'

She laughed and said, 'Not Ma-o, Ma-ya.'

I had seen Maya around town for a long time, as one sees girls in a small town, or hears about them, long before one meets them. My parents had often talked of her parents, 'Church' Mary and B. A. Peter, so-called because she spent most of her day in church and he loudly proclaimed himself to be the first BA-degree-holder in his parish. But the Maya I was seeing now, after an interval of about six months, was a plainer, more intense Maya. I could see the tell-tale signs of the converted: no make-up, no hairdos or hairclips, no jewellery except for a few red plastic bangles, hair falling down below her shoulders like a village girl's, a simple white handwoven cotton sari over simple white cotton blouse—the radical's rejection of bourgeois conceptions of beauty. All of which made her more startlingly beautiful. Despite her radicalism, she still walked with a demure, bowed head, holding her sari tight about her, as if in church, because that was the way saints and good Mangalorean girls walked (which also, incidentally, helped them avoid making eye contact with boys).

'You're a Marxist, I suppose?' I said—respectfully, having a sudden inferiority complex about my unconverted state. I hadn't completely squashed my *own* recent capitalist dreams. Perhaps I would become a capitalist pinko—using my initial pile of ill-gotten loot to publicize socialism, distributing copies of *How to Win Friends and Influence People*, and *I'm OK—You're OK* to greedy capitalists, and by this means achieving their conversion to decency and universal love. Solving most world problems at one stroke.

'I don't believe in labels. It is action that matters.'

'Well, you're a beautiful Marxist,' I persisted.

'"Beauty" is a bourgeois concept.'

'Oh come on,' my friend Jawahar, who was sitting next to me, joined in. 'Your dad has a car. How could you call yourself a Marxist? You'd have to bomb your own house first.'

'What about you?' I said to Jawahar, the son of a farmer who didn't have a car, true, but who owned dozens of bullocks and acres of paddy fields. 'You shouldn't be here eating beef curry from a clean plate, you should be eating rice and sambar on the floor.'

Maya laughed and said, 'Just because my Daddy has a car means I'm rich or what? But we don't think of ourselves as rich people. Daddy always makes us pick up our plates after meals and place them in the sink. And he never sends me to class excursions. He says, "All that is for big people. We are poor people."'

'Look at your skin,' said Jawahar, persistent, as I frantically gestured to him to quiet down. 'Smooth. Upperclass. You can't be one of us.'

'Rubbish! All nonsense!' said Maya, pugnacious. 'I'm Kannada medium, and Kannada-medium people cannot be upperclass. Tall-like-a-ladder Beatrice—she's upperclass. She has short hair like Bombayites. And she speaks English so nicely. Uses the fork and knife. She's always making fun of me for mispronouncing English words.'

She was right about Beatrice, who lived in a grand house on top of a hill facing the sea, a house named 'Chateau de Woof Woof' by her father, after their favourite, deceased Alsatian, Woof Woof. Beatrice was part of Mangalore's Westernized upperclass or bobcut set—'big people' as my father simply and realistically described them. Blueblooded, they described themselves, and claimed, by their choice of surnames, to be connected to high Portuguese officials such as Albuquerque, the Portuguese governor most responsible for Portuguese colonization in India. So Westernized and unlike the rest of us, that their blueblooded and booze-reddened eyes became moist when their imported stereos played "House of the Rising Sun" or "This Land Is Your Land"—as if they were a bunch of old Dixie Republicans listening to the Stars and the Stripes Forever. Beatrice had made history when her estate-owning father, to bolster her election effort for student council president, had had leaflets proclaiming 'VOTE FOR BEATRICE' and 'BEATRICE FOR PROGRICE' air-dropped on the convent, on the heads of the amazed nuns who lip-synched quick prayers to Mother Mary while bits of orange paper littered the convent grounds and tiled roofs.

Rich people. Despite all one's egalitarianism, one had to admit one was weaker in their presence. That despite all the kill-the-filthy-plutocrats rhetoric, one was always easier on them, letting their bullshit pass unchallenged, letting it pass with pilot lights and a motorcade. As if in knowing them there was security, for that possible future time of starvation, every poor Indian's terror, when one might need them.

In any case, Maya was unattainable for now, because she had been swept off her delicate feet by her recent conversion, and by her Converter-in-Chief, the city-bred Mr Marxism Personified, a Marxbearded twenty-two-year-old named Harry Moopanar ('Moops to you'), who moved about with the burden of being the only Indian to fully understand Marx.

'Consider the poor homeless woman whose only garment in the world is a single sari,' Moops had mournfully told a crowd of students, in a speech trying to impress on them the pathetic poverty of the Indian masses—which was on exhibition right outside our windows. 'The only thing she can do is wash half her sari, wait for it to dry, carefully unfold the other half while rewrapping the first, then wash the second half and wait for it to dry.'

There had been not a dry female eye in the house. By the time the speech ended, most of the women had fallen for him. In the discreet catfight that followed, Maya had won—for the moment.

For a while, I contrived to bump into her, to walk with her on the streets, pushing my bicycle alongside her as she walked home from college. But in a small town, all movements are reported instantly to headquarters. Merely being seen walking with a girl—it's more likely to get noticed than making love to a sheep in a market-square in Stockholm. The next day, Maya's father sent a note through his servant to my father.

'Tell your son not to move about with my daughter,' Bhat the Elder wrote cryptically and imperially, signing the note with a curt, 'P. Bhat, B.A.'

It was a sticky summer day in 1972, and assorted young men and women in jeans and flowered satin skirts could be seen draped casually over assorted chairs and tables in the lounge of the newly whitened Jesuit Seminary at Old Goa, in a setting of coconut palms and white churches. Here, at the CSU's National Leadership Camp, I asked a bearded, self-described Christian Marxist named Thomas Madtha, a rebel priest who had acquired fame in radical circles:

'Christian Marxist? But Marxists don't believe in God!'

'I say, look here. Who did Christ love: the poor or the rich?'

'The poor.'

'So if he returned to earth today: would he be on the side of the capitalists or of poor workers?'

I saw his point. I imagined Christ waving a red flag outside Beatrice's bungalow, demanding better pay for the servants, food for the beggars. And I was ashamed of my slumbering, anti-Communist past. Father Maximus's intellectual mentorship had been lazy, lackadaisical, woolly-headed, and without balls. I was angry with my former Educator-in-Chief, and felt ashamed of my abasement before Western penfriends, Jackie Kennedy, success books. My dreams of millions in my bank account and bouncy women in my bed seemed soiled and silly and selfish, compared to the travails of the masses. What a fool I had been, to trust *anyone* over thirty . . . .

Ah, what a heady and absurd time it was: rebelling against industrialization and material prosperity and monotheistic absolutism in a country that had yet to achieve any of the above.

Just then, Julia and Lucette, two Goan girls with hot pink lipstick and loose and svelte bodies and lavender, sheer nylon dresses swayed past us.

'Hellou, Vijay! Hellou, Thomas! Hee hee hee hee!'

That voice, a smoky velvet! My prick zoomed up in instantaneous, respectful salute, while revolutionary politics vanished instantly from my brain.

But why should a Marxist consciousness puritanically banish sex? Marxism gave power to the People—and who the fuck were the ruling classes to tell the People not to fuck? At least we could start by taking back our sexual capital . . . .

Behind me, underneath a mango tree, a Marxist was engaged in kissing a female member of the non-working classes. A man of action, I thought enviously. Exploiting the exploiters; engaging in oral indoctrination.

A classless society! What a beautiful dream! For in such a society, these male, mostly poor, and completely sex-starved armchair communists could easily climb into the pants of the sexiest Indian girls—girls who were mostly upperclass. Whose thighs now closed instinctively the moment they sniffed the approach of an economically disadvantaged male.

But in the meanwhile, Marxtalk worked. Because it was so dashing, *so* daring, *so* idealistic—and to many a female audience, *so* sexy. Leading me to suspect: *All philosophy proceeds from the search for an innovative way of landing a fuck.*

The top camp attractions were the fifteen or so Goan girls, some with part-Portuguese blood, who were to our hometown girls what the flappers were to Iowan cowgirls: Viola, who strummed a guitar as she sang hippy songs such as "Blowing in the Wind" and "This Land Is Your Land" (we had long ago, without knowing it, been co-opted in the American Dream); Lucette, who said, 'I know you are a witty chap, Vijay, but . . . .' Just to have these fresh flowers of womanhood within sniffing distance, charming and ladylike as they had been taught to be, and to be dimly—very dimly—conscious that naked beneath their unhampering chiffon or rayon dresses (decorated with bows and ribbons and such delicious frills) was the real thing, unabridged, uncompromised, absolutely begging to be taken. *It was the cause, my soul, of my taking up the Cause.* The Cause was the capitalistic dragon that we would slay with verbal swords, allowing us to claim these fair-skinned aristocratic Goan beauties whose breasts suggested the creamiest, Milkmaid brand milk.

On the day the camp ended, taxis, cars, mini-buses were crowding into the front driveway to pick up the departing campers. And then, it hit me. People were *kissing* each other goodbye! Kisses were flying in every corner! Sticky kisses of repressed sexuality, rising from the meeting of lips and cheeks like bubbles, seemed to float up and stick to the ceiling. I saw about me a sea of lips: lipsticked lips and nude, wet lips, cinnamon lips and caramel lips, sensuous lips and thin lips. Within thirty seconds, I had overruled my small-town fuddy-duddy's culture shock and done yeoman credit to the astonishing adaptability of the human species. Camouflaging my intentions in exceedingly fervent goodbyes (we had just met, for godsake!) I kissed, thanks to Father Maximus's good offices and for the first time in my life, females other than my mother and Aunt Meera: fifty of them in the space of an hour!

It wasn't what you think. Dear reader, I confess: I tongue-kissed my first girl when I was a shamefully old twenty-two! No *Sphuritakam* or throbbing kiss was exchanged here, nor an *Avapiditakam* or greatly pressed kiss, nor a *Jivhayuddham* or fight of the tongue, nor even a *Pratibodhikam* or kiss that awakens. All I did to these fifty was kiss them on their cheeks, occasionally with my eyes closed, sometimes with my lips slightly apart, sometimes lightly grasping one shoulder, for balance, on one occasion, with one foot raised slightly off the ground, for style and effect and soul. Behold me standing thus, in my green trousers and orange shirt and light moustache and dense hair-mop, thin as a reed, kissing with feeling, with heart, with the pent-up emotion of a millennium, of a suppressed race that had almost forgotten its *Kama Sutra*. Not something that would impress your average thirteen-year-old Swede or American (not a few of whom, I am told, can lay proud claim to fatherhood or motherhood), admittedly. Just a little innocent merriment, some camaraderie with the comrades. But, given what the priests had *done* to us, that just to be in the same room as a beautiful girl was equivalent to a Grade III American orgasm (or a Grade IV French orgasm)—*this* was extraordinary.

Meanwhile, I had noticed that the flashy boys, the leaders, and those with the gift of the gab, got the girls.

This was when I began to develop my speech, and my reputation for truly free speech, for *risqué* humour. Yes, the next thing that happened, in those busy busy years, was the liberation of my stiff, prayer-sprained tongue.

I remembered the day two years before when a classmate named Devdas had asked me, innocently, 'Do you smoke?' I, seventeen at the time, had sagely replied, referring to my never-repeated one-day aberration of ten cigarettes on my tenth birthday, 'I gave up smoking seven years ago. And I have also given up drinking!' By drinking, I meant the little swigs my soro-swilling uncles would allow me from their own glasses when they were high, and I a sallivating, tiny eight-year-old pup.

Devdas's face lit up with joy and relish and gratitude, as at someone who had set himself up for the squelching opportunity of the millennium.

'*Have you also given up fucking*?!' he retorted, to the roars of the surrounding benches, putting a complete stop to the boring political science lecture, the lecturer smiling timidly in the direction of the merriment.

Prissily disapproving of the joke as improper and vulgar, I quoted him, on the spot, *Reader's Digest* as an example of wholesome, truly funny humour (which set him and the onlookers, Bhola and Raghu and Madhusudan and Subramanya, all worldly members of the college hockey team, laughing even harder). The best wit and the high-minded did not need to stoop to *vulgarity*, I said.

But soon, aided by a classroom study of an unexpurgated *Hamlet* dense with 'country matters', I had begun to respect vulgarity as a kind of high masculine wit, a vital bond with our animal natures, with wholeness, with the earth. Besides being a device for disinherited Danish princes to let off steam, it was also a democratic function, by which the proles breathe free and assert their rightful ownership of language, and of their own vocal apparatus. Through it, commoners may thumb their noses at the lexicographic lords of language, who have so unnaturally fragmented the language into vulgar and nonvulgar. The Queen of England doesn't need to say 'Fuck you!' because she can, without saying the words.

I had by then earned a reputation for creating my *own*,

off-the-cuff, off-colour jokes. The one most often quoted: 'There are two types of sins: sins of commission, and sins of emission.'

Meanwhile the reputation of my earthy classmate, Devdas, had soared into quite another league. Having surged on to the next year with the rest while I repeated the class so that Father Ivan could compliment himself on his unbending uprightness, this Devdas, whom I'd two years ago lamely reprimanded for a vulgar joke, had become a student political star.

Tall, dark, and in a rugged south Indian way handsome. A winning smile lit up his face when he saw you approach, a smile that burned the distance between you both, vaporizing everything, human or animal, in between.

He was no weaver of words, no churner of philosophical systems. It was just that at every moment he feltright and didright and smiledright—and, filling the surroundings with his lanky, villager-rude, but forceful presence, made the bullshit flee. His moralistic, philosophical, and political vocabulary consisted of only a few words: right, wrong, will, yes, no, justice. Especially justice.

Unlike him, *I*, now a rebel with a million causes, having exchanged my hirsute and gangling form for a more elegant haircut and leader-like clothes, was a spinner of words: 'Down with politricks! The university belongs to the students! Power to the little people!' There was something about that time, that age, that gave me an air of pure moral righteousness, which in turn let loose words. Words that made the faithful and the fence-sitters laugh, and the faithless rail and rant. I used and misused words, tricked them and tweaked them, while twitting the adults who, in my opinion, had made a mess of the world with their hypocrisy.

It was good theatre and Devdas enjoyed it enough so that when I, a political tyro now and forever, decided to run for Vice President of the Student Union just when he was running for President, he accepted me as his running mate.

It was a smashing victory for us, and a first taste of political power for one who, in a more primitive, natural, un-Platonic world, might never have sniffed even the crumbs of power. There was only one moment during all this when I doubted my sway over the People, and that was when I stood up to make an election speech, and waved to the crowd like Churchill or Nkrumah or General MacArthur, and was nearly drowned by a wave of laughter in return.

But no matter. I had a title, and I was a leader. What I really needed right now to round up my worldview and my new leaderly status, I told myself, was a chick of my own. I would build my world around a woman and love, soaring, grand, head-spinning love.

Love's Labours Lost

THIRTY-FIVE MILES north of Bangalore, like a pair of mammoth blue boils, the hill-station of Nandi Hills rises from the surrounding flat plateau of rice fields and eucalyptus plantations and shrubbery, two towering black rocks joined together and crowned at their apex by the fuzz of a botanical garden, a few box-like guest houses, and a stately British-era bungalow in which Queen Elizabeth II once took a snooze and dreamt of her recently-liquidated empire. And it was at Nandi Hills—named after a sacred bull—that I became bullish again about love. For it was here that I met my first true love—that is, my first violently passionate *and* two-sided love.

And thanks again to Father Maximus, who selected me one day to attend a leadership camp there; though I was already under suspicion for leftist, ungodly leanings, he was short of representatives who wouldn't make an ass of their college.

'But no armchair radicalism, ah, got it?' Father Maximus warned.

'I promise to uphold the Stars and the Stripes,' I replied smiling, making a dig at his having just returned from America with an accent.

A week later, as my bus droned up the steep and winding road, a sign chalk-scrawled on a large black rock commanded, 'Stop for Jesus. Jesus Saves.' But the bus drove on, unloading me at an ancient, white, red-tiled traveller's bungalow on the western slope.

At 4,500 feet above sea level the next morning, under a bright blue sky, the camp's first session progresses lazily on the lawn. The forty campers, lanky, wispy youths from sixteen to twenty years in age, boys and girls in equal numbers, some in slippered feet, nestle lightly on yellow cane chairs; the smell of grass and of bathed woman is carried by the wind (because there are only two bathrooms, someone or the other is always having a bath, thus ensuring an uninterrupted supply of the erotic combination of soap and woman). The mid-morning sunlight has the whiteness of skimmed milk, but the cool breeze renders it gentle. Minds are churning overtime: what shall I say next to the girl next to me? What shall I say when the boy next to me says what he says? Lozenges are chewed, hair brushed back, imaginary flies shooed; the place crackles with an erotic tension.

Then I am struck by the sight of Anita, a soft and buxom beauty in jeans and a light pink crêpe shirt sitting next to me. And I am emboldened by the surprising fact that the previous night the campers have elected me Camp Leader.

I was simply too weak to resist using my power—my power as Leader to smile and flirt without reason—with Anita. About eighteen, she had a soft quietness in her expression, made more sensual by a mole on her left cheek and a dimple when she smiled her full-lipped smile, so rich with promises. Promises reinforced by her almond-shaped, hazel eyes, and long, lush black hair falling down to her waist in curly tresses.

'Get me my Programme File from the Director, please?'

'Yes, Camp Leader,' she replied, looking at me briefly, then looking away.

Above all, it was her eyes, and the way she rolled them away from you and then back to you, that set me on fire. Eyes, the most erotic organs on a woman, particularly the Indian woman, who simmers with unexpressed, suppressed, inexpressible longings. I confess: Except when angry, depressed, exhausted, or in love with Anita, I've always fallen passionately—even if momentarily—in love with any reasonably good-looking woman whose eyes I've looked into—provided she has allowed me one pure moment's admittance.

Her huge, ripe breasts, I didn't dare look at directly. It would have been too forward. Too forward for the fuddy-duddy I then was. Knowing dimly that they were there, enough pleasure for a thousand moons, I was happy merely to see her breathing. I concentrated instead on her face, her delicate nose which had a nosering with a ruby the colour of her lips. I fantasized licking her nose all around that nosering, licking it endlessly, with nothing but a smile to keep me going.

I would seize the day. I appointed Anita Official Time-Keeper to the Camp. Her job was to circle the camp five minutes before the commencement of each activity, ringing a warning bell. My true love, ringing a bell: my heart pealed for joy!

It was the Pavlov effect inverted: whenever my mouth watered for her, I asked her to ring a bell.

In the late afternoon, the group of young and faltering Catholics decided to pay their respects to Lord Shiva: to celebrate our liberation from foreign monotheism, our respect for our Hindu heritage.

The Shiva temple sat on the edge of a cliff which dropped off one thousand feet, and the path to it was strewn with variously sized rocks. I held her hand as if I felt she needed help balancing—when really it was I who did.

Disguises, disguises. I still didn't dare.

Inside the temple, I borrowed a few of the jasmine flowers she was holding in her hand, meaning to offer them to the idol.

And when the time came to shower the idol, I showered the flowers onto her. She gasped with surprise, laughed, blushed. Without knowing it, I was practising the highest form of Hinduism, in which God is within all of us, rather than in a piece of stone.

Had I exceeded my Leaderly writ?

It didn't seem so because when we walked back to the bungalow she chose to walk with me again, holding my hand delicately as if enfolding it with silk. My ungovernable fingers slyly wriggled in hers. We exchanged electricity.

Helping her down the last rock, I knelt down in mock chivalry and kissed her hand. (In my imagination, it was a kiss so grand that it would have made a watching Romeo want to go into retirement.)

In all this time, and through all this unprecedented impulsiveness of mine, not once did we speak the overt language of love.

But when the camp ended, and Anita returned to her vice-proof, male-hating convent hostel in Bangalore, and I returned to warm, humid, and lustreless Mangalore, after a night-bus journey overpopulated by thoughts of her, I sent her a letter through a friend's sister, her schoolmate. My letter was tentative, my lack of confidence masquerading under a certain British reserve:

Dear Anita

I think I'm in love with you. But if you don't think you are, would you mind at least being my pen-friend?

Vijay.

Her reply was a complete shock, a Gangotri of suppressed emotion. *I love you with all my heart.* And on and on, for three pages, which I read three hundred times.

I danced in the streets of my imagination, distributing sweets to passers-by. I climbed mountains for perfect strangers and won wars for armies of liberation.

There followed more letters dense with love-song prose, written on sensuously smooth bourgeois stationery imprinted with her kisses. Letters that completely belied the mildness and shyness of her behaviour in person, letters that showed her to be a complex, wilful, sophisticated, self-assured young woman. I read them over and over, carried them with me to class in the pages of my textbooks, re-read them secretly during lectures, inhaled their perfume when no one was looking. Yippee! I had said goodbye forever to my kashtigaar world of boblen curry and rice!

Sometimes she made my small-town, unsophisticated soul anxious. *Vijay, I want you to be rough with me—to hurt me sometimes. To be gentle at times. Lord, Vijay, I love you.* Or a letter that ended with a drawing of a flower, and the words 'Flower Power'.

What next? How? When? The 200-mile bus ride to meet her, the hotel costs for my stay there—it seemed as daunting to me as seeking India must have been to Columbus; and Columbus had a ship, but I hadn't even bus fare. And when I reached, what should I do: just ring the bell?

Pessimism began to infect the true course of love; my letters were soon arguing the fated impracticality of our connection. Her father was a famous surgeon, mine a retired nobody; would it work, or was it the desire of the moth for the star?

You love me for my qualities, for my external achievements. But do you love the real *me?* I wrote.

My Sweet Lord: I do, I do, silly. Your achievements are *the real you, see?* she wrote back.

I'm controlling myself, because I think in terms of future generations (ours, too), not just of one year of blissful love, I wrote. *It doesn't matter that we don't see each other soon. I have to study for the exams and establish a future for us.*

Her replies, sometimes tender, sometimes passionate, now betrayed exasperation (*You are a bloody bastard at times,* she wrote once, quickly following with, *Here, I'll give you a flying kiss to make up*). Starting at an exhilarating four letters a week, the volume of her passion had begun to dwindle, until one day two months after that ecstatic first letter, this letter arrived:

Dear Vijay

Anita asked me to write to you. She can't write anymore. Her father found out about you, and he was very angry, and he made her promise never to write to you again. Can you please return her letters?

Anita's friend, Annie

It couldn't be. It was only a minor hitch in an eternal love. It could be fixed, with my persuasive prose, so successful at winning college essay competitions. I wrote back gently, lovingly. Again. And again. It took me some while to reach the level of half-confirmed suspicion that I floated in for the next three years: that the letter from 'Annie' had been the anaesthetic to dull a premeditated rupture, because forty thousand fathers could not have dammed up Anita's quantity of love or her individualism.

My golden hour, the one time in my life that I connected simply and beautifully with a woman . . . and it had burst so soon? Insecurity—*my father's revenge!*—had gotten to me. I felt like a king who, having won a battle, had chased away the prize.

Then I heard, from a male spy of mine with connections to inside sources, that someone else, a young member of the business gentry from Bangalore—*with his own car*—had taken my place. I didn't realize that this made my chances of retaking my kingdom far less than his chances of keeping it; possession and physical presence are, after all, nine-tenths of the love game (and the other one-tenth is having a car). For two years, off and on, I wrote letters, rational, legally perfect letters explaining why it was best that we continue our eternally destined love, why she'd like me *now*, why she'd *adore* the new, improved me. And for three years, despite the thunderous silence from her side, no one could replace her in my imagination.

In the meantime her letters—which I furtively carried in my trunk through twenty world cities in the next ten years—were the physical proof that the whole thing had really happened, that it was an inextinguishable part of me. Evidence to my fantastically insecure self that I was loveable, that one human being out of four billion had, at one moment in the history of the world, loved me.

Though I carried my hope with me for the next few years, like a dirty secret, like a packet of pornographic snapshots carried in a secret compartment of my suitcase for emergency rescues, I often suffered *Hamlet*-like bouts of self-accusation at first. And I vowed that I would never allow myself to be rejected again, never be replaced by someone with transportation, never lack for means of transportation. I would arm myself—with success!

Something else happened now to steel my resolve to save myself. The town's student community, in the grip of foreign slogans such as 'student power' and of the idea of clean, idealistic youth against a dirty, corrupt society, was now re-enacting tiny bits and pieces of the Paris Left Bank show of 1968, and the Kent State University Opera of 1970. For this once-uneventful little town most remarkable for the thump-drag of its filarial population hobbling to church, deadly stuff.

It had begun one March day when a short-tempered classmate named Venugopal insulted some son of a bigshot bus owner, who had the cops arrest him and beat him up. We had gone to present our complaint to the Deputy Commissioner, Devdas and I, but had waited all afternoon outside his office to no avail, lazily studying the list of important local historical dates, the Mchistory of Mangalore, inscribed on mahogany panels and hung on the walls:

1523—Portuguese capture Mangalore. Franciscan friars begin preaching.

1581—Portuguese burn Ullal for tribute.

1695—Arabs burn Mangalore in retaliation against Portuguese restrictions on trade.

When we went back and reported our frustration to the student body, it was as if we had thrown a lighted match on a kerosene-soaked hut. Before we knew it, five hundred students, led by apoplectic Devdas and myself, were marching towards the D.C.'s office in a procession, shouting warlike slogans, demanding apologies and suspensions. The cops blocked our way with their Black Marias. Outraged, a few students flung *jully* stones and rocks at the surprised cops.

'Stop, hey stop, wait now, are you mad or something?' Devdas and I, not expecting this turn of events, shouted at the stone-throwers.

But the crowd had swelled with infiltrators, non-student goondas, who set fire to a shop and a parked car, knocked out streetlights, caused the cops to panic. Three cops fired, two missed, and there was a blood-curdling scream. The crowd was aghast, and there was a stampede, as I noticed a large stain of blood spreading over the white trousers of a classmate. The bullet that didn't miss had lodged in his thigh. We carried him on our shoulders to the Winelock Hospital next door, the one that had treated my dog bite.

There, we heard later, a nurse goofed, and the student's gangrenous leg had to be amputated. The student's parents came to school and wept, saying to everyone, '*Why* did you do this? Why *us*? What have we done to deserve this punishment?'

It was a kick in the seat of my tight pants. I simply hadn't expected this. But it had been naïve of me not to understand the unpredictability of street politics by which a parade to redress a small injustice results in an injustice of far greater magnitude. The world is a mess, baby, and damned if I am going to set it right by leading stone-throwing students to silly bureaucratic offices. Besides, there but for the cops' bad aim go I.

Not that it fundamentally changed my worldview; it just subdued my brash exterior and changed some of my priorities. Two months from my final BA examination, I dusted up my ill-used textbooks and gobbled up print as if for the Last Judgement.

When newspapers flashed my second rank in the university's exam, Dad was briefly disoriented, while I was pleased as a Brahmin priest after a wedding meal in a rich home. I'd get a national scholarship now and be able to study indefinitely at government expense!

Then came the shock: that the scholarship money only arrived at the year's end, because of the typically perverse inefficiency of the government. In the meantime, fees and living expenses would have to be paid by oneself.

'I can't afford to lend you money,' Dad said. 'I have other children. I had to walk to school barefoot! With my books on my head! Sometimes, I was thrown out of class by the priests because my fees hadn't been paid on time.'

So it meant that grinning half-wits among my classmates would shortly join the university pursuing master's degrees while I pounded Bombay pavements looking for *any* job armed with a University of Mysore bachelor's degree not fit to wipe a crow's behind. I thought bitterly: Greatness, Destiny, here I come.

'You said you would earn millions. Now let's see how you feed yourself,' said Pop, letting fly his parting shot.

III

KAMA

Delicious Undertakings

Dancing School

THE FIRST THING I remember about my arrival one month later in Bombay, the place where I was to have launched my search for journalistic success and fame, was that I *had* to go.

So I went. Extricating myself from the chutnified humanity that was the Dadar Railway Station, I took a cab past smoky slums and endless grey buildings to my Uncle Paulu's apartment building, hoping to board with him by exciting his compassionate filial feeling until I found a job. Uncle Paulu was my only relative in Bombay other than the once wild and now greying and cranky Aunt Meera, who had been jilted by boyfriends and abused by employers and now lived a lonely life; and Aunt Meera had become an unforgiving enemy on account of a tactless letter of mine suggesting that, since she didn't have any children of her own, she could lend me some of her spare Hong Kong savings to help launch my writing career.

Knocking at Paulu's door, I realized he wasn't at home. The saintly Paulu attended the Sacrifice of the Mass every morning. My needs at the moment were somewhat less than spiritual. Desperately needing to use the bathroom, I knocked on his neighbour's door, revealing my relationship to his good neighbour Paulu and my too-human need. Somehow, in my uncle's ancient book of etiquette, this was a monumental *faux pas*, a colossal transgression by which I had browned his family coat of arms and soiled his escutcheon. His eternal shame was that I had introduced myself to *his* neighbour with a shit-in. And that thenceforth, that neighbour's opinion of him would eternally be framed in *doodoo*.

'What will they think?' Uncle Paulu said, running his fingers through his distraught, receding hair, twitching his right eye, which was larger than his left. 'How can I face them?'

'Uncle Everest sends you his regards,' I said, trying to change the subject.

Paulu was Mummy's brother—and my Mom's family I had always thought of as sentimental, soft, hospitable, old world: 'Have you eaten, baa? Why don't you have some rest, dear, a nap, you must be so *tired*?' But Bombay, with its plutocentric values, its pavement sleepers, its brutal mafia, did something to people, something violent and un-Indian. Bombay—it is a city without a soul, where pure capitalism, self-interest, and hedonism vie unmolested. A creative centre, yet also an oasis for cockroaches, rats, and rat-like men. No other city, I would soon feel, made you feel so wretched, so subhuman, for being without money—pots of it.

'Have you tried the YMCA? It's a formative place—for the character,' said Uncle Paulu.

While most Mangaloreans in Mangalore were known for their warm hospitality to outsiders, most Mangaloreans outside Mangalore, I found, would introduce themselves to non-Mangaloreans (and sometimes to their own) as 'Bombayites' or as coming 'from Madras' or Delhi or 'Cawnpore' or 'Cal' or 'New Yawk'. A few lied outright and passed themselves off as Goans, as if there was some shame attached to being Mangalorean (the source of which I would discover later), just as for Uncle Paulu there had been shame at being associated with that primary human element called shit. In any case, there was little help coming from them.

Thus did I, a twenty-year-old recent BA lugging around a plastic folder bulging with certificates, dispossessed by my father, spend the next four months twice reaching the verge of starvation, often fearful for my next meal, ready almost to beg or sell my soul.

But then no place, not even Bombay, can be so poor or depraved that a young man of twenty, his balls brimming over with zealous and earnest sperm, his files bulging with glowing credentials, can go hungry for long. Yes, my balls had brought me my credentials, and my credentials had given me my balls. I, Vijay Prabhu, University Rank-holder, had come to collect my dues.

I asked for help, and got it. To survive, I touched one bishop (I recommend it highly as an experience that will have you laughing all the way out of the Bishop's House), a padre acquaintance and two old school pals including Jawahar.

When I met Jawahar in front of the Sanman Restaurant near Churchgate Station on a November evening, I had landed my first job.

Jawahar, who in Mangalore had been a long-headed, big-eyed, prematurely mature-looking sort three days behind his razor, now walked with a spring in his step, had the well-starched look of a salesman with an exclusive foreign firm.

'Congratulations!' he said, in a suave accent that was new as his hair-over-the-ears haircut.

We walked into the air-conditioned restaurant, an icebox to the steambath of the outdoors, and chose a congested formica-partitioned booth with sofa-like seats. The menu, which proclaimed 'South Indian Vegetarian', had an entire section devoted to idlis: Idli Sandwich, Idli Fry, Idli Butter, Idli Dahi.

'I'm going to have Idli Butter *and* Idli Dahi,' I said. 'Packing ladies' underwear is an exhausting job.'

Indeed, I had been appointed as an 'export assistant' in a firm that exported Kolhapuri chappals (lovingly made from the best Indian water-buffaloes by village maidens with little bells around their ankles) to Europe, and economy ladies' underwear to Africa. Our boss, Mr Bopatlal Patel, a young rake who had just returned from the US with an MBA and new-fangled ideas, believed that his new assistants, two of them young engineers frustrated by the employment market into accepting just any job they could get, should accumulate hands-on experience in every aspect of the work. We would laugh giddily when no one was looking, trying to picture the surprised African derrières that had tried to fit into *desi* undies, the sound of hundreds of simultaneous rips roaring back across the Indian Ocean, mixed with the laughter of delighted husbands.

'Nice tie,' I said to Jawahar, just as he dipped a piece of crisp vada into his stainless steel container of sambar. 'I mean, imperialist noose.'

Jawahar, a radical in college, laughed graciously. No one talked about Marxism in Bombay; life was so harsh, it caught you so by the balls, that it took real nerve to talk about things like revolution.

'People always treat you better,' he explained pragmatically, after a pause. 'Whenever I walk out of a station wearing a tie, man, the ticket collector never checks my ticket. Saves time.' He grinned.

'Who else treats you better? Now why are you grinning? Come on, come on.'

'I have a girlfriend,' he confessed sheepishly. The word 'girlfriend' gave me such a start, bringing back for a moment the vacancy I had been feeling within me at the memory of Anita, that I spilled dark brown filter coffee on the blue-formica tabletop.

But that wasn't all, Jawahar continued, spilling meatier details, and climaxing with a piece of friendly advice: 'Take my word for it, Vijay. If you kiss a girl down there, she'll do *any*thing for you.'

Helped by his detailed descriptions, my Paleolithic, breast-cupping imagination was slowly able to picture this astonishing scene. Kissing a girl down there! And I believed him, believed even his statement that the lucky object of his oral attentions was a young Gujarati from the higher commercial and banking classes, an early taster (as well as *hors d'oeuvre*) of the sexual revolution that was soon to come; for Jawahar's face had that sassy grin that was tailor-made to get him into compromising, down-there situations. I imagined him, naked except for his inseparable necktie, sipping at a woman's source, her cup of joy (and his too, shortly) running over.

But this imagined scene of X-rated frenzy only increased my frustration. Because, for God's sake (to point out a tiny logical flaw), how does one *get* to the point where one is able to kiss a girl down there? Especially when one is hardly *ever* introduced to any girl, or can barely stammer out a few words even if one were?

So I briefly consoled myself with a piece of my unenlightened thinking at that time: *that this was a part of the politics of sex; that Jawahar wouldn't really have wanted to do it*—except that it was the unappetizing price he was willing to pay to get to know her cervix . . . . 'Well, Bon Appetit, Monsieur Jawahar!' I thought to myself, remembering that the practice was reportedly a French speciality and main course. 'But I think I'll wait for the next course.'

Still, I envied Jawahar as he spoke of his babe's complete subjugation to his will. And I couldn't doubt his tale, for his bovine eyes were two pools of light radiating self-confidence, telling all that he had ridden the filly of success. That he was on his way, baby, filled to the foaming brim with *joie*. How had the ordinary mortal Jawahar, once known far and wide as the villager whose mouth was a fly trap, and later as the guy who acted the Guardian Angel or the deaf spinster in the Konkani dramatic performances at school, transformed himself so?

Well, the answer must lie in his background, his childhood. He had all the luck, the lucky *sala*. He was the only son of a large, male-worshipping rural family consisting, besides his mother, *of seven others of the cleaved sex*: nice, soft, and pneumatic *sisters* who bumped into him all day around the house in *déshabillé*, who brought armloads of girlfriends into the house, who worshipped him and probably washed his cock for him, who cooked for him, who sang over his lingam as they bathed it in ghee: 'Vive la différence!' What could he understand of my neurotic and loveless childhood, the forbidding and castrating women who ruled it at its most tender and impressionable moments, and now frightened my fragile little id from suavely claiming what I badly, truly wanted?

'When do you get the time for all this?' I asked, enviously.

'Oh, in the afternoons. I pretend I'm going on sales calls. Or prospecting calls, ha ha. I visit her, see pictures, go to the Asiatic Library. Read Camus, Sartre. Just read *The Stranger* the other day, in two afternoons. Bastards, what do they care?'

No kidding! Not just Kama, but the seminal Camus Sutra! The one must-read book for admission into Indian intellectual circles! Frenching it on company time! And Frenching his wench too!

What Jawahar had always had: security. Security was a terrific thing, because it bred more security. When you have always been sure that you will eat—however simply—because you have *land*, and the fertile, monsoon-drenched West Coast land could be trusted to look after you almost without prompting, year after year, as it had from time immemorial . . . then, life and job searches (and finally, down-there searches) are more of a game, played for the cool pleasure of it, and not a grim, shit-in-your-pants matter of life and death. So you nonchalantly took big chances, and often, you won.

Yes, Jawahar, with his happy childhood, was a blissful nipple sucker at the Megatit of Life. But someday, despite my pain, I'd overtake him on the highway of life and pleasure, I promised myself. I would reach the hundred-woman goal before him, *and* show my Dad.

Still, lacking Jawahar's sassy grin or his susurrating trail of sisters, I had to pick up a quick trick or two that might make women have hot pants for me. I would learn to dance! To beat my feet, to boogie woogie woogie, to trip the light fantastic! The idea was suggested by tiny ads in the astoundingly free *Free Press Journal*, for dancing schools with names that might have done honour to a university—Empire Academy of Ballroom Dancing, National Institute for Dancing Studies.

The next evening, after work, I walked towards the National Institute, past the roaring and honking mess of internal combustion engines entangled around Flora Fountain, past the Fort pavements where periodicals and self-improvement books and smuggled perfumes and pornographic playing cards lay spread out side by side, to a mildewed building in a *gali* or lane behind Dadabhoy Naoroji Road, and walked up a dingy flight of stairs to a couple of sleazy rooms.

'My name Kokila. How much time you want dance?' said a wafer-thin, long-plaited shyly smiling young woman before I could say a thing. She had on a blue-patterned cotton sari and cheap plastic bangles.

'Twenty-seven-and-a-half minutes.'

'No, fifteen minutes, thirty minutes, only is possible. Twenty-seven-and-a-haap minutes not allowed.'

I paid her fifteen rupees for fifteen minutes, and she hand-steered me into a garish plywood cubicle, the screens rising from ankle to head level, so the supervisor could watch out for any hanky-panky.

I was soon teasing Kokila, demanding that she pay *me* for teaching *her* dancing. Actually, I had no reason to complain: even without the occasional straying I permitted my hands, it was bliss just to feel the lightness of her angelic form, her soft skin—real human skin on skin!—her delicate childlike palms and ninety-pound frame, to make that prehistoric connection with her animal warmth through her thin sari, to hear the click of her sandals next to mine. And I thought: who cares if she doesn't understand my jokes? This *is* good enough. God, this *is* good enough.

Besides dance, the other thing I could do was prepare for the Moment of Truth. Gain Knowledge. So that when Ms Opportunity knocked, I could suavely lead her, over a trail of rose petals, to my satin-sheeted bed.

In Bombay, you could pick up knowledge from the pavement. Literally so. In addition to Western classics such as *Everything You Always Wanted to Know About Sex But Were Afraid to Ask* and *Sex from A to Z*—which I learnt by heart—and the rather academic and coy Burton translation of *The Kama Sutra*, various enterprising Indian authors had begun to package condensed sexual knowledge from various ancient Indian classics in tiny, badly-printed books wrapped in yellow cellophane, from under which a half-dressed, whorish cover girl usually winked at you.

So I learned, from one pundit distilling the essences of *The Kama Sutra* and *The Koka Shastra* into forty pages about 'sexual congress', that there were four types of men—hare, deer, bull, and horse—classified according to the size of their organs. (Does the size of the organ have any relationship to the sweetness of the music? I wondered.) Women were divided into the Padmini ('like lotus'), the Chitrini ('like picture'), the Sankhini ('low and passionate type'—the author seemed to use the words synonymously), and the Hastini ('fatty and wicked'). In other words, if you wanted someone who truly liked to fuck, with unfaked orgasms that would bring down the house, check out the fatties. The book went on:

> Pandit Koka says that if a man having a male organ of 12 inches meet a women of 6 inches deep vagina, it will be a troublesome job to cover the whole organ inside during conjugation and thus no enjoy can be had.

You got it, old boy, you sly old wizard of mechanical engineering, I thought. But this knowledge didn't solve my problem, because not many of two million nubile Bombayites remained after I disqualified the women the pundit warned me to beware of:

1) Very much laughing girl.
2) Very fat or very thin.

3) Aged lady over 45.
4) More talkative and proudy.
5) Stylish and roaming girl.
6) Pros or women in nurses.
7) With a tight vagina.
8) Having a broad forehead.

Pity. Because it was a well-known part of the local pseudo-scientific folklore that sex cleared up pimples, which are in fact the body's protest at insufficient sex or none.

But life has its consolation prizes; a week later, just as I was toying with another offer of a low-paid trainee journalist position, an entrance exam paid off: I was selected as an officer in the Bank of Golconda in the north Indian city of Lucknow—a job with security, status, salaams! See you later, fellow-agitators! Even the normally-unflappable ex-boxer T. S. Rex, my Malyali Anglo-Indian landlord who had spent the past few months loftily retailing me job-hunting advice and conducting mock job interviews during which he pulled my small-town legs, gave me respectful, slightly-sheepish grins for the next few days.

I celebrated by splurging on an unheard-of *six* bottles of Golden Eagle beer (our family bought two bottles a year, during Christmas, dispensing it like precious nectar), storing them in Rex's crowded refrigerator, and treating myself to a judicious half bottle every night, sipping with every drop the dream of my liberation, thinking my nightmare was over.

But it wasn't because of money *per se*, or the scary experience of having been penniless and hungry, that I was temporarily betraying my literary dreams, I told myself. It was love, and the lesson I learned—money, and only money, bought you love (Anita's, my Dad's—it was all for sale in this soiled world). Each time I moved up one rung on the 'success' ladder, I would write a letter to Anita: '*Now* you must want me. *Now* you will be proud of me.' And every time her silence dejected me, I hoped in some secret portion of me that the next rung I climbed would really satisfy her. So (like a monkey) for the next few years did I climb ladders for Anita and her sex.

City of Nawabs

LUCKNOW! ANCIENT CITY, home of the fabled Nawabs of Oudh! Microcosm of medieval, Muslim India—only sharper and tangier and earthier, like a Rubens nude just back from a mud-wrestling contest! A city whose domed architecture, seen from the heavens, seems appealingly mammary.

The story that sums up Lucknow for me tells of a certain nawab, whose satyriasis was remarkable even in a dynasty famous for its devotion to sensual pleasures: he had bare-breasted women line up on both sides of the staircases and corridors as he walked about his palace, so he could have tits in both hands as he passed by—so that no moment of his life would be titless . . . .

And I can tell from experience that underneath the misleadingly calm purdahs of Lucknow life crouched an unruly sensuality that could disturb any peace. It was impossible to live in Lucknow and keep one's innocence for long.

About seven years late in all my major stages except toilet training, I was about to embark on a marriage of my own. Because, for the first time in my life, I had a room all to myself: a paying-guest room in a small lane behind Hazratganj, the street where convent schoolgirls and hawkers strutted their stuff as rickshaw-wallahs pedalled and cursed, and oversexed males walked funnily by, desperately trying to camouflage their permanent erections.

It was lucky my landlady, a devout Goan widow who packed the embers of her life with novenas, didn't suspect the manner in which her room would be immortalized. For in her bare, cold, stonewalled room, in which a dim night lamp reminded the insomniac of Jesus, the Sacred Heart, did I embark on my first historic night with myself.

I remembered the moment four years before when my classmate Zuzey had introduced me to the amazing concept, though not the specifics, of masturbation. With the authoritative air of a native-born Kinsey, he had informed me that I was absurdly behind the times.

'Ninety-nine per cent of all college boys are shakers!' he had declared passionately, as we stood on the tarmac before the grey St. Stanislaus Chapel. (The American Shakers would have been surprised to learn that 'shakers' was the Indian word for masturbators, and that their Indian cousins directed their lives according to the theme song: Shake shake shake, shake your tootie!)

And as he told me this, his face glowed warmly in the evening sun that shone behind me over the Arabian Sea, and began to resemble, in my imagination, the tip of the masturbated penis he was describing—especially since he had a habit of shaking his head as he talked.

'Never done shaking? Never rubbed your plantain, I say?' Zuzey continued, in utter amazement.

But I was in no mood to accept sexual condescension from someone whose head looked like, let's face it, a prick. I was about to retort that God had created my plantain on the sixth day for nobler purposes than shaking, when I remembered that I had already disproved God's existence in class, and could no more use Him as a crutch.

But Zuzey, after all, was a loser. He had joined the B.Sc. merely because, as he inaccurately described it, eyes popping like a frog's: 'In B.Sc. textbooks, they have pictures of completely *nakkid* men and women.' What a tremendous misallocation of resources, what a mind-bending excuse for the misdirection of an entire academic career, this salacious hope of seeing a few broads bereft of their panties . . . but what a quintessential Indian story! (Just multiply this story by the total population of Indian males, about 350 million, and you get the broad picture.) To consider that instead he could have for a mere fifteen rupees picked up the most detailed, imported nudie pictures from the sidewalk smuggled-goods hawkers of Bombay! Pictures so detailed you could count the pubic hairs on them! And so, despite Zuzey, I had always rejected the idea of self-satisfaction as second best, as an admission of defeat; besides which, any waste of erotic energy—of the sublime erotic fluid, the Ether of Life, the Oil of Man, the Creative Juice of the Universe—was, in a cosmic sense, a sin, so long as legions of the Unsatisfied remained. For these sublime reasons, I agreed with the anonymous Indian pundit that 'hand practice' was to be avoided.

Now, after six years of ducking the issue and aiming for something higher, my disillusioned fingers are finally embarked on the unsteady course of self-love. Up, down. Repeat.

Fifty repeats later, nothing has happened; at least, nothing has been contributed by my digital friction, since I have already been excited to the limit by the very idea, even before I had touched anything. How come, I think, are there no 'How To' books on the subject—some shelf-help on the art of sexual self-help? Why shouldn't it be the assigned duty of some accomplished Village Elder to instruct newcomers in this handy, much-heralded, universal art?

Five thousand repeats and one hour later my hand has almost retired from the fray and I have trouble keeping my enthusiasm, not to speak of the object of all this fuss, up. I realize that what goes up must sooner or later, when overcome by the forces of boredom and inanity, come down. And if so, why not sooner rather than later? I'll give my partner a rest. He is just beginning to understand that life can be more than just a matter of being shoved around, of passing water, of pointless and painful expansions and contractions; but he needs more time to get accustomed to the idea of pure pleasure.

A few nights later. My landlady, Mrs Fernandes, has put on her only nightdress, a pink cotton number of the laundry-bag school, and locked her door behind her for the night, leaving me alone in my section. My pajamas are off within seconds, my legs up in the air, and a silent whoop escapes my lips. At the end of an evening's progressively more skilful assaults on Mount Everest, my entire face and scalp tightens, a shudder travels down my spine, down my surprised buttocks, up my electrified balls and stem and—spurt! spurt! spurt!—there is a sticky shower of gratitude, and I can almost swear that my balls are leaping about the scrotal sac like happy puppies. It's been a power shoot of intense joy; I laugh now at discovering, as I turn on the lights, that I've inadvertently hit the Sacred Heart. Henceforth, I shall have to arrange for a containment vessel, lest the old lady get wind of my manly pollutants; so I hit upon old newspapers—old copies of the pompous *National Times*—which somehow enhance the joy of my wickedness and the wickedness of my joy.

I imagine myself going to confession the coming (ha ha) Saturday.

'Bless me, Father, for I have sinned.'

'Yeah?'

'Yeah. One successful jack-off since my last confession.'

'Yeah?

'Yeah. I fucked an old newspaper—but a prominent one.'

'Yeah?' in an obviously excited voice.

'Yeah. I was revenging myself on journalism—for rejecting me.'

'Yeah?' The padre is breathing heavily now.

'Yeah, I yellowed journalism. With the whipped cream of the cream, 250 grams, pasteurized by white-hot thoughts.'

'Jesus Christ!' says the padre. 'Stand back, son! No, oh, oh oh, Aiieeeooo!'

'I forgive you, Father.'

'Thanks, son. Mine was half a kilo. Six weeks from my last emission, you see. I myself prefer the *Sunday Herald*, it's more absorbent.'

'Peace be with you, Father.'

But it was no more possible for me to make a confession. I had long since ceased being a Catholic. Besides, I was now a true Shaker.

Meanwhile, in my rounding up of Lucknow's monuments and hot

spots, old palaces and mosques such as the Imambara and Jama Masjid, and girl-rich shopping avenues such as the Hazratganj, there were the outings with the outrageous Om Singh, the babyfaced neighbour who has just latched himself on to me: he with the light-blue pants in which his perfectly globular hindquarters were unhappy tenants; he who was horny as a hoot owl. Om had a childlike, Eden-like approach to pleasure: he *wanted* it; and he couldn't understand why he shouldn't pluck it from whatever tree it grew on, regardless of the circumstances.

The fruits that most excited Om's passion were those that bobbed on a healthy woman's chest. A typical Om run went thus: Om would enter a crowded bus, and his two hands would energetically go about plucking every breast within reach—big and small, tight or droopy—with all the innocence of a boy pulling girls' pigtails. Pluck. Two-second pause. Pluck Pluck. Five seconds. Pluck Pluck Pluck. He did all this with a childlike giggle that seemed to say, 'Oh, what fun we are *all* having!'—with an expression of such innocent wonder that, somehow, the female response was more surprised than violent. (It can't hurt to think of him as a Harpo Marx with a weakness for titties.) And whenever he talked about 'mangoes', as he called these feminine wonders, his voice bubbled with pleasure. It was in this inflammatory atmosphere that the stage was set for the second attack on my dubious status of Shamefully Overaged Demi-Vierge.

A compassionate friend, Moti Kumar, having nearly shed tears for my virginal predicament, decided my shame could be tolerated no longer.

'This is bloody nonsense, I say,' he said grimly, shaking his massive head, a prize turnip with a moustache. An Indian Government scientist once sent to England for training, he had been inflaming me with his seamy tales of the former Mother Country. His most unforgettable memory of England, which he never tired of re-enacting, was of the evenings at the local pub, where the revellers, male and female, would rhythmically thump the table, while chanting into the late hours: 'Fucking, Fucking, Fucking! Fucking, Fucking, Fucking!'

It changed this UP Panditji's outlook forever, this chant. Uttar Pradesh, India, all his Brahmin learning and mantras, the world itself could never be the same, in this post-Fucking! Age. Against its awesome power, its promise of unbridled sensuality, the syllable 'Om'—which according to the Upanishadic nuggets passed down to him by his Brahmin Pop was the most sacred syllable in the universe—was powerless.

I, too, had changed. Not only was I now regularly wearing bell-bottomed trousers, flaring to twenty-one inches at the bottom, and polyester shirts custom tailored as to leave a maximum distance of five millimetres from skin to cloth at any point (which guaranteed that out in the hot sun after fifteen minutes, tributaries of sweat would race around my skin looking to merge and head out into the open, via a sleeve), but the powerful and lingering idea that sex was dirty and evil had been banished to a dungeon in my unconscious. On the contrary, the Act itself was so sacred, so important, that in an imperfect and unjust world the means by which I accomplished it were insignificant—mere mechanical details. And so, when Moti said he knew of a hard-up Muslim man who would lend me his daughter for the night, I agreed.

At our dusk rendezvous in the now-deserted bazaar area, I pay old Jephthah; and something clad in a black burqa climbs beside me on the back seat of the cycle rickshaw. A cloak-and-dagger cloak that leaves me uncertain of the sex or possibly even the species of the creature within. But on the long ride to Moti's apartment, as darkness envelops us, I lose no time exploring thighs and breasts. The breasts are steep, warm, alive, the topography inspiring, talking back to me. This is how I feel: like Columbus discovering America.

At Moti's place—the Good Samaritan has gallantly agreed to lend me his bedroom while he sleeps out the night on the living-room floor—I discover—or perhaps we discover—that my magnificent-busted mate-to-be is menstruating. She—let's call her Maimuna, what the hell, why not Maimuna for her mooners, her bubbas—she tells me this is a sudden development. She's sorry, but now that it's happened she can't possibly entertain my manhood—my by now significantly enlarged manhood that's been waiting twenty years for this Significant Moment. She'll arrange for a refund of my eighty rupees the next day, she says. Since it's too dark to return home now, she'll sleep the night anyway.

By now, I'm maddeningly excited, so as she sleeps I touch various portions of my Maimuna's body and try to lift her skirt on occasion to get a whiff of her womanly centre, trying to salvage a portion of my loss. Whenever she wakes up and finds me taking my pleasure in this manner, she remonstrates with me, warning that if I continue with this illegal pilferage, she'll have to reconsider the matter of the refund.

Then Moti knocks at the door. 'How's it going, Vijay,' he asks, his voice quavering with vicarious lust. I explain the situation. He whispershouts: 'You see these mosquito bites, Vijay? That's how much I'm paying for your fucking. But you are *not* fucking! Menses? So? Do you know what a *lucky* bastard you are? *Fuck* her, dammit!'

I am not sure I understand his reasoning, but I trust his expertise, and am touched by his friendship, by his having taken up the destruction of my virginity as a Noble Cause, noble enough to suffer mosquito bites for.

I return to the bedroom, wake up my coy mistress, and impart to her the garbled, lowbrow, unpersuasive equivalent of 'Had we but world enough and time . . . that refund, lady, might have been no crime. I know we are in a sticky situation; but isn't stickiness a relative thing? So why don't we do what we came here to do . . . what Allah intends us to do?'

But she's too sleepy now, she can't, and will I please stop being a *harami*? I am thrown by this sudden shift in argument, and too embarrassed to return to Moti for strategic and legal consultations. So as my Dream Princess sleeps, I remain awake throughout the night gazing wondrously at the form beside me (the mere fact that it *is* a woman, yoohoo!), half-wondering if I am in a dream, ejaculating in trigger-happy oblivion at least three times all over the room (with a little, but not too much help from my hand—Oh, balmy breath that doth persuade, Justice to tickle his sword!).

'Damn it, you fucker!' Moti said to me irascibly, a week later, that he had sent all the linen to the laundry but still couldn't rid the room of its extravagant odour of seminal fluid; that his once-excellent canopy was now ridden by a congregation of foul and pestilential vapours. Well, what if I had not yet learnt to regulate the effluents of love, to maximize the utility of old copies of the *National Times*? He should feel honoured to thus sniff at the sacred seed. So thinking, I smiled, shrugged, threw up my hands and shouted with a gurgle of remembered half-pleasure, 'Yipppeeee!'

'You can write in your spare time,' Father wrote in his letter, which Babu Lal the seasoned and pockfaced peon handed over to me with a wink, as if it were from a mistress, and I should be tipping him to buy his discretion. 'Jobs like this don't come by every day.'

He meant: Jobs like this don't come by ever, you lucky bastard!

I had just been selected as a Probationary Officer in the National Bank of India, India's premier bank.

For my father, my appointment was a bourgeois dream come true, a resounding kick up the social ladder. For you were not only what your father was, but also what your son had become. My father said 'National Bank of India' with more reverence than 'Holy Father'—it being the only Indian bank then to offer the magical four-figure starting salary: the Great Wall that separated Them, the haves, from Us, the have-nots. In his eyes, I had reincarnated myself into a class he had always regarded with sad envy.

I had often felt secretly ashamed of myself in the past few months. A vague urge to do great things, to pass my time in this universe with distinction, to be more than a user, gnawed at me sometimes. I was ashamed of not having read the authors others were talking about, ashamed of my BA, ashamed of never having done a solid piece of writing in years. But, living from monthly salary to monthly salary, I had no possible means of escape. And besides I had to settle the much-delayed business of my manhood. If not one hundred women, then fifty, ten, five, three—God, I had to tame my overpowering urge to know, to really know womankind.

So I joyfully embraced my good luck and job for the moment, thinking, as an added consolation: At least Dad can no more doubt that I can feed myself.

One evening while in Delhi on a training assignment, as I strolled through Chandni Chowk past hawkers selling second-hand sports jackets and silver jewellery and leather goods while buses and motorists dodged burqaed women and donkey-drawn carts, who should I run into but Maya, the Marxist of the Tirunelveli camp?

'Maya!' I shouted.

How a year-and-a-half of adulthood—of independence, movement, and red meat—had changed us both! Her cheeks were full and almost rosy from the north Indian December cold, and her liberal use of bright red lipstick and mascara might, in Mangalore, have been branded hussy-like. She wore a pink chiffon sari that hugged her hourglass figure; under the sari her breasts, tightly encased in the green silk of her blouse, heaved. Her fair bare midriff, dominated by a gorgeous navel, exuded heat rays. Passers-by turned their heads to look at her and she seemed to enjoy the attention.

'What are *you* doing here?' she said, her flace flushed with the joy and excitement of seeing someone familiar in unfamiliar surroundings.

She was in job training with her companion Juliet, she said, when I asked her the same question. And swan-necked, giggly Juliet, loaded with jewellery and paint as if on her way to a wedding, and a bit of a *bizalli wu* in the circumstances, giggled at the mention of her name.

'What for, to bomb the Parliament House? And did Moops give you permission to dress like this?' I said, boldly bringing up her Marxist boyfriend.

'That's finished,' she said, laughing. 'Actually, I always loved to dress well. Even before I met Moops, I was a rebel. My dad wanted me to wear my skirts below the knee, but the moment I was in the car on my way to school, I would raise my hemline by two inches and clip it there with paper clips.' The old Maya, direct and confident, in what seemed like a new body.

Well, I too was a new Vijay talking to her. And what I had understood about women was that they too want it badly, like us, but are oppressed by being conditioned not to ask for it under any conditions. The only way to break this stupid social impasse was to grab: fortune favoured the grabber!

'Come on, let's have some ice cream or something,' I said.

She agreed, and after cooling our hot bodies with ice cream at a well-known Connaught Place joint, we took an autorickshaw home, the three of us in a single autorickshaw bumping and whirling through the blackness of the Delhi night, and this was when I was seized with the notion that to seize the moment was to seize Maya, and so seized both Maya and the moment. I planted on Maya a fat kiss, rather to her surprise and the greater giggly surprise of Juliet, who said, 'Such passion!'

Maya recovered and said, 'What *are* you doing?' I thought I discerned sexual excitement as well as respect in her voice.

And I said, 'Kissing you of course,' and smiled sheepishly, and flashed a look that said, 'Here comes another'; and here indeed it did. Here's to a new threshold. And here's a new barrier to break: as once the four-minute mile, so now the four-kiss minute.

Was she responding? I tried to burrow my memory for the advice contained in Little Koka's sex manual. I remembered it saying:

> When the women get passionate her eyes become like a drunkered one, red like blood, her breath flows fast. At that time the man can make use of any organ without any objection.

But it was too dark to ascertain whether Maya's eyes were red like a drunkered one's.

Besides, alas, I'd also have to check Juliet's eyes. Because what if *she* objected to my using my organ on Maya? And what if my organ fractured when the autorickshaw hit a pothole? Damn! The superstructure of our lives was a plot against us. She was mine only during this bumpy, jam-packed, brief autorickshaw ride, because our lives otherwise were tightly packed into pre-set schedules, surrounded by the chaperoning environment of colleagues, training supervisors, and training schedules, and limited by our inexperience, financial timidity, embarrassment. To expect us to plot a two-hour escape from this environment and to check into a hotel room as man and wife: that would be like expecting a Bantu to arrive penniless in New York and the same day to make a killing—a financial one—in the stock market.

There was a brief moment of touch and squeeze—more touch than squeeze, perhaps, of her buttery flanks—'Stop it, Vijay, Juliet will tell *every* one! You've changed so much!' in a half-whisper, half-giggle laced with erotic excitement—and that was it, and the ride was over. There were some farewell witticisms, of a higher order than those that had begun the day—my brain having been fertilized by the limited successes of the past half hour. A hazy and meaningless goodbye followed, neither of us having the foggiest notion of our future, let alone of another meeting: we were both travelling on the crests of different waves, each wave with its own secret social purpose.

Nothing in this brief exchange was the stuff of inexorable romance; it had been one small squeeze for a man. Beyond the physical prodding, the wake-u-upper of sheer sensual presence, cuddly and cuddlable, what had made me take the leap from talk to physical expression? My impression that women who will, will; and women who won't, won't. And while the usual way to separate the wills from the won'ts was to put the question physically, I knew in my heart now that Maya was a girl who would—time and place and God and menstrual cycle willing.

In the meantime, I headed off to Murshidabad in India's Wild East, on a transfer, reconciled to one more postponement of my dreams.

The Real Thing

Kalaharupam Suratam, sexual combat: Sexual intercourse can be compared to a quarrel, on account of the contrarieties of love and its tendency to dispute.
  —*The Kama Sutra*

HOW THE MAGIC show of the world changes, the old magic giving way to the new! Within three months, when I realized Bengali rural culture was driving me insane (those beautiful rustic babes bathing in the tank or drying their hair in the sun), I decided to escape for a week (and later for another week, and still another) from Murshidabad's gloom to the greatest show in India's East: Calcutta, city of seven million, a sensual beast haunting the banks of the Hooghly River, that polluted daughter of the sacred Ganga.

It was a balmy February, nippy and foggy in the mornings, gloriously warm and sunny at noon. My hotel, the Empire Hotel on Chowringhee Street, had like Calcutta and the Empire itself seen better days; the peeling plaster on its walls was a metaphor for all three. The city still reverberated with the echoes of the recent violent Maoist Naxalite revolution, such as the occasional shouting procession of red-flag wavers. Besides which, Calcutta crowds had a disorderly density and energy about them, as perhaps Paris in 1789, which made it appear that a revolution could break out any minute.

But after I had my breakfast of eggs fried in mustard oil, and had walked out onto the dusty Chowringhee and the Esplanade, warm childhood memories flooded back: trams with destinations such as Esplanade and Tollygunge and Ballygunge still weaved about the city, carrying overflowing crowds.

But the pleasure they afforded me was brief. For on this my second trip to Calcutta, at twenty-two, my outlook was more purely informed by what my childhood catechism book so delightfully called concupiscence: I had read my fair share of Western sex manuals, could recite my *Kama Sutra* backwards (though Indian progress seems to have been arrested at about the first millennium, any book that describes *sixty-four* varieties of embraces, *and* something described as a 'throbbing kiss' cannot be all bad). Also *Sexercises* were the only form of physical exercise I would consent to spend my precious energy on, and I had some kind of inner confidence that I had been sent to this world to bring love to all women who didn't have it (I could have said: *Le concupiscence, c'est moi*).

The sights that grabbed me now were different, and the Calcutta air smelt, now, of a woman in heat. My new obsession was breasts and bulging crotches, and my eyes ricocheted from one to another as I ambled up and down Calcutta's fashionable Park Street, stumbling against pavement ledges and bumping into ballooned-out Bengali matrons in the process. Park Street was the Park Avenue of stolen sexual ecstasy: American and Continental hippie women in endlessly patched jeans wearing see-through white kurtas with the inevitable two brown patches, browned by the sun and my brown and pink-poor imagination. Westernized Bengali upperclass girls in jeans that rebelled at being pushed around by their owners' sweetmeat-fattened, rossogolla-soft buttocks.* The more purely-Bengali middle-class women, the delicate, married-or-about-to-be types, whose maddeningly soul-deep eyes—and eye-caresses—quickened the heartbeat and

---

* A truly innocent—honest!—culinary diversion: What you celebrate in a rossogolla is the purity of it, the whiteness of it, its spongy consistency, its balance between sweet and not-sweet, its near-perfect sphericality, its miraculous status as an *objet d'art*. Some of the same things you would in a buttock.

left no doubts of their intentions in the event a nuclear attack was announced. Bangladesh refugees who thrust out an alms-begging arm in unison with a breast that thrust out of its skimpy or buttonless blouse.

Some of the refugee women had mammoth breasts, or at least breasts that looked ample in contrast to their otherwise thin frames. I was desperate enough to want even them: if only they could be put through an antiseptic car wash to hose off their dust jackets . . . . After all, my Constitution prohibited discrimination: all tits were equal, regardless of colour, size, racial origin, education, experience, religious or political opinions, economic background, or the current exchange value of the dollar. ('Tits': a word that bubbles in the imagination—so, you Puritan tormentor, would you keep your sexless 'breasts' to yourself!)

I wondered if this was what was meant by 'living the life of the imagination'. An unpalatable fate, since this was my ideal for The Thing: the whole thing, or nothing. But what was a twenty-two-year-old involuntarily virgin male with a sex drive as powerful as a Napoleonic army to do? Especially one who had discovered masturbation (or being a ministering angel to oneself) too late to enjoy it and who thought it unnatural, an admission of defeat, a final capitulation to sexual inequality? (Women had only to clap, and there would be a queue at the door; but not vice versa.) Hath not a man hands? Hath not a male an organ? (Would it have been right for the twain—hands and organ—to meet in North-South dialogue? Never.) And in this condition to coexist on the same planet as Western youth who were fatuously complaining of Sexual Revolution Fatigue and had switched to EST and assertiveness training?

Yet those were also the days of elation and hope. I wasn't angry that all these women didn't notice my bulging pants and sweep me off to the nearest bed, bath-tub or kitchen table as in Henry Miller's novels. Though logic told me they should, as statistically ninety per cent of women in the Land of *The Kama Sutra* had never had, never would have a real orgasm all their lives; that they would meet their Maker without ever having been well made. And there I was, sent by God into the world to dispense orgasms to women who had no hope. An unrecognized Saviour. True, other men had penises; but I had *attitude*: an amalgam of infinite compassion, infinite love and infinite erections. I not only had a brave penis, but a gospel to back it up with: coming into women to save this world. I couldn't understand why people were so obsessed with fighting wars and petty ideological quarrels, why they couldn't see that the crystal clear answer to their frustrations and lack of charity towards others was the joy that sex provided. I was a Lawrencian even before I'd read *Lady Chatterley's Lover*. What I didn't have was the pubic relations savvy to put this gospel across persuasively.*

Most of the time, therefore, I throbbed with iridescent optical orgasms that left me unexhausted and insatiable for more. I would soon be the first human being to have seen a million breasts, draped or undraped, individually, pair by pair. My eyeballs had become super-dexterous tit-detectors, like those heat-seeking air-to-air missiles used by the Israeli Phantoms in the 1967 War. Calcutta street crowds have the density of platinum, so my eyeballs had to move from one tit to another at laser speed. Dieting tits, prize-cow tits, pointy tits, tits under a choli, loose-bloused tits gloriously revealed from a high angle of vision, 'Want these, mister?' tits under sheer chiffon, 'One-at-a-time' tits in which the sari diagonally bisected the chest thus highlighting the exposed breast, a babel of tit messages sent out into the universe, so many tits and so little time. I did not have the leisure for a moon-landing glance, even though some half moons deserved to be preserved in the Hall of Fame. It was as if I wanted to make my million tits before I was thirty.

Before that could happen, or much else of anything on my third and fourth trips to Calcutta, I had to change my base station. I was sent on my bank-propelled way to Bhubaneswar, my next stop after Murshidabad, and also a night's journey from Calcutta.

---

* *Bhaiyon aur beheno*, I speak as a creature of deprivation; and I speak not only for myself but for a class, for possibly five hundred million Third World males, half of them my countrymen, who must wait out ten, fifteen cruel years of sexual maturity, until they are twenty-five or thirty, to hold a woman in their arms. I am all suppressed men.

Bhubaneswar is a concrete monstrosity of a city squatting on the primitive rump of Orissa, a backward and tribal state that I saw as more recognizable to Cro-Magnon man than to your average jet-setting Pithecanthropus. This was where I was dispatched to learn the intricacies of cheques and ledgers; and, along with three ledgerous male colleagues, I rented the top floor of a two-storeyed house there.

One of these colleagues, who soon became a bosom friend, was thirty-year-old Sanjay, a spirited, quasi-debonair bloke who looked considerably older and more important than he had a right to—somewhat like a baby with a handlebar moustache. I found it queer that so many men—and women—regarded a mid-thirtyish look more fashionable, sexually attractive, and morally worthy than my mid-twenties appearance, my sex-only eyes (Could it be that these women preferred boardroom eyes to bedroom eyes?). However, Sanjay included me in his Brotherhood of Man. Between us existed the fellowship, the understanding that has existed between horny men since ancient times, of mutual conversational masturbation. Sanjay stroked my penile fantasies and made my *real* testicles throb with envy when he implied sexual communion with his girlfriend: a rare bit of luck for any unmarried man in my circles. She was a Christian like me, and this secretly troubled me: from a macro-economic viewpoint, he was fucking up *my* fucking.

But one day I was able to floor him with a conquest that made me his equal. The Brahmin housewife who lived on the ground floor was washing her hands and face in the centre-courtyard below. She was wearing only a white cotton sari loosely draped over her breasts, blouse-less as is the natural and sensible fashion in pre-'civilized' and rural Bengal and Orissa. When she bent, the sari became an arc that highlighted the glories within. Like many Brahmins she was fair-skinned, and her nipples were two pink roses growing atop two snowy mountains. Those pink roses glowed like embers in my brain for days after, continually sending sparks that ignited the pleasure centres of my brain. Depending on who was around, I would either jump in the air emitting a high-pitched 'Yaaaaaaaaah!'-like victory yell, or burst into a silent-movie version of a scream of ecstasy. My advantage over Sanjay was that he, being a prisoner of his bourgeois decency, couldn't possibly provide a detailed geography of *his* girlfriend's knockers, whereas I could deify *my* tits (they were *mine* because I had seen them first), boost them to Himalayan proportions.

That ecstasy lasted me for about four weeks. It was time to move on.

It was a fifth trip to Calcutta, made from Bhubaneswar, that brought me the high adventure that I was looking for.

By now I had already formed a kind of erotic partnership with the flamboyant Mohan Singh, a twenty-five-year-old colleague working at a Calcutta branch of the bank. Mohan had made an inter-city reputation for his rumoured seduction of two Greek girls, allegedly named Erecta and Ejecta, who were visiting Calcutta as part of an International Understanding and Brotherhood Week sponsored by the local Marxist government.

An Anglicized Punjabi who had spent a semester in London, Mohan was a greyflannel-pants-and-powderblue-shirt dandy who, with the help of an investment in a pair of pink-tinted lenses (to camouflage occasionally red eyes), managed to relay a world-weary condescension towards everyone he met, whether his inferior or superior.

The secret of his charm, however, was an infectious smile, halfway between a smile and a silly grin, which he accomplished by thrusting out his generous cheeks and displaying a set of white teeth that fluoride toothpaste makers would have loved to set their flags on. All you had to do to make Mohan smile his sunniest smile was to say 'fuck'. It was a magic word, 'fuck', (the esoteric possession of upperclass urban young men, the Indian equivalent of a Playboy Club key), a word that danced on the tongue, a word that brought the driest subject to life. He (and I at the time) could never have understood why Westerners would use this joyful word to express anger or exasperation. Its existence in the Oxford English Dictionary was the secret of his happiness. I wouldn't have been surprised if he carried on his person a note addressed to that little bastard 'whomsoever it may concern' saying: 'Dear Whomsoever-it-may-concern: If you're around when I'm dying, could you please say "fuck" for me?' Hearing the word on his deathbed would have launched him into eternity with a smile on his face—a smile the devil himself would have found too subversive for hell.

Since I myself had an iconoclastic attachment to the word 'fuck' at the time, my plebeian company was good enough for Mohan. When on subsequent visits I arrived at the Calcutta Railway Station, which in the daytime crams in more people than some Australian state capitals do, I'd give him a call.

'Hello, Mohan—it's *me!*' I'd shout over the preposterous noise of the not-to-be-pooh-poohed choo-choos, adding as identification, '*Me*, you *fucker!*'

Soon after, he would be at the station, his smile along with him. Then we would taxi off into the Calcutta sunset, dreaming of an Indian fuckland that was never to be.

'Heh-heh, you bastardo,' Mohan would chuckle in the taxi at some new *bon mot* I had come up with—my mind, hyperactive at the thought of Calcutta, had been busy making up and hoarding witticisms during the train journey.

And I would chuckle back at the 'bastardo', which he said while making with his lips a perfect 'O', like an expert fellator. As far as I could guess, Mohan was the only person in the world who said 'bastardo', having fixed upon the following formula: that adding an 'o' suffix to an insult would result, instead of broken teeth, in a laugh. I imagined someone rolling on the floor, senseless with laughter, as Mohan hurled insult upon insult, each followed by an 'o' sound.

After I checked into my fleabag hotel, Mohan and I would agree to meet later at Flury's, a posh restaurant serving Swiss pastries and star-shaped chicken patties. Flury's had a fish tank and turquoise glass lookout windows on Park Street for those who liked to watch the big fish. Mohan always liked to be associated with the exotic, the continental, to eat at places such as Blue Fox and Moulin Rouge. Ismail Restaurant and Ghasitaram Mithaiwala, which might serve tastier food, did not merit attention because they did not have European names. It was a sacred ritual: we would set sail on our exploratory voyages into this oceanic city only after we had sipped coffee and exotic erotic memories (tits-to-remember, our-most-unforgettable-arses, who's-fucking-whom-or-almost-could-be) at Flury's.

Mohan and I would then make our expeditions up and down Park Street, his eyes out for the South Pole, and mine for the North Pole. No planting of flags would result, of course—but that was our karma.

Except that, on this fifth trip to Calcutta, at last, a significant part of me finally entered a significant part of a woman. And here was how this piece of karma came to pass.

All the time that Mohan and I roamed about Calcutta in search of high romance that would lead to transcendent, nonstop sex, you see, bells were ringing. The bells hung from the man-drawn rickshaws lazing about the shady alleys behind Chowringhee Road, and the rickshaw-wallah would follow his tinkle with '*Chaliye*, saab.' (Sir, let us go). Words that to the sexually underprivileged—or to the Vastly Overaged Virgin—had the compelling power of Moses's 'Let my people go'. Occasionally, the rickshaw-wallah might spell out the obvious: 'Saab, you want *maal*? We have Chinese! Assamese! Nepalis! Punjabis! Anglo-Indians . . . !'

It was the end of another unsuccessful, largely-in-the-head week, and I was walking alone on a hot summer evening, when the rickshaw-wallah's last words—'Anglo-Indians!'—suddenly registered. The trouble with *purely* Indian women, I decided—extrapolating from my own Christian, but what I assumed to be purely Indian experience—was that their upbringing, which told them sexual organs were dirty, precluded their ever enjoying sex, making them regard it instead as a necessary evil, a means only to romance, marriage, and children. But in the Western movies and novels of my experience, women actively and joyfully participated in sex—all for the orgasm of it, and damned be the rest. And since 'Anglo-Indian', to me, was almost as good as 'Western'—indeed, I imagined, the part-Indian blood, the balmy climate, and the spicy food made their natural hotness hotter still, guaranteeing besides a suave and naughty English vocabulary that promised *communication*—I saw in this mating call the prospect of romantic banter, of an erotic, multi-megaton exchange of minds, besides of course robust, creative, sweaty sex. And afterwards we would laugh lightly at the socio-economic vagaries that had brought us together, and easily move on to a higher plane.

And so the leather-skinned, ancient rickshaw-wallah was

soon weaving through the narrow and malodorous lanes of Calcutta, making so many dizzying turns in the gathering dusk that my disorientation finally gave way to resignation. Suddenly he stopped on an unlit street in front of a rotting, two-storeyed building fronted by a tiny courtyard and a gate and asked for his commission, he had to be off. I insisted on seeing the girl first.

A heavily painted, healthy-looking, and thirtyish woman soon joined me in the rickshaw. In this black Calcutta night (gosh, what a set-up, even the heavens had been enlisted in the conspiracy!) that was all I could see, or thought I could see. So I tried to probe her Anglo-Indian essence with a few soulful questions—which somehow she managed to evade with monosyllabic 'Yes'es and 'No'es. Despite ominous forebodings, my growing excitement now overpowered my discretion. I handed over full payment.

I was led to a lighted room, where it became immediately obvious that my rented Juliet-for-the-night was a pedestrian (though pleasantly healthy), light-skinned Punjabi. Quickly she pre-empted my budding objection with a heavily accented and gruff Hindi equivalent of, 'What's the matter, an *Indian* pussy is not good enough for you? Who do you think you are? Laard Mountbatten?'

I had hardly recovered from this jolt when a boy entered with a basin of water and demanded an additional ten rupees. Ever the consumer activist, I protested.

'Pay the ten rupees,' she said.

I protested the louder, explaining to her the immorality of such trade practices as concealed extras and un-bargained-for-boys-with-basins. But when I realized she wouldn't budge, I coughed up and removed my clothes.

She unhooks her white, double-strength, anti-terrorist bra. Knockout breasts, the colour of robust, fair wheat, plop out. My tongue falls out. All the memorized lines of witty and erudite conversation—'Pardon me, but are you a Scorpio by any chance? You couldn't of course be a Virgo.' 'You'd never guess how Will Durant defines "civilization"'; 'Did you know that the Ancient Egyptians did it with their sisters?'—evaporate as I watch, frozen by the spectacle before me.

Now she lies down, lifts up her white petticoat, and proceeds to freeze. She is shaved—about four days since last shaving—a slight touch of class, a whiff of high sex here, I think, naïvely and salivatingly. But what dominates the scene is her jutting clitoris, an angry purple knob that stands guard and directs traffic in this shabby room, lit by the yellow light of a tungsten bulb surrounded by cobwebs.

'What are you looking at? Something wrong?' she asks.

So what should I reply? 'I think you have a mole that needs taking care of.' 'Have you tried Wilkinson Sword?' 'I think I saw something moving—should we call the police?'

But all my great expectations for such an event, all my laborious study of techniques and twelve-types-of-kisses and so on—it quickly evaporates as I consider her crass, commercial face and think: Finished. Forget the communication bit, just attend to the mechanical details, and get your ass out of here, quick. A naked woman is a naked woman, and that's no small achievement, for *you*. So be grateful, do your thing, and be done with it.

She must have been reading the general direction of my thoughts, because she said, '*Kaam karna hai tho karo aur jao.*' (If you have work to do, do it now and be on your way.) By *kaam*, Sanskrit-poor I understood her to mean work, not *kama* or love. So that's what it was to this working woman.

So I proceed to do what a man's got to do, or what my catholic, apostolic, non-discriminatory cock implores me to do. My lean and hard body, consisting of a slight chest, wiry arms, slightly erect chocolate nipples surrounded by a thin corona of long, curly hair, hairy belly, lean hairy thighs, tight dimpled slightly quivering buttocks, descends slowly and softlands on hers at the usual points of joining. And I'm ecstatic that finally I have joined the 'in' crowd. In my mind, a chorus intones, 'This is it! This is it at last! The world will never be the same again!'

Not that it was all smooth sailing.

First, she forbade my upper torso from parking on her upper torso. The moment the hairs on my narrow intellectual's chest grazed her nude nipples, she blew the policeman's whistle on me, as it were: 'Stop, you can't touch those. That all you can't do.'

A disconcerting attitude. Because how could I possibly stay suspended in the air above her breasts thus for more than a few seconds, without my chest brushing against her twin chocolates? And I thought: all these years, I've been clandestinely practising pelvic-twisting sexercises as convoluted as an Olympic gymnastic event, because one never knew when the moment would come when somebody's honesty about her too-human, universal needs coincided with opportunity. Why hadn't someone plainly told me just to practice push-ups?

And then, after about fifteen puffing minutes of in and out, '*Ho gaya?*' she says. 'Over?'

'Not quite,' I reply. *Ho gaya* my foot! I was just settling down, blast it, for the longest recorded fuck in history. How does she expect me to finish when all my energy is expended in push-ups? This is why I had asked for an Anglo-Indian: to avoid an encounter with the *Ho gaya* school. Damn it, weren't women supposed to give their eyeteeth for such a fate, to sing Hosannas and burn incense before the man who took his own sweet time?

And after about fifteen more minutes, though it is screamingly obvious that I haven't 'finished', she serves notice that my time is up anyway.

Sorrowful yet pleased as hell at the enormous geostrategic achievement (something of mine having entered something of hers; or what literary critics, if they fuck, might call a minimalist fuck), I walk toward my hotel. To be so abused and derided and made a plaything of by Strumpet Fortune, yet to walk home stone hard, hard as never before at the thought of my wickedness of a little while ago. I had reached the Tao of hardness.

(Actually, I was the victim of another physiological trick. I was pre-orgasmic, Doctor Kamala Kannan of Dadar General Hospital Urology and Sexology Department told me years later while with her big, chocolate-cherry-coloured pouting lips she rained kisses on my late-blooming, underprivileged pecker, her Hippocratic empathy soaring to dizzying heights. As it happened, while Dr Kannan was engaged medico-pleasurably thus, her long south Indian plait accidentally tickled and aroused my posterior and sub-penile portions with extra-medical effect, surprising us both a few seconds later with the astonishing therapeutic results that followed, and requiring the changing of Dr Kannan's lab coat.

'You zee, Veejay,' she said in her Kerala accent, adjusting the buttons on her new lab coat, 'your peenila skinna was underazensitizeda.' In other words, a skin that didn't *know*, didn't *understand*. Didn't understand, baby, that the waiting was over, that the long years of being a pore miserable pisser were over, that this was it. That this was the fucking big time.

That understanding would take just a little longer.)

Shillong

NINE MONTHS AFTER that first semi-successful experience in the essential driver's seat of masculine being, I was in Shillong, hill-top capital of the north-eastern hill state of Meghalaya, learning to drive a car while I waited for the next and fuller gift of love. The car belonged to Robindra, my muscularly intense, golliwog-haired housemate and oily-faced co-officer in the National Bank.

When you drive in the mountains in a 1940s model Prefect that's just been resurrected from the dead, whose brakes have never been replaced, merely 'tightened' (as if the solution to every problem were a matter of mere tightening); when you race down roads never knowing what vistas or dangers the next turn will bring (and it is just turns on a Shillong road), your brakes being not a matter of mere mechanics but of persuasion, prayer, faith, hope—all of which must act in concert for about ten seconds before the brake decides to respond . . . the most likely explanation is that you are (and we *were*) in a flush of youth so potent that it makes foolhardiness an everyday staple.

And as we fooled around with clutch and gear, in the car we had nicknamed Garuda Junior, tottering past the market with its Chinese restaurants and deliciously rose-cheeked, berry-selling, berryberry beyootiful children like living dolls; and as we raced down careening slopes, our gears in petrol-saving neutral and our hearts on fire; and as we oohed and aahed past sweeping views of sunlit or misty valleys from in between majestic blue pine trees—red rooftops, shiny tarmac scratches, pine blankets, firs, the scars of occasional buildings—our hearts thumped in anticipation of the spectacular delights that awaited us.

Thus in Shillong did I fool around with life and limb and love and lay claim to my inheritance as a hot-blooded, oversexed male.

Robindra fundamentally agreed with my vision, or a gastric version of it, fortified as he was by his two-LP record collection consisting of Engelbert Humperdinck and Tom Jones, both of whose songs resonate deeply in the Indian soul—or in our Indian intestine, to be precise, since we are always singing melancholy songs as if in the throes of stomach-ache: a universal Indian experience, as defining of Indianness as being drunk on beer is of Germanness. Touched by my Dale Carnegie-inspired appreciation of his head-banging renderings of "Delilah" and "Lonely Is a Man Without Love", Robindra co-opted me as a very-junior partner on the girl-hunting dream safari that was his life.

To young men streaming in from the plains, so weighed down by the life-repressingly puritan late-Hindu and Muslim majority culture, Shillong was the place for such dreams. Yes, this so-called Scotland of India, with its pines and lakes and orchids, its mild-mannered and contented people, who lived life the way nature meant them to—their tranquil, Mongolian faces conveying their unwillingness to make life an occasion for stress and strain—this Shillong was the capital of hope.

What seemed so spectacular, for this plains-reared man, about Shillong's women, was the presence they emanated, as if they *owned* themselves. The more sophisticated among them, especially the Mizo and Naga students from the neighbouring hills—they wouldn't have looked out of place in Piccadilly or on Fifth Avenue. It was as if they possessed the keys to their own bodies, giving them away if and when they so desired. That was what made them charming and magical—their true freedom from social rules and dictatorship, from the tyranny of neighbours and family.

Then came the dance. It was in Robindra's house—a two-bedroom, white house with thin white wooden walls and a green wooden roof, on the Larchmere Hill overlooking the downtown area. Robindra had invited three Khasi girls and one Assamese colleague, Abhay. At pitch-dark seven, as Englebert Humperdinck crooned "Killing Me Softly", the girls arrived, attired in their loose, robe-like native garments that fell, in what seemed like a miracle of air-conditioning design, straight down to mid-calf while hinting at their shapely, all-woman forms. There were only two choices on the evening's menu: Diplomat whisky and Chicken Fried Rice. Everybody had whisky, of course, diluted with water, of course, along with their Chicken Fried Rice, of course. Then, without further delay—what was there to wait for?—Robindra switched on a borrowed, zippier Pink Floyd, who pumped us with a 'political' passion.

"Us And Them."

But after all, we're only ordinary men.

Ordinary men, perhaps, but we'd reclaim our inheritance; we'd fight it out for cunt-ry and for a queen of the night. So thinking, we trooped into the dance room, like peasants about to tear down the Czar's palace. The lights were turned off, except for a two-watt red bulb specially and cunningly mounted for the occasion.

'I'm Vijay. May I have the dance?'

The girl glides up. She is about 5'4" and curvaceous, wearing her loose, Khasi kimono of green silk. In the red electric light, her face is demure, happy with life.

Taking her right hand in my left hand, as if I have done this all my life, I casually and effortlessly place my other palm on her buttocks, democratically divided between her two grateful globes. Thus feeling her warmth stereoscopically, my chest feeling hers, excruciatingly awake and sensitive to her two points of sheer bliss, we dance, as if it were the most perfectly natural thing in the world. The no-nonsense freedom of the Khasis! If this is what a boy and a girl want to do, this is what they will do! Q.E.D.

Now I place my lips on hers and seek entrance. I am surprised by her fat and wet tongue also seeking entrance—entrance to me. She obtains it—ladies first, naturally—and moves it about like someone just given the freedom of the city, which, God knows, she has. So this is how it is done, I think. I mustn't fall behind. But now there's a traffic jam of tongues, so first I retreat, then she retreats, now I follow. Now, hypnotized by her musk, I bend slightly and lift her robe.

God, she's wearing nothing!

Yowweee!

Yes, oh yes, and though I had deduced as much from the hand on her buttocks, it is this empirical confirmation that is the trumpet blast of the welcome that Shillong has finally given me; it so overpowers me that I graze in her pubic forest and get my fingers wet in what is the first democratic sexual transaction of my life, and a completely wordless one too. As Engelbert Humperdinck wails, 'Strumming my fate with her fingers . . .' my fingers thrum within her, her breathing grows heavier, and then *my* breathing grows heavier. Nothing in my education or experience has prepared me for this, for going straight to this point, but this seems to be the point, the point of it all.

The point is this: I have soft, long, and agile fingers, fingers made for writing beautiful sentences, I think, dual-purpose digitals also designed for making love to beautiful women. What a neat trick: the fingers disappearing, disappearing, disappeared, my lingam engorging, engorging, engorged . . . I have gotten my fingers wet and my soul too. She puts her tongue in my right ear, then allows it to flutter over my right earlobe, sending electrical sensations down the side of my body, down my virgin buttocks, to my near-virgin balls.

Engelbert croons "The Way It Used to Be". While I, fingers busy, nearly crying with happiness, wonder if this was the way it used to be, before we screwed it up with words, rules, permissions, 'Do Not Enter' signs . . . .

As the others dance on, possessed by their own possessions, I am sharp, finely tuned, cool, living in the moment, floating in space . . . .

But soon it is party-folding time, my partner agrees to join me for a cinema show the next afternoon, and the three girls leave in a group, Abhay following. I return to my tiny room and close the door. And then I regard myself and the past few hours with ecstatic, exhilarating, almost disbelieving joy. 'Whooppeee!' I scream, leaping into the air, my arms reaching for the ceiling.

The next afternoon, at the cinema, the girl and I sat quietly and without any demonstrations of affection except for accidental brushes, as befits the requirements of public behaviour in India.

But outside, when I asked her to follow me to a restaurant (hoping to continue this rendezvous in some bedroom somewhere), she regretfully declined. And then this girl, who had seemed so grateful to me at the time for having made her evening compared to the other klutzes who danced at a romantic distance from their own partners, said: 'Sorry, no can meet you another time. Our community boys get angry, they say no go out with outside community. It not safe.' So saying, she turned around and disappeared into the crowd and down the hillside, before I could pursue her and convince her otherwise. And I, too embarrassed to ask Robindra for her address, never saw her again.

So life returned to normal, or rather to a more desperate wanting, a wanting with a recently carved hole in it. Until one day another colleague of mine named Alok, a sleekly coiffured fellow who wore broad flashy ties and walked energetically with his behind high in the air as if he were a ship (and at the same time a practical and worldly-wise fellow with a feeling for the passage of time and life), had an idea that would help us both. In my part of India, small-town students, who are often strapped for cash, would often go to a restaurant and order one-by-two (one tea divided into two cups) or two-by-three (two teas in three cups). Alok proposed a natural extension of the one-by-two: by sharing a woman we would double our joy, besides striking a blow for true democracy, brotherhood, and thrift. What's more, the resourceful Alok not only arranged for a high class lay (a young freelancer who had been recommended by a friend for some amazing tricks she apparently had up her love-sleeve, a true courtesan in the ancient, highly respected tradition), but through his high connections managed a room in the Legislators' Hostel which, by its awesome aura, was Vice-Squad-proof. And so could our loving continue into the night, protected by the law of the land, by legislative immunity, by the Supreme Will of the People!*

And was she classy! Let me begin with a joke told me by a

---

* Despite legislative immunity, there was no guaranteed immunity from the poking around of chowkidars—who are enemies of love, of life, and ultimately of the life of the mind—so we kept no lights on, managing with the light that came through the translucent glass panes of the bathroom door.

respectable Indian girlfriend, and which none of my un-prudish and cosmopolitan upper-middleclass countrymen will find unfunny. Indeed anybody who *objects* to this joke will be laughed out of the room:

Q: What's the difference between a circus and a striptease act?

A: A circus has cunning stunts.

Now then, what would you think of a lady who combined the cunning stunts of a circus artiste with the stunning sexual charisma of a stripteaser? But wait, I am getting ahead of my story with my verbal stunts. And since I already have interrupted my story, let me first say a few words in praise of stunning artistes. Or what I thought that night, after my stunning experience.

I thought, after my woman left, of the millions of males—and females—all over the world, the vast majority, who would entrust themselves, all their lives, to rank amateurs doomed by their inhibitions never to reach professional standards. And I thought of virgins who would be turned off the act of love forever thanks to a fumbling initiator, and thereafter join the Enemies of Love, the battalions of prudes, the venomous censors of others' joy. I thought: what a waste! Why not, as in some wise ancient tribes, let an experienced woman (or man) initiate the young virgin? And, in fact, have a University of Love awarding Bachelors of Love and Masters of Love degrees to its successfully graduating professional initiators for what is perhaps the most crucial experience in a person's life?

Beginner's luck perhaps, but as it turned out, I had hitched up with a Ph.D.—a Doctor of Love. And to think that when I began the evening, I would have been thankful for an S.S.L.C.(Failed)!

Dr Love was a Nepali, a mixture of Indian and Mongolian, lithe, tough, extremely vigorous. She had curved eyebrows, a nosering on a short yet delicate nose, and an expression with a twinkle in it, as if she were about to break into a laugh. Her skin was young, and her breasts were muscular and healthy and remarkably large, and . . . I watched in amazement as she stripped off her salwar kameez with Olympic speed, as if not wanting to waste a single moment of stark naked pleasure. For she was, Haré Krishna, starkers under her dress, and I caught a vision of swollen lower lips and milk chocolates despite the coarse black hair that cascaded down to her hips, and sent electrical sensations through my half-nude, underweared body as she moved forward and backward, artfully uncoiling my serpent (swollen with pride and joy) from its proletarian prison, occasionally kissing and nipping at my nipples and chest.

And now, this take-charge woman assumed the superior position, the *Purushayita Prakarana* (acting as a man), as if it were the most natural thing in the world—which it must have been for her, for her bounce spoke not only of well-developed muscles, but also of a natural, almost genetic flair. Indeed her whole body was a muscle, and like ten thousand expert micro-tongues it hastened the sole object of its concentration towards the inevitable spasm. It was the Mare's Trick that she was up to: the *Samadamsha* technique in which she gripped the penis with her yoni's vice, squeezing and stroking it, holding it inside her for a hundred heart-beats. Was it a true passion for fucking, or some ethical business principle such as 'Service with a smile!' or 'Give it your all!' or 'The customer comes first!' that gave this freelancer her energy, I wonder now, for she had me dizzy with her tricks.

Watching the quickening in my face now, she said cheerfully, 'Liking fuckee fuckee me?'

'*Oui, Oui,*' I said.

But the hastening I had just felt was just an illusion, and an illusion that was the source of considerable ecstasy. For this, O dearly beloveds, was work—though divine work. On this sweaty, warm-for-Shillong night, even with her on top, my ass was doing ninety miles an hour, uphill. But soon, about twenty-five minutes after we had begun—and I now understood dualism or *dwaita*—my unaerobic body wanted to retire and apply for a pension, while my beastly little member was going strong, protesting underemployment even. So I hastened very slowly, surprising my hitherto-jaded queen, who after trying the *Samuptam* or pair of tongs manoeuvre, and then the *Hansabandha* or Swan manoeuvre (she sits upright upon you, her head thrown back like a rearing mare, bringing her feet together on the bed to one side of your body), and then the incredibly whirling *Chakrabandh* or Wheel position (lying upon you, your beloved moves round like a wheel, pressing hands one after the other on the bed, kissing your body as she circles), finally couldn't resist asking, with obvious respect, 'You're taking so long?'

(At which point a muffled sound also came from behind the bathroom door, 'Hey, don't take so long!' It was the impatient Alok who, having gallantly given me the first turn while he sat it out in the bathroom for what he expected would be a five-minute wait, was now concerned for his turn.)

I tried to answer, to my love partner—to my Nandini, my cow of plenty—that I was doing my best. 'Too good this fuckee-fuckee,' I said, using her expression. 'But I too tired from pumping-pumping.'

Whereupon she decided to do her best, too: and her best was a thousand times better than my best. Concentrating now like a yogi about to perform a miracle, she began a controlled and unbelievably pleasurable quiver over certain Prohibited Areas of her anatomy, mostly invisible. For a short while, I was stunned, so surprised by this sudden burst of new improved free extra pleasure, that my expression must have resembled a half-wit's.

But the quiver demanded an answer, and soon the answer came, and the answer was a roar from all levels of my being (followed by a shout from one level of her being, 'Haré Rama!')! Joy at coming into the world. O Joy, gratitude, love. *Oh God. Oh My. Ah, Ah, Ahhhh . . . . At last. Free at last.* It had been a soul-destroying, ten-year wait for my first complete, unabridged fuck; but these forty-five minutes almost made up for every minute of it.

At which moment, an urgent shout also came from behind the bathroom door: 'Hey, don't make such a racket!'

'Bravo!' she said.
'You mean the writing, or the fucking?'

'Now now,' she laughed. 'No comments. Just an involuntary ejaculation.'

'When you drive with me, you leave the ejaculating to me,' I said, parodying the Greyhound song.

It was my editor, pulchritudinous Pam Gardner—as wonderful an editor as any man dreamed of. (Because that's what we writers were placed in the world for: to dream dreams.) And I had been reading my book aloud to her on a warm summer day with her apartment opening out onto Central Park, the glorious June sun from a clear blue sky shining on our nude bodies, shameless as those of the pre-apple First Parents, as we spread out on the plush scarlet rug, my head resting against the swell of her remarkable breast after an earlier session of Vijrimbhitakam.

'And I think you ought to end your book here,' Pam said now.

'Here?' I was shocked, and turned around. 'Sweetheart! Just after a successful screw? What does this tell the world about who I am—a chap whose only yearning in the world is to stick his silly little tool in some soft place? OK, I'm not, anymore, ashamed of screwing, not ashamed of having a thing dangling between my legs. But isn't there something more that we all reach out for? Isn't there some statement to be made about the human condition?'

'Look, love,' Pam said, tenderly, 'what could be more human than a young man finally getting his rocks off? There could be no story that is more human, more universal, more timeless. Fine: we all yearn for meaning, for philosophy, for depth—but where does all this life and meaning and so on begin and end? In someone getting his rocks off!'

'True, true,' I said, my affection aroused deeply by her passionate way of making her point. And as I listened, I fell to fondling her breasts, playing with an erect and pink nipple that jutted out two centimetres like a button on an extraordinarily user-friendly gadget.

'Be an artist, if you must,' she continued, with her admirable concentration. 'But be an artist in the presentation of the everyday story, the universal human story. Not in artificial sophistication. Not in fancy-schmancy literary-philosophical tricks.'

'Mmmm bbblub!' I said. Her hard, pink nipple was now fully in my mouth, along with most of her gigantic areola.

'Nine years of deprivation, of heroic endeavour! And then he has this glorious fuck! It is the natural conclusion to one part of his life, and the beginning of another,' she continued. 'His coming is a symbolic *release!—from constrictions that have been put on him since he was born. A freeing up of the whole self! An empowerment. Now he can do anything! The world lies before him.'*

I was now sucking devotedly at my blonde adviser's glorious breast (is it true that literary gentlemen prefer blonde editors?) and her arguments sounded delicious.

'Now he can do anything. It's the phallic-pen thing, do you understand? His pen is now, shall we say, flowing freely; now he can write about his past! A great moment to end the novel.'

'What about a few more chapters?' I pleaded, not very coherently, between groans, kisses, and licks. 'A few more chapters, to unfold his growth, development. His search for love and meaning. And the rest of the plot.'

'Great moment to stop,' she repeated. 'Save all the rest for Book Two, the sequel. Don't spoil the, ohh, nice, moment!'

'Don't spoil the mmmmomment,' I mumbled.

An hour later: 'You're not telling them about this are you?' she said, a little shocked. The manuscript was all over the bed and floor now, having in the course of an energetic hour edged itself interestingly into various nooks and crannies. 'The End' I salvaged from in between her bottom cheeks) and absorbed some of Pam's distinctive womanly smells.

'Why not, Pam?' I said. 'Let them know that a writer's life is not as deprived as some people think.'

'I suppose it's OK,' she said thoughtfully, once again hungrily and too hopefully caressing my declining member. 'They'll probably think I'm only a creature of your fantasy. Like all the rest.'

'But please,' I said, somewhat more in control of myself now, having bitten into a sirloin sandwich to regain my recently-spent energy, and put one hand affectionately around her body. 'This book is about a search for love . . . the human condition, the emptiness within. It's wrong to stop it just after a physical release, however transcendent.'

'This disease of our civilization, this embarrassed stiffening at the mention of sex, this sudden, urgent rush for Meaning . . . when in fact human history is merely the history of our **stupidity**! It's stupid! It's unbecoming!' She was sitting up in bed now, and the coverlet had fallen from her breasts, which looked all the more rosy in her emotion.

'Tell me,' I said, trying not to get distracted. 'Why aren't people happy, even those who have everything? Because, even if we don't know it, we're searching for some meaning . . . .'

'Why can't some people just be content to be poets of fucking?' she said, *passionately and a little disappointed. 'We have poets of angst, poets of love, poets of nature, poets even for each individual toe, but not one poet of fucking, not one since Ovid. Except maybe D. H. Lawrence and John Updike. And Lawrence can be so straightfaced about it, it makes you want to laugh.'*

'You shouldn't be lecturing me *about this,'* I said, *touching her arm gently. 'However special you are to me, it's* my *book,* my *vision. What about your editorial integrity?'*

'Look,' she said, *'I'm only trying to liberate you from your puritanism, which you think you're free from, but aren't really. Like* Playboy *putting philosophy and political analysis between its nudes. But at least* Playboy *has to sell ads; you don't. You're writing in the freest country on Earth.'*

'Freest country? With you lecturing me on what I should and shouldn't write? What about your editorial integrity?'

'Editorial integrity?' she said—*and then, placing her gorgeous lips around my cock, she added, with some difficulty: 'What's* that*?'*

She had made her point: That for tit, tit for that, tara ra boom deay (no, nothing profound going on here). Within seconds, we were laughing so hard we were rolling on the floor, naked. Which, let me put to you, is a metaphor for human happiness. Or the Revised Eden.

Soon after the burst of erotic firecrackers with which Shillong welcomed me to the world, the *real* world in which birds did it and bees did it, it gave me a farewell party. I had made it!

I had made the list, flashed by national newspapers, of the one hundred and fifty Indians selected for the Indian Administrative Service (IAS) and the Indian Foreign Service; it was the fruit of an exam I had written just before arriving in Shillong, during a six-month branch-training stint at Silchar, a mosquito-ridden sewer of an Assamese town. Despite the handicaps, I had made it—to the most élite by-merit-only class in India.

The bankers, soon to be my ex-colleagues, surrounded me with fawning compliments. 'Big shot, IAS saab!' they said. They confessed to sudden urges to take me out to dinner and ply me with Golden Eagle beer and murgh makhani.

How could this have failed to recharge my sense of confidence, only recently assaulted by an encounter with graduates of St. Stephen's College, city slickers steeped in existentialism and oriental philosophy, who began every second sentence with 'The Tao of . . .' I still didn't know the Tao, but perhaps a brighter, more spacious, more accepting, intellectually sparkling world lay in wait for this perennial outsider, this small-town kid, this grandson of a kashtigaar or underwear wearer so mortified by his past, so desperate to join the clubs that had so far set their dogs upon him. Dreams, dreams, dreams. There always would be a new dream.

IV

MOKSHA

Endless Laughter

The Tao of Power

WHAT FOLLOWED NOW were the two weirdest, unrealest years of my life—so remarkable had been the mutation in my fate. It was like a starving insolvent hitting the lottery jackpot. Or rather like a street bum marrying a Rockefeller heiress, then discovering that she kept a dungeon. And that the price of staying on was taking your quota of nightly whips like a, er, man.

To sum up: it was a story of power.

Power! Now that I had it, after years of hating it and fighting it, of calling it corrupting and evil, it seemed . . . OK. Well, more than OK: sexy. It swelled your balls.

What Power Was Not: Power was not merely, not necessarily, ego-boosting, nefarious control over other people's lives, or the power to require bended knees.

What Power Was: In its most ebullient form, power was Life asserting itself over Death. Power was the *opposite* of weakness. The opposite of knock-kneed meekness. Of acned hiding. Of hungry hoping. The opposite of impotence. Of unrequited love. Of penile self-help.

From the moment the news flashed across the country's newspapers, carrying the results of India's most famous power lottery, the Indian Civil Services exam . . . it was a tale of power. Because we Indians, having for centuries been ruled by the *danda* and the license, bowed meekly before the *gaddi* or seat of power. And in the popular imagination, the essence of the Indian Administrative Service's (IAS) power lay in the fact that every IAS officer would, within eight years, become a Deputy Commissioner or Collector of a district—which, arguably, is just a democratic euphemism for king.

What made this system unique in the world was that it didn't matter who you had once been; so long as you made the top hundred-and-some-odd places, competing against perhaps eighty thousand graduates in a gruelling, eight-subject examination, you had made it for life.

Two future colleagues of mine, Pankaj Khullar and Baldev Dhingra, who had, like me, 'made it for life', were postgraduate hostellers in Haryana when the newspapers published the empowering news of their administrative knighthood. Celebration time! Come on! They drove across the state border, bought a huge quantity of booze, and were returning to the hostel, when the Excise Police at the border check-post stopped their jeep.

'You can't do that,' the cop said.

'Why not?' they asked, feigning bland surprise.

'*Kanoon hai,*' said the cop. It is the law.

'*Kanoon? Kya Kanoon? Hum log kanoon banaate hain!*' (Law? What law? We are the people that make the law!) the boys roared, as they zoomed off. A trail of giddy laughter and dust hit the open-jawed cops.

Two hundred miles north-east of New Delhi in the town of Mussoorie, atop a hill-station that rises seven thousand feet above the surrounding plains to merge with the Himalayan foothills, lies the C. D. Phawade National Academy of Administration. The Academy is an architectural jumble of about ten buildings sprawling across a hill of its own. These buildings, having expanded from the now-defunct Happy Valley Hotel, and bearing such melodious names as Happy Valley House and Kateswar Castle, are surrounded by tennis courts, badminton courts, and a riding field, and consist of various auditoria, dormitories, a library, and a refectory. From the windows of the Library and the Refectory one may see the steep northern drop of the hill on which the Academy stands; beyond, spectacularly occupying almost the entire range of one's vision, rises the Great Wall of the Himalayas, an unending patchwork of dark-blue forests and dark-faced mountainsides topped by resplendent snow peaks. It's a sight that can, on a clear day, hush the most raucous of human beings; before the highest mountains in the world even the proudest human being cannot help but pause.

Such a natural corrective to one's ego is sorely needed in the Academy, the place where the barely post-pubertal winners of the country's most-widely-attempted power lottery had assembled before fanning out to its nooks and corners.

It was a power lottery for which the ticket was merit—democracy's imperfect way of bypassing the entrenched feudalism of a country that, accustomed to despotism and class division for fifty centuries, couldn't be expected to become a true democracy overnight, and so needed the symbols of power and authority to make its government work. After all, it was power for good or evil: having once been used by the British to build an Empire and make of us loyal and useful subjects, it could now be used to make the masses willing—and if need be, unwilling—participants in vast social and economic transformations. If in reality the letters 'IAS' after a person's name worked like an American Express Gold Card of power, instantly accepted at locations throughout India, opening Travellers Bungalow suites, freeing hidden seat reservations in trains and planes, sometimes providing meals and official vehicles, provoking smiles of embarrassment and reverent recognition, it was because they spelt potential power. In every district, in every corner of our vast nation, an IAS officer was the Deputy Commissioner. Which, in a rural district particularly, meant the embodiment of the State. In a country where centuries of tyrants and foreign powers had made State power something to be mortally feared, you did not take this power lightly, just as you did not tweak a lion's moustaches in sport.

After one sexless, sometimes giddy, sometimes anxious year of training in the Academy, I, the future Deputy Commissioner, was on my long rail journey home for my first visit in three years. In the last hour of the journey, the Mangalore Mail, a 2,000-foot-long steel python richly stuffed with roasted and sweaty passengers, chased the evening sun that flashed through the coconut palms screening the Arabian Sea. Ascending now onto the old red Ullal Bridge, the train left in its wake petrified pedestrians, farmers, hawkers, and idlers, who clung to steel girders on the narrow, pedestrian path. And now the sun could be seen dipping into the sea for its head bath of the day. The orange glow spread out over the tiled roofs, the spaces between them filled by trees, barking dogs, autorickshaws, children and adults who had stopped whatever they were doing to gape at their only excitement of the day.

In a few minutes, the train arrived at the Mangalore Railway Terminus, where I was surprised to see Dad waiting to receive me, eager to help me with my luggage. 'Welcome, welcome home! Everybody is talking about you. Everybody is asking about you!'

In the over twenty-four years of our often-stormy acquaintance, I didn't remember ever having seen Dad in such high spirits. He was sixty-five years old but had an insolent skip in his walk; his rough, sunburned face glowed, and his bald head shone stubbornly and solidly; he hadn't aged in the three years since I had last seen him. The tone of his letters had become decidedly more self-confident and bourgeois each time my social status had vaulted, and my present achievement was, to his mind, the clincher. A priest—yes, a *priest*, the vice-principal of St. Stanislaus College no less—had come to his house and asked whether I would, when I arrived, be willing to give a talk to his students. He told me this on our way home in the taxi, like a child reporting a compliment he had received for the best essay in class.

'How's Uncle Gaulbert doing?'

'Oh, very well, very well,' Dad said. 'He is now worth thirty lakhs.' The smell of boiling water poured over a freshly plucked, just-killed chicken came from the kitchen: a festive smell.

In the next few days, succulent rice cakes—apams, mutlin, panpale, and sannan—rich, coconut-milked chicken curries, and dark beef curries appeared on the greasy and tattered tablecloth of our humble dining-table without pause, as if every day were a day of celebration. Dad sat before me and listened to everything I said with the utmost attention, like a docile *shishya* before his renowned guru. Whenever Mom, sitting at the table, head resting on her palm, regarding me with bemused love, pride, Mother Henness, tried goodnaturedly to interrupt or offer her little conversational nugget, Pop would shout her down with, 'What are *you* talking?

Let *him* speak.' Never before had I been treated thus in my own home—as if I were a star.

In a day or two, Dad started dropping hints. 'You know the Coelhos, the Lighthouse Hill Coelhos? Mr Coelho dropped in the other day, asking about you. He was asking when you were due in Mangalore.'

'They have *two* coffee estates now,' he continued, after a pause. 'They must be having lakhs and lakhs!' Dad always got a thrill, flavoured with a touch of hopelessness, from contemplating king-sized bundles of money—other people's money. But the hopelessness wasn't as conspicuous today. He spoke like a businessman who had just forked over a few lakhs.

'Aunt Rose was saying to me the other day, "Your son is the most eligible bachelor in town," ha ha,' Mom said now, her voice both chirrupy and shy.

It was a fact that no Mangalorean had passed this exam in a decade, and many itched to have a son-in-law in the corridors of power, a 'connection' who would lend them the status, and perhaps the licences, they craved.

I understood but said nothing. Either I would find the girl I loved through a natural expansion of my natural—or well, slightly artificial—contacts, or I would die a bachelor (not very likely, of course, given my shoot-first-ask-questions-later yearnings).

But in Mangalore? In a town where girls didn't want to be seen with a boy before marriage, lest people 'start talking', how could I entice a girl to come out with me? Dating didn't exist except in an unstated way—for rich boys who had cars and could give girls 'lifts', tempt them with parties and ice creams and drives to the beach. Going for a drive in a car! *Any* old *latpat* car, so long as it moved! In a secure little cocoon of metal and plastic and comfort and exclusivity, to be lifted out of the surrounding dust and heat and everpresent eyes by a knight on a white-horse of a car, and to speed away to some oasis of beauty, or wherever the heart desired, just somewhere *else*, time and effort compressed, to be taken, taken, taken, deliciously powerless and imprisoned by wealth and power, flesh touching flesh, nudge nudge nudge—as indeed it had to be in the crowded confines of an Ambassador or a Fiat . . . . It was an offer that few middle-class girls, however long coached in virtue, could refuse (luckily, motor cars had been invented after the Commandments, and no one could recall any specific prohibition against car drives). And it would be a long time before I, with my government salary, would be able to afford even a second-hand car . . . . Still, wasn't the alternative worse: to be a commodity in the marriage market, available for handling without my permission by any grubby-fingered purchaser who thought he could pay the going price?

One day, I was surprised to see a sparkling new Ambassador negotiating the narrow and humble mud lane to our house and parking in our hitherto-virgin yard, a destination only for humble bicycles or autorickshaws. Out came the glittering, terene-clad Mathiases, another coffee estate family that would normally have not even come within sniffing distance of our plebeian abode—Mr Sylvester Mathias, Mrs Gertie Mathias, sons Maxie and Laxie.

Inside, on the proletarian furniture of our living-room-cum-study, the regulation Kissan squash and Glaxo Glucose biscuits were served and ritually tasted. A few minutes of exaggeratedly polite talk followed, Daddyji and Mommyji trying absurdly to be at their best, feudally-correct behaviour, I trying to balance proletarian hauteur with normal human courtesy.

Now the silk-saried, well-powdered, bobhaired Gertie Mathias fished out a photograph, then another, and then another. The photographs consisted of different poses, all socially proper, of a long-plaited, quiet-looking girl from their family tree, (a different branch, though, there being a lot of mutual back-scratching in this monkey business) a very good girl, good in *studies*, High Second Class Passed in her BA, Home Science major! No airs, talented, honourable, a hidden jewel, a girl who had moved around—but wisely and not too much.

This sudden, unprovoked focus on this girl, a good girl no doubt, continued for a few more minutes with the Mathiases generously holding forth in their cloying voices on the minutiae of her educational qualifications, her memberships in various sodalities of Our Lady and Her Lord, her preferred brand of shampoo: a very noble and unimpugnable brand, no doubt. And as they recited this veritable *curriculum vitae*, Father and Mother looked expectantly at me, confirming in my mind my theory of conspiracy with their remark, 'She is like us, a Brahmin.' It was the first time that my parents had acknowledged their consciousness of caste.

'Does her beauty hang upon the cheek of night like a jewel in an Ethiop's ear?' I said, addressing the Mathiases.

'Ha ha,' Mama Mia said nervously and hurriedly, trying to put a fuzzily benevolent spin on my remark. 'Vijay was always *first-first* in English and used to make hu*murr*ous speeches.'

'Or, to get down to basics: How much is she worth on a per-kilo basis? And is there a discount for wholesale?'

'What?'

'Well, isn't this some kind of marriage bazaar? So why don't we call a spade a spade and get down to the meat of the matter?'

This was when the laughter changed to shame-faced confusion, Dad and Mom now trying to drown me out with loud niceties and hasty goodbyes as the blue-blooded but now red-faced family walked out of the Prabhu residence into their waiting blue Ambassador, their not-cool drink half-sipped and Glaxo biscuits half-munched. Every dog must have his day; unlike most days, this was not theirs.

When the visitors left, Mom cried and said, 'What shame!' and Dad said, 'Why did you have to be so rude?'

'What do they think of me?' I said angrily. 'I didn't ask to see photographs! I believe in love! Why can't I have love, just because I was born poor? Are men and women to be bought and sold like commodities in the twentieth century? I'll meet my own girl!'

'You do whatever you want,' Dad said, disgustedly. 'What do I care? At least you could have been polite.'

'No one will talk to us now,' said Mom, tearful.

Later, I would regret my intemperate outburst. The brokered marriage, arranged by close relatives, was the Eastern way of doing things, and my fantasies of personal choice, acquired from reading and Western movies, did not change things for the vast majority, who had no opportunity to meet and choose their own partners. I ought to have tolerantly humoured them and politely declined.

Damn! News like this spreads, and people would shy away from me. Why had I, with such ill humour, closed the door to meeting new females? Part of me, like millions of my countrymen from my social class, envied the local Westernized rich, envied their free access to warm bodies at their inbred dances and parties, night after night, aloft on wings of freely-flowing beer and whisky.

I envied them their free kisses, their complete innocence of lower-class anxieties about food and acceptance, their perennial preoccupation with fun fun fun. I was now a powerful pauper! Power did not automatically put money in your pocket or guarantee late-night cheek-to-cheek dancing with hot *haute-monde* belles . . . . Why had I let my anger explode? At this rate, I would end up spending my fifteen-day holiday within the same kind of gloomy, cobwebbed, dusty and lemon-juice-serving middle-class walls that I had spent most of my life in.

Besides, my posturing didn't change realities. A few days later, when another estate owner, Lawrie Saldanha, stopped his car to offer my father a lift to Hampankatta—the first time any member of the upper classes had acknowledged his existence thus!—he came home visibly shaken from the experience.

'So kind of him. They are such big people,' he said again and again, with utter sincerity.

'That's because they are so full of gas,' I said deflatingly, at which he smiled with slight embarrassment, dutifully but without conviction.

It was futile of me to try to explain that, given who I had recently become, Saldanha was only being kind to himself. He was only investing in a cheap official insurance policy that would assure favours and minimal harassment from the powerful bureaucracy. I felt a pang of sorrow for this my father, this shrinking man, this man awed by every stuffed shirt's position, even mine. The army had made a trembling feudal serf of him so that he could never shake off the secret feeling that he and his sons would always be social inferiors to those exalted at birth. It made my egalitarian blood boil.

My vacation was over. And on a rainy July morning in the middle of the south-west monsoon, I stepped out of the spit, phlegm, paan and garbage mix that was the Mangalore Bus Station into a red government bus that was soon climbing up the winding, misty Western Ghat mountains, only three decades ago the haunt of fierce tigers, bears, snakes, and wild boar, now being fast destroyed by poachers and timber smugglers. There had been a landslide somewhere up the road, said a downcoming bus driver, stopping his vehicle to shout the news to our driver; but we drove on through fourteen hairpin bends and fifty miles of monotonous green forest and occasional paddy fields, then in turns rocketed down and groaned slowly up on the leaf-carpeted, hill road which wound through this thickly dark-green, misty coffee estate country and descended towards the flat plateau that was Shimoga—where I would begin my practical training as democratic potentate.

'Saar, you want to see the DeeSee? What is your good name? Oh, IAS Probationer, saar? Very well, saar, I will send the jeep right away, saar,' crackled the voice on the bus stand telephone, instantly shifting from arrogant to obsequious.

Intoxicated with the contemplation of my power, full of youthful lust and hunger, I realized it only dimly at the time: *that what my education, and even power itself had done was to make me a stranger in my own country*! No one in this, the real India—where corruption, irrationality, and inefficiency had been a way of life for centuries—wanted us of the lost urban intelligentsia or bourgeois class poking in with our new-fangled ideas, with our gratuitous moral code.

Nor, deep in our hearts, did we want this, except as a dung-smelling stop on the ladder of ambition. Our minds were elsewhere, in the world of Western movies, of Candice Bergen in *Soldier Blue* and bare-breasted Jacqueline Bisset in *The Deep* and Sophia Loren in all her voluptuous, scantily dressed, Eternal Woman roles.

In the Academy, well-stocked with Anglophiles fresh from their breeding grounds in our exclusive urban colleges, one of my colleagues, 'Pinker' Singh, was such a rabid P. G. Wodehouse fan that his trademark was his ability to quote pages and pages of Wodehousian dialogue. We often greeted each other with 'Pip pip!' 'Bung Ho!' and 'Tally-ho, old chap!' Our fantasy was to go to a district and have our personal Jeeves, carrying in a tray of gin and lime and carrying out our commands with a flawless 'Very well, Sir' and 'Certainly, Sir!' Instead, we got pockmarked fellows whose hair dripped with coconut oil, whose idea of formal dress was striped boxer shorts and dirty banians. These dusty and misshapen louts with bare feet and imperfect hearing, paid by the People so we wouldn't have to mix with the People in some greasy curry joint, brought us proletarian Chicken Fry when we asked for upscale Mutton Shahi Korma, and responded to our bewildered protests with, 'Yes, saar, Sicken Fry, saar, Sicken Fry, saar!'

My personal peon spent most of his People-subsidized time having siestas in broad daylight on the bare cool floor of the veranda outside my Travellers' Bungalow room, dreaming of the wife and eight children he had left behind in the areca nut-growing village thirty-five miles away, (as far away to him as Mangalore was to me) in the hope of 'saarvice' to the 'saars', and a permanent appointment that would be financial moksha for his family. He too was an exile, coming from a three-thousand-year history of agricultural labour, feeling as organically connected to the alien official papers he lugged from place to place as a Burundian is to unicorns.

'Shall I sugar you?' asks the Minister for Family Planning, passing the sugar to his brother politician at a Circuit House.

'Thank you, sir,' replies the junior Minister for Animal Husbandry, passing on the milk jug in return. 'Shall I milk you?'

The gathering of ten officers sipping Shaw's Vissky and munching chicken tikka at the Shimoga Motel, a concrete-box enclave built to shield precious white-skinned foreign tourists from accidentally gazing on the shamefully uncool natives, burst into high-pitched, effeminate laughter at this joke from the bald, dark Mr Subbaiah. Subbaiah's standard greeting, parodying the politicians' English, was: 'How are you? I am in the well, thank you thank you!'

We were exiles, all. India was full of exiles, exiles at every level, even in towns like Shimoga, which was crammed with petty district officers always plotting to get a transfer to Bangalore, and in the meanwhile trying to milk their local office for all it was worth and lay the foundations for their comfortably creamy urban futures. Indian-made foreign liquors, 'nonveg' or off colour jokes (amazing how often the functionaries of the Licence Raj are licentious chaps themselves), non-vegetarian food eaten with decadent glee, cash under the table.

But even if most IAS officers then still had a relative reputation for honesty, the agenda was often set by someone else, which was why our country had been so slow to develop, as I learned one day, in a premonition of my life to come.

I was in the Deputy Commissioner's chambers one morning, when an excited clerk burst in with a wireless message: the President of India, an ex-politician who had been kicked upstairs into the job so he might be an embarrassment to the country rather than a nuisance to Her, had decided to visit Shimoga to 'inaugurate' the golden jubilee celebrations of Nanjundaiah College, a college so obscure that it would have thrived in its well-deserved obscurity without his help.

A microsecond after learning of the President's plans, the D.C., a short-cropped no-nonsense ex-army officer, a natural big samosa who outgunned everyone else in protocol matters, sprang into action with a catlike smile on his face. This was his opportunity to get back at all the other departments, to force sullen Superintending Engineers to do idiotic work he wouldn't normally have dared ask a First Division Clerk to do. Gigantic meetings were summoned, the halls overflowing with compulsive notetakers, the official compounds a mess of jeeps, chauffeurs, and chaprasis. The Circuit House or chief official guest-house, a huge rooming complex situated on the town's only hill, was completely commandeered by the D.C. and swept clean of its occupants, many of them homeless junior local bureaucrats too poor to afford hotels, now forced to lug about their beddings and lotas looking for any shelter they could find. Private cars were requisitioned by official fiat for the motorcade, endless drills held, roads repaired and potholes filled, unsightly huts (and people) along the presidential route disappeared (not as in Argentina; these squatters were just told to get lost). A spare electric generator was shipped in for a possible emergency. Every official, big or small, was commanded by a suddenly muscular and omnipotent D.C., (now functioning On His Exalted Excellency's Service) to drop everything else on his schedule or on his friggin' mind, to snap to it and rehearse his visit-related duties, even if these were merely to stand and wait at an obscure stretch of the seventeen-mile Presidential route, should some unforeseen eventuality (no one could imagine what) result in a sudden demand for manpower at that very point. (And even standing and waiting took talent, took mega-rehearsals, what?)

I of the IAS thrice-born (twice-born as a Brahmin, I had been

born again into the IAS supercaste) was luckier: gratifyingly, in
deference to my outstanding class and sophistication, I was
appointed as the Liaison Officer between His Excellency the
President and His Mortal Mediocrity the local Assistant
Commissioner (the minor cheese who was to make all the physical
arrangements for the President's comfort). If ever the President
wanted anything, just anything, from the Assistant
Commissioner—*Ginger Frog Legs with Minced Dog*, for
example—he could sleep soundly knowing that I, Vijay Anthony
Prabhu, stood by ready to speed his message over land and sea
without rest. Who knows, the President might even decide to have
some liaison with me, and just me, and nobody but me, just for the
bloody heck of it, and to hell with the Assistant Commissioner, the
boring stiff. We might hit it off famously, trading wicked limericks
and Vedantic philosophy into the night, discussing political
philosophies until the President exclaimed, 'Corblimey! I have
been wrong all along?'—and changed the direction of this
700-million-strong country. Future history textbooks might rank
our momentous meeting next only to that between Stanley and
Livingstone, Solomon and Sheba, Raisa Gorbachev and Nancy
Reagan. I launched immediately into memorizing my *Penguin Book
of Quotations*.

With the trip now only a week away, a high drill is unfolding on
the hot and humid open spaces of the Shimoga Aerodrome. It is a
rehearsal of every moment of the ritual, to anticipate the bizarrest
eventuality. On the tarmac the slightly overdone Divisional
Commissioner, Mr Appamma, and the medium-rare Deputy
Inspector-General of Police, Mr Balajirao Saheb, neither of whom
has piloted even a toy plane, are arguing over which direction the
nose and the tail of the plane should point—for some obscure
reason, a crucial element in the arrangements—and the Aerodrome
Officer is watching in bemused disbelief (but he must defer,
because these Lord Highs outrank him by a few dozen rungs). Four
score assistants and hangers-on, including dutiful stenographers
poised with pads and pencils in hand (and an extra one behind
each ear) ready to fire at the slightest provocation, and senior

officers who look depressingly outranked and reduced to superfluity, are watching the drama. Suddenly, a bespectacled and white-shirted assistant all but canters from the terminal building in great excitement and heads directly for the Deputy Commissioner. The argument screeches to a stop, and all eyes rest on the babu as he utters the momentous words, 'Saar! Wireless message from Madras just received, saar! President is sick and Visit is cancelled!'

The entire anti-poverty programme, the entire administration, the daily needs of a million democratic citizens—all of these put on hold, frozen in their bullock cart tracks, for an entire month, all on account of a proposed visit by an airheaded figurehead. A visit that was never destined to be.

With the President off our backs, we went back to fighting poverty (many of us our own poverty), and the people of Shimoga went back to their everyday lives. So did I, until an old but now irresistible force thundered into my life, quieting my fears about careers and stilling my trembling about my ultimate purpose. The name of this force: Maya.

Of Human Bondage

In the pleasure room . . . they should then carry on an
amusing conversation on various subjects, and may also
talk suggestively of things which would be considered as
coarse, or not to be mentioned generally in society.
    −*The Kama Sutra*

WHEN I RAN into a common friend on Bangalore's Brigade Road,
and he told me Maya was in town, working as a field-worker for a
mildly leftist organization reaching out to help slum dwellers and
raise their 'consciousness', I nearly freaked out.

For a year now, in lonely, one-horse Shimoga, where the peak
of the day's excitement might be a crazed cow stampeding through
the vegetable market upsetting onions and potatoes, I had been
making trips to Bangalore, plotting every possible
ruse—discussions with the Chief Secretary, consultations about
the anti-poverty programme with the Development
Commissioner—to escape my banishment from civilization and
make weekend jaunts to this city. The only real city within a radius
of five hundred kilometres, a city dominated by a mammoth
marble edifice called the Vidhana Soudha—one quarter temple,
one quarter mausoleum, and three quarters sheer balls—a city
bursting with rose gardens and gulmohur-lined avenues,
provocatively dressed convent-school Lolitas, palatial English
movie theatres, Chinese restaurants called Rice Bowl and Bamboo
House, salacious cabarets named Three Aces and Roxy, and a
spiffy rock group called The Human Bondage.

And all the time, the last Marxist I had ever kissed, the girl I had kissed in a dusty and bumpy Delhi autorickshaw three years before, whose crevices and chest bumps I had feverishly felt . . . this girl was in Bangalore, and I didn't know it?

The realization hit me like a glass of fire-hot Andhra rassam downed in one long gulp.

I merely had to conjure up Maya's come-hither eyes and Oh-Come-All-Ye-Faithful figure, and remember that she was in Bangalore and alone—and what spurted out with demonic force, like a long-suppressed oil well, were the juices of tenderness and hard-on-ness. As fast as thought, the end of the story was written in my mind: we met and mated.

It only remained for me to carry out the *physical* details of the script that had been stamped and approved by every cell of my being.

On my next weekend trip, having arrived in Bangalore and checked into the Hotel Woodlands, and then having located my special flower and gotten the address of her apartment, I called her up. I sputtered only two words on the phone: 'I'm coming.'

There was a cause for this unstoppable urgency: last time's four kisses and three squeezes had, during the four years of absence, magnified themselves in the chamber of my mind into a Zhivagoesque passion. I bathed with Mysore Sandal Soap, slapped on some Old Spice, and pulled on my tightly tailored trousers—I had stopped wearing underwear, finally at twenty-five rebelling against confinement, emancipating my manhood. I brushed back my wavy black hair, having wet it with a little upscale Pantene for Men, slipped on my naturally air-conditioned Roman sandals and my orange striped shirt—I always dressed casually now, the confidence of power achieved and constitutionally guaranteed for the next thirty years—clicked on my dull, metal-braceleted West End Swiss Watch, a ten-year-old discard from an uncle, and jumped into the nearest autorickshaw. 'Richards Town *hogu*,' I imperially commanded the driver. The three-wheeler wove and farted through traffic into the gathering dusk.

Arriving at my destination, I ran up two flights of the red stone staircase, dodged one little servant girl and two bony kids, and breathlessly arrived in front of Maya's apartment—which had a

Mickey Mouse sticker on the door and a coir doormat saying 'Welcome'. I knocked the hell out of Mickey. A kurta and jean-clad Maya, long hair still slightly wet from a head-bath, opened the door, and Old-Spiced I, almost without checking to see if I had the right girl, rushed into her arms, she surprised and protesting and laughing, I moving dialectically like History, as if the Zeitgeist were working through me, inexorable and argument-repellent.

What what, what you doing, what you, how're you, hee, doing, doing to me, so dashing, huh? Enthusiastic, a little too much? Sit down now, Vijay, let's talk. It's so nice, you a big man and all, such a surprise. Wow! *Such* a *surprise*!

Conversation irrelevant, badly-timed, unhinged, unpegged to reality, ungrammatical even for this B.Sc. (Physics) (High Second Class) girl.

So we proceeded, now, to an unbuttoning of our separate, multicoloured existences—zip; rip; then the thlap, shlap, of two bodies on a Dunlopillo foam bed.

Her light brown body, lean but with a twenty-four-year-old's oomph and bloom; her two dark chocolate nipples matched by two similarly coloured moles, one each on left thigh and right upper chest, so erotically quadraphonic. I gasped. She looked at me half shy, half proud.

And what struck me now was the magnificence of her pubic forest—a new vista of beauty I had never before imagined. Her hair spread out from her pubis almost to her belly, and sideways to her groin, leaving her, like Sonia Braga (owner of the world's most famous pubis?), hardly any belly, but a gloriously sculptured belly button.

And the breasts! I was reluctant to touch them at first, as if afraid to spoil their ivory smooth, visual perfection with an intrusion of my hairy, masculine fingers.

I let my face hover closely over them, and after a while, closed my eyes and tasted them, softly, not rudely, as if invited to take just a single taste of the world's best chocolate.

And now, following the masculine imperative—go for the thing, man, the good old missionary position—my muscled young body, my near-virgin body, prime beef, lay on top of this other divine body, acutely conscious and sensitive of every contact from every quarter, scalded nerve-endings collecting field reports of ecstasy, bringing them to my consciousness, now a sex-filled Howrah Central. Two bodies in their prime, now interlocked in slow motion.

Rather, exterlocked in slow motion: because of one slight missing detail. What was happening here wouldn't impregnate a flea. It was just a chaste sport[*] devised by our atavistic imaginations to circumvent our pre-birth-control reality. A rubbing together of skin against skin, like two particularly sensuous cats rubbing against the fantasied sofa of the other. All over her body was light, silky down, each hair of which conveyed an erotic message for me.

'You're so beautiful, inside. I had no idea. No idea you were here,' I say.

'Two years.'

'*Two*. Damn! Oh God.'

'Vijay, please, oh!'

Me, happy to be here, too happy to be happy merely, happy only to thus simulate like some understudy to a temporarily-incapacitated male star, having gotten a lucky break with the bombshell heroine, enacting a steamy love scene until the director says 'Cut!' For my courage had somehow fizzled at the final stage, the Real Thing being somehow too much to ask for, too greedy of me, too unkind, too risky, too Malthusian in flavour, likely to spoil my chances, me sensing she sensing me sensing she had limits for me, at least today!

'You're beautiful! Your skin—glorious!'

'Oh, you all say that.'

'You *all*? Who?'

'Oh, men.'

It wasn't in Maya's constitution to be deceitful. Her honest, Frieda Lawrence pride in her liberation, her belief in total, uncensored candour between men and women—this came from a truly revolutionary passion. And it made her tell me her story during breaks in our loveplay.

From what I soon heard, Maya belonged to nobody but everybody; she deserved to be declared a national treasure.

---

[*]   In a more American idiom, a 'dry run'.

'You seem to have a hard time saying no to hard men—these are the hard facts of your life,' I said to her teasingly.

Luckily (for me—because I was possessive), few were the men in those sex-shy times who could translate their hardness into the question, 'Shall we?' And thus, though the men who had had her, and who were having her presently—among others a banker, a rocket engineer, four students, and a seminarian—added up to a sizeable number, they could at least be gathered together in one large room, not an auditorium. And though she had three current full-time lovers, none of whom knew of the existence of the others—despite their having her at interlocking schedules so unkempt that her closet must occasionally have hid living skeletons—still, she made room for an occasional another, such as myself today.

All this excess was of course post-Moopsian (Moops being the revolutionary she had fallen in love with many years ago, the fellow with the 'Love me, love my Marx' look, and a mind so Marxist no sensual pleasure could violate it). Now, in this post-crisis moment (the crisis having been actually circumvented by a few million sperm landing on her thigh, she squealing with laughter as I mopped the little wrigglers up into the interstices of a Turkish towel), her nakedness being a spur to truth and confession (if only politicians could be required to be naked while they made campaign speeches), (I thought: Ha ha, Prime Minister Maya being probed by ace investigative reporter Vijay, using the tool of his trade), Maya told me the story of her affair with Moops.

'Moops—what a character!' she laughed. 'But complex.' Pausing thoughtfully, she now said in her Sphinx-like manner, 'I liked his mind; and that's exactly what I had against him.'

'What do you mean?'

'Like, he was a curious person: his thirst for knowledge extended to everything except to what was inside my chaddi.'

'Ha ha.' I saw that her face had a pink flush, her movements the sureness of one who had known men, and acquitted herself very well in the process.

'He was such a prude. Once, at a camp, when we were all sitting on the floor having a discussion, he objected to my leaning against another boy's back. It had been such an innocent gesture.'

'He was snatching eroticism from the jaws of continence,' I said gleefully.

'You've captured the very arc of the situation,' she hit back. Like me, she loved repeating some high-sounding expression she had read somewhere, comically out of context: this is where our mutual arcs of zaniness intersected.

'Arc arc arc aaaarc!' wailed I, clownishly imitating the archetypal novelistic orgasm.

She continued: 'Moops had some funny ideas. He kept boasting about his self-control, how he could use it to stop a fever. Queer fellow, except for his mind.'

I, jealous, 'But why are you so obsessed with his mind that you have to keep singing its praises all the time? Does it really matter?'

Missing my joke, she continued, 'Well, because there was nothing one could find attractive about his face: thick glasses, small eyes, jungly beard. To love him, one had to get past that facial block and contemplate his mind. The content was good, but the form terrible.'

'Then why did you choose him in the first place?'

'Because my father wanted me to look for a "decent, Konkani-speaking Catholic boy". So I had no choice but to choose the opposite.'

'Take me then. I'm an indecent, English-speaking, lapsed Catholic.'

Passion between two red-blooded young human beings being what it is—it has its *mounting* quality—we attempted now to make *progress*. Now that I knew she was no virgin, I didn't need to be so restrained, did I?

It came to me, the advice in the pundit's book picked up from the Bombay pavement:

Now insert the male organ into vagina for getting pleasure of life for which king Edward VIII left the throne and saints their sacrifice.

But progress there could not be—not tonight: because she was too small . . . or perhaps I was too big . . . or maybe it was simply the absence of Vaseline, artificial or natural . . . . Maybe, in violation of the advice of the sex pundit whose book I had once picked up from a Bombay pavement, I had washed my organ too much, and had failed to take 'ten to fifteen drops banian milk' daily. Never mind, we'll leave a future Einstein to sort that out. In any case I, the soul of kindness and consideration, oversensitive to the look of hurt surprise on her face as I began to bore my way in, had to bigheartedly relinquish the thought and my dismay at the crazy disproportions that steal away some of life's creamiest moments.

She continued her story of her other men as I, the frustrated writer and forever voyeur and virgin in the true ways of the world, listened in open-mouthed fascination to her narration of her post-Moopsist-sensualist phase.

She told me now about Frederick the Ex-seminarian, who entered her life—and shortly thereafter, her—when he sent out a mass mailing to all the women on a campers' address list. The letter went: 'Dear So-and-So: Is it true that you suffer from an awful inferiority complex? I could help you.' Frederick's years as an almost-priest conferred a shamanistic aura on him; his stentorian voice enhanced it; his self-defrocking (he left of his own accord) was a sexy coup. The letters netted him more than one girl, and one of these was Maya.

'He's still so much like a priest,' she said. 'That seminary training must scar you for life.'

'Why, does he bless the spot before he enters it?'

Then there was the banker, a member of that rare species Macho Indicus—an oxymoron, some would argue, considering Hinduism's accent on pacifism and bovine meekness; yet there are some Hindi film heroes playing the character, probably one product, in real life, of a diet of cowboy novels and the Upanishads. The banker had a habit—strange for one who preached the conservative gospel of *savings* deposits—of withdrawing a few seconds before the moment of truth and expending himself on Maya's creamy breasts; and while doing so, instead of the customary 'Aaiieeeoo!' he would exclaim: 'If any other man sees your naked body, I'll skin him alive!'

She didn't tell him that there were more cats, cool and uncool, than a mere banker could handle; nor did she let her family in on her secret life. For the mere fact of her unmarried state, her carefree singularity, had been upsetting to her father, a bastion of the Sodality of Our Blessed Virgin and a great hit in social gatherings of bishops and mother superiors with his super-clean Saint Peter jokes. The holy man (her father) only faintly suspected the richer details, which would have made him faint if known. He had tried to beat back the tide of men in her life, reading all incoming mail from young males—there were many such all over the country, whose flybuttons popped at the very thought of her—and tearing most of it up before it reached her eyes. Still, he had missed the Moops affair. As her aunt commented sarcastically later, 'Whole village knows, Mother and Father don't know.'

'And he had to discover and stop our innocent meetings,' I said, ruefully.

'He was just being careful. Actually he thought highly of you. In fact my entire family admired you, used to talk about you.'

I supposed she meant my academic prizes, my essay and debating victories, all of which impressed Mangaloreans more than they should have, which impressed *me* more than they should have, too. Mangaloreans, lacking other social activities at the time, kept tab of such prizes, in little notebooks, it seemed, translating them as 'goodness'. Though it pleased my ego to think that she had heard of me before I her, the downside was that a reputation for goodness, even though acquired chiefly while I was in shorts, was hard to shake off and had probably kept lots of fun-loving young women away, women who had probably gone to other men for their intimate satisfactions, fearing a pious reprimand and a lecture on morality from me. How costly this reputation had probably been to me, I thought morosely.

God, I ought to have taken her then. It is more blessed to take than to half-take. Because a half-taken woman is a woman scorned. What a greenhorn I was! How excessively sensitive, stopping at the slightest suggestion of concern in her face. It could have been managed, with patience, with sinuous ingenuity. My instant retreat must have seemed so callow. Women like men who are sure of themselves. She had once confessed to me that the fictional scene that made her moistest between her legs was the troglodyte one in *The Godfather* in which Sonny Corleone forces himself on his sister-in-law.

But Maya soon left on an employer-sponsored trip to Brazil to train for six months in slum development and agriculture. When I saw her next, calling on her at her office, she was a different woman, made larger, smoother, and more self-assured by her foreign experience and perhaps a few all-night sessions under the approving gaze of the statue of Christ the Redeemer. I could see her breasts had thrived on it. She told me she had grown out of her experimental zeal, was going steady now.

But as I talked on, bringing back warm memories—we were both suckers for reminiscences of childhood follies, and we both considered ourselves rare 'survivors' of the Mangalorean System—she gradually agreed to a tryst at Kempegowda Circle. In that jungle of red, bleating city buses, bell-ringing cyclists, irritable autorickshaws, ant-dense crowds, I was too inhibited to kiss her, to do anything more than say 'Hello'. In 1977, sexual intention was still illegal in India, at least in that part of town. Being too inexperienced, too green, too excited to impersonate a married couple, we had to play brother and sister (India was extraordinarily full of brothers and sisters; you couldn't throw a stone without hitting a brother-sister pair).

'Why did you ask me to come *here*?' I asked, pained. Why this rowdy bustle of humanity and not a park or some cozy Cantonment restaurant, for example?

'Well, you wanted to go out with me . . . and this is out, isn't it?'

We walked aimlessly for a while. And then, like a dog light-headed with lust, I led her into one of those janata-type restaurants that had cabins or plywood-partitioned nooks for 'families'.

'Aha, a family cabin,' said I.

'As if we aren't *all* part of one large human family,' said she.

This particular joint, the Imperial Hotel, had muddy blue cabins: slightly better than muddy green, the only other and more popular colour (preferred by three out of four dentists surveyed) for sleazy restaurant cabins.

Lowering myself onto a steel folding chair by her side, our eyes facing the door and watching out for approaching trouble (such as sexually-frustrated part-time sleuths and guardians of public morality who cruised the family cabin scene), I commenced my softlanding advances on her.

She had on a conservative sari: a smooth and light cotton material with a design of endless bluebells, a fifty-rupee lower-middleclass garment used by smart local women to blend with the crowd and thus repel the unwanted attentions of professional skirt-chasers. And which, because of its tightly knotted, fortress-like positioning, repelled all conceivable intrusions. Which said: 'Don't even *think* of parking here.'

The waiter, a curly haired, oily-faced rascal in maroon tight pants and pointed shoes in Tamil film hero style, entered, deposited a greasy menu, and stared at us. My eagle eyes, as if by some encoded genetic programme, quickly zeroed in on the menu's most exotic offering: Partrege Moghlia, which I took to mean Partridge Moghlai—which in turn I took to mean a dish having some connection to an exotic bird called the partridge (a bird I had only heard of, coming as I did from a sweatfarm of a town monopolized by crows), in which chopped strands of the hapless bird were blasted with spices and overcooked and presented in unrecognizable form on a greasy aluminium dish. And yet, for a connoisseur of *nouvelle experience* like myself, a must.

'Partridge Moghlai,' I said, eagerly, letting my *haute cuisine* instinct temporarily override the carnal.

'Butter chicken, yes,' said the waiter rather abstractedly. He had the heavy Kannada accent meant to repel English-speaking invaders from the other, more-fashionable part of town.

I was in no mood for semantic arguments. I had other birds to attend to. But, tired of the too-familiar Butter Chicken, I suggested something else: 'Mutter Paneer?'

'Butter chicken, yes,' said the fellow again.

'You have Mutton Sag?'

'Butter chicken, yes.'

Damn fool! Having attained the butter chicken track, the man seemed to find himself stuck in it.

'OK, butter chicken,' I said finally, pragmatically acknowledging defeat, wanting to put a stop to this nonsense.

'Mutter Paneer, yes,' the scoundrel nodded back to my momentary astonishment.

'OK, *yesyes, and four parathas!*' said I without further argument, hurrying him on his way, remembering that we had come here not to eat but to fornicate, at least as far as is possible fully clothed. We laughed as the outsmarted waiter left with his precious menu, like a dog with his tail between his legs.

I looked at Maya, and then pursued her with my lips, trying to nibble at her mouth.

'I'm hungry,' I explained.

'Eat me, then,' she said.

Alas, she didn't mean a single word.

She knew what 'eat me' meant, of course, having probably picked it up, like me, from some naughty American novel. But this was simply provocation.

That was the kind of woman she was. She walked the demure, bowed-head, eyes-downcast walk of the Mangalorean woman walking to church (an activity that seems to consume about half the average Mangalorean woman's life); yet in some moods, her pouting lips and intense face seemed perfectly cast for the heavy fellatio part in an X-rated film. At other times it was a face that, with its peering, watchful, sad eyes, surprised you with its sudden, golden laughter.

Underneath the gossamer nun's veil of her modest, churchgoer's exterior, her eroticism heaved and smouldered. Yet it was an eroticism given life by her domestic puritanism. To really respect eroticism for the blessing and pure pleasure it is, we all must begin in puritanism. As Maya and I had.

I started kissing her again, probing her tightly closed thighs with caressing, persuading touches through her sari material, thin enough for a little warmth from her upper pubis to pass through to me.

'Open Sesame,' I whispered, hoping she would relax enough to let me feel the contours of her warm triangle.

'Sorry: my lips are sealed,' she said seriously—then laughed. It hurt me deeply to see her thus before me, so warm, so incendiary, yet so far.

But the next time we met, her hardness melted towards mine. I had just received a promotion into a position of real power, which had filled me briefly with a can't-take-no-for-an-answer ebullience. She agreed to join me for an afternoon tryst at a multi-storeyed hotel known to cater to such trysts.

Checking into the Hotel Staylonger under the antiseptic, ultra-virtuous pseudonym F. L. Gandhi, I took the elevator to the fifth floor, while chivalrous she, to avoid suspicion or recognition, walked up via a little-used side staircase.

Once inside, having embraced deeply, we shed our clothes in a hurry. And on white starched sheets, as traffic noise and bright daylight filtered through the translucent white curtains and illuminated by light-brown love, she licked the skin of the forbidden fruit. I remember her face still: at first, full of cautious concentration, as if she were licking jam from a sharp knife. And then, she proceeded very seriously to try to swallow more of my lingam than her full-lipped mouth could possibly accommodate: the whole process, because of her imperfectly restrained teeth, becoming a mixture of pain, pleasure, sacred ritual, and high comedy: a toothy fruity job (Yes, we have no bananas; no, we almost lost a banana). Two tyros doing what they believed had to be done (a ritual as fundamental to sex as the Sign of the Cross is to Catholicism), but ignorant of its finer points.

Yes, it was Murphy's Law of Blowjobs in operation: Either you're good at it, or you're not; there is no middle ground. (Especially if, like me, the recipient had a penis that was oversensitive to pain, undersensitive to pleasure.) But what does Murphy know about the excitement of the first time, of the joy of doing the immoral, the cock-fattening, and the probably illegal (somewhere in India's Victorian legal code)? Even though, as Murphy might have pointed out, nothing else went right or came right that afternoon?

Soon after this unconsummated episode, and perhaps, I consoled myself, due to my physical absence from Bangalore and the influx of new lovers into her incredibly energetic life, she began to avoid me.

Still, I was so inflated with penile confidence at the time (and despite everything else, she loved to talk to me), that I tried again.

The next time I landed in Bangalore, I gave her a call from the bus station.

'You just come into town without telling me. Then I have to drop everything and be with you.'

'Reasons of state,' I said. 'I never know for sure, until the last minute. And then, I just want to be with you.' That, and a goofy lack of organization, and of some understanding of women.

'OK then, we'll meet. But no touchie-touchie, feelie-feelie. Only talkie-talkie. OK?'

'What? No prickie, prickie?'

Having bargained over the matter much like Henry Kissinger and Le Duc Tho over the shape of the negotiating table (like Kissinger, I had the missile, and like Le Duc Tho, she had me by the balls), we finally met at the open-air, vegetarian Airlines Restaurant, a place where vegetarian leaves and non-vegetarian birdie-poop plopped into your dosa or dahi vada at no extra charge, and where sunlight and openness, sworn enemies of love in India, foreclosed all possibilities of foreplay.

'The best way to approach the subject is to enter it,' I began craftily.

'What else can there be but pricks and cunts? Why, after all these years, are we beating around the bush?'—she shot back, shocking me with her frankness, making me feel like a coy prude.

I need her as a volcano needs an arsonist, I thought. And yet, I did. While she, licking her lips with pleasure at my neediness, needed me not and played with me.

Talking to her was like talking to an assortment of neurotics simultaneously. In turn came the nymphomaniac, the paranoid, the depressive, the curmudgeon, the subversive, the wit, the punster. It kept my mind and my tongue nimble.

I had given pet names to our private parts: Julia and Maria to her tits (in the photograph, standing erect, from left to right), Portia to her pussy, and Julius to my sub-imperial member.

Now I said, assuming she would understand my references: 'Shall we confer in private? *All* of us?'

'Where are the others?' she asked with pretended innocence, refusing to play the game she had begun.

'What is it you find lacking in me?' I said, suddenly serious. 'Is it that I don't have a V-chest?'

She laughed.

'OK, is it that I don't have a V *on* my chest?'

She gurgled with pleasure. It was an arousing, provocative laugh. Actually, it didn't matter what we talked about, politics or philosophy or pop psychology, there was hardly a moment with her that I did not have an erection.

Then, noticing that she always talked of Marxists with respect: 'Do you mean to say that each of your lovers has to pass a quiz on Marxism before he can go to bed with you?'

Stupid me, to provoke her thus! I didn't understand strongly enough that Marxism was a faith to her, a faith that defined her war with her repressive past, a faith to which she was true, for which she made commitments and sacrifices. Besides which, the passionate incantation of Marxist terms was a sort of foreplay, a lip-service necessary to get her in the mood, to wet her more significant lips. She also got her kicks from handsome men regardless of political beliefs . . . .

Then it hit me: her latest lovers (none of them Marxists) all had motorbikes!

I should have saved and invested in a motorbike. Bangalore was overrun with motorbike-mounted Lotharios: human pistons, their helmeted heads penile knobs, their sweaty, sun-soaked faces and necks symbolically seminal, moving with fluid ease, in between the just-liberated, just-opening thighs of India's upper crust.

So the intellectual crap was really an excuse?

Win or lose, I would persevere. Because she was good for me! She sparked my sense of humour, brought out my noblest pie-fighting impulses, brought forth an atmosphere of primal permissiveness in which the only justification for words was the laughter, the intellectual frisson they produced. She was my living, breathing lifeline to my barely-awakened artistic soul.

But there is probably an easier, biological explanation for my stubbornness. It is power. Power, the power of a new and substantially bigger job drove me now and pumped up my already-bursting balls. And power, too, explains why Maya in turn didn't more forcefully banish me from her sight.

Toil and Trouble

I tell women who have difficulty having an orgasm, 'Fill
your head with fantasies. Think about Burt Reynolds.'
    –Pooja Bedi, Indian film actress, in an
        interview with the *Sunday Mail*

AT HIGH NOON on a Tuesday in September 1978, a stranger rides
into town, strides up to the local big boss and says, in effect, 'I've
come to take charge of the town and everything else within a radius
of twenty-five miles.'

Does the Bossman say, 'You little shit! You better make your
ass scarce or I'll have you arrested'? No. He says, 'Wait, have some
tea pliss.'

The Bossman's name is Shri U. Ugraiah, and his appearance
is very unbosslike: the stubble on his unshaven face and the
sweat-stained khaki balaclava on his head ('I have a cold,' he
explains, and loudly blows his nose into a large green
handkerchief).

The tea soon arrives. The tea is consumed. Bossman orders
more tea. More tea gets consumed. Between sips there are phone
calls, irrelevant conversation, conspiratorial whispers to
conspiratorial assistants.

Then, at 2:30 p.m., a clerk with the tell-tale fountain pen in his
bush shirt pocket arrives with a dirty brown folder containing
some pieces of paper, and says to the stranger, 'Sign here, pliss,
sahib.' The stranger signs. Bossman smiles, shakes the stranger's
hand, and offers to exchange seats with him.

I am the stranger, armed with a government order that empowers me to take over Mr Ugraiah's job as Assistant Commissioner of Yellanagara Subdivision; and this elaborate charade about tea happened because Old Ugraiah did not wish to hand over charge during 'Rahukala'—the time of each day, determined by complicated astrological calculations, that Hindus consider inauspicious moments for important work.

The town of Yellanagara, the headquarters of Yellanagara subdivision, is one of those nameless market towns of Old Mysore State, with roads that radiate out from the denser, gaudier urban homes towards hesitant, dung-splashed shacks squatting amidst grain fields on the outskirts; in which the bus station is the centre of, almost the only justification for, and often the only sign of life; and where everything else of importance, including the bazaar, the high school, the college, and the hotels are on one main road. This road is usually the highway that bifurcates the town, conveying buses that have more important places to go, but will condescend for a piss-stop anyway. The buses and loaded lorries hurtle along these highways at great speed, barely missing cows, coolies and kids, their piercing horns battering away at small-town eardrums, their tyres whirling dust into small-town faces and astonished, open mouths, onto exposed foodstuffs on carts, their exhausts spewing carcinogenic fumes into the pedestrians' pitiful lungs.

It wasn't my idea of glamour, working in this town dominated by the odour of cow piss. But it was power all right, my first, heady taste of power—such power at age twenty-five as most human beings would never know in their lifetimes. Grown men trembled before you, sometimes lunging forward like terrorists in sudden attempts to touch your feet; peons awaited your commands, hanging around even when not needed, just in case the Sahib changed his mind and thought of a command; village chiefs awaited your arrival with garlands and lemons, the way these characters had greeted honoured guests for generations; large audiences listened to you with respect or at least silence, regardless of your speech's merits; chauffeured jeeps and the largest and gaudiest rooms at government guest-houses awaited your pleasure.

There is a secret monarch in all of us, however democratic and idealistic we may be; a megalomaniac child that cannot but be gratified at being treated like a king. If it was the power that turned them on, my colleagues were too decent to admit it, being bound by at least some of the democratic, egalitarian idealism that most Indian postgraduates must pretend to. Yet, when we had gotten news of our postings at the Academy, we had rushed to the library to pick up a district gazetteer and survey our territories, our kingdoms.

And now, three months later, my heart is thumping. It is past midnight, and I am on the Yellanagara-Singladatta Road, under a cool, starry night sky, but the air I'm breathing has diesel fuel mixed with dust.

'Saar, communal riot has broken out, saar, come immediately, saar,' the Tahsildar had said on the phone, waking me up with a nightmarish jolt.

We're now entering Singladatta; the diesel jeep, like a loudly neighing steed, surprises the quiet night, the engine hum echoing off shabby houses in pitiful narrow streets. A half mile into the bowels of the city, the silence gives way to a tumult of shouting and murderous epithets. Suddenly, huge stones and bricks are flying in the air in front of us and breaking against the stone-scattered street. I duck, my head between my knees, hands raised to protect my head; my driver, Subash, bends only slightly, one hand raised to protect his turbanned head; with the other, he drives on. Miraculously, the stones stop to let the unarmed jeep pass. Brave Subash. Relax, old chap. We haven't lost an A.C. yet.

The jeep, dodging stones and barricades of cow-dung (recently deposited on the road by obliging cows, our country's honorary traffic cops), heads for the Taluk Office, where the portly Tahsildar, looking rumpled and unhappy at having to be up at this late hour, awaits me, his immediate superior in the feudal chain of command. Before the Tahsildar can explain what is happening, there are shouts outside; and a dozen dirtied and bloodied—but mostly dirtied—warm bodies are hauled into the police station next door, apparently suffering from the hangover of their recent warlike overindulgence. More prisoners follow, as do more shouts and curses—I've rarely noticed a police operation not accompanied by a lot of noise and self-hypnotizing hectoring.

'It was really just a fight between two groups of drunks,' I tell the Tahsildar irritably, after the Circle Inspector of Police has filled me in on the details. 'What made you think it was communal? Couldn't you have handled it yourself?'

'Sorry, saar; Yes, saar,' says the poor, indecisive man. Then, 'Saar, please sign this order, saar.'

I read it. Unbelievable. It is titled: 'Section 133: Offenses Against the Pubic [sic] Peace.'

'I have no objection to offenses against the *pubic* peace,' I tell him. 'For me, pubic peace is the peace of the dead, do you understand? The government ought to *encourage* people to violate the pubic peace. Then, they might be too busy to violate the *public* peace.'

'Saar. What, saar?'

In my little room, With no pants on
I'm hiding away, With no pants on
And planning to stay, With no pants on
Cause I've nothing to do, With no pants on.

–Parody of song popular in India.

I of the IAS Cream of the Cream, the most powerful human being in an area of a thousand square miles inhabited by one million people, having shed the ill-fitting clothes of power, was jerking off—relieving myself of the cream of the cream of the cream—in an old bungalow, the shell of its former glory. Is that power, or impotence? I ask you. Impotence, I say, because the price of this awesome power is 'respectability', which in the local vocabulary of the time meant No Fucking Whatsoever! As an IAS officer, I had to conceal the fact that I had a prick. My contract required me to 'behave' myself, to do the eunuch-y namaste towards women I wanted to do calisthenics in the sack with, to pretend to be an impotent potent-ate.

With no pants on, the frustrated and erect Assistant Commissioner suddenly decided he had had it with the mosquitoes that were whooping around him, launching guerilla attacks on his nude but exalted frame. I jumped into a karate stance.

'Come out, you fuckers,' I shouted, profaning the hallowed residence. 'Let's settle this, man to mosquito.'

God, what was I doing here? I, who once dreamed of making the world his stage, in this hole in a corner of India? Because what's so big and meaningful and noble about a prick running about in a jeep—affixed though it be with the seal of august officialdom?

I was not even a good magistrate anyway. I thought I knew better than my subjects—yes, that's how I looked at them. I was often more severe than I might have been had I reminded myself of my own shortcomings. I was annoyed at them for crowding my life with work, for not being able to settle their own disputes about streams flowing in the wrong place or direction, about land demarcations running in the middle of someone's kitchen. I would have been happy to judge whether the tea should be poured first or the milk, or whether the defamation of a famous restaurant's cuisine by a food critic were justified. I would have been most happy to decide, say, a divorce case in which the groom disputed his bride's virginity and wanted me to be the final judge of the matter, with a field trial if and when His Honour so deemed it necessary. I would have loved most to be a member of the Indian Censor Board, taking unseemly joy in, and asking for endless repeat showings of dirty foreign movies or Hindi movie kisses which it would be my duty to protect my fellow Indians from.

That evening at a small travellers' bungalow in Tumkur district, I had a tryst with my colleague Chowdaiah. Chowdaiah, with his hirsute sideburns and extra-dark glasses and beige and blue safari suits, belonged to the Kannada Film Star School of Administration—administrators and politicians who believed that imitating the loud, rakish style of these film heroes would project the right, 'power' image of dynamism and virility.

'What, hahn, Vijay, A.C. saheb?' said Chowdaiah with his usual ebullience.

We got down to talking of my boss, the D.C., who had become my mortal enemy because I refused to be too lenient with the perennial requests of politicians, as he wanted me to be.

'What he needs is a good fuck,' said Chowdaiah.

I thought: The Fucking Theory of Indian Administration. Something in it. Because when you took your irritating, difficult-to-understand, mean colleagues—male or female—one by one, and tried to understand them in their domestic contexts, you realized it may come down to this: they weren't getting enough or good enough. And their reservoirs of unspent spunk or joy juice caused misery to everyone around them. All you had to do was imagine them well-fucked, and you could practically picture the smiles on their mugs. For a small investment in high-class studs and fillies this medieval country would take off, and guided by its three million scientific and mathematical geniuses who currently languished in bureaucratic prisons or in unemployment lines, would zoom out of its surprised fifteenth-century underpants directly into the twenty-first century.

We drank to this, our joint discovery, downing our glasses of UB Export Lager. It is an article of our national faith that 'export' quality is always the better quality in almost any field, including, sometimes, the human; the government believes in keeping the junk for the domestic population of human donkeys who will eat anything, while the best coffee, tea, shrimp, et al, is sacrificed to the dollar god—the latest addition to the Indian pantheon.

'It isn't what I bargained for,' I said now of my job, suddenly turning serious. 'I'm too individualistic, too driven from *within*. I cannot let myself be subsumed by some "national purpose", see?'

'Then why did you join the Service?' asked Chowdaiah, rather taken aback at my odd passion. '*I* at least expected this. It was still better than teaching economics to idiots. Who would go on strike to get themselves promoted to the next year, I say!'

'I did it to please my father, I guess,' I found myself saying.

Perhaps I *had* done it for my father. What a transformation my new position had wrought in him. It had been his victory over his brothers and his world. And my chance of love, acceptance, pride.

But here I was now, stuck in a hick town, performing tedious and empty rituals for a power and a purpose whose glamour had already grown stale.

My sense of purposelessness came to a crisis when I discovered that my dreams of Maya had become history. In Bangalore, where we met at the open-air Lovely Milk Bar and sat across each other drinking 'Milk Sheiks', the truth had burst out from her like water from a tender coconut pierced at the right spot: she had married Ganesh, a confidence man who had virtually abandoned her after three months of rather kinky non-sex. Ganesh's life's purpose seemed to have been to keep germs out of his territorial air, and to keep mosquitoes from biting his secret parts. He also liked to walk around the house nude (it allowed his skin to breathe in oxygen), so it was Maya's privilege to follow him around, watching out for mosquitoes and killing them before they entered the forbidden zone—that is, his twelve-inch territorial limits. Ganesh's fear of bacterial contamination was so great that he was always washing himself with antiseptic soap, with Dettol-laced water. So that a nutshell biography of his life would run: Wash hands. Wash face. Wash thing. Repeat.

'Still washing your plantain?' she would call out from the bed, naked and expectant.

'Yes, Amma,' he would reply—Amma being his pet name for her.

'Well, sure you are not saying, "Out, out, damned sperm?"' she would tease him.

'I love him still,' she had added, stubbornly. 'He'll come back.'

I left her and took a bus to Mahatma Gandhi Road, where I started drifting aimlessly amidst the voyeuristic crowds of the evening, groups of tight-panted 'City' males standing out in their emerald green or vermilion trousers and blatantly shining wrist watches, despondently ogling confidently sexy convent girls completely out of their sexual reach.

It's all over now, I told myself, shuffling past India Coffee House and the Blumoon complex and beggars spread out on the pavement to trip up the uncharitable. In India, I was a man without an audience. I had had an audience, once, during my late student days—an audience that would cheer even at my philosophical discourses on Australian sheep; but it had been dispersed by the cruel hands of Time and Reality, by the compulsion to look for jobs, husbands, security, whatever. With so much more to say now, I needed an audience even more than before.

At the corner of Brigade Road, by a bhelpuri stand smelling of red chilli powder and gingelly oil, I ran into Chowdaiah. In the circumstances, better than no company. In fact, my jadedness in the realm of humour was still low; I could still appreciate his sometimes-crude jokes.

'There is nothing in it for me anymore,' I said now to Chowdaiah, in between bites of the Chicken Chilly Fry he had ordered for us at the Bamboo Restaurant. 'This job is as dead as the Mughal Empire.'

'But you play an important role in society, I say,' Chowdaiah said. 'In no other country this opportunity exists. A personal ladder to the top. And tremendous capacity for good.'

'All this "doing good" and "serving the nation" and "alleviating the plight of the poor"— it's all someone else's crap. You really think we're serving the nation. No we're serving the ruling class.'

Besides, what 'important role'? In the immensity of India, I wasn't even a fart, I wouldn't even be permitted a fart without a ten-page application that would have to pass ten different levels.

At Chowdaiah's insistence, we were soon sipping beer and inhaling tenth-hand smoke at the Savera, a garish joint showing 'Kannada' cabarets, a low-level form of entertainment that had replaced the 'Western' cabarets banned by a zealous police commissioner for having displayed too much art besides a few things else. The dancer looked like a plucked, overfed hen trying desperately to fly. The more she uncovered of her many rings of fat matching her age, the more I wished she would simply put her outlandish costume back on and split the hell out of there. Finally, after two Kannada disco songs belted out by the grinning band, she reached the compulsory stage of wrapping herself in a translucent shroud. Underneath the shroud one could notice pale pink panties large enough to ensure the modesty of a respectable giraffe. Instead of arousing me, she was making me laugh.

'What job would make you happiest, I say?' An uncharacteristically mellow question from brash, cynical Chowdaiah, whom the dancer and the high-glycerine beer had made a little morose.

'I would be *happiest* being a pubic hairstylist,' I replied. 'But I would be reasonably happy being a writer.'

The next dancer, wearing a heavy skirt that looked like it was designed for X-ray protection, danced like she had ants up her bottom and liked them being there. Then, in a sudden move, she dropped the skirt in disgust, and, clad now in underclothes which looked like the armour of ancient Indian warriors, she flapped about her idli-fed arms. Surely there must have been some people to whom this flapping about was ecstasy, such as the goonda-faced chap in front of me with shaved head, green beret cap, cream white safari shirt unbuttoned to the level of his nipples. In her own way, she too was serving the nation, and alleviating the plight of the poor of imagination.

I continued: 'Once, I had a dream. I betrayed it. For safety and security and comfort. For my father. But I am going to follow it again.' For years, I had carried it within me, like a secret shame: my inadequately tutored, insecure soul.

But the hole in me: it was more than wanting to become a writer, getting understanding, fighting for justice. There was also that deep spiritual-biological need, and it came back to me, that old theme song of my subconscious, engraved there with an adaptation of the Vincent H. F. Purblind formula, submerged for a time by a college radicalism: *A hundred women.*

Well, even if I wasn't going to be that goal-oriented . . . *some* women.

Quite simply, my heart did not belong here; it was in the world of witty men and beautiful women (and vice versa), abundant and generous sexuality, philosophical discussion, theatre, glossy foreign magazines and books; my stage must be the world—not this backyard of civilization. I wanted to vamoose from this, the world's largest guinea pig camp, the world's largest experiment on how not to run a country; or what the US State Department termed the world's largest unimportant place. The only way to escape from this was to fly to America, to study there, become the writer I always wanted to be.

The West owed me something, because it had given me dreams. It had used my life, made me a tool in its grand intellectual design of global primacy. Saintly fantasies, a Western consciousness, misfitness, Bertrand Russell, a love of rationality, a yearning for technological solutions, Alvin Toffler's *Future Shock*, sexual super-consciousness, clitoral versus vaginal orgasm, sexercises, *I'm OK—You're OK*, Will Durant, *Reader's Digest*, Laughter the Best Medicine, vertical spaceship cities, endless love, a yearning for streaking and be-ins, linear progress, success, How To Become a Millionaire, private Cessna airplanes, Marilyn Monroe, Stop in the Name of Love. In sum, it had pocketed my country's original destiny for me and replaced it with one made in the West.

As my autorickshaw droned and trr-phutphuted back to my cheap hotel near the city railway station, the words now came in torrents, in sentences that made me feel wiser than I was in everyday life (for in everyday life I often talked like an ass). There was an old friend that I wanted to pass this on to. Though I had long since given up mailing letters to her, I used her as a mental peg to hang my thoughts on in an epistolary form—a device an old American writing guru had suggested. In my room, I fished out my airmail pad, then wrote:

To
Jackie Onassis
c/o The Empire of Aristotle Onassis
Athens, Greece.

PERSONAL/CONFIDENTIAL, PLEASE

Dear Jackie

As the chewing of tobacco leaf was to my grandfather, it has become a habit with me now, writing these one-way letters to you. Forgive me, but insanity runs in my family, like a cowherd chased by a crazed bull. Though one day, I know we will meet, and you will write to me. What can I say but: *Me nobody, You star, So what? Man's gotta write what he's gotta write.* Well, here are some thoughts fresh from my brain, written in an Indian cow town by a lonely man (who knows more than ever before about America) dreaming of America and analysing his American Dream. Little thought-snacks for your mind to munch on, while you devour Ari's caviar and shout, 'Beulah, peel me a grape!'

Jackie, have you ever wondered, like a lot of Americans, why the Third World is such a persistent pink sore in the West's fat white arse? What explains its restiveness, unhappiness, wars, revolutions, and love-hate relationships with the West, decades after it has attained 'freedom' from its former masters? Or the psychological slavery of the Third World male (who, admittedly, still reigns in the Third World)?

My answer: The power of the Western media. Yes, Jackie, the fate of the Third World is now decided in Hollywood and in New York, as once it was in Buckingham Palace and Whitehall.

Because, Jackie, just a few decades after Thoreau and Plato and the Bible educated Gandhi and Nehru and our country's other liberators, and even as *Time* Magazine's Guide to the World lulled India's ruling class into thinking correct and wholesome thoughts, something of a more fundamental nature was happening. Western motion pictures and books and magazines, flooding the Third World in search of international royalties and superprofits, really began to make Western women and men—female and male sexual symbols—accessible to India. To a huge Indian middle class, who were now fed erotic caviar, long distance, electronically. McLuhan's global village—it turned out to be a village run by the American pop culture syndicate.

So Love—vitamin-enriched and spicy Love, Hollywood style—became the new commodity of export-import, the new source of Third World indebtedness. Once upon a time, the white man taught the coloured man that nakedness was naughty, then sold him clothes (and sometimes a new religion to see that he kept those clothes on); now that most clothes are no more produced by him, he teaches the coloured man that sex and love are cool, and sells him textured condoms and other masturbatory, blonde fantasies. Oh how he'd love to sell Sheik Ali (the man) a Sheik (the condom) and the Sheikh West (the luxury Park Avenue condominium—this is not a prospectus). And also *Penthouse* magazine and *The Joy of Sex* and Harold Robbins and Mills and Boon (the last two being co-authors of mass-produced British romantic pulp, the limey version of Harlequin romances, that is devoured by Indian women). Ask any convent-thoroughbred Indian girl-woman between fifteen and twenty-five to name her favourite authors. One might answer: Dickens and Mills and Boon. The second might say:

Milton and Mills and Boon. A third will say: Shaw and Mills and Boon. The literary stiff will vary, but the Mills and Boon will be as solid rock.

I see now that through all my variably intense romances with Indian girls—and I speak now only of the convent-educated, English-speaking, urban minority—Mills and Boon were the Unseen Puppeteers, deciding when I would be granted nookie, and when not (mostly not). And just as the blond and dashing heroes of Mills and Boon with their determined jaws (they *always* have determined, un-Indian jaws) have captured Indian female imaginations, so indeed does the *femme fatale* of our male imaginations wear an easily-lifted skirt rather than a demoniacally knotted, vice-repellent sari; her come-hither look, her come-up-and-see-me-some-time dialogue, her athletic abandon in bed—these power our fantasies now.

And so we Indian men sometimes fell short in the fantasies of our capitalistically-aroused women, and they (less so), with us. It dulled the magic that might have been between us, soured marriages sometimes. Kneeling by our bedsides every night (metaphorically speaking), tears in our eyes (truly speaking), we would pray to God to grant us our fantasy (you and your sisters), to right this horrible imbalance of gifts and assets to equal citizens of Republic Earth.

Why this boundary-crossing erotic fascination? Is it that, metaphorically, pubic hair is blonder on the other side? This fixation of the Third World male—Japanese, Arab, Indian, Bangladeshi—on about two triangular inches of Western territory, after having allowed the West's plunder of millions of square miles of their own territory—isn't it absurd, farcical, tragic?

Oh, Jackie, what a mess it all is! In India, my own country, there is no more place for me.

Love (without import duties, without cost),

Vijay.

For a brief moment I dreamed of a Jackie, in a black and brief swimsuit or none, on a balmy Mediterranean day, lying on her back in her private yacht, laughing hysterically as she read my letter.

And then I folded the letter and dropped it into my personal file, unsent, like about two dozen others.

Things moved quickly after that. At Nandi Hills, I had another tryst with Chowdaiah. He was wearing a grey safari suit stitched so tight you could see the impression his nipples made against the Japanese polyester. On the croton-bordered lawn, swept clean of rumpled villagers for us by rumpled underlings too eager to please, we looked abstractly down at a hazy view of villages and irrigation tanks and ragi fields two thousand feet below. And I confessed to him my American Dream. But how would I finance my trip and my first semester, until I found a scholarship?

'What are roses for if not for plucking?' Chowdaiah cackled, not completing the racier ending to that piece of verse, then adding dramatically, 'What is money if not for helping friends?'

'What?' I was stunned.

Chowdaiah said he could lend me some money from his 'family funds'.

I knew the sort of family, usually of a business or landlord class, which, despite endless resources of irrigated lands and cash—which they secreted in numberless bank accounts, hid in mattresses, converted into extra gold and jewellery—lived utterly simple, utterly basic lives, wearing handspun white cotton shirts and wrinkled, dusty, baggy pants, indistinguishable from poorer neighbours in every detail except for a secret light of confidence and authority in their eyes. The money would not be missed; and I would do it justice. I jumped at the offer.

Once again, Camelot signalled to this American dreamer. America was the beacon of hope, the New Frontier, Marlboro Country, where all the excitement was: Famous Writers' School, streaking, nude beaches, discos, Campbell's Cream of Chicken Soup, women who wore black lace underpants and often, none whatsoever. I began to salivate over the offerings in the lavish and colourful university catalogues that soon flooded my desk, like the starving man who has never in his life tasted anything other than ordinary bread suddenly placed before a king's table, not knowing where to begin. Joining Abdul from Afghanistan and Pia from Pakistan and Iskander from Iran and Zaman from Zanzibar, I would respond to the Statue of Liberty's welcoming fart: Give me your horny masses. Fifty years of progressively more unclothed American films had sent a universal message which it was not in the call of this mere mortal to ignore. Yes, America beckoned to me like a woman with three sequins, all of which itched.

And I said soundlessly, into the darkness of the valley below, through whose light blanket of mist occasional streetlights twinkled: Yes, I am coming. Just wait for me.

Faraway, a dog yelped in answer.

America

'YOU HAVE SWINGING?' I eagerly asked the young, lean, weirdly shaven-headed American next to me on the Air India 747 to Washington ('swinging' was to my unsophisticated sensibility at the time a catch-all word for sexual calisthenics), barely able to contain my excitement at our approaching arrival in the land of nuclear-tipped lingams.

'I swing for the Lord Krishna,' he said. He went on to inform me that he was Bill Stein, originally a New Yorker, now of the Haré Krishnas, Arlington, Virginia branch. He happened to be one of the few non-Indians on a plane full of Indian doctors, engineers, and computer scientists, part of the historical Westward movement of capital and brains.

'Visit us some time for a vegetarian feast,' continued Bill cordially, passing me a business card. A vegetarian feast! When my dreams were of miles and miles of steaks and roast beef and baked hams and not a carrot or boblen in sight!

Disappointed, I returned to my fantasies, dreaming that I might catch a glimpse of the Statue of Liberty from the airplane window, with Dale Carnegie and Napoleon Hill dancing on each tit, flinging self-help and get-rich-quick manuals at all newcomers.

So began my Adventures in Cowboy Land.

It's a glorious country, America, and in some moods, I could even conceive of punching someone who says it isn't. But someone should have told me a few things before I started out.

Such as, that if you are a Third World greenhorn planning to live in the United States for the first time, Washington D.C. at the height of winter is one of the worst places to start.

It was a sub-freezing day in January when I arrived in Dulles Airport, having watched, with mute excitement and foreboding, a snow-blanketed New World approach from my airplane window. It took me fifteen minutes to figure out how to outwit the escalators at the nearly deserted airport, because of a 'This Way Out' sign that, as you stepped off the escalator going up, merrily pointed to the escalator going down. And then, unprepared for the weather—coming from a region where winter usually signified such chilly temperatures as seventy degrees Fahrenheit with gusts that made it feel like sixty-eight degrees—I had to fish out my two substandard Indian sweaters and wear them on top of three shirts. It wasn't easy to manage my numerous bags after that. The bags had been crammed with mucho mucho quantities of Hamam soap, Vajradanti toothpaste, and Brahmi hair oil (the last containing secret Ayurvedic ingredients), and even some bananas, because my Indian advisers had suggested I take along a six-month supply of everything I might possibly need and be able to carry, so I could conserve the precious foreign exchange that was to last me till the expected scholarship materialized and I could live like a prince.

The silver, monster bus, no cousin of the rickety Indian buses I was used to, sailed into the city from the airport, passing miles and miles of uninhabited, snow-carpeted countryside. Was this the capital of the world's most powerful country? Or had everybody, having heard of my arrival, decided to stay home in protest? And then the bus crossed over the Potomac river and I arrived at the heart of all that whiteness, the heart indeed of the whiteness of the world, and I checked into the Hotel George Washington, and began to see my money disappear.

It was a Saturday morning, and with blustery Arctic winds blowing outside, I had no choice but to stay in and watch television in my seedy hotel room. At the touch of a tiny switch, the black-and-white box exploded into life, sounding harsh, foreign, absurdly hyperactive and merry in relation to the bleak coldness of the life outside. In the next few days I lost a small fortune to soulless food machines whose intricacies I couldn't fathom, and whose offerings looked much more attractive than they tasted: my losses seemed enormous because I kept converting them into rupees and calculating my vanishing savings.

I had to change buses twice to get to my university; waiting for the bus in below-zero wind chills with my second-rate clothing was no picnic, saar! Because I had bought the cheapest coat that promised me some raw bulk, a fifteen-dollar, synthetic piece of Taiwanese industrial packaging that kept me warm for exactly two minutes after I left the store. In the meantime, I sometimes tried, in that desperate cold, to hitch a ride—America, I had heard, was the country that invented hitchhiking—and was flabbergasted, then quickly dismayed, when people glared at me for trying, as if I had shown myself to be an unspeakable turd. Fluids oozed from my eyes and nose—from the cold, not the sadness. But I was too stunned at that point with the harsh novelty of the place, its complete opposition to my expectations, to be ready to mourn my American Dream.

There had been a culinary component to this dream, built up by brightly coloured ads for Campbell's Cream of Chicken Soup and Swanson TV Dinners in my uncle's imported *Reader's Digests*, by news reports of an abundance so sinful that the country periodically dumped oversupplies of food into the sea. Now, tearing greedily into cans of chicken soup and a single 'TV dinner' from the Safeway, my astonished reaction was, 'They forgot to add something: Taste!' (As for the suspiciously coloured cream of chicken soup itself—what exactly had the chickens been up to when they produced this cream?) Even the eggs, mass-produced by unhappy, incarcerated hens who lived to eat and lay and ate to die, were bland, nothing like the earthy taste of eggs from free-roaming Indian chickens, bland as this snow-covered country with no smells, no noises, no humanity.

No humanity indeed, for more chilling than the frozen aspect of Nature during the North American winter was human coldness. The utter indifference on most faces, an indifference that occasionally went further and said, 'Don't bother me, asshole, I don't give a rat's ass about your stupid, fucking existence'—this penetrated deeper than my bones; it stirred and woke up the hibernating heart of the darkness within me. I had heard of anti-social moods in great philosophers while in deep concentration, but one million people in Washington couldn't simultaneously be thinking deep, profound thoughts.

One day I was walking to my university when I began to understand some of that coldness. As a blue Chevy zoomed past, two white sophomoric types stuck their heads out and yelled, 'Go back to Eye-Ran! Asshole!'

Ah, well, perhaps we all need to get shafted once in a while, so we are forced to stop and question our bird-brained existence, our beliefs, our illusions, our unkindness to those less fortunate than we. From India's top two per cent to America's bottom two per cent—ah, what a beautiful metaphor for universal brotherhood, though a well-deserved lesson in humility. And now, I saw it all. Disillusionment: that, to me, is the universal Philosophy 101; without it, you may spend years at the graduate philosophy departments at Cambridge or Princeton, and still fail to get it.

There was a lifting of my mood soon enough, though, because of a force I hadn't bargained for: spring. Most Americans endure winter knowing in their bones that spring will eventually come, but a south Indian in particular, never having experienced strong changes of seasons, doesn't. When spring arrived, it put a better face on everything, from the trees that began to sparkle with cherry blossoms to the women who shed their dull outer layers and began to smile foxy, seductive, or tentative smiles. I found a library job paying $2.10 an hour (if I was good, I might even get a raise to $2.40 by year's end, my superior informed me in conspiratorial tones). Not much, but safer than working off-campus as a well-tipped waiter (really, that was as far as I dared to dream by that time), since Immigration hounds were reportedly going around trying to catch 'illegals' who looked Eye-ranian. And I now rented the living-room portion of a one-bedroom apartment from a fellow university student named Carson McDermott, who pumped iron and ate pumpernickel bread and steaks by day and pumped women by night, often keeping me awake with the creak of his bedsprings.

And as spring matured into warmer weather, everything seemed to open out. Golden girls! All-American beauties, spread out on the lawns in brief shorts, on the steps of the various campus buildings, babyfat thighs (The Collected Twinkies) spread out, milkmaid breasts thrust out in your face, daring you to pluck!* It seemed the country was awash with copulation; relatively, the birds and the bees were behaving like monks.

---

* To those laws, thought systems, colour and class bars and prejudices, and assorted oppressors who would keep beauty like this away from me, I say: You're too beneath me to be insulted in anything but a footnote.

But when I tried to speak, even relatively innocuous stuff, I met with glassy-eyed non-recognition. Even women who sat in my classes made an art of walking by saying 'hi hello bye' without missing a beat. Jesus, I'd heard of flying fucks (I mean, I'd heard the expression), but flying 'How-are-you?-See-you-later's? One need not declare one's racism like Enoch Powell or George Wallace, I thought; one can deny another's humanity simply by refusing to look at him, simply by making an invisible thing of him.

I wrote in my diary:

Political Idea Number One: To create a society with equality of sexual opportunity—the ultimate equality. I call it lustice—for it is the ultimate justice. Imagine: every man will be entitled once a year to a one-hour ride in a sports convertible on a summer day with a gorgeous woman by his side, her hair whipping in the breeze. And every spinster will have the right to spend one night a year with a state-paid hunk; and if he fails to punch her ticket, she has him free for the rest of the year. (And so on: Send $9.95 for the complete manifesto.)

Then came summer.

The summer of 1981 was a wild summer, a summer of wild hopes, wild dreams, overpopulated fantasies. The perfumed presence, sometimes inches from my nose and popping eyeballs, of millions of American women roaming about, their multiform butts clad in brief, towel-textured shorts (some towel-manufacturing capitalist was making millions making asses of these millions), was catalysed by the new and provocative knowledge building up within me—the knowledge that, here in Freedom-land, nothing (but the will to act) came between me and media reports of the country's loose fads: Plato's Retreat, swingers' clubs, nudist camps, horny and liberated and yearning readers of *Playgirl*. I had as attractive a body as any man, I thought vainly, admiring myself in my room-mate's full-length mirror. Some day soon my secret assets, now camouflaged by my unfashionable attire, would be open for inspection to any discriminating customer. And then, there would be no looking back.

Call it cowardice, shyness, or the childhood fear of punitive women and the canes I had known them to use, but I merely feasted my eyes on the dishes that were before me, and waited. For my fantasy was simply to be *taken*. I wanted life to be as in Henry Miller's books, gorgeous-kazooed women with not a stitch underneath their short skirts sitting on my lap and wrestling me down to the carpet and devouring me like animals. I wanted women to burst into the bathroom when I was having a pee and say, 'Can I have that? Please? Give me that lovely big thing of yours.' But I would never ask. When my time came, *they* would come to me.

One bright evening a day after the following Christmas, sauntering about listlessly in an unfamiliar part of town, I suddenly followed a young brunette with an exquisitely thin waist, exquisitely round and firm buttocks whose every mood could be observed through her thin silk dress. 'Take me!' the buttocks seemed to shout, in the ancient animal language that our DNA had stored over millions of years. 'Ravish me like an animal!' Mesmerized, I tailed this devoutly Christian posterior into a house of worship. The first Temple of the Lord I had entered in five years. The First Baptist Church of Arlington, where a fashionably-dressed crowd was slowly gathering for what seemed like a theatrical extravaganza, while I knelt behind the chick whose behind I now idolized.

'My brothers and sisters in sin!' began the telegenic preacher, inaugurating this special Christmas programme. And as he exhorted me to recognize the Lord and my miserable sinful state, I was recognizing the enormous power that the Lord's female creations exercised over me.

The highlight of the programme was the unveiling of the 'Human Christmas Tree', a dark forest of a tree from which, to my surprise, beautiful, promiscuously-dressed blonde babydolls (and a few dull men in suits, unfortunately), started revealing themselves one by one to a spotlight, and joining their voices to a cascading Christmas song which soon became a polyphonic roar. Music that soothed my soul as syrup soaks and soothes a gulab jamun. If Christianity had been this much fun in my childhood, so misspent in kneeling bare-kneed on sadistic surfaces, I might never have abandoned it. What a rip-off: that the Western countries, which dump inferior, obsolete, and dangerously outdated drugs on Third World children, often do the same with their religions.

One day, I vowed, I would have for Christmas, for my first real Christmas ever, an utterly human and humane Christmas Tree made solely out of gorgeously naked women, a United Nations of nude fillies wearing nothing but Santa caps and toothsome grins, with bells around their ankles, rose-coloured nipples just begging for my delicate touch, leaping out of the tree to take me, clawing and biting each other like Kilkenny cats just to have their turn.

When I reached my apartment it was past midnight, and I simply turned off my lights and got into bed and under my quilt and dozed off within seconds.

I am arriving at the Waldorf Astoria in a black stretch limousine. Press photographers' flash bulbs explode as my security guard opens my door. I wave to the crowd milling outside, smile and walk in, surrounded by bodyguards. I walk to the salutes of the manager, bell boys . . . . A tall platinum blonde in a black pilot's suit glued to her tightly packed body drops her room keys into my bodyguard's hands, others follow suit. I wink at her and the rest and say, 'I'll try. Can't promise anything.'

I take a private elevator to my fiftieth floor, permanent ten-room suite.

A blonde, statuesque secretary in a sheer negligée gives me a list of messages. A list of famous beautiful women, movie stars, ex-wives of Presidents, have left messages, wanting to know if I'm free for the night.

I stop my secretary as she reels off the messages. 'That's enough for now. I'm not in. Even if the President calls.'

I'm going to be having a small powwow with the boys tonight: David Rockefeller, Robert Redford, Henry Kissinger, Prince Charles, and the latest Henry Ford, whoever he is. We just want to chat over the state of the world, about what is to be done. Johnny Carson has promised to make it too after doing an early taping of the Tonight Show.

I proceed to the master bedroom where half a dozen Penthouse Pets, hand-selected by Bob Guccione from a list of dozens, plus one or two surprise guest stars, are waiting for me. As I sink back into the colossal bed, covered with sheets and pillows of red satin, they approach me in various stages of undress. One is wearing a black diving suit that has a cut-out over her red-haired pussy. Another, a dark-haired Latin beauty with long hair is in sheer harem dress. The third, a blonde with ice-blue eyes, has on a leopard skin bikini. But her impatient fingers have yanked out one breast with one hand, while the fingers of the other hand are buried in her pink, wet lower lips, on the outer reaches of which fine, light gold fuzz gleams. There are scratch marks from her long, painted fingernails, and her middle finger seems to have disappeared inside. She is moaning. The fourth, a tall mulatto, is wearing a short, frilly pink dress whose fringes flirt at crotch level; as she dances mesmerized to the smoky Teddy Prendergrass song coming from the stereo, it exposes her treasures and covers them, teases you with alternate views of a gorgeous bum and a completely hairless sex whose dividing line opens and closes and slants and winks as she dances. The neckline of the dress is deep, revealing the steep slope of her mountainous breasts, giving occasional views of chocolate nipples.

The wiggly circle of lust-crazed bimbos surrounds me, leaps onto the four-hundred-square-foot bed. Tantalizing me with tongues or fingertips or nipples, they slowly unbutton my clothes, down to my jockeys. Now two of them, fully nude, oil themselves and massage my legs, face, and chest with their nude bodies in alternate directions, one with her scissored pubes and breasts, the other with the cheeks of her rear end. I beg them to stop. Then two other chicks on either side in matching crotchless red-leather pants and nipple clamps remove my Jockey underpants with their teeth. They nearly scream when my erect member bounds upward. Whereupon someone who looks like Brooke Shields—it's hard to say for sure, her face is painted with war paint, her large brass noserings gleam, her hair sticks out like a wild beast's—springs out from behind a velvet curtain. With an unexpectedly lusty animal cry, without so much as a 'by your leave', she quickly clambers onto my majestically erect love pole. I see her mascaraed eyes widen with surprise and then close with ecstasy. With my left hand I clasp the pink bottom cheek of a girl who is bending away from me with catlike languor, to remove her stockings. I feel the buttock's silken softness, glide my fingers gently down her rear crack to her gaping moist cunt, and then suddenly ram my fist up into it. She screams, 'AHH! Ah! Ah-ha. Ah-Ah, Aaaah. Oh God, I'm coming. Ahhahaha.' I feel a tongue lapping at my balls and perineum, God, how did it get there?! From between two bodies a large, pink and erect-nippled breast floats towards my open mouth. I suddenly close my lips on it, like a predator, and suck. I get sweet milk. I suck furiously, ravenously. Milk floods my mouth, nearly choking me, while tears of joy flood the owner's eyes. After drinking about three-fourths of a glass, I stop. And burp. They all laugh.

Now I feel mouths and tongues nibbling and licking and biting and exploring various orifices, erotic surfaces I have never known to exist. My visual horizons have been narrowed by two massive pink udders rolling over my face. Like one soaked by foamy wave after wave of a rough, afternoon sea, my body is drenched with pleasure. I'm sinking deeper and deeper, into a womblike darkness, so dissolved in bliss now that nothing else exists, it cannot go on much longer, and I . . . .

Explode! Resurfacing into consciousness even as the first wave of explosions has begun, I wrench my cock off Brooke's slit and point it at the ceiling. Hot white sperm spurts out like an erratic fountain coming to life, and four utterly naked beauties leap, mouths open, like flying fish, to catch my ejaculation in mid-air at its ten-foot apogee just below the crystal chandeliers. They gobble it down, smacking their lips with delight at this snack more precious than caviar. Their bodies are radiant as one by one, they sail out the open window.

America was a splendid country for a dreamer, I mused to myself, waking up and changing my stained pajama.

Les Misérables

With money you are a dragon; without it you are a worm.
 – Chinese Proverb

BUT ON ANOTHER level, my life in America, Part I of the American Dream, was quite another cup of tea, or rather of 'processed' hot chocolate from a food machine, in which chocolate seemed an almost theoretical and insignificant ingredient. With five hundred dollars in my savings account for emergencies and two-hundred-fifty dollars a month from my part-time library job for my chow and roof and everything else, I, a recent Mover and Shaker of Old Age Pension files, a recent personification of state power in cow-dung country, saw myself as dog-poor, and looked upon the System, upon America the Beautiful, as an underdog does, see? Exploitative, heartless, cold. As a bonded Indian coolie looks at a Kuwaiti Mercedes whizzing by, or at the insides of a Kuwaiti palace.

So did it happen that I was the one outside the restaurant looking in at all the beautiful and happy people looking out. Looking out at the wildlife—yes, such as me, a strange, unruly-haired, bearded freak who had probably come from some unpronounceable country and had some unpronounceable name. I was the chap trying to stretch his haircut, trying to stretch his ill-fitting tropically tailored clothes—not such a contradiction as it may seem, because they were tailored in India by small-town tailors so out of touch with what was cool, that they seemed to have been tailored by a devilish mind precisely to make me look crummy. To separate the jerks from the Rest. I looked like a disorderly ape with an excess of testosterone.

Thanks to the glorious free market operating in the realm of human worth, I was now a chartered member of the American underclass. For the only things that separate your society gent from the fellow he regards as garbage are his haircut, his suit, and the amount of money in his pocket. (Give a man a bad haircut and you may as well hang him—a skin-deep truth, I know, of one far far away from buddhahood, but at the time I was in the grip of skin-deep truths and lived among the skin-deep, in thrall to the insanity of desire.)

Money was the price of admission to everything. To restaurants. To good stores. To shows and spectacles. To exclusive suburbs and parties. To life. Without money, I was not worth diddly squat. When I walked into my embassy one day, the Indian Embassy, and they saw me—when they saw me, an unaccommodated man, stripped of the armour of confidence I wore in India with the backing of a premier civil service, and dressed instead in a Taiwanese polyester-filled bomber jacket, a hooded parka that was the favoured uniform of hoods, a jacket that one didn't want to be seen in the same suburb with, I was to them son of Melvin Prabhu, kashtigaar, villager, buffalo boy, fit only to fashion cow-dung cakes, not one of them—and they didn't want me. Drunk with their petty power and status consciousness, they didn't want to acknowledge me as one of their own, their own brothers-in-the-civil-service, to whom respect and help was due in this strange and frightening country.

Simply because I was cash-poor, and to them, part of the degraded class of the American poor.

To think that until I came to America, I had been like most Indians, who explode with wild laughter whenever the words 'American' and 'poverty' are joined. 'We'll tell *you* what poor is,' Indians say. 'Poor *isn't* not having new clothes for Christmas. Poor is children running around naked, their bodies caked with dirt, because they don't have a single item of clothing to their names. Poor is searching through Indian garbage for scraps of rotten food—because, man, nothing that is remotely edible ever goes into

Indian garbage. Poor is sleeping on the pavement without a sheet under, or a blanket over.'

Now I realized that poverty was relative, a state of mind. Poverty in America was not having what all your neighbours had and took for granted: an occasional meal outside that was not fast food, a warm and comfortable home with a variety of cooked food in it, and the money that would enable you to be in the sexual market—for as a male without money in America you weren't entitled to sex, and without sex in America you were the wretched of the earth.

So the Golden Arches were the outer limits of my culinary fantasies in those days, and it took me years to justify the purchase of a soda when water was available free, and I would still try, in the student cafeteria, to dissolve as much sugar into my coffee as it could physically take, so as to satisfy my daily caloric needs at the lowest cost. Sometimes I would buy an extraordinary Safeway packaging brainwave called 'chicken backs', the cheapest calories in America at seventeen cents a pound. From the way they tasted, those chickens must have spent all their lives with their backs to the wall. Chemical, plastic fat with bones attached. Safeway was such a sharp supermarket operator that it would have packaged chicken penises if there were a few pennies to be made from them.

But I was young, and the wind was in my hair, and Paris was waiting for me, and always would be . . . .

On to what happened.

It was a late midsummer Saturday, a humid, sweaty, dog's testicle of a day of relentless sun in Fairfax, Virginia, a suburb of Washington. I had only that morning given in my used car, only recently acquired, for repairs. My first and only car, a growling, power-packed baby, freeeeedommmm! They had virtually taken apart the car and then told me the car needed a brake replacement, costing two-hundred-sixty dollars.

Now auto repair shops in America, they are the cynical quintessence of theft. The thing they have called a 'labour rate manual': it is the bible of twentieth-century thievery, so cynically corrupt that it is worth two million hollow laughs, so brazenly cunning that Machiavelli would have committed suicide on coming upon it. Every shred of faith in human nature you have patiently collected from twenty years of life in a small Asian town . . . it cannot survive one trip to an automobile repair shop (I'm sure Mother Teresa must only use bicycles).

'Two-hundred-sixty dollars to replace the front brakes,' said the man in charge, a gorilla with a baseball cap.

'What? The car itself cost me five-hundred dollars.'

'Two-hundred-sixty dollars. Parts and labour. According to the labour rate manual,' he replied, without breaking the one-two rhythm with which he was chewing gum.

'Can you not make it one-hundred-fifty, please? I'm a student. I have to live an entire month on this money.'

'Two-hundred-sixty dollars,' said he, with absolutely no change in expression.

They were going to rob me of half my remaining savings: the few miserable greenbacks that stood between me and utter nothingness (yes, I was such a perfect pigeon that I had defined myself by the amount of money I had—exactly the kind of thing They want you to do).

Money: to a man with little of it, it loomed so large in his life, it made him shit in his pants merely to contemplate it. (I understood my father now, his absurdly exaggerated fears of doom, his petty stinginesses.)

Money was a rack on which the poor of the world were tortured—yes, even in America. For example, a plastic glass of soda selling for one dollar in a fast food restaurant, actually costs the restaurant ten cents, the soda and the glass together. Now if you take a dollar from someone who earns three thousand dollars a month, he doesn't notice the difference. But when you take the same away from someone surviving on two-hundred-fifty dollars a month (of which two hundred and thirty are going to rent and food), and it's a hot summer day in a strange part of town, and he *must* have the drink—for God's sake, you can chop the hate in the air with an axe.

What did it mean, this perverted, unjust value of money, of exchange rates, by which an Indian farmer or clerk, couldn't make in a month what his American counterpart made in less than a day? Why is the sweat of one human being worth so much less than that of another?

Smouldering thus with dark thoughts, and an entire day to spend waiting and carless in the meanwhile, I decided to stroll through the sprawling white Fairfax Mall next door.

The reason I had chosen Fairfax, a suburban mall, for my auto repairs, and not some place in Washington itself? A large ad in the *Washington Post* proclaiming a one-day sale with 'FREE CONTINENTAL BREAKFAST UNTIL 10 A.M.' at the Fairfax Mall. This special, patriotic sale was in honour of the birthday of some dead President of the United States—Jefferson, Lincoln, Grant, Harding, I don't quite remember which.

A Continental Breakfast! For one who had been stuffing his reluctant gullet every morning with cheap, processed, plastic-flavoured white bread with margarine that tasted like lizard oil! Visions of ham, bacon, French and Swiss cheeses, croissants, muffins, corned beef—all flown in from Europe—piled up before my imagination, like a banquet spread in a beggar's dream. I had woken up at 8:30, so there was no time to shower. Quickly brushing my dishevelled hair, and slipping on yesterday's slightly soiled polyester shirt, I dashed into my car, and sped towards Fairfax on Route 50, which was clogged with twenty thousand other Suckers Americanuses also dreaming of their free continental breakfast and showering blessings on President Whatsisname.

When I reached the scene, at 9:45 a.m. or so, I found out that the store's definition of continental breakfast was one styrofoam cup of watery coffee with one greasy Danish pastry.

To make the best of a half-ruined day, I had decided to entrust a huge auto repair shop with my car—and had found myself in my present soup.

A couple of hours later, oily and vaguely hungry and unhappy, an open bag hung over my shoulder—I am a compulsive bag carrier, ever since Granny with a Bag deprived me of one—I entered a gigantic department store, stuffed with more consumer goods than many an entire Third World country. Thirty brands of toasters, thirty-five models of children's bicycles, and a whole floor, like a transvestite's Disneyland, displaying tens of thousands of feminine unmentionables. God, I thought, remembering the days in India, when the sight of one pair of panties absent-mindedly left on some clothesline might have made my day.

Finally I entered the menswear section. I sauntered listlessly, looking at the shiny, polyester shirts, shirts that looked like the colourful skins of tropical snakes, shirts that looked so much smarter (maybe, just richer) to my hick mind than the cheap stuff I had on.

It just so happened that this was my worst day of the century. Unbathed, uncool I, my shirt revealing a forlorn swatch of chest hair because of a missing button, shying away from women because I thought I looked so bad, while Muzak from concealed speakers got under my skin.

Ah, Muzak, that vicious American invention, designed to kindle so much trepidation within you that you can only counter your indefinable angst by spending, spending, spending. The Muzak system had just blasted me with the three songs that I hated most in the world, one following the other: "Somewhere My Love", "Pearly Shells", and "Stop in the Name of Love". These had been preceded by the most insincere announcement possible, 'Shoppers! We Want To Give YOU Extra Value Today! So Check Out Our Home Appliances Department For Amazingly Low Special Prices Only For YOU.' At that moment, if I had a machine-gun in my hand, I would have sprayed a hail of bullets at every suspected source of sound. And if I were a judge, the Muzak Defence should beat a murder rap thrice as easily as the Insanity Defence.

But this wasn't all. A few hours earlier, at the repair shop itself, I had begun to feel the withdrawal of Librium, a Luciferian chemical to which I had become addicted recently in the effort to drown out the anxiety of a callous, newly xenophobic America directing hate at everyone they could fit into a quasi-Iranian label. But my absent-mindedness has always been far stronger than my pill-taking need, and rushing out that morning I had forgotten my Librium dose. There was an edge of despondency in me now, and a dulling of my discrimination.

Now I often do silly absent-minded things such as forgetting to zip my fly, and have at least three times after that day caught myself, heart thumping at my discovery, almost on the point of leaving a store without remembering to pay for the item in my hand.

But on this day it wasn't forgetfulness. This was a wilful act, even though the premeditation was for about a confused and disoriented two minutes or so, when the impulse seized me with a savage force, drowning out any thought of consequences: So what if I took a shirt, and wrested back about fifteen of the two-hundred-sixty dollars the Bastard System had just cheated me of?

My hand moved as if robot-controlled. Within terror-filled seconds, the hand had slipped a shirt off the rack and into my open bag.

Whereupon an alarm rang, and two beefy white men, cowboys in neckties, came racing towards me, and it was all over.

I had ignored the first law of larceny: Never steal small. Be patient, wait your chance, and then steal so huge it blows their mind, they don't even call it theft, they call it enterprise. Because for petty thefts, they slap vengeful handcuffs on you. For thefts in the range of hundreds of millions of dollars, with you kicking back part of your loot as political donations, they give you Ambassadorships, they name towns and university libraries after you.

What happened then was simple. I was arrested, arraigned, and spent a month in a cage.

The thing that struck me most: a Christian country is the last place you can expect to find some mercy.

'Please, sir, I'm not a criminal. This is a mistake,' I remember telling the cop.

'Now shut up, or I'll gag you,' the cop replied.

'This county is tough on crime,' the judge said at the trial. 'It is a message to criminals: Don't even think of coming here.'

The jail term: It was so traumatic, so unimaginable to me, that it is now as blurred as a night spent on a train while pissed. Nothing remains, no jailhouse rock, nothing but a dim memory of feeling like a naked animal in a cage, your sins and your private needs open to public inspection, and a vague memory of insipid boiled green potatoes and mashed potatoes and plastic processed meat patties handed out in plastic trays. That combined with a deep sadness, and a few thoughts: the country that I had admired since childhood, that I had for most of my life dreamed of being merged with, had booted me into its penal system, squashed me under its gestapo boots, shut me up in a cage with people who were . . . animals! With people I had never spoken to in my life, could not relate to ever . . . . Yes, even though they were indeed—I see that now—my true brothers and sisters.

At first, I simply couldn't face the shame of what had happened to me. And yet, the shame was really in the 'being caught', and because of the punishment attached to it. For we are engaged in theft much of the time, aren't we—whether consciously or unconsciously, with fancy rationalizations or with none. We do it every time we take more than our fair share from the common till. Every time we charge a hundred dollars an hour—or twenty thousand dollars an hour—for work that someone else, with less bargaining muscle, can only get three dollars an hour for. Every time we order a sixteen-ounce prime rib of beef or load our plate at the buffet cart and waste half of what's on our plate, while some brother or daughter of ours, in another part of the globe, starves. (This society is so unjust and fucked up, God, where can we begin?)

But in any case, that was not how They looked at it. It was not how even some of my friends would look at it. So I would have to lie.

'Where were you all these days?' Wendy Wulitzer, my library co-worker asked me, when I got out of jail just in time for the Fall Registration and ran into her on campus. 'They were so upset, at the library.' Her blue eyes showed concern. A straw blonde with a homely, clean, round face, she had leaned on me as an extra, available listener to whom she could retail her marital troubles in between handing out magazines to borrowers.

'Oh, an uncle of mine came to New York suddenly, for a holiday. I had to leave right away.'

So I lied. Once I was free, I suppressed the incident completely. It was a blunder, an ugly aberration that didn't belong with the rest of my life. And gradually, amazingly, I expunged it from my memory. When a cop passed me, I would experience brief cardiac tremors, that was all. The memory of what had happened never resurfaced in my brain of itself.

If only I had told the truth . . . . It might have humanized me, revolutionized me, I would think later. For once you puncture the myth of respectability, that great social lie, we all become so much like each other, so much like brothers and sisters, links in a universal chain of protoplasm . . . .

There were other times in the following years when I would see what had happened as being the inevitable harvest of bitterness. Life shafts you and shafts you, unequally, you see; and the bitterness builds up, see? It is dangerous, the build-up of bitterness, whether between children and parents, husband and wife, or man and society. Like tartar rotting away your teeth, bitterness builds up and eats into your soul, corrodes the wholeness of your perspective, the perspective that should make you see yourself as not separate at all, but a part of the grand show of the universe.

Still, I couldn't be too hard on myself, because if I did I would also be hard on the blacks who form an overwhelming portion of America's prison population, the world's largest. Poverty, injustice, class differences, the creation of desire without its automatic satisfaction, all of these had some part to play in the story, after all?

Consider. Bonnydale's, a department store subsidiary of a huge oil company, charges fifteen dollars for a shirt it has bought wholesale for three, having been tailored in some Third World sweatshop by a worker who was paid ten cents for her labour, so that Bonnydale's managers and major stockholders can snort A-grade Colombian cocaine and get highclass blow jobs and feel as virtuous as Mother Teresa when they leave ten-dollar tips for waitresses who are privileged anyway to be in such jobs earning as much in a night as many a minimum-wage earner makes in a fortnight. What a triumph of glorious capitalism, of social trickle-down. The tale of a shirt made by some half-starved Third Worlder, a shirt that later in its capitalist career gives another unfortunate Third Worlder a one-month jail sentence for having dared to fantasize owning it.

When really, the only moral and civilized punishment for a needy person who 'steals' something so wretchedly insignificant is to say to him, 'You need it so badly? Well, then, help yourself, it's yours free!' That itself should be humiliation and punishment enough . . . if indeed humiliation and punishment is what we desire to inflict on those who are fashioned of the same clay, only with different pasts and different presents.

Anyway, it amazes me now that by lying to myself enough, by pretending I was normal, another starry-eyed immigrant in search of the American Dream—by virtually erasing the memory of what had happened, drowning it in television and everyday living and a renewed ambition—I soon became 'normal', soon resumed, indeed, my pursuit of the American Dream almost as if nothing had happened (except that money of itself would always stand corrupted for me from then on, never be as important to my Dream as its other components). By lying—and this is a terrible truth, but a truth nevertheless: by lying I became whole again.

Maybe—I sometimes (and only sometimes) think—maybe it is imperative that we lie in this world, for its very currency is lies, its very substance is a tissue of lies—*maya*, if you will, divinely-ordained illusion, if you must. To tell the 'truth', to even think the 'truth' in these circumstances, is often dangerous to our sanity, or our survival in society. And maybe it is that if we didn't keep lying to ourselves and each other, we couldn't survive for one minute.

Running Away

AS ALL IMMIGRANTS do, in time—or so the myth goes anyway—I had become a survivor. So much for success and how-to books and zillions; from now on, I was simply on a survival track, like my four billion brothers and sisters on this planet. I had learned to do my low-rent thing, to cut my coat according to my loincloth, to have my cake and microwave it too. Library jobs, illegal jobs, term-paper typing, scholarships, assistantships—America was addicting, because America forked over a few dollars every day, just enough to hang on to the frayed coattails of your hopes. Even if your life at the moment was drab as a toll collector's, as sleazy as a soggy hot dog handed you by a scabrous pervert, there was always television, and in some still-virginal, illusion-friendly corner of your mind, the boob tube fuelled your dreams as powerfully as rajmaan fuelled farts.

Then I met my next passion, who woke up my recently suppressed libido as the racing Madras Howrah Express wakes up a coolie napping too close to the edge of the platform.

And in good time too. In another year I would be thirty, and according to the goal I had set myself at sixteen, I had ninety-six women to go.

It began with a course called "Philosophy and Literature"— the kind of hybrid and grandiose course that had made my saliva drip on the University's slick bulletin in the first place. Professor Hucklehead, a tall, fifty-ish, philosophically-bitter man with a stubble that matched his grey tweed jacket, introduced the reading list: Dante, Hamlet, Sartre, Kundera. His smile was a thing of ugliness, a snarl of a man condemned to hurl meaninglessness at things beyond meaning.

'They're geniuses,' Professor Hucklehead said despondently of the literary greats he had chosen to teach, as one aware after fifty years of life and academic striving of his utter emptiness. 'Nine or twelve rungs above the rest of us.' Meaning: Forget it, buster!

In any case, he consoled himself, 'Shakespeare was also, once, a snot-nosed little kid who wet his pants. Until he began to feel his stride, crossed the threshold, came into his own.'

This was new to me: literature explained through folksy American idiom.

'How did they have the time to do all that creative work, I don't know . . . . After all, *they* had bills to pay, *they* had to go to the bathroom . . ?'—a homespun, American, correspondence-school interpretation of genius. What would he do next: expound a thesis analysing the relationship between Dante's mortgage-payment history and his flashes of genius?

'Dante—picks up an obscure reference and takes it for a ride,' the dismal don continued. 'He knows how to take the ball and run with it.'

Yeah. Just as you know how to run with your fifty-thousand dollar salary and cosy office and three-month vacations—I whispered to the leggy and fluffy blonde sitting next to me.

Ruth had attracted my attention many times before, with her soft, slightly husky, pained voice mouthing woozily-pinko thoughts, her curly blonde hair always tied in a different style of lap-dog or pony, her gentle, happy-sad smile, full of large slightly-yellowed teeth. And the swell of her breasts, the outline of the nipple against the soft dress. From every angle, she presented a different, equally ravishing prospect, a new pleasure in its own right. She had no unflattering angles. Her physique possessed the right weight, the right aspect, the right fullness, right tits, right buttocks. She was pure gold. She was the quintessence of what was right with America, even though with leftover Sixties' rebellion she occasionally sighed and expelled a long list of things that were wrong with America.

Today, Ruth was wearing a short, flowery dress, lots of purples and light greens and pinks on a background of black. Black stockings, black shoes. A rich gold-chain watch.

The flowers on her dress hijacked my stream-of-consciousness to unmentionable contemplations of her inner orchid.

Whereupon a nerd in high-powered glasses, trying to increase his visually challenged grade point average at the least cost, burst in with a loudly squawked comment—'diaphanic'. Which thrilled the professor, who got fifteen minutes of mileage from it.

'That's because it reminded him of his plump wife's diaphanous nightgown,' I whispered to Ruth, encouraged by her laughter at my earlier sally.

This meeting of liberal, irreverent minds continued in class; but outside, she always seemed to be rushing somewhere or the other, except for once, when she asked me whether every Indian wasn't terribly poor or deprived, and I answered, 'Well, I was. At home we had five cats and all of them were named Pussy, and all of them ate leftovers mixed with rice. Later on I met city-bred upper-class Indians who had cats named Xerxes and Mephistopheles, and they actually drank milk from saucers.' The trademark sadness had again fled from her face, as it exploded in laughter and I had my first instant hard-on in years.

I didn't see her for the whole of the next semester, and then one day in the following summer, we ran into each other at a theatre showing *Starting Over*. Suddenly, my feelings for her were all aflame, fanned by the low red blouse she was wearing, and the jeans that were so tight they cut into her vitals, making me ache for her pain. She seemed more beautiful, more approachable standing there alone, unrelated to some awesome university, alone in the lonely city like I was. We saw the movie together; after which we almost wordlessly got into her car. She drove me to her apartment, a mile-long ride during which I felt as if I were suspended between two movie scenes, waiting for the action to begin in the next. But I was excited all through the drive. As we staggered in her door, my thing pushed against my jeans with a fury and an expectation that I hadn't known for some time now. As soon as she closed the door behind her, I kissed her. And then kissed her again. And again. There was a last kiss that would have cost five dollars on long-distance.

That kiss! It made her drop her keys and handbag right on the floor where we stood. My hands went to her blouse. She was breathing heavily. I yanked up her lacy bra and kissed, oooh, slaveringly and with utter devotion, her high, warm breasts. I knew, for the first time now, that light-pink nipple tips were real (as real as the Pope and my purple-pink glans), and not, as my sceptical examination of *Playboy* magazine had led me to suspect, painted, cosmetically alluring illusions.

And then, kissing her still, no, sucking on those pink nipples, I slipped my hand below her jeans and thrilled to the smoothness of those buttocks, to the fact that my finger prints were leaving their mark: 'Vijay Prabhu was here, August 1983.'

She had begun to moan. I knew I could unzip her now. I did, with an expertise and speed that surprised me, with one artful motion pulling down her jeans to her knees and then, while I kissed her smooth, creamy belly, her pale pink panties that didn't half cover her wild, gold pubic hair, I slid my tremulous fingers in and found her wet and hot! I kept telling myself, 'This is real. Who said it could only happen in my imagination? This is real.'

I exclaimed, 'You're beautiful!' almost without effort, without premeditation, just flowing from the natural emotion of the situation, as Adam must have to Eve in that first passionate moment, without coaching, 'I love you!'

I got a squeeze of love in return.

I didn't want to rush things. But I had let fall my own pants now, wanting to banish any potential impediments to love.

She was fondling my reverend member with a reverence it had not been shown in years: softly rolling her fingers around the shaft, and occasionally, almost timidly, reaching with one finger for that ecstatic region where it connected with my tight balls.

And then I slid her pants all the way down and nudged her towards the bed, which was about six feet away.

Made it! I was thinking: I had made it! No matter the deflating jokes that circulate from time to time about penises ('It's not the penis that counts, but the ass on the other end', and 'It's not the length of it, but what you do with it'), I had known, even in my limited experience, that once I had gotten a girl to fall in love with my cock, to connect with its hotness and hardness and its flattering *enthusiasm*, I could virtually lie back and watch the world go by from that point on. Because a bond had been established, an ancient bond that was a heaven and an earth more potent than your current philosophy. Which made it a *fait accompli*, man, a frigging *fait accompli*!

But then, as Uncle Gaulbert always said, life is different! Life—it never ceases to surprise you (which is why I am not your average suicidal Mick, because I want to be *in* on the next fucking surprise, and not dead!). As it turned out, travelling the six feet to her bed proved to be the longest distance I had ever travelled in my whole life. For, the moment I had drawn her jeans completely down, she began to slow down and acquire feet of clay. So long as I tongue-kissed and fondled her, my hands moving in multiple directions and subduing multiple territories, she moaned and dripped; but my gentle attempts to propel her toward that bed were subtly foiled.

'Wait, this is not right,' she said.

My hands ground briefly to a cease-fire halt. What wasn't right, I asked, my expression serious, half dumb.

'This. It's too fast.'

'But aren't you attracted to me? I have felt your very centre. I *know* you are.'

'I hardly know you.'

'Well, I can't think of a more delightful way of getting to know each other,' I said, laughing. 'Look, do we have to play by some rule book? So long as we're giving each other pleasure, what does it matter?'

'I suspect pleasure,' she said.

Suspect *pleasure!* What an unstoppable argument, in this pleasure-mad world, this distrust of pleasure. For a moment, I was stumped.

She took advantage of the pause to yank up her jeans, but I didn't want to let the momentum slip so easily. It had to do with a certain philosophical conviction: I'm not sure that I exist, but if I do, these are the only moments that are true and beautiful and worth every other moment of my non-existence.

Again I kissed her, again I unzipped her jeans, again I bared her smooth, rubescent bottom to the air-conditioned elements as she stood there. Again she thawed melted poured, and tongued the roof of my mouth. Again we ascended to the passionate point where the logical next step was for me to nudge her towards the bed. Vertical love, love standing up with one's jeans around one's ankles—it has its own wild, slightly freaky pleasures, I admit, perhaps harking back to that time when our ancestors wanted, at all times, to be poised for escape. But right now my fantasies yearned for the less-restricted horizontal position.

'It's not right. I have someone else,' she said.

God, that final step always seemed to bring on a new objection! If only I had the gymnastic physical flexibility to skip that move altogether: a standing fuck, at this point, was no more objectionable to me, if only I could wangle it, wiggle, wriggle it, whatever.

'Look, he can't be that important. Or we wouldn't be here.'

'Honestly. He moved to Chicago. But we haven't quite broken up. He visits me once in a while. And I'd have to tell him.'

'Look, trust your instincts, Ruth. All I know is that at this moment I want you, and you me.' I was searching desperately for the corny phrases I may have accidentally caught from the airwaves while switching television channels, dimly recognizing that my moves may have been somewhat sudden, may have rung those ancient alarm bells warning against savage Violators from across the seas.

'It *is* my instincts. I'm just following a sudden hunch not to go on.'

'Maybe you misread your hunch. Maybe your hunch said we shouldn't be doing it swinging from the ceiling—for today at least.'

Again she laughed, and melted as I went through all the steps, until we began making the pilgrim-snail's progress towards the bed, it was looking so good now, and suddenly, with a complete finality, she said, 'I'm sorry, Vijay, I can't. It's not your fault, it's me. Sorry.'

I gave up. My face contorting with dismay and exasperation, I yanked up my own pants, rudely shoved my still-uncomprehending and expectant and non-cooperative member into its cruelly vertical space, and stomped out onto the streets.

And then a surprising thing happened. I began to suspect pleasure too. In fact, I began to hate pleasure, for it had brought me only pain. Or rather, I hated sexual pleasure, or more precisely, the quest for sexual pleasure.

Sex was a nuisance. So long as it was an open question, it elbowed everythi·;g else out of the brain. And that was why my intellectual gifts had lain fallow all these years: because the quest for cunt had dislodged the study of Kant.

And what was it, after all? Twenty minutes, thirty minutes—forty minutes if you were lucky—of ticklish, electrical sensations around your penis, after which you went back to life as usual: you still had to wash your dishes, eat your baloney sandwich, sell soap or weenies or whatever for a living.

For a moment, now, sex became to me the most hateful three-letter word in the English language, much as it had decidedly been for the nuns of my childhood and allegedly been for a lot of priests. A plot of the devil to make cartoon characters of us; to provide laugh breaks for the roasting residents of hell. I felt deceived, betrayed by the years of wasted searching, as I once had by those squandered years of striving for sainthood.

What was sex but the need to be good, to be approved? Good sex (in which the woman was 'pleasured', as the new texts horridly expressed it) was hard work, ending with a virtuous pat on one's own back for a job well done. But I didn't *want* to be good, because goodness had been tainted for me by Sister Domina Mary, who had tried in my childhood years to impose it on me with a cane. And as for work, it was for the booboisie.

Good sex. You had to unravel the complex attire of a woman while she stood there like a dumbstruck statue, without the slightest awareness that she might help, at least by suggesting, 'The hook is in the front, not in the back.' Then your central command had to organize a multi-pronged but harmonious assault on her spread-out and not-equally-accessible properties. Thighs to be spread? You use your valuable muscle power—so crucial to the unilateral push-ups lurking around the corner—and spread them yourself. And then, your lips kiss her earlobes, your right hand does shuttle duty between her buttocks and her Reverend Mons, your left hand does clockwise, then counter-clockwise motions on her left areola while your tongue complements with antiphonal movements on her right, your pubis bumps and grinds against her thighs and belly when your unzipping, slyly peeling hand is not in the way—so that you might enlist her lower regions into your grand conspiracy. You're doing a more complicated job than Zuveen Mehta conducting the New York Philharmonic, because jolly old Zuveen doesn't have to bump his pelvis against some violin or unzip a tuba (on the contrary, dozens of violinists quite possibly wait in line outside his exclusive apartment building for the pleasure of unzipping him); yet compared to Zuveen, what are you getting paid? Zilch. Compared to his standing ovation at the end, all you're really getting is the permission to do it again the next time. And boy, are you supposed to be pleased!

Yes, there are a few droplets of pleasure, a few globules of sticky joy to be squeezed out of it, some diversion from the bump and grind of life, and well—slightly less chance of semen stains on your ceiling, but at what cost? These occasional satisfactions—if you could call them that—and more often, the mere dreams of these satisfactions, have you hooked. I was constantly a performer in some erotic play I had written. The rest of my life was merely footnotes, directions for stage scenery. A performer I was, solo, cast opposite an endless number of erotic actresses, who entered unannounced and left without a trace, except for a face maybe.

You might say that I gave up too easily, didn't try hard enough except in my mind, jumped to conclusions too soon, and like my father responded catastrophically to isolated defeats. But you are not I, so shut up—please. And understand, if you can, my fear of rejection, and of moralizing women, modern versions of my mistress Sister Domina Mary, women who whipped out the New and Updated Ten Commandments (with five-hundred sub clauses) the moment they saw a penis. I remembered my Academy friend's words: 'I want only a woman with the morals of an alley cat.' But since my type of intellectual stick-in-the-mud could never enter that social world wherein such amoral, free-as-the-birds women, the rare and blessed Marilyns of the world floated about, I decided to give up the world of women—forever.

Still boiling, I decided to write a letter—or different versions of the same letter, tailored to editorial taboos—to newspapers, magazines, and groups all over the country. The letter would announce the formation of a mass movement called Humanity Against Sex.

I wrote:

Dear Sir,

This is to announce to your readers that I have discovered the root of all evil in the world. The name of this evil? Sex. It breaks up families, turns teenage children against their parents, friend against friend, brother against brother.

Sex: the most overrated three-letter word in the history of language. The cause of the downfall of the Roman Empire. And now, of Western Civilization.

I say: We don't need it.

To save mankind, let's have an international moratorium on sex for the next ten years, enforced by the United Nations. With US air support if need be. B-52ing to eradicate evil thoughts among men.

To wake us all up, and our fellow human beings, I say to all of your readers who feel as I do: Let's march on Washington on the second Sunday in May, to demonstrate on the steps of the Capitol building.

Any of your readers who wish to help this cause may send their contributions to:

Vijay Prabhu
Acting President, 'Humanity Against Sex'
6521 W St.,#415
Washington, D.C. 20016

Sincerely,

Vijay Prabhu.

I rushed to a nearby library, xeroxed multiple copies of the letter, addressed envelopes from a couple of directories, and mailed the letters out to about a hundred publications and organizations of all stripes, some from backwater southern and midwestern towns. I pushed myself, shouting down my mind whenever it began to berate me for doing a foolhardy thing I would later regret.

Soon, the telegrams and letters poured in. 'Jesus Lovers Against Copulation', 'Romance Novelists Against Pornography', 'Citizens for the American, Asexual War', 'American Business

Against Immorality', SIDS (Sex Is Dirty So Don't Do It!), 'Feminist Ex-Hookers For Retrospective Justice', 'No Coming Until the Second Coming', 'Families Against Erotic Provocation'—these congregations of good and solid American citizens seemed to pop up from nowhere and pledge their support and unwavering loyalty to me and my cause. And while the Society for the Dominance of the Missionary Position promised only partial support insofar as my Humanity Against Sex march discouraged 'perversions', Evangelist Jimmy Sugarbaby clipped my letter from his local newspaper and hallelujahed over it in his Sunday sermon. Contributions started pouring in: cash, cheques, pledges, even supermarket coupons. I didn't suppose the Reverend Jimmy had intended to cite me as anything more than an example in his unending crusade against immorality; perhaps his followers had misunderstood. I was stupefied as I opened the envelopes, read their crackpot contents, and counted the enclosed cash: if I pocketed the money, I could return to India and lead a cozy existence.

And when the paid speaking invitations started trickling in, I must confess I had brief, tempting visions of gurudom: private jets, worshipping followers—especially those accommodating, spiritually ecstatic female devotees that have made gurudom and the manufacture of new religions such an attractive prospect for men since the beginning of time. Perhaps most fads and religions had started in some such insane moment of individual rebellion, anger, or revulsion, or drug-high—and having quickly garnered a following, had then acquired a life of their own.

But it wasn't for me. I was tired of scripts in which I played an instrument of larger purpose. (It may be that a divinity shaped our ends, but why did it have to kick my butt so often?) I would find myself, be myself. I would write my own script. I knew now that I had to flee this growing mob and this crazy country, but I didn't want to be a fugitive—even though it was tempting for me to be the instrument that would part these fools from their money. I decided quickly to return every penny that had been mailed to me.

The phone rang.

'Praise the Lawd!' said the male voice in a very Southern

drawl. 'Your letter saved mah life! And I'm gonna help you save other lives. I done gonna come over to your place first thing Saturday morning, and we're gonna plan this march together.'

Two radio stations called in the next hour. Then I unplugged my phone and decided there was no time to waste. I had to get away before the mad swirl of events overpowered my weak will. It had been a mistake to supply my address to these kooks, these cartoons, these people from whom I was removed by dozens of wavelengths.

God, what *was* I doing in this bizarre country? This land of gum chewers, lukewarm hot dogs, tasteless 'crap of cow' burgers, women who flaunted their chemically deodorized privates right under your nose but gave you nothing, not even a flicker of recognition? Why was I masochistically surrendering myself to this antiseptic land of loneliness, of fiercely loveless lives, of idiot box dependencies, of kick-ass excursions into foreign countries, of random criminality, danger, and depravity lurking behind the blandest faces? It was nothing but a colonial script that I was playing out, one that had been written for me and my babu brethren by Lord Dalhousie and Warren Hastings and Sir Winston Churchill—he who wrote glowingly of the 'excellent moral effects' of poison-gassing Iraqi tribes, then went on to oppose Indian independence. I needed to be whole, to understand, to get back to my roots, my people.

It had all been one long mistake: Running in the opposite direction from Benares, how could I achieve my salvation, my moksha? India *was* the place for me. India, where rich smells of tamarind, rose, cardamom, and mango honeyed the balmy air. Where people knew your name. My countrymen: they were warm. They had time to talk to you. They didn't give you the bum's rush. Unlike in America, where every man's house is not his castle, but his fortress, shutting out people and human warmth and connectedness, Indians invited you in, offered you coffee and delicious snacks: Mysore Pak, bondas, bhajjis, any of a thousand delightful surprises. They were happy as puppies in a pound when they saw you. They remembered friendships from long ago, valued them for their own sake. They did not judge you by the name of the crook etched on your polo shirt. *It was the more civilized country.*

I would go back and, liberated from my quest for sex, write the book I always had wanted to, always had promised myself I could. I would look for my roots. Meditate in the Himalayas, perhaps. (Maybe even in Poona, at the Rajneesh ashram? I thought briefly.) I didn't have to work immediately, I still had a few rupees there, some arrears of salary owed to me. I was seized with a mad nostalgia for my friends, revolutionary as well as not, with whom I could spend days and nights talking, laughing, exchanging jokes, creating fresh ones, fresh insights. I would seek them out, these doomed people, embrace them, hug them like long-lost brothers . . . .

But what about my ticket? All I had was four hundred dollars in my bank account. Oh, yes, there were also some brass thingumajigs I had brought from India, which people had persuaded me would bring me a fortune from naïve and art-hungry Americans. But commerce had arrived in the US before I, and many African, Indian, and other Third World students had also come to Washington with the same brilliant idea, leaving my brass bowls to collect dust. Still, I would go to Wendy, my library co-worker, my one friend in America, and say, 'I know this is not the most profitable financial proposition you have run into. But could you possibly let these thingumajigs decorate your living-room until I return you the three-hundred dollar loan I'm now asking of you?'

Wendy had not only helped me with money, she had lightened me of luggage, and there was very little to pack into my suitcase, which I lugged in my hand through the subway ride to Union Station for my train to New York from where my plane departed that evening. I made it just in time for the check-in at JFK International. And, as the hordes marched on Washington D.C. in response to a wild scheme I had launched but seemed powerless to control, my Air India Jumbo sailed the Atlantic sky on its way to India, with me in it singing, 'Got no bag or baggage, to hold me down!' As they shouted in their D.C.-headed buses, 'No Sex! Free us from Free Sex!', I was flying to freedom, and peace—far away from the 'land of the free'. As they yelled, 'Lust Kills Family Values!

Lasting Love, not Lusting Love!', I was going home at last, and travelling light. My wanderlust had been stilled, and so had my lust.

Return

THE LINE OF Ambassador taxis that ferried travellers from Bajpe airport to Mangalore town began to race each other on the winding, hilly stretch beginning a mile from the airport, trying desperate James Bond-like manoeuvres to resist being overtaken. And soon after my taxi passed the initial stretch of shrub-covered red hills and emerald green paddy fields, I began to notice the traces of modernization that had settled on the suburbs, some houses having acquired a new dress of plastic paint over their original whitewashed frames, garish greens, pinks, and blues, and the ratio of houses to huts having increased—signs of the influx of Middle East money, of material progress by ex-coolies and clerks and small landlords slaving for Arab masters. A purdahed woman rode sideways on the back of a scooter, her arms tightly enfolding her husband's midriff for reasons of survival rather than of romance (though the effect of the tips of her nipples grazing his back might well have had an unintended romantic result). A coolie woman in a torn sari carried on her head a haystack that was twenty times the head's breadth, fifty times its size, and perhaps two hundred times her brain's volume. As we entered the town limits, all houses and shops now, a sweeper swept the road in the traditional way, the dust flying back with the wind onto the road, resulting in a socialistic redistribution of dust.

I couldn't wait to get home and surprise my parents, but when the creaky brown door opened in answer to the doorbell, it was I who was in for a shock. Dad had grown older, so much older. His cheeks had sunken, his teeth were rotting, his frame was shrunken and bent, and his embrace was a half-embarrassed, half-bodied one, following which he slunk back into the shadows of the house that looked smaller and less fit for human residence than it had when I lived there. Mom looked dishevelled, soiled. Her face, like her faded sari, was smudged with soot, and seemed to signal a menopausal surrender of her womanly state. But her embrace was tighter than Dad's, plus she had a kiss for each of my cheeks.

I was shocked to see what the intervening four years had done to them; I felt rising within me that protective urge one feels towards ageing parents, whose preservation suddenly becomes as important to you as the preservation of old photographs, of family heirlooms, of your own precious organs. I almost felt personally responsible.

Having no pressing engagements—I was still a refugee from the world, a man adrift, trying to endure my coming hence as I had once celebrated my going thither—I settled in for a few days of rest, recuperation, and re-evaluation. It was January, but already too hot for my expanded and mildly American-fat-coated body, used now to air-conditioning and cooler climes. Walking around shirtless was the only sane, if less than middleclass-proper, option. A mosquito bite on my forearm had bloomed into a one-square-centimetre boil. Unable to scratch it into submission, I tried painting it with my blue Uniball pen, hoping maybe that the next mosquito alighting on the spot and trying to drink deep would develop a stomach ulcer—maybe even food poisoning.

'How's the weather been?' I asked Dad. The Sunday lunch of sannan and Chicken Rosachi Kadi glowed within, the spicy coconut milk radiating warmth and goodwill throughout my body.

'One keeps oneself busy. Don't have time to worry about the weather,' he said, smiling weakly, then returning to his melancholic expression.

One of Dad's worries today was the family's middle-aged grey cat.

It had died all of a sudden, after a day of apparent lassitude. Dad was contemplating the various options.

'Bury it,' Mom said.

'How? We can't dig a hole deep enough. Just throw it in a gutter somewhere,' Pop responded, ruminatively. A slight improvement on the traditional remedy—throw it into your neighbour's compound. I thought: the cat had spent its last hour-but-one nuzzling up to me, trying to sleep in my lap. Yet, in a brief resurgence of my weakness for being irritating to cats, I had worried it with my Uniball pen and tried to hypnotize it. Had my hypnosis proven too much?

'Aunt Meera died, you know?' Mom said.

'What?!'

'Gramophone needle. It was rusty. She had bad eyesight. Got tetanus, it was too late.'

'God,' I said, with a sinking feeling, floating for a few seconds in warm memories of young love, raw regrets for a peace never made.

'God, yes. I'm worried. No job, you got to get a job,' Momma said suddenly changing the subject with her old alacrity.

'I've just come back one week now, Mom.' And almost shouted, voicelessly: I am not what I have achieved, Mom! I am what I am. And I am worth it!

Damn, I was losing my cool in this burning place. So my escape from America had been no return to paradise—only the start of a new quest. Peace was not to be for me—not yet. I thought of Maya. Should I just jump into the next bus and barge into her life?

As for my parents, they would never change. The way they saw it, I was unmarriageable, unredeemable, despite my 'American' card. Poor Mom, she needed her worries. Without them, she couldn't be a good Christian. Because to be a good Christian was to be a sad, suffering Christian. If you weren't crushed by troubles, then maybe Jesus didn't love you; and then you'd *really* have to worry.

Her face, which once had a Madonna's serene beauty, was now porous and wrinkled from the ravages of tension, neglect, and middle-class wifehood. Worry lines zigzagged over her features. People would look at that face and, without knowing why, become tense themselves.

Was I getting fed up with India already? Had my conversion to Western ways been too deep for my understanding, beginning perhaps even before I was born? Who was I? I had fled the geographical America, but I hadn't yet conquered the America of my mind. It still nagged at me, this confusion about who I was, about who pulled my strings. An old, nearly-forgotten urge came over me. Hurrying to my old study and finding the same desk there, I dusted it, brought out a letter pad from my suitcase, and started to write:

Dear Jackie

We all go a little mad sometimes. As I did, in America recently. And may have in my letters to you.

Blaming the West for our sexual colonization, it is not the entire truth. Because you have fantasies about us too. It is a corollary of the human condition.

Thus it is that American males go to the Philippines looking for young and submissive wives, and English males raid Bangkok panting for that explosive Oriental lay, while young American women, à la Jong, slouch around Italy, fantasizing the addition of a few notches of manly perfection to their love belts.

Is it something in our genes, this impulse towards racial diversity? Is it in our archetypal unconscious? (Do you think about these things at all, Jackie, or just about dresses and fashion and the Kennedy mystique?) Or is it that, as Plato pointed out long ago, man and woman are the two lost halves searching for the other all their lives, looking for love? Asunder, they yearn to join (yes: and joined, they often yearn soon thereafter to break asunder and rejoin in newer combinations, but that's another story).

What I'm saying is: I know it isn't all the West's fault. Even before the West goose-stepped in, we Indians had lost much from the Muslim invasion and conquest; *The Kama Sutra* had been a dead treatise to all but a few horny Brahmins. Hollywood love, free love—it was all a breath of fresh air into the stale state of male-female relationships in India.

So what's the problem? Not the new international trade in love—which, commercially, benefits mainly the West. Not even this trade's overtones of a slave-Massah, man-Sex-Goddess, robot-inventor relationship. But that those sons of bitches stole our identity! That, to me, is not something that I can so easily live with.

But I say: After me, the deluge. I have gotten back at least some of my identity—my Indian identity—even though I had to go to America to rescue it. What makes me truly joyous is that this is my last letter to you. I don't need you anymore, Jackie.

Best wishes,

Vijay.

That was the end of my American connection, I thought to myself. Goodbye, America.

A dog barked in approval.

It was Doggie the Seventh, the family's dog—or rather, my father's dog, since he didn't seem to relate to anybody else around. He was the joy of Dad's joyless life, this nondescript, brown mongrel of uncertain age who had just wandered in one day a few years ago and decided to stay, who went wild with joy when he heard my father's rust-stained bicycle's kirikirikirikiri as it brought him home from work at his bus-company job. My father would feed Doggie by throwing meat pieces on the floor, shouting down my sanitation-freak of a mother when she weakly protested that it attracted ants. Doggie the Seventh was my father's only reason to smile, his only consolation in a country full of people ... but people, and his children, had failed him. I wanted to make amends.

In the making of amends, I had come upon some unexpected good fortune. In the rush to escape back to India from the looneys who had suddenly fallen for my Anti-Sex Campaign, I had accidentally packed in my writing files a few dozen of the envelopes containing cash 'donations'. I had found them only the other day, when attempting to restart my stillborn literary efforts. In rupees, these contributions translated to a fortune. It seemed stupid and even impractical, at this point, to locate my donors and persuade them to pass that cash on to a *real* crook.

'Would you both like to visit Goa with me? Some nice hotel on the beach for a week?' I asked, wanting to give him a holiday from his sad, dull routine. 'I'll pay for everything.'

'Nowadays, home is best. You eat your little bit of conjee and are comfortable. Outside, there are too many problems.' My father's stoic, tired, slightly careful response. We never really had made peace.

'You better go to a dentist, Dad. Your teeth look infected,' I said, trying to change the subject. 'I'll pay.'

'These dentists and all—it's all rubbish. Salt: it's the oldest, cheapest, and best remedy. Just brush my teeth with salt.'

Just then, there was a clatter of the iron gate: a visitor.

Uncle Everest, carrying around scraps of unread newspapers and a plastic bag to save leftover bones for his dog (a see-through doggie bag for an unseen animal), has dropped in. My mother's cousin, the one-time Rebel and black sheep, a fascination to us children—now, to my grown-up self, his presence is like that of a living ghost, his mind like a broken record. He has come for an unscheduled visit at his usual, psychologically correct time: mealtime.

This is Everest's life now: he evaluates the different events of the day—weddings, First Holy Communions, inaugurations and muhurtams, festivals, openings of stores—and the chances of getting free food and refreshments at each; then, through a crude mental version of the Critical Path Method, he settles on an itinerary that will take him from food point to food point while expending the least possible energy and bus fare. Despite a wealth of such experience, qualifying him as a consultant for the government's Energy and Transportation Departments, he is angry at the time wasted in this circuitous search for food—a lifestyle that interferes with his reading goals, his hundred pages a day, his thousand best books of all time, or whatever.

He's been barred from the houses of some relatives, because he doesn't wear 'decent' clothes—by 'decent' they mean freshly-laundered and untattered and appropriate to *their* station in life, which might be compromised by the social visits of a rag-tag relative. He does his reading, particularly of matrimonial columns, at the various bookshops in town, while evaluating, on a second and concurrent mental track, the proximity of free watering holes and feeding troughs. And he's anxious about the way the country is being run: *everything* the government is doing is wrong.

'For someone who has no mother,' he says, all of a sudden.

My attempt to bring the conversation back onto the main line by asking about his books spurs a lament about the deterioration of his collection: 'Books of Shelley, Wordsworth, or what. They're in sacks, trunks, all over. Then there is this Vysya Bank officer. He lends me money. What to do . . . .'

What to do. Of course I should be able to answer that, shouldn't I?

I, the soon-to-be preachy writer and bloody know-it-all, who imagines himself capable of advising, and doing a better job than, every major head of state, pope, and ayatollah. I, who am as filled to the gushing brim with advice as Kuwait's entrails are filled with oil. Yet Everest's simple question 'What to do' stumps me as an eternal question to which I have no answer, nor expect to have, ever.

And then, after that depressing and sobering visit from Uncle Everest, ex-Rebel and sometime Hamlet like me, now hunting for food and women with less success than his Paleolithic ancestors, I begin to get worried myself: Will I end up like him, as Dad had prophesied?

And then the revelation came.

I was casually conversing with Dad and Mom, sitting on the blue plastic sofa after a heavy lunch, when I asked how our landlord was.

'Oh, he sold his property and moved to Bangalore,' Mom said.

'Sold? To whom?'

'Well, we bought the house, you know,' Mom said. She added after a pause: 'Spent all our money. Had to borrow a little.'

It astonished me, this revelation. All these years, I had believed they were nearly penniless, and my father completely dependent on his pension and the few hundreds he pulled from the bus companies. The scorpion sting of betrayal poisoned my mood.

'Dad, if you had only loaned me a thousand rupees after my college, until my National Scholarship money came, I would by now have had a Ph.D. at government expense. And I could have started teaching. Who will give me a job now, with a mere BA? You lied to me, when you said you couldn't afford it!'

'At least you had a BA. I had only an S.S.L.C., and no shoes, and no trips to Bangalore, and no guitar!' Dad shouted back, stormily, and went into his bedroom in a huff.

But the next day, a letter came.

The letter, an apparently routine government one, woke me up with a shock: by some bureaucratic mistake, my resignation had never been processed. So I was still a government employee, treated as if on leave of absence. I was free to return if I wished, with all the power and capacity that my present seniority entitled me to.

I was seized, in a return of my childhood piety and passion, by a desire to return to a new, purer, more-serious incarnation of myself. It wasn't entirely idealistic, this impulse, because I also realized it might endear me to Maya—my only hope of life and love. I would become an IAS officer less selfishly absorbed with the Western, individualistic idea of 'fulfilment' or 'self-realization'. I would dedicate the rest of my days to India's weak and poor, who were still as poor as ever.

But first, I would visit my former colleagues and seek their report on what really was happening in India. They must be powerful chaps now, I think, excited about their capacity to help people and change things.

Three days later, in Bangalore, a peon in a frayed white uniform and a dishevelled, worn face leads me defeatedly up two flights of stairs into a large, coir-carpeted room with a large desk situated under a whirling fan. From behind the desk, its perimeter walled by three-foot-high piles of files—symbols of his overweening ambition—beams the fuller, porous, intelligent but tense face of my colleague Bundlemani, who has on a white short-sleeved shirt, the regulation dress of the in-crowd of bureaucrats: Brahmin, deadly-serious, dependable. It is 6:30 and nearly dark, the huge office building quiet; but Bundlemani is catching up, after a foreign jaunt on 'official' business. Ganpat Lal, another colleague, a north Indian muscular type, hearing of my arrival, comes by in one of his fleet of chauffeured official cars. They are mystified that I want to return from the fabulous United States—the land where everyone owns two cars, one for office use and one for vacational use and decadence—to this primitive, gadget-poor life of theirs.

'So you had lots of babes in America?' says the burly and bulldog-faced Ganpat, coming straight to the point and surveying me greedily.

'Couldn't keep their hands off me,' I say, knowing that's what Ganpat wants to hear. 'That's all they want.' I say it convincingly, because Ganpat's eyes look envious for a moment.

'Administration is shit,' Ganpat says unequivocally, while Bundlemani laughs equivocally and continues to burrow into his heap of uniformly brown government files, throwing occasional polite glances in our direction.

'I don't know. I want to see if I have something to contribute,' I say. At which Ganpat laughs brazenly.

'Contribute?' Ganpat says, 'To what? *It is all gone. It is finished*!' What is finished, I gather, is their idealism, and their hope that India is ever going to change for the better. 'Everybody confines themselves to their personal interests and forgets about the Service. That is the way to survive.'

'Say, how do I get tickets to the Bolshoi Ballet?' Ganpat now asks Bundlemani. The ballet's Indian tour includes one sold-out show in Bangalore. 'Everybody here is saying, "If you haven't seen the Bolshoi Ballet, you are nothing!" One officer got five hundred complimentary tickets for distribution to other officers and VIPs, but sold three hundred of them on the black market!'

He sees he will get no answer from the file-busy Bundlemani. 'I say, stop that file shit!' he says. 'Give it up for today!' And Bundlemani is embarrassed by that tone of *command*—a command disguised in pally good humour, but still a command: north Indian, imperial! He secretly thinks, dimwitted bastard. But stops as commanded.

I consider Ganpat in quiet amusement: the willingness to say 'Shit, Man!' and laugh loudly was the foundation on which his muscular personality was built. He had no opinions on anything; but most post-adolescents (and perennial post-adolescents like Bundlemani) from the mild-mannered south were too stumped to respond to a sudden burst of foul language, and this was enough to shut them up.

'Where is Chowdaiah working these days?' I ask Ganpat.

'You didn't hear? They found about fifty lakh rupees in unaccounted money in his house! He was dismissed,' laughs Ganpat.

I was stunned. So it was his ill-gotten money—the hundred-rupee bundles he had handed me—that had financed my loftily-conceived American fiasco.

Honour and dishonour were all so mixed up! The purest and most self-righteous virgin began in a filthy act of lust! So nobody (and never mind already-corrupt me) could remain unsullied by the corruption that seeped into the earth, in turn nourishing the food they ate and the very blood that coursed through their veins.

My brief, self-flattering fantasies of idealism, of making changes through an administrative position—it now seemed as irrelevant as the flying brontosaurus. Most of my once-'idealistic' friends now spent their time plotting to get plum jobs, which they rated according to the number of cars, guest-houses, air trips, five-star-hotel meals attached to each. Another colleague's house had recently been raided and a fabulous two crore rupees in unaccounted cash seized! What was the point of playing Boy Scout games, trying to lecture humble village accountants on honesty.

All was entropy, all was decay. The only way to counter this universal force was to understand it, to be at peace with it, to seize the present. In my case, it meant fleeing my depressing past, at least everything after the dogbite: not literally fleeing it, but mastering it by writing about it—and damn the money. But I had been creatively fallow for far too long. I needed something that would jump-start my stalled brain.

And the answer to this seemed to be just one: Maya. The only woman I had ever known whose mere presence made the blood rush simultaneously to all my major organs: my brain, my heart, my prick. What would I not give for the salt-sweet taste of her skin, for one night's grazing rights to that magnificent pubic forest?

I took the next bus to Mysore, and called her from the bus station.

'What are *you* doing in Mysore?' she asked with a start that apparently sent something crashing to the floor.

'Dying to meet you after this long. Aren't you?'

'Oh yes!' And then she added, as if it seemed relevant, that she had a current boyfriend. It made my spirit sink momentarily, but I couldn't take her too seriously: from what I had known of her, to have just one boyfriend seemed the moral equivalent of having joined a cloistered convent. In all probability, what it really meant was that there was room for a half-dozen more on a slightly sparser schedule.

'Is the atmosphere conducive?'

'Depends on what you want to do,' she replied. The old, quick-on-the-draw, triple-entendred Maya.

'Just want to talk, get back in touch. I'm writing a book,' I said, trying to bolster my case with Art.

'I'm surprised you remember me,' she said. I could hear the old warmth and sharpness returning to her voice. 'Most people, once they go to America, think they are big shots. Too big to mix with Indians.'

'That's true of people who went to America as nobodies and returned as big shots,' I said. 'I went to America a big shot and am returning a nobody.'

She laughed. 'See you about six,' she said.

That evening, I almost gasped to see the new, older, somewhat-domesticated version of Maya opening the door. She had cut her hair short, Liza Minelli fashion, but her light green cotton sari seemed to hint at a return to a revolutionary, non-sexual simplicity. All she had on by way of accoutrements was a pair of simple gold earrings—the mark of the non-destitute woman—and the mangalsutra; nothing else, not lipstick, not even talcum powder: the basic woman. Still, there was that light in her eyes. Old and suppressed feelings leaped within my body.

But her proffered handshake, after a four-year gap, seemed a cold insult, a denial of everything I stood for: the brotherhood of man, caring, compassion, sisterhood under the skin . . . . I wanted to squeeze her in my arms till she was out of breath, till we were both out of breath.

'A friendly hug, please,' I said, fixing her in my gaze with my most stirring, Et tu Brute? voice.

'What if the hug gets more than friendly?' she said.

'Well,' I shot back, losing my cool at her lack of charity, 'if my fly-buttons hit the ceiling, and your diaphragm is seen exiting from your rear end—*then* we will know that our hug is more than friendly, OK?'

She laughed her soft, flattering laugh of surprise and gave me a feather-light hug to mollify me. I was surprised to find my old 'wit'—my old, chutzpah-born-of-horniness wit—returning.

We sat down on her wicker furniture in the modest sitting-room with its bare white walls and cobwebbed corners.

'I heard about your Anti-Sex episode,' she said, smiling. Some Indian in Washington had probably recognized my name and passed on the news.

'I don't know what came over me,' I replied, shyly, recognizing by now that the episode had been a kind of madness, an extreme reaction to another kind of madness. 'But all of that is over. Anyway, tell me about yourself.'

'I've changed a lot too. I know you thought of me as some wild nymphomaniac. But at that time it was political, you know. I wanted to do all the things they said I shouldn't do.'

'You've *really* changed? Why, you're only on your third sentence, and you've launched into the subject of sex.'

She laughed, and her eyes met mine in that deep, copulating manner she had of making eye-contact, and then she laughed again. Then she excused herself and brought me a glass of diluted Kissan squash, that watery solution of fruit essence and saccharine that has unfortunately become the modern, lazy version of traditional Indian hospitality. Then she lay back at a forty-five degree angle on her makeshift divan. She contemplated me now, more calm and thoughtful than usual. She watched me sip my drink.

'Don't tell me you got *no* pleasure out of it. I won't believe you,' I said.

'Oh, sex is all right.' She seemed contemplative, changed. 'Except for the icky part of it.' She laughed. 'God screwed up. He should have made sex electronic. So there was no washing up to do. Just a meter to show how much pleasure each of us was having, ha ha! I hate germs, you see. Germs make me sick. I mean, they make all of us sick, but they make me sicker. They've psyched me before they have even gotten into me. I surrender without a fight. And all those fluids are full of bacteria. Even kissing is nothing but a large-scale swap of germs. Like Iran and Iraq exchanging prisoners of war.'

Maya always had been stubbornly quirky, and this sanitary obsession of hers now explained her old attraction to Ganesh, the washing maniac. Did she think of me as a large germ, or an agglomeration of germs, I wondered.

'Actually,' she continued, 'sex isn't that much fun, because I'm so petrified thinking of the germs . . . . What I most enjoy is my power over men. They want it so much, you can see it in their faces! They're so grateful when they get it. And when you love a guy, it's the least you can do.' She paused. 'And when you don't love a guy, it's still the least you can do . . . . 'Not that I used to do it with every Tom, Dick, and Harry. I did it with a lot of dicks, yes.' We had once alighted on this knowledge together, from reading an American novel: that 'dick' was American slang for penis. So snappy and hilarious and right did it sound on the tongue that we loved the word—almost as much as she should have the object.

We laughed. And damn it, listening to her juicy, ballsy conversation was getting me horny—a long time since I had felt this way. Thank God her mother never washed out her mouth with soap. Or maybe it was precisely because her mother was strict and prudish, making her kneel on grains of mustard once because she had said 'but', that she was now like this.

'Actually, I never give *in*,' she continued. 'I *give* when I choose. I like to be in control. I like to see the faces of some of the fellows who think they are going all the way. And then, when they realize they aren't. That's funny.'

'I can imagine,' I replied, having been there. 'Like Hillary when he's within fifty feet of Mount Everest's peak, being told, "No, you can't come up here, old chap. We don't have your reservation. Sorry, speak to our Manager in Delhi about that. If you ever get back there alive, ha ha!"'

'You see, in the past, I would feel I was striking a blow for liberation each time I blew a guy,' Maya said. We laughed; I was amazed to see her verbal naughtiness return. 'Actually, I never blew too often; like I said, the germs piss me off. But sometimes, it was just the right thing to do. Maybe I had found myself licking his knees or something. And then, I couldn't just make a long jump back up to his face. Do you understand? It would have been impolite.'

'Etiquette and the Art of Erotic Maintenance!' I interrupted, but she was too much in the mood to stop.

'Then I got tired. Guys stuck to you. They didn't understand that I was just playing around. That it was a political thing. They had had such lousy luck: frustrated Hindus who had seen too many sexy Western movies. Sad fellows with sad cow-like eyes. They now looked to you as if their moksha depended on you. They didn't take hints. Life became so hectic just handling these dicks—I mean their owners and their owners' problems . . . the dicks themselves were quick work, ha ha. But you see, fun is not fun if it is ninety per cent work. And then, I was always thinking of those germs.

'So after that I had only one at a time. I mean, the same one for maybe six months, like that. Purely charity cases. They gave me nothing, except may be pay at a restaurant sometimes. Men are such chauvinists about these things, not worth the trouble fighting them. But nothing else. In fact, most men, once they had me, would sleep over at *my* apartment and eat *my* food!'

'You never fed me,' I said chidingly. Again, she ignored my interruption.

'But you know, I became smarter . . . I found it was safer to have one steady friend at a time. Less chances that word would spread. I mean at work, people had already begun to talk about me, because I have a wicked tongue. I just enjoy talking naughty. And people think you're really that way. Some Hindu boys from Kerala and Tamil Nadu, if any girl *talks* to them, they think she wants to sleep with them. Because no girl has ever talked to them before. I sometimes think, if I'm going to get a bad reputation anyway, I might as well have fun. But the people I really enjoyed, all the people who talked revolution and free love, they have all left.' She paused, and turned serious. 'Got jobs, married safer women, once they had had their fun with me. So now there's no real fun. That's all.'

'Maya,' I said. 'Isn't it true: most Mangalore girls of your age, your class. They didn't like Mangalorean men, right? They were always falling in love with outsiders, rejecting us. Why?'

She smiled, fidgeted with her fingers, looked into my eyes and smiled again, fidgeted with her fingers again, laughed a little—as if my idea were revealing itself to her in stages.

'You're exaggerating,' she said. 'Well, maybe it's partly true. All those guys from Bangalore and Bombay—they were just more dynamic and confident. And spoke like gentlemen. And wore jeans. Like the heroes in those books.'

'What books?'

'Teenage books, I mean. When visiting my aunt's house in Bangalore for every summer holiday, I would read whatever my cousins brought from the circulating library. Romantic fiction. Mills and Boon, *Woman's Day*, *Woman's Own*, *Seventeen*. So all my romantic dream heroes are from those foreign magazines: broad-shouldered, narrow-hipped, ruddy-complexioned, blue-eyed, intense, long-legged, deep-voiced, tight jeans, spoke very little, when they did speak, they used romantic words. Heroes. Took care of you. Understood your moods. Compared to them, most Indian men are just consolation prizes. Except the guys from Bangalore and Bombay, they were a little like those heroes. Brown studs.' She laughed.

A funny thing was happening to me. Even as she explained her disenchantment to me, I was only half-listening to her. I was becoming attracted rather to the voice, magical because of the speaker's openness, her ease, her almost innocent provocative-ness—qualities all women should have but which many have lost in the process of 'civilization'.

'I've changed too,' I said. 'Unlike your other friends, I don't wear my philosophy on my sleeve, that's all. Yes, I have a comic, absurdist side. But you think I am less than your gloomy, pompous friends? I think what I have isn't so bad: my bullshit detector, and what Plato would call a love of justice. Beyond that, in a world that's soon going to blow itself up, I really know nothing. Except that . . . .'

I touched her hand softly, to her surprise, and continued: 'Except that, as far as I'm concerned, in the universal, timeless, ideal world, you are married to me, and he is a mere loafer. The fellow you say is your boyfriend, I mean.'

Smiling at first, she turned her head aside and blushed. There-you-go-again-tut-tut, her expression seemed to say. 'Vijay,' she said. 'I'm sorry, I just can't.'

'What do you want me to do to be worthy of you, Maya?' I said. 'Tickle your backside with deep thoughts?'

She laughed.

Recovering my breath in the room's silence, I stood up to leave. 'All the best, Maya.' I said. 'Goodbye.'

'Write your book, Vijay,' she said, in a changed, somewhat affectionate tone. 'I really look forward to reading it. Wait, I have a book of yours.' She went into what seemed like her bedroom, and returned a couple of minutes later with a copy of Plato's *Dialogues* that I had loaned her five years ago.

Outside, walking in the moonlit street to a sonata of barking dogs—three hours had passed, and it was 9:00 p.m. now, sleepy time in this somnolent city—I thought: Gone! The one woman in the world that I wanted with body, mind, and soul, because she was a challenge to all three . . . gone forever.

Try to make me believe in intelligent creation now. We're lost, I say—all of us, this universe itself. Lost in the pits of randomness, of no-sense. The one woman who's right for us, and she's taken. Taken, possessed, by another person, another idea, another ideology, another dream, another illusion.

I needed to start anew, to quit dreaming of what I could never have.

One thing she had done to me, even though it had dimly come to me almost as soon as I was on the plane returning to India, was to make me realize that for me there would be no escape from sex ever. Despite her conservative, no-flesh-exposed dress, her mere voice, her smile, the timing of her laughter: these had given me an erection.

To be a man was to be in a state of wanting forever. You could control it, you could divert it, you could threaten it with eternal damnation, but it would always be there. Only a sense of humour . . . but who the hell was I kidding? I had had a sense of humour for years now, but I was still horny. Anatomy was destiny. The only hope lay in the fact that as one got older, one got more tired, and one's choice of fantasies got fewer and fewer. The only other hope would be that one day evolutionary logic would give every man his own cunt and then he could say to the women of the world: 'See you and your vibrator around sometime!'

I decided I would send a recantation of my Anti-Sex letter to all the newspapers and groups that I had sent the original letter to.

No, no, not yet. There were things that needed thinking over. The fundamental assumptions of my post-Catholic life. They had been wrong too. Banishing God hadn't been the equivalent of banishing evil and unhappiness. If life was a getting from Point A to Point B, what were the elements in my past that had made my journey so stormy, so rocky, so zigzag, so completely irrational and unexpected? I needed to rediscover my centre.

Sankara, my guru in my teenage years, told me of an ashram near Pondicherry where one could occupy a room in a cottage, be undisturbed if one preferred, or attend philosophical and spiritual lectures. I decided to spend the next six months there, away from everybody and everything. Luckily, I could afford to. I still had money left over from the Anti-Sex envelopes, physical evidence that one time in my life some believers had believed in me just as I, in turn, had long believed in others.

Well, religion owed me something for all the years of my life it had stolen from me. Helping myself to this small bounty, as a down payment on my salvation from poor souls who were lost forever—it was the least I could do to renounce my saintly destiny forever.

Moksha Express

IN THE BROWN, hot, dry countryside of south-eastern India, a few miles outside formerly French Pondicherry, the pink edifice of the Universal Love and Om Temple and Ashram rested on fifty acres of parched red earth pocked with stunted trees. Here I spent six months in honest, deep meditation, looking for a fast lane to moksha or salvation—or if not moksha, at least the diluted version of it, understanding.

At first, in that remoteness from civilization, it was bliss to be alive. But the heat and the effort to concentrate and produce elevated thought seemed to me to be slowly evaporating my brain cells. My meditation exercises seemed to have gone awry. 'Imagine yourself on a nice beach,' was the suggestion of an assistant guru with a *faux* British accent; it didn't work, because when I imagined myself on an Indian beach, I saw in my mind's eye grown men lowering their shorts to answer the call of nature—which annoyed me. And when I thought of a non-Indian beach, I pictured a nudist beach on the French Riviera with spectacularly naked Frenchwomen with flaming red pubic hair saying, 'Oui! Oui!' My soul 'Oui!'ed them back with extraordinary enthusiasm, and the fantasy gave me a hard-on, which was vicious in a sitting down position, so I had to stand up and lose my mental 'image'. [Narrator's Note: A momentary pause here for your comfort, so that you, dear reader, can stand up for a few seconds as I had to.] I tried an alternate method: letting my spirit or 'I' escape my inert body through the dome of my head. Instead, I found myself visualizing brain cells rising to the top of my skull and up through the stratosphere, the ionosphere, and all those other spheres, finally becoming one with Brahman or pure being, the Great Oneness. With the result that Brahman was getting brighter, but I was getting dimmer!

This was my conclusion: When one arrives at the point where the *rate of memory loss* plus the *rate of confusion* exceeds the *rate of absorption of new knowledge and understanding*, it is time to give up one's quest for enlightenment. Surrounded by all the saffron-clad-absurd characters from Germany, France, and Am'rika, it was difficult not to come to the conclusion that all quests, including this one, are by definition quixotic, and even insane. Why else could it be that I, who didn't even know the meaning of the in-grown toenails on my father's weatherbeaten flat feet, was looking for the meaning of life, no less?

Besides, when one is looking for the meaning of life, one is usually looking for the meaning of one's own life—which in most cases is a mess. What if, like my father's quest for bourgeois acceptance, mine had been a quest for acceptance by clubs that would rather not have me as their member: the Marxistocracy, the GrouchoMarxistocracy, the aristocracy, America, women, the Francophile intellectual establishment. I decided I was playing a sucker's game, because after each acceptance, I'd find a new club that wasn't well disposed towards me.

'You have to believe in the great Om, the breath of life, the great I Am,' said my saffron-robed, clean-shaven assistant guru, a bearded young male who called himself Swami Aighedananda and who smelt of Old Spice lime.

'What "I Am"?' said I. 'I can't believe in the "I Am", because I keep asking myself "Am I?" "Am I perhaps a fool to be in this funny farm of a place"?'

'You are an incorrigible sceptic,' Aighedananda snorted, shaking his head again.

'I *was*!' I replied, laughing. 'Now I am just a combination of non-denominational bizarre individualist, sensual existentialist, rational secular Buddhist, and erotic human potentialist. As for THE TRUTH, I am just sceptical that we will ever know it, or even that it makes any difference to human folly.' What I was truly sceptical of was that *he* and dogmatic outfits like his would make any difference.

'Religion is a great formative influence for the young. It builds character.'

'It fucked up my life,' I said. 'At least the way they taught it to me. I'm sure it keeps a lot of people good and decent and afraid. But I do wish they would find a way to build character without fucking up one's life.'

'Well, nothing we teach you here will mess up your life—which is probably a mess already, so you have come here. We teach you to meditate, to accept the oneness of things, to find peace. I may not have answers to all your questions, but this is one way. So why are you hostile to belief?'

I thought for a moment, then said, 'I'm not hostile to *belief*. I don't know what I am. Well, let me meditate on this a bit more. See you later, Aighedji, I mean, Guruji. Don't merge into the Absolute before I come back!'

I went to my room, sat at my desk, and wrote:

Pondicherry,
June 5, 1986

Dear Sankara

A little report card to you, my original philosophy guru. A position paper, as it were. A state-of-the-brain address.

Thirty-three years on this planet. And what do I believe in?

I believe—on good days at least—that Love and Woman are the measure of all things (even though I presently have neither). I believe in justice—the word justice gives me an intellectual hard-on. Even though most people don't have it.

Or maybe these are less beliefs than fantasies. I don't know what I know, anymore. I don't know if I ever will—because, I fear, losing your faith through rationalism is like losing your virginity. You may cry and cry, but you won't ever get it back.

For how can one, at the end of twenty years of feverish, mind-numbing education, accept a philosophy that all is worthless, all is illusion, all is *maya*? Even if this philosophy were invented by my progenitors? I have invested too much in the other, the Western, scientific, Aristotelian viewpoint. This investment has corrupted me; indeed, our corruption starts at

birth, and our salvation, if it is to work, must start right then.
And how can I accept your confident assertion the last time we
met that Wittgenstein has rendered all of Russell's philosophy
meaningless? Is nothing sacred? Or is nothingness sacred?

Well, maybe this much I *have* found out, after 33 years on this
planet:

1. Vijay's Law of Barbers: No haircut will ever make you look
smarter than your barber, so take a good look at the barber first.
Vijay's Second Law: If you look incorrigibly stupid: then, the
more sophisticated the haircut, the more stupid you will look.

2. If Plato had been a graduate student in philosophy
condemned to write term papers on the meaning of life, he
would have been too fucked up to have written the *Dialogues*;
he would have written a completely obscure and opaque treatise
called *Idealistic-Theological Perspectives in Utopian-Fascist
Theoretics*.

3. Philosophy doesn't help common folks. For one scarred by
poverty, philosophy is a luxury. A poor man does not get up first
thing in the morning and ask: Why do I exist? He asks: What's
for breakfast today? What can I do today that will guarantee
that I'll never again have to worry about breakfast, lunch,
dinner? Even now, many gourmet moons later, I still climb out
of bed every morning and head straight for the kitchen to
consider and behold my breakfast.

So this is it, Sankara: I've quit forever my search for
understanding. From tomorrow on I eat, drink, and make merry
until I die.

Yours forever,

Vijay.

This was it for me.

In the meantime, to my surprise, I ran into Father Thomas
Madtha, the radical priest from Mangalore—fifteen years after the
Goa camp, when I had last met him. A beard stippled with grey, a
face scarred and weathered by severe acne, but still that intelligent,
insolent light in his deep-set eyes.

'Father Thomas! What are you, a Christian Marxist, doing in this obscurantist Hindu ghetto?'

'Not so loudly,' said Father Thomas, embarrassed, but joyful at seeing an old friend. 'And just call me Thomas.'

'Well, by God, Tomaas Saiba! What *are* you doing here?'

'Let's go sit down under a tree somewhere and talk,' he replied quietly and just a shade wearily.

We found a spot under an ancient banyan tree, an oasis of shade under the bright canopy of the sky. Until the crows started a racket we could hear a myna singing somewhere. We sat quietly for a moment and examined each other's faces, maps of experience, disillusionment, pain, and puzzlement.

He spoke. For fifteen years, he said, he had tried to balance a Christian ministry and psychological counselling at the local university with his radical thinking. There had been fights with the Bishop, who often threatened to throw him out for being too much of a free spirit. He had spent most of his nights reading, reading thousands of books. For all his doubts and his reading, he had been unable to walk away from the priesthood, because his childhood brainwashing, like mine, had been so complete. To leave his religion would be like leaving his human nature behind.

'But then, as I kept counselling our Catholic women over the years, I realized the damage the Church had done. One lady said to me, "Father, if I stop having children now after my seventh child, will God forgive me?" I laughed, but it wasn't funny. Contraception and abortion—if any woman had done it, she felt guilty and became dependent on priests for the rest of her life. Guilt, guilt, guilt. We have ruined them with our guilt.'

'The better side of guilt, I suppose, is conscience,' I said. 'Aren't Christian bureaucrats more honest than non-Christian bureaucrats?'

'What the point, if you can't be comfortable with your own body?'

'But isn't there guilt associated with sex in Hinduism also?'

'Not among rural Hindus. Among them, there is an ease of movement between the sexual and non-sexual. No duality. In the Hindu scriptures, a girl is supposed to be a *naganyika*—to be allowed to run around naked. Until she develops pubic hair. Then, she is withdrawn into the house and kept there until she is married.'

'So why did things change?'

'Foreign invasions. Then British education blended with Victorian morality. So only the middle-class, Victorian-educated Hindu knows guilt,' Thomas continued. 'He secretly fears his religion is inferior to Christianity. He is embarrassed about the *Kama Sutra* element of his culture. He wants to stop women from going naked in Saundatti, but is happy enough for his daughter to wear a swimsuit! Because the Westerners have told him *that* is okay.'

I had found out about it only recently: that in Saundatti in Karnataka at an annual festival, thousands of women stripped down to their birthday suits and dashed forward in an ecstatic act of mass streaking. And I had always felt nervous and shy in the presence of Hindu women, thinking them more conservative. How complete had been my separation and my alienation from my Hindu heritage, how hermetically sealed my Catholic world from the supposedly nefarious influences of Hinduism, supposedly a worship of stones, snakes, and devils. Thus had I gone to America in search of streaking, unaware of Saundatti.

Then I thought about Maya. What was it that had changed her and mellowed her? She, who had once been a Mangalorean rebel, and therefore so interesting (the only Mangalorean Catholics who had interesting minds were, coincidentally, all rebels)? Had she had an abortion, perhaps, while I was in America? Had she then been swamped by a wave of guilt when she could no longer fight alone?

He yawned and smiled at me. 'You seem to be in another world,' he said.

'But things are changing right? Sexual revolution and all that? I wish I had been born fifteen years later. I wasted so much of my life simply fighting against rubbish,' I said.

'You should consider yourself lucky,' he said. 'What about me? I discovered my life was a mistake when I was forty-five. I can't begin a sexual life now. After sublimating myself for forty-five years! A forty-five-year-old virgin! Only the Catholic Church could have achieved this.'

I broke out laughing, then apologized. 'I laugh because I am completely incapable of shedding tears,' I said.

'On the other hand, being a priest and a confessor, I know it's not so much better for our married people. Many of our Mangalorean women, when they reach thirty-eight or forty refuse entry to their husbands. Pleasure for its own sake is sinful, they think. After that, the men are traumatized. They booze harder. Often, after that, the women become the power in the home.'

Before I could ask him more, the bell rang. We walked, brooding, across the parched lawn to the large hall, decorated with banana leaves, where people were gathering and stuffing themselves in the corners to listen to the big Swamiji's lecture. After the lecture, I would hop on the bus to Bangalore, stop for a few days, then return to Mangalore.

The lecture was packed. Swami Dayananda, a bearded middle-aged man with bovine eyes, baby-smooth skin, and a gentle voice, began: 'Once, Indra, the god of the sky, thinking himself all-powerful, decided to build a massive castle. His architect, exhausted by Indra's endless demands, approached Vishnu, the Supreme Being, for help. So Vishnu, taking the form of a little boy, appeared before Indra. The little boy was sitting on the ground, watching a train of ants, and laughing. "What are you laughing at," asked Indra. To which the boy replied: "To think that each of these thousands of ants was once an Indra in a previous birth, reborn an ant because of his bad deeds. And all of these Indras come from just one day of Brahma's life. The life of each Brahma is 311 trillion human years. And I am creating new Brahmas every day of my life."'

My head felt giddy. There suddenly came to me, like a gift from above, a kind of grand perspective that made my little worries somewhat meaningless! I was smiling. The fresh breeze that blew in from an open door seemed the most beautiful thing in the world.

It was just a story, yes of course, but so what? A myth that you choose for yourself, with no strings, canes, or meal tickets attached—no pressure no threats of damnation, but simply of your own accord, simply because it wasn't imposed on you by foreigners. This was a myth that had taken root in my own Indian soil; it had probably been woven by my Brahmin ancestors.

Hinduism—I had long underrated it, long dismissed it as the mumbo jumbo of priests looking to make a buck. More recently, I had been charmed by the depth and profundity of its philosophy, but had not seen how I could reconcile it with my individualistic bent. But there had long been budding within me a perception that we are all matter, all combinations of atoms, leaves on the great tree of life, thinking ourselves different and utterly free, but completely determined by the genetics of the tree, by the pattern set by tree-ness long before us, thinking ourselves immortal, but immortal only in our universal essence, in our oneness, in our interconnectedness as matter. Now I found that a Hindu story and the philosophy behind it expressed this same perception with so much more elegance. A little story had given me a sense of scale. If the life of the average Brahma was 311 trillion human years, and there would be millions of Brahmas, and everything that had ever happened would happen again and again, your little problems become somewhat less earth-shattering than you had imagined them to be. Your children have leukemia? Your brother is an alcoholic paraplegic? Your father likes cross-dressing? So what? Here, let me tell you about the time that Indra, in the thirteenth *manavantara* of the last *kalpa*, decided to build an even bigger castle . . . .

'It happened that at the very dawn of the present day of Time,' Swami Dayananda continued, 'that the Earth was captured by the Serpent King and taken to his Abyss. So Vishnu, the Highest, Absolute God, took the form of a boar, and rescued the Earth. Of course the Serpent King was part of Vishnu's substance; of Vishnu as the Absolute, containing all opposites. But as a god and creator, it was his role to fight the Serpent, which was an enemy of creation and evolution and progress.'

He paused for a whole minute and then said slowly, to the hushed audience, 'Fight, fight, and enjoy the fight, but don't take it too personally. Because the Other is also you, and your separateness is an illusion.'

As I walked through the ashram grounds that evening, a swarm of little flies hovered about my head, irritating me. I jumped, and flailed wildly. They split for a second, and settled again into their preferred orbit around my highly desirable coconut. I swore. And then I said to myself: This is the way I have been reacting all my thirty-three years. Swearing. Misbehaving.

Chips on my shoulder. And hey, these flies could all be little Indras. They are all me, in another life. That little black one there is Vijay, and that fat one there is also Vijay, and so is that hyperactive one right now softlanding on my nose. They are all little Vijays, extensions of my essence in another form, and they are merely doing their thing: congregating round the nose of the larger Vijay. Sharing the common space. So long as they occasionally let me do my thing, why get so worked up?

I walked on. Outside the ashram gate, a mud path led into the village. Naked dark-skinned children played in the street, a cow in an advanced state of relaxation occupied the middle of it, and an occasional farmer on his bicycle swung past, marvelling at the visitor.

And I thought to myself: All Indras. All Vijays.

I heard a dog bark. The bark grew louder. I thought to myself: Another Vijay. The dog had decided to pursue me. A voice in my head said urgently: Vishnu says, Run!

I sprinted back towards the ashram, to the amazement of the flies circling my head, to the laughter of the children.

And Sister Domina Mary was you too, and racists and colonialists were in you too, and your father and mother, and Ruth and all those bouncy women who had denied you love. And Maya: she too was in me, and I didn't need to seek her out.

You are that which you are searching for.

The next day in Bangalore, the southern capital of vice and booze, of skirted nymphs and Chinese restaurants I learned of the presence in that city of Father Maximus, my former mentor.

Father Maximus in Bangalore, now a retailer of divine inspiration and pious jokes at a city Retreat House! The thought was like a glass of rum punch, or a well-remembered and dear anecdote.

I got him on the phone, and he quickly accepted my invitation to dinner at the Bangalore Club the following evening.

Next evening, I was taken aback to find his famous face and once-strong body shrunk by his years into harmless, *Reader's Digest*-condensed editions of their former selves. I stole a few glances at this my former mentor, as a waiter with goggly eyes, a hungry look, and a faded white homespun uniform appeared, trembling. The waiter was a ghost of the Club's former imperial glory, admittedly, but at least he now served Indian masters, not British ones. In one trembling arm the waiter bore, in accordance with an order placed by me earlier in the evening (Father Maximus had given me *carte blanche* on the à la carte), French Onion Soup, Fish Tandoori, Chicken Kalmi Kebabs, two naans, and Mango ice cream.

Father Maximus's face glowed and almost recovered some of its youthful fire. 'I don't often get rich food like this. I rarely have ice cream.'

I was mildly awash with compassion and something akin to love for this man. In my childhood's deprivation, I had imagined the aromas emanating from priestly dining-rooms to mean that being a priest was a continuous feast. I felt more kindly towards them now, realizing besides that priests must have gastronomic pleasures to compensate for the more vital ones they are forbidden.

A few ecstatic bites later, he said, 'It isn't every day one gets an invitation to the Bangalore Club.'

This was a shrunken man, a shred of his former self. Where was the awesome Father Maximus I had known?

Suddenly, I realized our old relationship—me a goggle-eyed adolescent, scrambling for the pearls of literary and worldly wisdom he would drop ('To read *Reader's Digest* is to have a world view')—was shattered forever. This seemed preposterous: I was repaying his *Reader's Digest* quotes with chicken kebabs.

In fact, he was repaying me with some of his own awe, implying that I was one of his handful of 'enlightened and illustrious' students. And he treated me to the unaccustomed confidence that the Jesuits had curbed his life with their narrowmindedness, that they had 'junked his collection of magazines', selling them for peanuts to the wrappers of peanuts. That they had warned him not to go around town on a bicycle with his cassock scandalously up.

Those same Jesuits were the gods who had ruled my boyhood and adolescence, the makers of our Catholic civilization, in whose hands generations had surrendered their souls! I had once contemplated joining their number! Shortly after that, I had hated their number. To find one of them so weak and inconsequential now, bitching about the pettinesses of his tribe to me, who once trembled before them . . . .

'I never understood the meaning of loyalty to India,' he continued. 'I was so brainwashed. I remember, when my father and I first saw British women in Ooty, we trembled . . . trembled in front of the *conquerors*.'

I imagined him in Ooty, the south Indian hill-station enclave once reserved for the white-skinned conquerors and their personal servants alone. So he trembled in front of the conquerors, and I trembled in front of the priests, and my own peons trembled before me. And so we tremble on.

But where does it end? I asked myself. Even though I had made a conscious bid to expunge my colonial past—the subservient and self-hating side of it—how could I know if I had really succeeded? When I speak, and think I speak freely, am I really My or His or Our (Colonial) Master's voice?

In any case, the Mangalore of yesteryear was no more. And never would be, again. It made me almost weep to realize that I was a Mangalorean no more. Except for my incantatory, obsessive, repetition of the word 'Mangalore', nothing about who I was today anchored me to that place, or to any place at all, except generally and vaguely to Planet Earth.

Except that now, in some way, we were all the same—part of the universal substance, the Absolute.

Still, there existed a real world, and real forms. And at this real moment, in some smaller, barefoot Indian town cocooned in a time zone twenty years behind Mangalore's, a St. Juliana's Convent, a St. Stanislaus College, and one or more Vijay Prabhus existed, inchoate and voiceless, grappling with life like blind, prehistoric beasts. I would write my story for their sakes.

After all, the people I loved, and the places I loved, with all their imperfections, were dusty, poor, Indian. They were me.

In the second-class train coach to Mangalore, as the sun set on baked farms outside Bangalore, I opened my copy of Plato. The copy I had possessed since my early twenties, and that had spent the last five years with Maya. Flipping through the pages, I came upon a folded piece of airmail paper.

It was a letter from Maya. She must have slipped it in the book before returning it to me.

It said:

Dear Vijay

> You are a dear friend, a special person. But, don't ask me why, we cannot be lovers. Well, why does it have to be me? With that always-hard thing of yours, you shouldn't be lonely for long.

Maya.

I burst out laughing, and then barely suppressed myself, for the sake of my staring co-passengers, who could see a flood of feeling transform my expression.

Her words had been just the signal I had wanted, the kind words of affirmation from the female of the species. Something in her words had released me, released me from a bondage to her.

I'd look for a woman with big hips, with lust and fire, a woman untouched and unscalded by the religious hot iron that was Mangalore. A graceful, slender-waisted *Padmini* with the passionate and eager ways of a *Sankhini*, and a woman versed in the sixty-four arts besides.

But I was once again in unswinging Mangalore and at home, and the mosquito-embodiments of the Absolute that were now biting me were true residents here, unfazed by the faded white ceiling fan that noisily and wearily blew at them. Father sat with his usual solace, his glass of feni distilled from genuine Goan cashews. I noticed he had lost most of his teeth: the very ones whose treatment I had offered to pay for before I left for the ashram. Their absence made him comical, especially when he smiled: like some cinematic buffoon rather than the all-powerful father of my childhood.

'So how was Pondicherry? Had some french fries there?'

'Sautéed frogs legs in sambar,' I said, laughing. After just a few decades, Pondicherry had little to show for its French history, and had quickly reverted to being a filthy, mosquito-ridden south Indian town.

Even though we hadn't formally made our peace, in this sense we had: he tried less now to change me, and I him. This was our wisdom: changing someone else was impossible, especially when changing our own selves was nearly impossible. All said, he did what his fate said he had to do. And perhaps he had to fight worse demons. Only the other day this man, scarred by shrapnel from the American bomb that nearly killed him, had like a true believer of *Reader's Digest* been exulting over the American bombing success in Libya.

Once, he had had a soul that loved music, that played a violin, dammit, a thing of infinitely sweet melody. But he had been forced to sell his soul to the army, in return for a job, security, and the wherewithal to feed his parents and brothers and sisters. Life had no more delicate notes for him; he had been prevented from loving me.

And then, Dad told me the news about Arun. Arun, my elder brother, who had suddenly become religious in the extreme, had joined a fundamentalist Christian group called the Charismatics.

'Jesus, Jesus, he says all the time,' Dad said. 'The fool. Won't get a job, just talks about Jesus. Says, "Look at the birds in the air, they neither sow nor reap." But he won't eat like a bird. He must have meat and fish every day.'

So my parents, once great fans of Jesus, were in the strange position of having to de-emphasize the Lord while their son reminded them of the Holy Name twice in every sentence of his. And just the other day, in the obscure North Indian town of Jabalpur to attend a Charismatics convention, Arun had been nearly run over by a speeding cycle-rickshaw and was in hospital with a broken foot. The telegram to my father, conveying the news, had ended with the words: 'Praise Jesus.'

I couldn't help but laugh. Mischievously, I went to my room, picked up a leaflet I had preserved from my American days. The leaflet said:

MRS STELLA SAYS
Don't give up!
This Southern born spiritualist has helped thousands of people who have been CROSSED, HAVE SPELLS, CAN'T HOLD MONEY, WANT TO GET RID OF STRANGE SICKNESS. If you are seeking a sure-fire woman to do for you the things that are needed or WISH TO GAIN FINANCIAL AID, or PEACE,

LOVE and PROSPERITY in the home, see her in the morning, be happy at night!

I scrawled on the back:

Dear Arun
    I know you have a high opinion of Jesus, Arun, but maybe it is time to give Stella a try?
    Just a joke, okay? Get better now, dear brother of mine.
    Love,

Vijay.

I returned to the sitting-room, where Dad, his chest bare now, sweat droplets crowning his bald pate, was sadly picking at boiled salted peanuts in between sips of his feni. Once again, I wanted to make him happy—to make him a gift of happiness. He had been dreaming of owning a television set. The recent arrival of television was the most sensational thing to happen to Mangalore since the Tipu Sultan captivity and even the most middle-class Mangaloreans suddenly seemed to have found the means to buy at least a black-and-white set: suddenly, TV had become the preferred route to moksha. One of the few Western programmes shown on Indian television, *Lassie*, was one he—and his favourite personal dog, Doggie the Seventh—could enjoy. But I had shushed him with my pompous pronouncement that television was a Faustian bargain, a modern-day evil. I could easily buy him one, partly from money set aside for his dental treatment.

'As the Bible says, "Blessed are those who have no teeth, for they shall be rewarded with a television on earth,"' I thought, and must have mumbled.

'Wha . . . . What's that?' Dad said.

'I'm going to buy you you a television,' I said, laughing. At first, my merriment had come from my own surprise at my new softness: offering to buy him what I had once called the brain-extinguisher.

Slowly, his face lit up at the thought, and then he joined in my laughter. And at the sight of his face, and his toothless laugh, I couldn't stop laughing.

Epilogue

THE ROAR OF a low-flying jet seemed to shake the Bombay airport terminal's glass windows as I wheeled my luggage towards the check-in counter. I had a one-way passage to America in my hand, an air ticket bought with the money still left over from my evangelical experience. My single suitcase had nothing much in it except a nearly-completed novel.

'Stay,' said Maya. 'Don't go.' There were tears in her eyes. She was wearing a purple silk salwar kameez, and her hair fell loosely over her shoulders and back. Her expression was tragic but she had never seemed more desirable.

'It is too late.'

'It's never too late,' she said, wiping the sweat from her face and the tears in her eyes with a handkerchief. 'I always knew you were mine if I wanted you. You can turn around right now.'

'A year ago, you would have been right. But I have other plans now.'

'But why return to a country that tortured you the last time? You are just courting disaster! You're being masochistic,' she said.

'Maybe you are right,' I said. 'Or maybe this time I won't be defeated. I am harder now. I have fewer illusions. And I have things to say, people to reach. And I just know that America, with all its faults—and which country is without faults?—that America is still the place that will give me the chance to say these things and to reach people.' Besides which—and I didn't dare admit this to her—the United States was a quiet country, a country of almost unnatural, comforting, solipsistic peace, where the pitiful cries of hungry and sick babies and of children being whipped and of dogs being stoned do not rend the air letting reality leak into your dream-bubble all the time.

'But how would you feel fulfilled there among people you don't feel connected to? You're leaving us and joining them.'

'I don't believe in Them and Us anymore,' I said, conscious that I was being somewhat pompous. 'Freedom has no nationality. And I've come to realize the Enemy is as much within me as anywhere else.'

'Come on, what if you make the same mistake twice?'

'Well, like one of my favourite characters in *Catch*-22, I believe in seeing everything *twice*, Maya. And I'll never leave India. I'll take India with me wherever I go.'

'I was wrong. You were always the one for me. Don't turn me down simply because I turned you down once.'

'Don't be mushy now,' I said. 'You're still my best friend. And like Bharat Mata, you will always be with me.' And kissing her suddenly and ferociously, I wrenched myself free of her and darted across the security line separating my mother country from the outward-bound passengers.

'So what is the moral of this book?' Pam, my editor, asked.

We were at her apartment facing Central Park, a spacious but eclectically furnished apartment dominated by an image of the dancing Shiva and perfumed by burning joss sticks. Greedy pigeons pecked at a window sill, looking for handouts. I had recently moved into Pam's, there being no sense in keeping two apartments in New York, where so many human beings had not even one. It was now five years after that farewell to Maya, and Pam had become my literary mistress—the best kind of mistress a writer can have, work and play all rolled into one cuddly bundle, and extremely helpful in developing good working habits, since you can do your writing and your editing and your fucking at the same time (which is the best kind of life). Pam had just energized her brain with a headstand that ended her morning session of nude yoga (the only way to do yoga, in her opinion, and one that not only helped her to access her serpent power, but also consumed hundreds of calories, because we often ended up making love, I having been inflamed by the sight of her yoni, a proud yoni, a yoni that—I fantasized for a moment—had probably launched a thousand first novels, besides the usual quota of epic poems and limericks).

'Pamela, my puss,' said I, 'Plato begat Saint Augustine. Augustine begat numerous illegitimate children and Christian puritanical attitudes to sex and the body. Christian Puritanism trounced The Kama Sutra 64-0 in two short centuries and in the process begat advance-resistant underwear and Mangalorean society. Which in turn begat Sister Domina Mary and Father Maximus and our anti-hero's pater, Melvin Prabhu. But Father Maximus and Reader's Digest and Western media gave our anti-hero a taste for the Kennedys and the West, which in turn begat Joy of Sex and Time Magazine and Herzog. Which begat an American Dream, a yearning to take off his underwear and to travel; which begat disillusionment, and a renewed and revised appreciation of The Kama Sutra and the American Dream. Now, the moral of that is pretty clear, right?'

'Get out of here!' she said, slapping my nether cheek affectionately and with delicious sexism. 'On second thoughts, stay right there. I have this sudden yearning to take off your underwear.'

'To continue,' I said with great difficulty, as she teased my bounding tickler with her fingertips. 'There are no easy morals.'

'Only easy women?' Pam interrupted, rubbing my deeply perturbed dingalingaling between her rose-nippled, warm, ivory breasts, then letting her hand slip between her legs as my excitement aroused hers.

I continued, summoning all my cobra power of concentration: 'But maybe the real moral is this: If you want to have a one hundred per cent happy literature that offends no one, create a race of eunuchs. Or, a better moral still: spare the rod, spare the child. Best of all, exterminate the artists! Ban the act of writing. After all, we have twenty-four-hour TV now; who needs books?'

'Who needs writers? What do writers do anyway?' she sighed, breathy and hoarse as she sank fully back on the plush carpet and my head dipped towards her centre, the source of our existence—and presently, of my happiness and my utter peace.

Narrator's Whimsical Glossary

artha: Life in the world, including business, family, acquisition of wealth – the art and practice of. One of the four supreme aims of life according to Hindu scriptures, the other three being dharma, kama and moksha. Some of our businessmen are such whizz kids at artha that they don't need to give a damn about dharma, or whether their wives kama; as for moksha, it can be achieved by paying off your favourite god with ten per cent of your under-the-table profits. For our gods, unlike Western gods, are very human.

ayah: A maidservant, usually child-care help; occasionally helps out the man of the house in the task of attaining moksha or salvation, in ways not usually spelled out in the contract.

babu: clerk, low civil servant. Also a term of respect used by the illiterate when addressing the moderately literate; an insult if directed at the highly literate, of which India has an unfortunately high number. In Konkani, though, babu pronounced baboo is an affectionate term for a little boy.

banian: undershirt or formal wear, depending on your social class. Doesn't go with a bow tie. Dirtiness and sweatiness are required characteristics; to say 'dirty banian' is to be redundant.

batlivalla: hawker who goes from house to house *buying* up your old newspapers, bottles, metal cans, et al; in other words, paying you for the pleasure of recycling your garbage.

bhang: a derivative of marijuana, usually blended with flavoured milk – whereupon it becomes the milk of human kindness.

bhen chot: (or 'barn shoot' in the *Oxford English Dictionary*) meaning sister-fucker, it's a popular term of invective as well as brotherly address in north India – which may or may not be indicative of a high prevalence of incest or brotherly love in those regions. See also: *sala* or *saley*.

biknas (K):* the edible seeds of the jackfruit, notorious for their flatulence; consequently, a lowclass snack. 'Eating biknas' is an expression implying one who fritters away his time in undignified pursuits.

bimbli (K): the acid fruit of the *averrhoa bilimbi*; Konkani slang (diminutive) for penis.

bizalli wu (K): wet lice; a girl without enthusiasm or a sense of fun; a spoilsport in a potential sex encounter.

bokro (K): an innocent, a sheep.

chai: always-sweet milk tea presented in a small greasy cup.

chappals: leather sandals which are the preferred and copyrighted instrument of the Indian women's movement (traditional branch) in Hindi movies. Also used by rural Bihari police in the making of garlands.

conjee: boiled rice served along with the water it was boiled in. Fed to Robert Clive's troops (by silly self-sacrificing south Indians)

---

*   (K) indicates a Konkani word.

before a famous battle, it directly resulted in a victory instead of, as is usual, lethargy and sleep.

Dada: Big brother. Big Shot. Thug. A term of address that signifies you have arrived. See also *goonda*.

desi: Of India, made in India. Among Indians it is a popular Indian synonym for 'second-rate' and 'doesn't work'.

dharma: complex word meaning, in various contexts, righteousness, doctrine, Sacred Law, a momentary configuration of events.

Didi: the female form of Dada. Big sister. When a man diddles a didi, he becomes a true bhen chot.

dwaita: school of Hindi philosophy that regards reality as dualistic; its practitioners are often businessmen who maintain dual sets of account books.

four-letter words: (i.e. the narrator's preference for short anglo-saxon words like piss): Yes, I use Anglo-Saxonisms or short Latinisms to describe the basic functions, and that is because throughout my childhood and adolescence, I've so choked and gagged on 'organs of generation' and 'reproductive system' that I now find any synonym of *La System* longer than four letters to be indigestible. I become testy at 'testicle'; and 'urinate' makes me furinate.

Gandhi: a man whose experiments with truth and naked women launched thousands of Gandhi Roads, Gandhi Parks, Gandhinagars, and statues of bald men.

ghagro (K): petticoat. No decent woman will allow herself to be seen in one, or suspected to be without one. Indecent women and *phirangis* (the same thing) have no need for it.

glossary: aid to intercultural understanding or colonialist hangover, depending on your political viewpoint (the dominant fashion among Indians, who rarely *buy* books, is to regard a glossary in an English novel as traitorous, given that no Western novel explains its terms merely for the benefit of Eastern readers). But if, like this one, your glossary trips up rednecks, whether brown or white, it ought to be called a subversary.

Glossary, purpose of this: to light a fire under the ass of the world.

godachi mutlin (K): rice dumplings filled with a mixture of jaggery, coconut, and cardamom.

goonda: a tough, who usually has bad manners, wears loud or rakish clothes, let out a mean whistle, and spits great distances.

gulab jamun: north Indian sweet consisting of brown sticky balls of flour fried in oil (oh, it's tastier than it sounds – and most Indians of either sex would run a mile in broken chappals for balls such as these) flavoured with the essence of rose petals and soaked in syrup.

I: Not I, but *I*: a character born of the process of the author putting his pen to paper.

India: Popular tourist destination for such Westerners as Robert Clive, hippies, and low-budget British tourists who, whether armed with 'How to Outwit the Natives' guidebooks or not, find they can wheedle out astonishing hospitality and amazing bargains from the gullible or outsmarted natives.

India (Definition Number Two): a geographical pot pourri and political fiction inhabited by diverse peoples who spend most of their time plotting each others' downfall.

Indians: The term, even though I use it myself, is a Western conspiracy (starting about the time of Alexander the Great) to pigeonhole a people as varied as humanity, thus annoying most Indians and doing justice to none. To take a tiny example, North Indians, traumatized by the Partition and repeated conquests, have few illusions about human beings, while most South

Indians are as innocent and idealistic as Tahitians were before the French made them run around in ridiculous skirts and shorts.

Indian Censor Board: Men whose holy mission it is to protect the purity of Indian women by preventing Indian men from learning to kiss well. In fact, by preventing Indian men from making love without looking like idiots.

Indian English: e.g. 'What all you are talking, you stupid fellow!' Neither this nor 'babu English' represents the jumbled, biryani English in which *I* [see definition of *I* above] write now, a potpourri of butler English, Victorian English, American comic-book slang, American sitcomese, black speech, supermarket checkout-girl speech, standupcomicese . . . Yep, I am a linguistic Marco Polo, having travelled across the terrain of five languages, two continents, and so many disparate Anglo sub-cultures. Thus speaking a postcolonially raped international biryani diction beyond repair, I say to thee: if thou desirest purity of syntax and historical eras, get thee a *Webster*-certified virgin.

kakkoos (K): toilet

kama: desire or physical love; satisfaction of bodily needs like food and sex. But it is wrong to suggest that the majority of Indian males, after sex, ask the woman, 'Did you also kama?'

kashti (K): kaccha, langoti—traditional male underwear or loincloth. Not usually manufactured under a designer label. One size ties all. An instrument of male bondage.

Konkani: my mother tongue, a language with over five dialects and over five million speakers.

lakh: Indian numeral representing 100,000. One hundred lakhs make a crore. A lakhpati is (or once was) a rich man.

lingam: Sanskrit for penis. An object of general worship (the

Hindus had their priorities right, knew what really mattered). Therefore, not a four-letter word, but easily handled by ladies. We ought to try introducing dongs into the rituals of Western religions, as a tool of transforming Western civilizations, ending its ridiculous mind-body split. If we did, 'prick' would no longer be a term of contempt but would connote an upstanding member, a pillar of society.

I delight in the various synonyms for penis: Jade Stalk, Yang Pagoda, Crimson Bird, Unicorn, Diplomat, Ambassador, General, Tiger, Monk, Cock (that's some bird!), and the Konkani *tendlen*, *mimi*, *bimblen*, and *bitto*—joyous, comic words. And as for me, lingam stands high in this company. I love the feel of the word. For this Sanskrit word for dick has the sound of sanctity, an aura of religious ritual to it ("Did you sprinkle your lingam with Holy Ganges water, Lakshman Bhai?" "I did, Dada, and sprinkled all over.") It sounds like something you could sell in the advertising columns of the holistic health magazine *Whole Life*:

> GENUINE GANGES-WASHED LINGAMS!
> Sizes Virgin, Intermediate, Economy, Family,
> Slutsized. Colors Black, Nude, and Vermillion.
> $19.95 each. Postage and *handling* extra.
> Stonewashed and preshrunk extra. Free "I Love
> Lingams" T-shirt with any order of three of
> more. (Sorry, no more applications for *handling*
> jobs will be entertained till 2091, except from
> spinsters producing hardship certificates).

lungi: A male lower garment, named after its inventor Muthu Lungiswamy, who discovered that it was a convenient device to answer calls of nature without interrupting social chitchat. White or brightly coloured, wrapped around like a sarong and knotted at the hips, sometimes folded upwards at the knees by the less inhibited. South Indian male drag, highly airconditioned. Besides reducing the distinction between the sexes, the lungi is accident prone, and hence keeps south Indian life interesting, and is the main reason why Keralites, its chief wearers, specialise in producing salacious movies.

maal: merchandise; in this case, sexual merchandise.

maidan: a large open public ground used for circuses, spitting, and assorted bodily functions.

Mangalore: a town famous for its nuns, nuts, tender coconuts, toddy, tile factories, pretty women, Gulf-bound accounts clerks, and audiences who refuse to laugh at jokes unless announced to be such. Located on the west coast of South India, it has its fair share of injected Aryan blood, in the form of the Mangalorean Catholics (also called Mangies or porbus) and Konkanas, who migrated from more northerly regions to watch cockfights organized by the local Tulu-speaking race.

Mangalorean Catholics, History of: Not enough space for that, so here follows a partial bibliography for the Portuguese invasion and the cultural history of Mangaloreans
- *The Christianisation of the Goan Islands*, by Anthony D'Costa
- *The Inquisition in Goa*, by A. K. Prayolkar
- *Kadamba Kula, A Sketch of Mangalore*, by Dr George Moraes.

mutlin (K): spherical rice cake, steamed, with a navel-shaped depression at the top.

namaste: The traditional Indian greeting of respect, usually accompanied by joined hands. To offer to shake hands with a traditional woman, instead of offering a namaste, might result in your being run out of town.

Octerlony Monument: if you had any doubts at all that imperialism was all about big boys whipping out their penises and imposing them on other countries (to put it politely), consider this amazingly penile monument erected (ah, what a verb!) by the repressed Victorians to dominate Calcutta's skyline. So uppity is this incredibly elongated dong that it points directly at God. And it looks like it has had one of those ribbed condoms drawn over it. The best you could say about it: it is the British yin to the Black Hole of Calcutta's yang.

paan: betel leaf, chewed sometimes with areca nut or tobacco leaf, to produce a red saliva often spat onto pavements and walls to make them colourful.

panpale (K): flat rice cakes, pan fried. Made with boiled rice, having a stronger rice taste than a dosa.

patolio (K): flat dumplings made from a mixture of rice and jackfruit paste and sometimes cooked in flavourful leaves.

payasam (K): kind of semi-liquid pudding using rice or vermicelli and milk or coconut milk, the very mention of which will make a south Indian's mouth water.

peon: one who sleeps.

phirangi: foreigner, usually white-skinned, but occasionally a brown-skinned expatriate; mostly contemptuous and comic. Though the Aryans were at one time themselves *phirangis*, the irony is that though they still revere whiteness in their search for the ideal marital mate, though they don't particularly care for its pinker shades of Northern Europe.

phirangi lovers: sad to admit, but most brown Indians with fake British accents are closet phirangi lovers, in effect the chief white supremacists of India; all they ask of their Supreme White masters in the West is second-in-command status and permission to fantasize about *phirangi women*.

phirangi women: Ah, what bliss. Even in our *own* men's magazine, *Debonair*, the *phirangi* women always bare more. It never ceases to fascinate Indian men that in an inversion of natural law, women from cold countries such as Sweden wear (and *need*) so little and look as if they were almost born to be nude, while Tamil women, who have never seen temperatures below thirty-two degrees centigrade, show almost nothing, and are considered daring if they expose their elbows. Though a trifle confused by this cruel irony of colonial history, we are always grateful for the sight of *phirangi* women travelling about our country, looking always lost, always a little frightened, and always gloriously underdressed.

Prabhu Family History: I give an oral version of my ancestry received from an old grand-uncle, one who had somewhat lesser respect for the Christian yearning to erase non-Christian histories.

The Prabhus, he said, had descended from a nomadic horseman named Kurgavir Pirahab, who lived somewhere in south-eastern Europe about two thousand and five hundred years before Christ, and came down to India in one of the conquering Aryan migrations of that time. One of his descendants, Vishwamitra Pirabham, was a small-time philosopher and soma-swilling Brahmin priest in the fifth century BC, who is rumoured to have had a penchant for creating catchy Sanskrit slogans, plus occasional, accidental bits of higher wisdom. One of his female descendants, Kundalini Pirabhatt, is reputedly depicted on one of the Khajuraho Temple panels performing a rather complicated act with three men, one of whose erect and oversized lingams she is in the process of ingesting. It was an act involving such creativity and mechanical precision that her mother, when she clamorously denied having taught her daughter anything of this nature, was instantly believed by her father. (But no doubt the profession of live nude modelling and group art was practiced with much verve and dedication in those days, though artists, the lucky stiffs, have almost always managed to have a good time.)

My more recent ancestor of the mid-sixteenth century, a Gowd Saraswath Brahmin named Padmanabha Pattinga Prabhu, was impaled on the nearest sacred object by Portuguese soldiers (under Major Bartholomeo Diaz, Mapuca regiment of the Portuguese Infantry, Goa Division), who were incensed by his refusal to convert to Christianity. His wife and children, watching his excruciating last moments, immediately begged for the Divine Light, and were baptized on the spot by the chaplain attached to the Mapuca regiment.

pudwem (K): the Mangalorean-style white cotton dhoti, or upscale loincloth, which makes the wearer look like Pan, the hairy goat god, from the waist down.

rajma: Red beans popular in the dense Gangetic heartland. While many have blamed cow farts for the greenhouse effect not enough study has been done on the contribution of 400 million eaters of rajma.

rossogollas: white, spherical, spongy sweet. Mouthwatering and the Bengalis' second greatest contribution to civilization, after the title of the nude musical, *Oh, Calcutta!*

sala or saley: a highly ingenious curse word common in north India (the north Indians are superior at this). Technically, *sala* is a respected relation: a brother-in-law. But if you address someone as *sala*, it means you have married his sister—and presumes you are sleeping with her (in other words, you are an upscale *bhen chot*, because the *bhen* you are *chotting* is *his*). The word also occurs as a term of humorous conviviality between male buddies, but try not to use it one someone to whom you have been recently introduced.

sannan (K): fluffy white rice cakes, fermented with toddy. Spectacular.

saunf: a grain-shaped, aromatic and digestive food, taken in small quantities after meals or in large quantities from restaurant trays.

Sita: the wife of the god-king Rama; a virtuous, shy, obedient wife. Every Indian bridegroom's fantasy, until he picks up a copy of *Playboy* or *Debonair*.

soro (K): liquor, usually signifying the local, colourless variety; low-grade hooch; booze; the unblushing Hippocrene, sometimes made of cashew fruit.

Srirangapatna, Captivity of: The incident recounted in popular

Mangalorean histories in which Tipu Sultan, the Anglophobic ruler of the kingdom of Mysore, angry that some Mangalorean Catholics had helped the British, vengefully marched thousands of their defeated and starving number two hundred miles to his capital, Srirangapatna. Where, in a perverse post-facto application of Middle Eastern penile doctrine, he deprived many of the male survivors of their prepuces.

tarlo (K): sardine; fishface; greenhorn.

Tat twam asi: In Sanskrit, 'That thou art'—meaning there is no division, no separation between you and another; separation and ego are illusions, since you yourself, in a sense, create the other. A fantastic pick-up line.

Third World: the difference between a Western and a Third World Country: a Western Country does things, a Third World Country has things done to it.

thoti: chappie involved in the carting away of human waste from the old-style toilets. Not a profession likely to get you into the Delhi Social Register.

Uncle Everest: What happened to Uncle Everest? Oops, I forgot. He was run over by a bus while trying to not miss the meat puffs at the wedding of Balthu Souza's daughter Minna. His brothers gave him a nice funeral (kingfish curry was served), and he was buried next to Aunt Meera.

Upanishad: Holy book of the Indians, by the Indians for the Indians, and only understood by the Germans.

Vijrimbhitakam or yawning position: In *The Kama Sutra*, the position in which the woman raises her thighs and keeps them wide apart. While you're at it, don't forget to try the *Vadavakam* or mare's position, the *Varikriditikam* or elephant's love-play position, and the *Avalambitakam* or suspended congress. Then you'll truly have come a long way, baby.